DELIGHTFULLY
DAMNED

ALLYSON KUEPFER

atmosphere press

This book is dedicated to Gary Kuepfer.
I love you desperately and appreciate your
unwavering support and inspiration.

TRIGGER WARNING

Hello there! You picked up this book, and therefore I very much like you as a person. Because I like you as a person, I have no desire to do you any harm. This book will be painful for those familiar with grief and sexual assault-based trauma. Additionally, if you are not a full adult yet, this book isn't yet intended for you. I'm not saying DON'T read it, but I am saying if you aren't over eighteen, please don't read it yet; come back to it as this was written for a mature audience.

'

NOT SIMPLY ANOTHER ANNIVERSARY

Christine glared at the menacing little hand of her alarm clock. It clicked, one irritating tick at a time, closer towards the large six, which would signal it was time to get up.

"Mornings belong solely in Hell," she grumbled at the purple clock as it sprung to life. Gravity felt stronger this morning as she sat up and, in a rolling motion, stretched some energy into her sore shoulders.

Her calloused feet scraped against the compressed carpet as she dragged them out of her bedroom and through her kitchen. She squinted against the attacking light as she slowly opened her curtains. One purple and the other black. She had gotten them for sale in a mix-and-match bin. Running a hand down the coarse fabric, she paused, appreciating just how much her best friend hated them. Amy had stomped her foot when Christine had waved off her disapproval.

"You may like them, but Christine... people can see them from outside. They'll know they don't match. Care or not, other people's opinions matter." Christine had hugged her and promised she genuinely thought the colors were a good fit.

Amy was from a cold, affluent family and could not fathom having zero regard for other people's opinions. Whereas Christine came from a colorful home of working-class love and parents who raised her, quite intentionally, not to care what other people thought.

Ignoring her overstimulated paranoia was a skill she had thoroughly crafted. Her anxiety may have been well-earned, but today, she didn't have time for it.

She shook the shiver from her shoulders and rubbed some warmth back into her arms. Looking up, she cursed a quick, "Fuck you too," towards the sunlight for subjecting her to this renewed anniversary.

She tiptoed to the bathroom, irritated she hadn't taken meeting a potential new therapist this morning into consideration when setting her alarm. Most mornings she had time to do her hair and makeup, but now she'll just have to look as tired as she felt.

From the reflection in the bathroom mirror, she could see the disarray that was her closet; a plain cardboard box caught her eye. Forcing herself to ignore it, she turned her attention back to the mirror.

Her curls contained memories of her mother; on today of all days, they shouldn't be something she allowed to piss her off. So, she worked some coconut oil into it with a ghost of a smile.

She rubbed a bit of lotion into the tawny tone skin that was a mix of her Irish Father and Spanish mother. That was one thing she couldn't skip today. This winter had been aggressively bitter. It was as if the season sought to be quenched of its dry brittleness directly from her skin.

Working on her hair was never quick. Today was no exception. Her baby hairs had decided to be persistently rude this morning, standing up in every direction defiantly. Vaseline helped her tame them to be smooth along her hairline.

Her mom had invested hours teaching her how to wear her hair proudly. For hours Christine had sat on the ground in front of her, enjoying the sound of her voice. Her mom had a way of expertly weaving hair care instructions together with stories.

Stories of a world with winged men and power.

Her elbows were suspended in the air, fingers full of hair and toothpaste was beginning to escape from the corner of her mouth as she caught herself staring at the box again. Blinking the haze off, she forced herself to reanimate and finish securing her hair into a tight bun. Well, tight enough, hopefully, to survive instructing a whole day of classes.

"Well fuck," Christine garbled through her foamy mouth, now standing in the closet, her hands reaching towards the box. Her outstretched fingers snapped into fists as she stomped back to the sink.

Her gums were raw, and the mint flavor of the toothpaste was mixing with an iron she could only assume was blood from her abuse.

The problem was, once she finished brushing her teeth, she would be another step closer to leaving her small sanctuary.

"This is all Amy's fault. I'm fine," she assured her own reflection.

With a deflated sigh, she tried to convince herself again, "I'm fine." Hearing her own uncertainty, she clung to the fuzzy void that was her parent's memory; since she didn't collapse in a heap on the floor crying, she assured herself again, louder this time.

"I'm fucking fine."

Non-professionals attributed her numbness towards her loss as strength and sometimes a coldness. But the professionals, and lord knew there had been many of those, had wildly different theories.

"This guy, award-winning or not, will be no different. Last one Christine. Do this; Amy deserves it for putting up with your shit. If they try to numb you with meds again, just leave." She pointed at her own toothpaste-speckled reflection, reminding herself that Amy had paid for this session. Blowing it off would be like spitting in her well-intentioned face.

The only reason she had even agreed to go this morning was because of the anxiety attack that hit her while with a student last week. Amy's concerned voice whispered through her memory, "Panic attacks are bad, yes. But only getting two hours of sleep a night is worse."

Her eyes rolled at the words Amy had jabbed her with on many occasions, including the night before. Truth was, the lack of sleep was annoying, but Christine felt she operated well on it.

Pushing her unsorted, hanging clothes back and forth on the different bars, she pretended to give thought to what she would wear. She would end up, like every day, in one of her rotating outfits consisting of jeans and a tee shirt.

"What is wrong with me today?" she snapped at herself, pulling her hand back away from the box yet again.

Maybe Amy had a point.

Maybe it was time.

Maybe she had reached a place where she could accept feedback and the help everyone said she needed and start to live this life her parents had traded for their own.

"Or maybe I am just being dramatic," she thought, looking for a way to justify canceling what would be her fifth therapist.

Finishing dressing, she pulled on boot cut jeans and a pink 'New York' tee-shirt that, in her mind, perfectly matched the green jacket she threw on top of it. She also stuffed two sets of workout clothes in her black, tattered gym bag before tossing it over her shoulder.

With one last glance over at the box, she had a fleeting moment of bartering with herself.

"Take it down. Go through it. Process it. Do that and prove you don't need this." Hands clenched into fists she stomped to the door, pausing at the hook that dangled her carry gun and holster. She took a second to strap it on, eyes flicking back to the box several times.

"Those are some bitch terms, Christine. Bitch terms, and you know it," she grumbled, unlocking each of the three dead bolts and door braces. While grabbing her keys, she shot one final angry glare at the triumphant box before slamming the door behind her with a final, "I'm fine," and aggressively re-securing each lock.

When she had first moved to the city, navigating high-trafficked areas was anxiety-inducing and bumpy, but now, she could expertly shift through the thick crowds of locals and tourists alike.

The thing she missed most about her hometown was the air. Back home she had never really thought about air. She missed that luxury. Here, just breathing on a busy street made it taste like you licked someone's tailpipe.

With each turn of a corner, she glanced over to scan the reflections available against the buildings on each side of the street. She did this to make sure there was no repeating face visible behind her, a necessary precaution in her line of work.

Amy had offered to pay for her cab fare, but Christine had never minded walking. Some people liked yoga; her meditation was listening to punk music and walking.

Standing at a cross walk, she smiled at the creased grin of a woman standing near her, who clearly heard the punk rock melody that Christine was slowly bobbing her head to and approved of it. New Yorkers tended to keep their heads down.

Being raised in the Upper Peninsula of Michigan had exposed her to how unkind 'small town niceness' could be. Yet, that 'smiling at strangers' way of life had been a hard one to shake. Today she enjoyed this small moment of solidarity in music tastes with this perfect stranger.

Still grinning, Christine pushed through the door of a tightly tucked in building that was nestled neatly in between two high rises, standing out with its quaint, clean architecture. She had to give it to Amy; this place already looked more promising than several of the pretentious thirtieth-floor offices of therapists past.

The clean scent of lavender hit her as she was waved in absently by a scruffy haired assistant who was tuned in to the TV adjacent to him. It wouldn't be right to blame the poor guy for how distracted he was. A rerun of the season premiere of Supernatural was on, and one of the characters, Dean, was escaping purgatory. She too had been completely immersed in that episode when watching it the week before with Evan. Before, of course, they got into a screaming fight when a certain news broadcast came on during the commercial break.

"Christine?" Pulled from her thoughts, she noticed the doctor, if you could call a therapist that, had come out to greet her. "My name is Ray; my office is back here." Nothing about this man could have been warmer and more inviting. Not the crinkled edges of his smile, the distinguished gray of his untidy stubble, or even the soft, muted blue of his eyes.

Yet, as soon as she met the pooled water in those eyes, they seemed to freeze over. The hand he had outstretched to her for a friendly greeting clenched closed, his head snapping back with an audible gulp as he stumbled back away from her.

Concerned, she stepped forward, thinking he was having a fit or maybe a heart attack.

"You good?"

The blue of his eyes melted back into a softer hue as his posture loosened. The tension dissipated as quickly as it had accosted him.

"Yes, I am well. That was not the best first impression; my apologies. I am thoroughly invested in this program and wasn't prepared for that." He explained, nodding to the T.V, that, at that moment, had a car commercial playing.

Deciding it wasn't worth drawing attention to his weirdness further, she held back a comment about how heavily he had started breathing.

"So, why don't you follow me, and we can get started?" he said, turning to lead her through the doorway into his office, his shoulders lifting slower and steadier with each step.

"Sure thing," she said, looking back at Mr. Man-bun, who was still staring, very entranced, now tuned into a commercial break. As a child who frequently constructed her Christmas want list from infomercials, she decided she was in no position to judge.

She pushed through the thick and not unpleasant scent of lavender as she broke the threshold of his office and glanced around, discovering the source rested on a windowsill, the little flame dancing a bit too excitedly.

'Funny,' Christine thought, 'I would have pegged him for an incense kinda guy.'

"Is something amusing?" he asked. He was sitting on a large leather armchair. It matched the one she had plopped her gym bag onto before making her way to the wall of books.

"I was remembering one of the first sessions I went to like this," Christine said, reaching towards one of the book-filled shelves and resting her pointer and index fingers at the top of one of the spines and pulling. As expected, four books pulled out attached to the one.

"Yup, she had fake books too." Christine added, pushing the display back into place before walking back to the big leather chair her stuff was resting on with a small cheeky smile.

"I feel as though I have witnessed a private joke." She would have expected him to be annoyed or at least embarrassed, but found herself happy that he hadn't taken it personally.

"Yeah, it's just a little test I do every time I see a wall of books like that. If none of them look like they are solely entertainment, I assume most of them are fake," she laughed.

"That is a clever game. I may need to try that myself. However, your friend had your files sent over, and I think it would be best to get started," he offered gently.

"Is it okay if I stand?" she asked, pushing the leather down with her fingertips thinking how unappealing being surrounded by that texture seemed.

"Is it okay if I ask you some questions while you stand?"

"Sure," she forced through her stiff lips.

He ran through a brief review of his notes on her previous files. After summarizing that her history with therapists had been rocky, he commended her for, on this day of all days, taking the right step toward healing.

Healing. That word seemed too ambitious. He knew only a mere fraction of the healing she needed. Her files were intentionally incomplete. The last professional she had seen was the reason she'd sworn off the entire concept of therapy.

She could still remember the women's pointed face telling her it was 'okay' that she had imagined things about her parents' attack. That 'delusions' regarding traumatic events were 'normal.'

That lovely, fueling rage simmered warmly in her gut as she continued to rock on her heels, leaning stiffly on her palms against the back of the chair.

"You appear to be answering on autopilot. If this is going to work, I need you to answer me honestly, and these responses seem rehearsed."

'Aaaaand here we go,' Christine thought. This could go one of two ways in her experience. Condescension or a full brush-off.

Placing his hands on the desk before him, he stood, and for the first time, she noticed his impending height and found it strange she hadn't noticed before.

"Christine. I am well aware of your disdain towards my profession. We want to help you. For us to do this, you need to allow us to. Based on the disclosed information, I think it would be wise for us to consider treating you for a delusional disorder. There is no shame in this diagnosis and no need for you to be evasive about it."

She ground her teeth, picking up her bag as she made for the door.

"Let us help you," he called.

She stopped for a moment and took a calming breath that did nothing but add oxygen to the flame festering deep in her gut.

"I know I am broken, but not like that. What I saw, the bizarre way my parents were killed, was no illusion. I gave the treatment a chance; it did nothing but kill the small bit of me in there I can still feel." This was one of those moments where her face felt the tingling sensation of needing to cry tears that didn't come.

She had stunned him, but pity quickly won him over.

"Before you lost your parents, did you struggle with such a limited array of feelings?"

That stopped her.

Before? How had she felt before?

Gripping the shoulder strap of her bag a bit tighter, she tried to remember before.

Forcing the memory into her mind was more difficult than it should have been. Those images were stale and almost too vibrant to reconcile with the dull lens her more recent life had filmed over with.

Reliving memories of her childhood was like watching a caricature of herself. A wannabe punk rock girl with black painted fingernails and curly hair that fought hard against her straightener. The sting of burnt hair still singed her nose as she remembered the upsetting results of her attempt at the 'punk look.'

Sarcasm was considered the first language in their household, but if she had to choose a second, it would be laughter. She was the only sixteen-year-old she knew who had an annual family roast. The first person to laugh was deemed the loser and had to make dinner; it was wonderful.

Her lonely smile shifted quickly into a pointed glare as her stomach clenched and heat spiked through her in a nauseating wave.

'Great, nothing like a full-blown panic attack in the middle of a shrink's office to get you locked up in a looney bin. I bet Dr. What's-his-name is loving this.'

Looking pointedly through the red haze, she noted the concerned agony on his face. This would be her last appointment with this guy.

"No. This wasn't an issue before," she spit out, unfurling as the pain subsided.

It took her approximately ten seconds to flee the building without looking back. It took ten minutes before her phone began buzzing angrily in her pocket.

"Ah, to pick up or not to pick up," Christine mused, knowing full well the scolding she was in for.

She decided to take the punishment over the phone now, instead of giving Amy an excuse to come over tonight and dish it out in person. She hit accept and placed the phone to her ear.

"Hello, my beautiful stalker. How are you on this fine day?" Christine asked with mock cheer.

"I was better before the call I just had," Amy said, with a disheartening amount of breathy disappointment.

Christine was lucky the appointment had only been a few streets from her gym. She had back-to-back classes this week and would have been annoyed had she needed to push or cancel a session for that waste of time.

"So much for doctor-patient confidentiality," Christine laughed.

"Are you alright? He said you had an attack."

"I'm fine."

"If I never hear you say, 'I'm fine' ever again for the rest of our lives, it will be too soon. You've seen the Italian job. You know what fine stands for," Amy scolded. Christine had forced her to watch that movie to prove 'bad guys' could easily be portrayed as heroes, given the story was told from the right perspective.

"Yeah, yeah. Freaked out. Insecure. Neurotic. And, of course, Emotional," Christine responded, still trying to keep it light.

There was silence as Christine waited for a response, fighting with her keys to unlock the alley door of the gym. Only after successfully getting the key in the lock and shoving the rusty door open did Christine decide to break the stalemate.

"I gave it a shot. I promise. I'm sorry." The words sounded as they were. Regrettably insincere.

"Sure, you did. Well, can I at least come over tonight so you aren't alone?" This question, or a variation of it, had become a daily ritual between them. It dated back to the night Christine had woken up in the hospital and discovered her parents' home could never be hers again.

Christine almost always rejected the kind offer of company. It wasn't that she didn't enjoy nights spent with Amy. They were always fun and filled with Indian takeout and movies, but she had self-imposed a rule to never say yes if the question was fueled by pity.

At this very moment, she didn't need to make up an excuse. Telling Amy she was working all night was completely legitimate.

The hallway inside the gym was lined with corkboard for flyers and class schedules. "Fucking Evan." Christine gasped, pulling a blown-up image of herself looking as irritated as she felt at this moment. It was from last week's top newsreel; a tasteless picture of a burning house behind her, as if she had been there in person.

What infuriated her most were the words, "Learn to save yourself." Followed by their business information.

"Can you believe Evan made fucking flyers about last week? What has gotten into him?" Christine hissed more to herself than Amy, whose laugh crackled back at her through the speaker.

"Um. Probably the desperate desire to make enough profit to make putting up with you worth it," she snapped in a failed jest. "Sorry, that was mean," she tacked onto the end.

"Yeeeah, it was, but I earned it." Christine smiled, feeling them wading back into smoother waters.

She locked the back door behind her before turning and opening the door to Evans's office.

To her dismay, there was a folded sticky note with her name written on it in a way that looked like he had been pressing the pen a bit too hard on the paper.

"Ope. Think I'm in trouble," Christine said.

"Shocking. Astounding. Gasp worthy," Chuckled Amy.

Evan had found her actual schedule. Not the printed one she had given him showing her fifteen paying clients. Nope, it was the real one that included the 'non-paying' students. High-risk individuals who couldn't afford to pay or could be endangered by paying her.

Three late-night classes were highlighted, and a note of "SERIOUSLY?" was scrawled along the top. She had saved it to the desktop, assuming he wouldn't bother with it. Obviously, he did since she was now holding a freshly printed copy.

"He gets so frustrated," Christine said, knowing she was in the wrong for hiding this and hoping Amy would provide validation for her actions.

"Dude. He should be mad." Realizing she hadn't yet told Amy why she was in trouble; Christine closed her eyes and pinched the bridge of her nose.

"He did NOT call you."

"Well... He's worried."

"So, what are you, my friend or my fucking keeper!?" Christine bit out, wishing she could snap her phone shut, cursing the inventor of the touch screen.

The reflection on the black screen looked back at her in judgment before obscuring it as she hit it against her forehead.

Before the professionals had decided to drug her, they had instructed she try things like 'take social risks,' and 'put herself out there.' She still scoffed at the implication that her great cure-all was to involve herself with more people and stop being 'closed off.'

She looked back at the very disappointed note from the person she trusted most on this planet and rubbed the center of her forehead. A bruise was beginning to form in punishment for treating the closest thing she had to family like shit. After her recent behavior, Christine couldn't fathom how the doctors could have jumped to the conclusion she was 'cold' and 'shut down.'

The small space of the room was cluttered as she leaned against the desk and guiltily eyed the photo of Evan and her up on the wall. They were smiling and cutting a 'ceremonial string' Evan had tied to each side of the front door. He thought it added a sense of occasion to the grand opening two years ago. He was right.

His bright smile pierced her heart. This gym was just as much a part of his healing and his purpose as it was hers, and she was running it into the ground. After swapping her outfit for workout clothes and re-tightening her bun, she plopped onto the tattered office chair, thumping her head down a bit too hard on the desk.

She had become a mere thread of the ambitious and self-assured girl her parents had known. Her very essence felt like it was thinning and stretching as it wound through time, tightening into a tenuous coil on the very verge of snapping.

That tension was present within her now as the cool wood of the worn desk did nothing to soothe the uncomfortable heat building in her scalp. Music, she needed music. Memory was a fiend, and music was her weapon against its constant intrusion.

Beginning to straighten her spine to a sit, she felt the whisper of a nightmare against her neck, *Little one…*" the eerie voice flitted through her, the look of his silver eyes sharpening in her mind as her lungs constricted in an unsuccessful attempt to draw in air.

"Fuuuuuck," she gasped, jumping to a stand, clothes damp with perspiration and goosebumps littering her chest and neck.

She had the nerve to doze off, so the Sandman had punished her audacity accordingly.

A simple clock hung beside their picture, displaying a warning that her first class was in a half hour. The first lesson was a group class of standard, paying clientele. Her waitlist for these classes was full, and therein lay her financial remedy, if only she could find the time.

Instead of resolving her own issues, though, most of her day was spent with desperate, high-risk clients who couldn't pay. These students were in situations where her help could be the difference between life and death.

Still slightly jittery, she grabbed her keys from the desk and walked to the metal grate that was rolled down at the front of the studio. She had students that enjoyed coming early to stretch or ask questions.

Through the obstructed glass, the shadow of a large man loomed just outside the door, halting her in place as she rounded the corner. Her pulse pounded in her ears as she forced herself forward.

'It is not him. It is not him. Maybe it's Evan; maybe he forgot his Keys again.' She reasoned with herself as she slid a lock into the door, opening it but not yet lifting the grate.

A very large, young man stood with his hands in his hoodie pocket, the hood framing the shy look on his face. All the tension immediately left her body. With the slump in his posture and the pleading look in his eyes, he was not here to threaten her.

"Good morning," she said, genuinely cheerful now that she knew this was not the middle-aged, silver-eyed, tanned man she feared was still out there plotting her death for unknown reasons.

"Yeah, I guess. Are you her?" His voice was broken, rigid, the sound of someone who spent the night yelling. Now her concern returned. Occasionally the abusive spouses of her clients took their issues directly to her, it didn't tend to end well for them, and she didn't feel like spending another night in the drunk tank for 'assault.'

Last week she had broken the nose of a client's abusive husband who tried to jump her in this very spot and had then pressed charges. After he tried to burn his wife and kids alive the same day, the charges were dropped though.

"I am a, her, yes. As to a specific chick you're looking for, I will need more to go on…" she said with a smile, looking at him through the rusty intertwined metal. She bent and clinked her key against it, knowing full well the lock was broken; it would lift if she just pulled.

"You the Christine from the news?" he asked. With a sigh, she threw her head and arms back, cursing the existence of all news broadcasters. The incident with the fire-wielding husband had made top news stories; her client had dropped her name. Praising her free lessons for saving her life.

"Yup, That's me."

"Damn. I expected you to be bigger. You know, more… jacked. The shot they got of you was a bit blurry and, I don't know, I guess I was expecting someone a bit more intimidating."

The grate rattled like a loose bike chain as she rolled it up and motioned for the man to come inside. The bitter cold was turning his breath into little white puffs; she could see from his shifting feet that being here was difficult for him.

His olive-colored hoodie reeked of cigarette smoke as he walked past her into the studio; she couldn't help but scrunch her nose, earning an apologetic shrug from him.

"I have a class soon. Were you looking to check it out? I'd have no problem with you sitting in for one." She put the offer out there but knew it wasn't her classes he needed.

He wasn't the first guy she had seen come through here, embarrassed, and reluctant to say the words 'I need help.'

"I don't mean to jam you up. They were talking about you on the news, about how you took someone on for free, and because of what you taught her, she was able to get out of ropes, saving her sons and herself from the house her husband had set on fire. That's impressive."

"I gave her skills, yes. But it was the work she put into learning those skills that saved her life." He nodded and sauntered away from her, walking around the open gym space, stalling.

"And?" she prompted. He gulped as he turned to face her, shrugging again.

"I uh." She busied herself with the coffee pot on the far side of the room, hoping to ease his feeling of being in a spotlight. "I read a bit on your website. There were these classes called low-impact defense...."

'Evan, the saint, has another calling. He is gonna kill me,' she thought, twinging, both for the man and at herself for what she knew she was about to do.

Turning to face him, she could see he was looking at everything but her.

There was heavy-set shame on his face; she knew it was for being here. For needing help, as so many others did. Others he hadn't heard about or seen. She stepped towards him and reached up, putting a hand on his shoulder with a small smile.

"Low-impact classes are designed to teach a method of defense for men that will not harm their attacker. We teach you how to defuse, escape, and, if necessary, gently restrain."

"Those classes are popular?" he asked.

"My business partner, Evan, is at the police station, giving a weekly lesson to our boys in blue as we speak. His classes are popular, but I think he may have room." He stepped away from her, the offer of a class getting too real for him.

"I was just curious. My girl, she got a temper, ya know? I love her; I just, I need to be able to do somethin' when she gets in her moods and starts swinging." It astounded her that it could be 2012, and men still felt the pressure of society to act as if it was impossible for them to be abused.

"If you have a minute, I can check Evan's roster and see if he has any openings."

He retreated a bit further, stepping into a beam of light. It shone through a gap in the curtained windows against his skin, revealing a gash behind his ear that stretched around his scalp to his shaved head, undoubtedly made by strong, manicured nails.

"They sound interesting; I wouldn't mind checking one out. I've got the time, I'm on leave from work. Are the classes high?"

She grimaced in knowing, "about fifty a class."

He scoffed, offended by her expression. "It ain't like that. I have a good job in finance. I make a good living. My wife and I had a little misunderstanding is all, and she involved the cops and called my work. I'll be back at work soon; the charges got dropped." The defensive edge to his tone had her regretting her lack of composure.

"No assumptions, no judgments," she clarified, holding up her hands. "I just know how hard fifty can be to come up with when you don't have a solid paycheck. I'm sorry."

His shoulders drooped and it broke her to see this man dissolve before her. Whatever he had constructed within himself to hold back his turmoil was cracking, breaking loose, his pain flowing free before her.

Tears escaped him in a silent, defeated cry. It took her a moment to shake off her discomfort, watching this man trying to hold it together before she stiffened her own spine. Luckily for her, Evan had trained her for this moment, just as she had trained him for the same, but with women.

"Look," Christine said. "The owner here is a big guy. His first girlfriend was abusive. One night she stabbed him because she suspected him of cheating. On reflex he shoved her, and she fell, hitting her head. He woke up in the hospital, chained to the bed, accused of attacking her. He spent five years in jail."

His tears stilled, and his posture straightened. The sun was gleaming through the shrouded windows, highlighting every particle of dust in the air. Their little dots illuminating this man as he experienced validation for the first time.

Christine continued, "Is your situation headed in this direction?"

He took his hands out of the front of his hoodie for the first time and pushed his sleeves up. Long lines were raised down his arms where he had been scratched.

"My wife. She's just a little thing. Just over five feet. But she is so fast and so fucking temperamental." Christine nodded. "Between the two of us sitting in a police station, both claiming self-defense, whose ass do you think would be getting locked up?"

He was right. Sure, his case was the minority. But it was just as tragic.

"Let me get you signed up. No payments for now. We will expect back compensation once you're stable, but Evan won't be able to turn you away. Follow me to the back. We need to document your injuries and take some pictures. We will open a file for you that we will only add to it what you approve." He shuffled behind her; although she was happy to see a new bit of hope in his eyes, she knew Evan would not thank her for this.

The rest of her day passed at a rolling speed. Each of her classes lasted the single blink of a second. Her one-on-one instructions with women ending within what seemed like the span of one excretion of breath.

In comparison, the time between her classes wheezed painfully by. Each of the ten-minute breaks she had scheduled was painfully lengthened by her growing anxiety of seeing a man walk into the studio. There were two she was specifically concerned about.

If she had the choice between a confrontation with her parents' seemingly extraterrestrial killer and the furthered disappointment of her friend Evan, she would happily take the murderer.

However, by nightfall her conviction shifted. Every day she feared meeting silver eyes, discovering the truth behind how he had done things no one could explain. Like breaking into her parents' house without being seen by the camera outside or breaking a support beam with her father's body.

Her last client had left twenty minutes ago; it had only taken her five to clean up. Sitting in the office, she stared at the picture of her and Evan again. Missing the easy way things used to be between them.

They had been surrogate everything's to one another for the last few years. They spent the night at each other's apartments, him sipping a nice red wine and her a cheap white while bitching about life. Occasionally playing the role of fake significant others to dissuade unwanted attention at parties. This well-earned comfort between them did not include Amy, who found their closeness inappropriate.

She clung to those moments as she heard the door creak open. The wall shook as Evan shut the door behind him; the force sent their photo shattering to the ground. He peeked his head into the office moments after, looking from the broken glass to her with a cautious smile.

"If you don't see glass as it breaks, is it still bad luck?" he asked lightheartedly, his thick Mexican accent blurring the ends of each word. This superstition was one of her mother's that she had shared with him.

He was clutching the silver cross that hung from a gold chain around his neck as he always did when he was uncomfortable. Based on the thick jacket he still had on, she figured he wasn't planning on sticking around.

"Oh, what? So, I get your bad luck, then?" she laughed and debated for a second not telling him about his new student. Just letting him figure it out tomorrow when it popped up on his schedule.

'No, that would be super shitty,' she scolded herself.

"So. I'm a shitty person, and I did a thing," she began. His light brown eyes lost the little bit of the whimsy they had been carrying, and he went slack.

"You are not a shitty person. A shitty business owner, yes. Sometimes a shitty friend. But not a shitty person. Do you have a new client, or do I?"

"You do," she said, pinching her lips and leaning back guiltily.

"Christine, Por que?" His question of why was drawn out with well-earned drama.

"Lo siento," she apologized; debating continuing on in Spanish as her fluency always softened him a bit but decided that would be manipulative. "He looked like he had been attacked by a big ass cat. She already got him arrested and cost him his job."

Evan's eyes hardened in remembrance of his own past. But unlike her, he fought against connecting himself to every person in need. He flexed his fingers apart, elbows at his sides and shook his hands toward her in annoyance.

"Woman. When am I to train him? Unlike you, I am not fueled by El diablo. I need sleep." She smiled at him. He was being kind to her, keeping his tone light, but she could see the weight she had just dropped on his undeserving shoulders.

"I know. I'm sorry. I, I just couldn't say no."

"I could teach you," he offered in a mocking tone, picking up the client application and skimming over it.

"Ah, yes, in English or Spanish, though?" she joked back, a bit relieved.

The last client she had taken on for free was for herself, and that disclosure had ended much worse. She wished he would yell at her; that meant they would be fine. When she really pissed him off, he tended to get very quiet and distant. Due to this, they had not spoken for several days.

She was smiling up at him. He caught her over the application.

"What?"

"Nothing, I'm just relieved," she explained.

"About what?"

"I thought you would be pissed." He dropped the application on the desk and crossed his arms stiffly.

"What have I ever done that makes you afraid to tell me shit?" It was a good question because the answer was nothing. He had his own trauma. This was one of his triggers.

"Nothing. Evan. Nothing. It isn't anything you are doing. I am just ashamed and we are drowning here, and I just signed you up for your time without asking you. I figured you would ice me out again."

"Ice YOU out? Are you serious? You have a phone too. This goes both ways. Fuck, this is your problem. You jump to these assumptions about people and how they will react and over-read into every little thing." Each word came out in a harsh breath of a man defeated.

Reaching behind him, he pulled forward a jogging bag she hadn't realized he'd had strapped on and pulled out a bottle of her favorite white wine. The blue bottle was muted in the low light of the office; he offered it to her.

"Christine. Please go home. Drink this bottle, and don't worry about coming in tomorrow." The cool glass felt good in her heated palms. She rolled it back and forth, opting to look at its muted blue glass over her kind friend. "I know what today is. You did it; you survived. Go celebrate; you deserve it."

She left shortly after, feeling a bit silly for getting herself so worked up all day. The foil-wrapped tip of her gift was peeking out of her bag and was the cause of the foreign feeling smile on her face.

***

Feeling better, I pulled my phone from my back pocket, deciding to take an active step towards 'healing,' as the therapists would say, to call Amy and invite her over. Evan had come in with the sole intention of instructing my last three clients and letting me know he had cleared my schedule for tomorrow.

The screen was alive, and I was pulling her contact up when I ricocheted off something hard enough to send me flailing to the ground. Sprawled out, phone lying beside me, the pre-existing crack in the screen lengthened, I looked up expecting to see the corner of a building and instead was looking into the face of a moving Greek statue.

The heat of the gentle sunshine warmth radiating from him was absolutely terrifying. He offered me one of his marble-like hands, but all I could do in return was stare unblinkingly back at him.

"Here, let me help you." Snapping out of it and taking his hand, I felt an unfamiliar blush run up my neck that radiated a bit too much warmth considering I was overtly unenthused to be touching this stranger.

"You were really moving," he chuckled while not releasing my hand. "My name is Pierce. It appears you may need some help in getting home safely. Share a cab?"

The comfort and lightness in his tone worried me further.

It wasn't his fault, though. Any man showing possible affection towards me, especially pretty ones, elicited this reaction. My experience had been, and many women could attest to this, that they, in particular, don't take rejection well. With how polished this dude was, he definitely was registering as more of a threat to me than a romantic possibility.

'I am so fucked in the head. Be in the moment, Christine, Christ almighty.'

He bent his head forward slightly, prompting me after we had stretched the time out, standing there awkwardly, him still holding my hand.

My chest was cracking open, molten contentment seeping

from me in a way I had only experienced during my childhood. To some, that may sound enjoyable, but the emotion was too misplaced to not raise alarms. After snatching my hand back, I focused on the swirling gray of the concrete.

"Thanks for the offer, but I don't know you, and I know better than to share a cab with random dudes in this city," I added some sneer to my tone in response to him taking a step nearer to me. By the crease in his forehead, I could tell my words successfully needled him. I could scold myself later for reverting to antisocial behaviors over a disciplinary glass of wine.

"Have a nice day," I said before shoving past him.

Thick, uncallused fingers wrapped quickly around my arm and spun me back toward him. There was a war of warmth and bitterness battling it out in my chest. He had pulled me far too close to him for me not to be introducing my knee to his nut sack.

Luckily for him, the state of disorientation I was in had me focused on fleeing, not fighting. I couldn't identify the full spectrum of the emotions overwhelming me, but I did know I wasn't wanting this interaction to continue.

"I apologize for grabbing you. I know that was rather rude of me," he said guiltily, dropping my arm. "I don't mean to be so abrupt, but it isn't every day a stunning woman runs right into you. As a firm believer in fate, I must ask, may I please buy you a drink? In a public place we can walk to?"

I was sweating from nerves, but I had nowhere to go but home. Sure, I could invite Amy over; we could watch movies, but that would still end with me sitting in the same room as the box containing everything I had left of my parents.

Reluctantly ignoring the sirens and trying to focus on that alluring feeling of warmth, I tried to look at him objectively. He was wearing a loose-fitting white button-up and jeans. I looked for and failed to sense anything malicious in his smile. He was thick with what I considered vanity muscles, and this was not a point in his favor. Skilled as I was, this beast could overpower me given the right circumstances.

"I know a place right around the corner," he added, reaching out and gently brushing dust from my arm. She put space between us again to avoid the heightened emotional fluctuations I seemed to experience at his touch.

"One drink." I very formally held up one authoritative finger.

The hours and drinks melted away as I reveled in the seductive way his presence seemed to bring me a sense of balance. I hadn't felt this good in years; my insides were molten chocolate.

Pete's Tavern was the bar's name; I was happily surprised by his choice. There are debates in the city regarding which bar is the oldest, but Pierce seemed confident this was the one. It fit the brand in the most charming way.

The dark wooden walls were tinged by a warm glow from the glinting red ceiling lights. The whole place was adorably adorned with ornaments and wreaths, as many places had done to celebrate the upcoming holiday. This was the most festive I had felt in years.

I debated sending Amy a selfie but knew she would show up if I sent it, and I didn't want to commit to any more time out; I could crash at any moment. The cozy cheer of the place had almost distracted me from the ominous way the red light hung on his features and from the fact that within the crowded bar, I could see several women attempting to get his attention.

One had even been bold enough to completely squish her way between us. Her long legs and slim figure casually pushed my chair a bit away from him as she did so to introduce herself. The confidence she was wielding was so enviable I couldn't help but root for her in her conquest. She would be much more fun than I would be anyway.

I glanced down at my drink and debated downing it and sneaking out, but when I looked back up, the woman was walking away with a disappointed pucker on her face, intentionally swaying her hips and pulling her long hair forward to show the small of her back, visible in her tight gown.

'Bravo, Great show Hun.' I had to consciously resist clapping for her performance and embarrassing myself.

Yet, he hadn't taken off after her or stopped looking at me. As a self-declared rom-com expert, I understood I should be all warm and fuzzy about that, but I couldn't have cared less. Even with the alcohol massaging my brain, I couldn't muster any desire toward him, which felt arrogant as hell.

"So, what's your thing?" his head tilted like a confused child at my question.

"What do you mean, my thing?" The sincerity in his tone had an admirable innocence that made me want to reach out and pinch his cheek. Realizing that I had genuinely debated doing that, I knew the alcohol was hitting me.

"The reason you're single, in New York, looking like, well..." I gestured to all of him.

He smiled wider and sat up a little straighter, carefully cultivating an answer. His eyes became slightly distant; a half chuckle escaped his otherwise stoic composure.

"A good friend of mine once told me I wasn't built to be with any... 'one.'" I narrowed my eyes at him. He looked more like a 'boy scout' than a playboy; I had a hard time imagining him juggling women.

"Come on, seriously," I pushed.

"Assure me you won't laugh?" He raised a brow at me, so I nodded my head back at him innocently. Sipping from my fifth drink, I used the straw pinched between my teeth to mix the separating red and clear liquid.

"My culture believes that lucky individuals are blessed by fate to meet a very specific match. Not necessarily a soul mate, but someone who makes your heart and mind do things no one else ever will be able to. Someone you're drawn to, unable to resist. And I have been waiting for..." he looked at me then, "her."

The effort I put into not laughing wasn't enough; a restrained chuckle shook my shoulders as I clenched my lips shut to avoid it escaping. He shrugged my condescension off and downed the rest of his drink, standing.

"So, when will I see you again?" He shot a smile at me while pulling a thick wallet out of his back pocket.

"Ya know, sitting on a wallet that thick is bad for your spine," I deflected, sipping my drink.

He leaned closer to me with my non-answer. The warmth of his eyes began overwhelming me with their heavy heat. That gaze held an expectation as it faded into something softer, causing me to shrink away from him, fearing he was going in for a kiss.

"I am far too drunk to give you an honest answer. How about you give me your number, and if I remember you, then maybe I am the mystical 'one,' and I'll call you?" A laugh cracked his composure then, and he pulled away, giving me the space I needed to breathe again.

"That is not an unreasonable request. If only I had a phone." I damn near choked on my drink at the absurdity of anyone not having a cell phone. There was no way he couldn't afford one based on the amount of cash he had stuffed in that leather spine bender of his.

"How do you NOT have a phone?" He lifted both my hands to his mouth and kissed them.

"Not even a landline?" I squeaked.

"I'm slightly old-fashioned, but I'm sure we will see each other again. I'll be securing a ride for you. Are you sober enough to remember your address?" My response wasn't immediate as my liquid brain hadn't caught up to his words.

"If not, I could always take you home with me now. However, I have a feeling you would prefer to sleep in your own bed tonight." I was still shocked that he was holding my hands the way he was, as I nodded yes.

"I know my address."

I sputtered it out, a heat rising in me that I had never experienced before.

'Is this all it is to want someone?'

Briefly, I considered taking him up on his offer. To allow myself this human experience, but along with that want was a slightly stronger feeling I couldn't explain, a wrongness warning me off.

It was like my body was rejecting its own hormonal response to this anomaly of a man. He went to drop my hands, and I reflexively squeezed his finger in response. Looking from them to me, his smile grew and only faltered slightly when I crushed his rising spark by declaring I wanted to go home.

"That is fine. I am confident fate will bring us together again soon. Trust me." He smiled that sunshine beam of a smile at me and walked away.

I stumbled out of the bar and into the red mini cooper Pierce ordered for me. After a very twisty ride home, I climbed out of the tiny car feeling the weight of too many long days draped around me.

My sketchy, albeit affordable, apartment complex was bright this time of night. My neighbors were busy with whatever illegal thing they did to pay rent. I was the girl scout of the building. The people here knew I didn't care what they did. I assumed it was because they were all kind to me. Almost like I was the little kid they all kind of adopted together.

Everyone here kept to themselves, heads low, not even passing nods. Just the way I liked it unless I happened to bring someone home with me. Then that someone got a long once-over by anyone we came across.

I won them over during Christmas every year. The last thing I did with my parents was watch my dad horribly burn Christmas cookies. So, in their honor, I made several batches and left a box in front of everyone's doors. During that week, I would catch smiles and friendly nods from the rough faces of otherwise intimidating individuals.

I fumbled with my keys, enjoying the cool of the metal against my warm drunken skin, but eventually made it inside. I pushed them and my holstered gun onto their hooks and surveyed the room.

After doing so, I poured myself the disciplinary glass of wine I had promised myself. Needing some food, I threw some popcorn kernels in a pot with some butter and oil and headed for my bedroom.

Five drinks later, and I was already sobering up. Hopefully, the gifted wine from Evan would be strong enough to hold me in the complacent state I was enjoying just a little longer.

'Today is almost over. I've almost survived another anniversary.'

Standing in the closet, I set the wine on the ground and lifted my T-shirt above my head. When I heard a creak behind me, my toes curled against the stiff carpet. I turned slowly, ready to grab the tiny pink handgun I had taped to the back of my closet door if need be, but, as usual, nothing was there.

I discarded my shirt in the hamper and looked at the box nestled in the back corner of the top shelf of my closet. Being a long walk-in closet with organizers, the space was tidy and busy enough to keep my attention off it most of the time. This morning had been hard; tonight, was inevitable.

I shoved my foot into one of the bottom slats of wood meant for shoes and hoisted myself up, appreciating my own handiwork of the wooden organizers for holding my weight. I had constructed them after watching a tutorial on YouTube, only cutting myself a couple of times. I hooked the edge of the box with my index finger and pulled it from the shelf, grabbing it as I hopped down.

Feeling the dry cardboard in my hands sent the same chill of bitterness and longing through me it always did. Placing it gently on the ground, I pulled the woven top apart and took in my parents' scent. Everything I had the frame of mind to grab was in this box. The house was still sitting there, untouched.

I technically inherited it but had never had the spine or funds to go back.

I pulled out a large Star Wars t-shirt, my dad's favorite, and pulled it on. He wasn't a big man by any means, but it was still large enough on me to be worn like a short dress. I closed my eyes and tried to remember the way he lit up with excitement when we went to see the premier of The Phantom Menace together. So many people seemed mad, but not my dad. He was just thrilled to be able to share in the experience of his geeky world continuing into a new saga with me.

The box had various items in it. Items that, in a normal person's life, would live on some coffee table or on display on some random shelf to be sifted through and reminisced about together as a family. The most frequently viewed items were on top for easy access.

A family photo album and their wedding rings on a chain I wore as a necklace during the holidays. A small bear I got on my fifth birthday made from my baby quilt, a little box with an assortment of jewelry that was my mom's, and a VHS with one of our home movies on it. Underneath all of it was my most coveted memoir. A bottle of my mom's perfume.

I carefully lifted the cylindrical glass bottle from the box, feeling the cool, smooth touch against my fingertips. It was dense and would be hard to break. But, if anyone's luck would warrant it, it would be mine. I lifted the top to my nose and inhaled deeply. The faint smell of lingering, sweet lilacs and cut grass drifted through my senses.

With the airy smell of spring, a clear image of my mom's shockingly blue eyes came into view. A deep spring green danced around my mom's pupils; her lips twitched into a smile. The memories made my heart warm in the way a child experiences when coming down the stairs and seeing the tree and presents on Christmas morning. My mom's clean and crisp voice soothed me, "It's okay, Krissy, everything will be just fine."

Those words were all I could really hear in Mom's voice anymore. She had said that so frequently it was etched into my memory. That was her go to. Failed an exam, everything will be just fine; lose a friend, everything will be just fine.

Man has you by the throat.

"It's okay, Krissy. Everything will be just fine."

I shouldn't be in danger. The man who killed my parents was severely self-destructive at best. The odds of him being alive and caring at all about me was highly unlikely. Taking in another deep breath, I lowered the bottle into the box and weaved the worn top flaps back together.

Abandoning the box, I grabbed my wine and threw myself on the couch. Remote in hand, I clicked around, looking for a familiar movie to watch in celebration of my emotional triumph.

The floor strained behind me; I felt the undeniable dread of another body being in my apartment. I jumped up, spilling a small amount of wine on my hand. Nothing was there.

"Great, I didn't turn the stove on to make my popcorn." Sipping my wine, I contemplated starting it now but decided it was too far away and settled back onto the couch.

Goosebumps electrified my shoulders; a knot set fire in my stomach.

"Hello again, little one." The words were quiet and rough behind me. Quiet, but crystal clear.

'It's in your head. It's in your head.' No matter how many times I thought those words, I didn't believe them. He went through my parents, trying to get to me. They died defending me.

I winced as the brush of fingertips tickled the baby hairs on the back of my neck. Before his grip could clamp down, I threw myself to the floor, sending the wine flying. For the second time that day, glass shattered a few feet from me.

Suffocating heat shot through my chest and constricted my throat, the way it always did when I was hurt or scared. 'Fucking anxiety.'

I pushed through it and reached out, grabbing for the gun taped under the couch. More broken glass shattered around me as it detached. Amongst the ambient ringing in my ears, I thought I could almost make out the faint pop-pop-pop of my popcorn bursting on the stove.

Cocking the gun, I pointed it at a frazzled man standing above me. I recognized him. I just had drinks with him. Surprising myself, I hesitated. It should have pushed me to fire, but somehow, I gathered that he wasn't even looking at me.

He was looking towards the windows behind my kitchen table. Another explosion rang out, heat blasting from my kitchen and the couch wasn't enough to shield me this time. I felt the sharp heat engulf me, and for the first time in eight years, darkness won me over.

TIME DOES NOT HEAL
ALL WOUNDS

I blinked a few times and found myself wrapped in Pierce's arms.

'Had I blacked out, and he caught me? Why are my feet cold?'

With a shove, I freed myself from his unwelcome embrace and looked down at the hardwood that had not previously floored my apartment.

'Oh, holy shit. I'm not in my apartment.' Dread settled in the darkest corner of my brain. My training kicked in. I backed away from Pierce slowly, taking in my surroundings. Everything was, in a simple word, charming. The temperature of the room was too perfect; the walls and furnishings were comfortable and cozy.

'Fuck. Nothing is blunt enough in here to use as a weapon.'

"Christine." My head didn't swivel to him; only my eyes adjusted to look at him.

I froze in my tracks at the sound of a voice I knew and trusted. "Hey. You're safe. No one here is gonna hurt you."

In a flurry, I spun on my heels to see Amy standing in a gently arched doorway. Her smile was sheepish. I didn't miss the way her fists were balled up and bouncing off her thighs.

Pierce approached from behind me, and I ducked out of the way, ready to send my knuckles into a sensitive area of his anatomy. Before I could swing out, he was, impossibly, standing in front of me.

"I am going to leave you in Amy's capable hands." Had he not vanished before my eyes, I would have head-butted him for gripping my shoulders with unearned affection.

"What the FUCK?" I demanded. As if to irritate me, her shoulders rose innocently. "AMY?" In two swift movements, she shut the door behind her and only turned to me after an excessively deep breath.

"Okay. Don't haaate me. This is Heaven. You aren't dead. Heaven and Hell are just different realms. I'm actually from here. The fates are real too. And they kinda, well, talked about you, and 'cause of that, I, based on my parents' position, was assigned to protect and watch over you." Amy's method of delivering information had always made me smile. This instant, however, my head was throbbing in response.

"That's the stupidest thing I've ever heard."

"Really? Pierce just teleported in front of you, and you're doubting me?" she said.

I blinked a few times, processing that what I had just seen was real. "By the way, teleporting is possible. They call it transporting, weird, right?"

"Wait, wait, wait. You know Pierce?" Amy smacked her forehead.

"That is what you took from this?" I nodded yes back at her.

"Yeah. Everyone here knows him. He's.... well... sorta, like God. As in he is stupid powerful and rules this entire realm. And we have all the same continents, so it's a lot...." I cut her rambling off.

"Let's pretend this isn't just an elaborate prank. So, what does any of this have to do with me?"

"Christine, the guy who killed your parents, knows your death would destroy the man who ruined his son's life. He JUST tried to kill you again. Are you so damn proud you'd die rather than admit you have a soulmate? Here, it's called being Fated. It's why you feel so strongly for him...." That had been my breaking point.

It had been too much.

When Amy uttered the words 'killed' and 'parents,' a crushing, coiling pressure slithered up around my spine. One familiar to those who have seen death in the eyes of someone they love.

When Amy said 'proud,' all I heard was Evan pleading the words, 'Por que?' as he had that very night when I, yet again, couldn't say no to a student. Now, I'd never banter with him again. A crushing weight dropped onto me as I ran to the window, seeing the skyline of a city magnificent enough I should be able to name it.

It wasn't one from my world. That was clear, given the giant, winged man, with glinting silver-tipped wings flying in the distance.

I ran, and when Amy stepped in my way, I shoved her with my full might, sending her skittering to the ground. She was crying now, but silently. My adoptive sister, my only family; I didn't care.

Amy hadn't said another word. She ran from the room, locking the door behind her. I dropped to my knees, watching the lock turn into place.

Pressure had mounted in me. It needed to come out; it did in a throat-tearing wail.

Pierce appeared before me; in my destitution, I actually allowed him to take me into his arms. The pain slowly faded and ebbed into a nothingness I was more accustomed to.

***

Christine stood a week later, leaning heavily against a rough, wooden window banister. As the sun lifted into the sky, she breathed in the last seductive bits of the morning dew scent, eyes closed, savoring the peacefulness of the moment.

Worn, wooden floorboards were smooth under her toes as she curled them. Breathing in through her nose and out through her mouth slowly, she focused in on the strange, neon finches cooing from the garden just outside the window.

The door to her gilded cage breached behind her, causing any sort of contentment she was experiencing to fizzle away. Contempt quickly took its place. One week here in 'Heaven,' and she had already decided Hell couldn't possibly be much worse. There, at least, she could seek out the river Pierce told her cleansed the disembodied souls of the dead. The souls of her parents.

Leaving the room felt dangerous. She had just familiarized herself with its soft color pallet, clean lines, and well-used wooden flooring. She had never felt softer wooden floors before and had wondered how old they must be.

Pierce explained to her that he had intended to introduce himself to her back in her old life. His intentions had been to let their relationship unfold naturally before telling her about everything. With her safety at risk, he had to take drastic measures. He assured her she was not a prisoner and this room was not a cage.

The door had been left unlocked, but she retreated within its walls, fortifying herself. She tried to retain her newly acquired knowledge of the realms existing around her own. The alarming part was trying to distinguish where her place was within them.

According to Amy, in their brief moment together before Christine snapped, the fates had once foretold of a Fated match for the ruler of this realm. Pierce had filled in the details. This woman was said to be Middle Earth born and would be equal parts a strength and weakness to him.

Being fated also meant being bound to each other for eternity. A rare and honorable occurrence for Angelicans. The woman tending to her had gone as far as explaining the honor was more so for her. No ruler, or High God, as they called them, had ever been known to share a fated connection, let alone to a mere mortal.

Pierce was convinced she was the woman from this prophecy; Amy believed him. Christine was far less convinced. His claim that he heard the Fates say her very name in reference to this prophecy wouldn't hold any weight with her until she could speak to these supposed 'fates' herself.

The woman tending to her was named Teena. She was mousy-faced and had been the one to let herself in, announcing to Christine that breakfast had been served. Pierce had proven he wasn't an immediate threat, so she saw no harm in accepting basics from him like food and water.

Her clothes had been provided by Amy and were surprisingly made with familiar fabrics. As upset with her as Christine was, she was grateful for the clothes. It would not have gone smoothly had Pierce tried to dress her.

Teena led her down a sparkling set of hallways. The tiles were perfectly laid gray stone slabs. On each side, an expanse of large windows were surrounded by cream-colored walls that gave the space the illusion of warmth.

Each hallway was distinguishable by the view outside. From one side you could see an illustrious garden, the other walked along an open courtyard. There was a disturbingly large fountain of Pierce himself made entirely of stone, with his arms outstretched. She noted the apparent vanity.

They approached a double-door entrance. Its gold handles and trimmings popped out against the plain walls. Teena knocked quietly before pushing the doors open. Pierce sat at the end of a massive table lined with trays of every breakfast food imaginable. Her stomach turned over at the sight of a sweaty tray of sweaty scrambled eggs. Breakfast food had always been her favorite, but seeing it now, made her nauseous.

Pierce was heavily involved with a projected screen in front of him. His eyes meticulously scanned line by line through whatever report he was reading. "Excuse me, my lord. Your guest, Miss Luvlynn, will be joining you this morning. Where would you like me to set her plate?" Pierce snapped to attention.

"Good morning. I'm glad you decided to join me." Rising from his seat, he approached her slowly, looking positively buoyant.

"Oh God, you're a morning person, aren't you?" Christine couldn't help but criticize. She wasn't sure how it was possible, but the smile on his face brightened. He took her left hand and casually brushed his lips in a kiss on her knuckles. An unpleasant shiver vibrated through her and then dissolved, along with some of her previous discomfort.

"God is a bit formal; you can call me Pierce," he joked with a quick wink. "Teena, good morning, lovely. You can set her plate to my right. How is your family doing? Did Cassidy pass her flight test?" he asked with casual interest.

"Good morning, Sir; everyone is well. She failed again, but I have hope this third try will be the one. She just needs to calm down, and she will have a better grasp on control. She just gets so nervous," Teena responded comfortably while grabbing a plate with some silverware from a large, overstated China cabinet that was tucked into the corner of the room. She piled the plate with a little of everything and set it to the right of where Pierce had been sitting.

Pierce was solely focused on Christine. His hand still embracing her fingers. "I am sure you are right. Let me know if you need any time away to assist her. Christine and I can handle things from here." Teena smiled in his direction and curtseyed before turning to leave.

"Thank you, Teena!" Christine called after her.

"You are very welcome!" Teena called back before closing the doors behind her.

The 'fated love' between them had cost her three lives. The lives of her parents and then, more recently, life as she had known it. A price Pierce was all too happy to pay. He seemed ecstatic to have her tied to him forever, but she wasn't reciprocal. She wanted to make that clear as she politely removed her hand from his and went to sit down to eat.

Breakfast food had been the second most frequent thing she shared with Evan. Their entire friendship was built on wine, violence, and bingeing breakfast food after all-nighters. She wanted to ask about him but knew Pierce's response would be the same as it was the first time she asked, "He needs to grieve you, and he will with time. Amy is working closely to ensure he accepts that you are gone."

Unless they somehow planted copious amounts of spattered blood across her apartment, there was no chance in Hell Evan would believe she was dead. She would have gotten a shot off at a minimum. She didn't know how long it would take, but eventually she would explain all this craziness to him. For now, she had to hope he would fill her role in their gym and maybe even thrive without her holding him back.

Feeling no need to perpetuate the fake niceties Pierce clearly was looking for, she poked at her eggs with a fork, debating if she could stomach them. Something about eating food he offered her felt like a submission she was unable to adhere to.

"Christine, I know you don't want to be here. I know you don't reciprocate my excitement about our approaching future together, and I am sorry for that. I will not push you or rush you into anything. All I am asking for is a chance to show you my world and give you time to adjust to it while under my protection."

She pondered his words. She was stuck here either way, that she knew. Taking a deep breath and exhaling in defeat, she finally, truly looked at him. Feeling a sense of mismatched warmth creeping into her chest, she regretted it.

"I will try to be more accepting of your accommodations.

But I can't promise I won't break your hand on reflex if you try to touch me. I don't know you. It's that simple. And I don't feel any sort of pull that one would think should exist between two people fated to be together. All I have to go on here is your word, and the complacency of your subjects, whom I suspect are incredibly biased."

His stunned expression told her he wasn't used to anyone being so candid with him; she felt slightly apologetic for it. Savious wanted her dead; the only reason she was breathing was because he had intervened. Giving him credit for that shouldn't be so hard.

"But I will try to have an open mind to the idea," she added, softening her rough statement. His face softened a little in response.

"That is all I ask." He lifted a glass of purple-looking juice in the air in a fake toast, hiding the concern he now felt. This was not going to be as seamless as he had expected. It injured him that she wasn't experiencing the pull between them because he certainly was. It grew with each rebuttal she threw his way; each grin and laugh she inspired tied her to him more.

Poking a piece of unfamiliar fruit and lifting it to her lips, she looked down at the plate as she hesitantly slipped it past her lips and cautiously chewed. He leaned back in his chair, brazenly watching her with interest; she lit up at the taste of krezzlebart. It was similar to mixing Kiwi and strawberry together and getting a cantaloupe texture.

Based on the enjoyment he felt emanating from her, he could tell she loved it. He would make sure there was always some available for her. Excitedly chewing, she popped more krezzlebart into her mouth and glanced in his direction. Catching him grinning at her, her eyes shot back down to her plate, face flushing.

This warmed him. He was raised to believe a woman's place was being guided, protected and cherished by their partner. Their initial interactions had worried him that she may have a hard adjustment to this way of life; her loneliness had hardened her. But if she was willing to give this a chance, he was sure she would grow accustomed to this world and to him.

"Will I get to see some information about the actual prophecy that brought me here? I honestly would love some video footage or any sort of context behind that," she asked.

"This world has a very complicated history; it will be more digestible if taken in at a certain pace and in a particular order. I am having a course put together for you as we speak. I promise you I will make sure you have access to the information you need to feel comfortable making this your home. It may just take a little time." His words were resolute.

His words were diplomatic but contradictorily sincere. She had spent days weighing her options and had already decided to trust him. This place appeared as a Utopia. She needed time to discover if it was real. If it were, she had hope of using the impact she had on this 'leader' of theirs to help all the people suffering back home.

"So, if this realm isn't where the well-behaved dead go, then what is it? 'Cause so far it looks a lot like mine, just shinier." Grabbing her coffee, she took a sip and couldn't decide if she was delighted or worried that it had been prepared to her preferences.

"Much is similar. We have evolved beyond your realm because we have had life here longer. We have been given gifts that nurture us, blessing us with extended lifespans, which allows us more time to learn. The greatest difference between the two is my realm celebrates differences. We do not wage war on them."

She couldn't help but feel a bit judgmental with the arrogance he displayed by claiming a whole world as 'his realm.' Even if the statement impressed her.

"So, there's never been war here, and everyone just unanimously agreed to hail you king almighty? Except the brooding boys you ousted and sent to Hell?" She wasn't buying his utopia sales pitch and was fine with being honest about it.

He pressed his fingers to her arm and lowered her coffee to the table before taking her hands in his, shifting them to be face-to-face.

"Christine. You were raised in a world of greed and fear. It is natural to be skeptical. You will not need to take my word as gospel. This world is yours now. You will get to see for yourself the different cultures and the unifying peace throughout them. My position allows for an oversight that ensures local governments function for the people and not for power."

His sincerity made her hesitate for a whole second before she deflated him by taking her hands back, grabbing her coffee again, taking a swig and hitting him with, "That is easy to say from your literal castle."

The enigma of a man before her didn't recede or blanch as she expected but smiled wider. "It is," he said with a laugh. "Which is why it isn't simply my word I expect you to learn to trust. It is the many voices of the countless people you will meet."

"Okay, but I retain the rights to judgment until your self-claimed virtue is proven. In the meantime, I will try not to give you too much grief."

"That is only fair."

He scooted away, maintaining a suspicious smile as he resumed his meal, looking as if he had just won something. Christine couldn't help but think about how the therapists of her past would be so proud, talk about 'taking social risks.'

***

Pierce worked hard to earn his status as the most patient man alive over the course of the next two years. He gave me space when I needed it and put visible effort into not pressuring me.

The first few months I spent here consisted of me being

paraded through the different territories of this land. I was constantly being bombarded with questions. Pierce ended up answering them for me because I always panicked with a microphone shoved in my face. The perfection of this place frazzled me. I hadn't even fogged up like that during the interview I had about my student. Granted, I had only told that reporter to fuck off, but still, I had done so confidently.

The questions I held now, years after being dragged into this new life, eclipsed the questions I had then. Questions Pierce acted eager for me to answer, yet actively limited the resources I needed in which to learn them.

One of the biggest backings I had in my faith of him was the people's consistent view of his character. He was their first, people-chosen High God. The man who was one of them, even if his bloodline was of the ruler's past, he was a symbol of independence that shone into the future.

And I could only muster enough affection for him to kiss, even after all this time...

His certainty did nothing to dissuade my unease. Pierce was sweet and an obvious sort of attractive; if I squinted and turned my head to the side, I could almost see what everyone else did.

'If only I could banish this nagging feeling I had in my gut.'

Something still felt wrong. I had been considering stomping that 'something' deep down and moving forward with Pierce. I had always trusted my intuition; ignoring it was becoming increasingly difficult.

His constant restriction of information didn't help. The excuse of 'needing to digest information in a specific order' had long since lost its power with me.

I had been sitting with my legs crossed in a padded window library nook, skimming through a book I had stolen during a dinner party we had attended a few weeks ago. He must have sensed the flipping of forbidden pages because he obnoxiously poofed into view. His presence always intensified any existing sunlight, turning my nook into a microwave.

"I didn't know I could summon you by reading. I'll have to misbehave more often then," I said, forcing a flirtatious response. His smile grew; he pulled me closer to him.

"You misbehave often enough, my love. I thought we agreed you would read only the material I provided you. It's a substantial amount of information, and it will be better if you read it in a certain order," he gently chastised me while tugging the book from my hands.

"Well, you may have decided, along with everything else in my life, but that doesn't mean I agreed," I countered, a bit of my now damped spark rising in me again. His eyes sparkled back at me in response; the storm inside me calmed before he changed the subject.

"I have a surprise for you. Amy needs an escort back to Middle Earth. I thought it would be a nice chance to reconnect."

I climbed out of the nook and pushed past him. The book Pierce had just snatched from me had confirmed that transporting was exceedingly rare, which was nice because it was obnoxious. I had stolen the book to see if Pierce had been honest about inventing the skill, and about my inability to ever learn it. The abilities I had been gifted with by him had not included anything useful for eventually leaving if that became necessary.

"She has made her disinterest in playing my babysitter any longer very clear," I said.

"When did she say anything of the sort?" he challenged.

"She would need to SEE me to tell me things. Absence speaks volumes." I crossed my arms; he grabbed them, still sitting on the edge of the nook, pulling me in between his legs to stop my pacing.

"It's fortunate then that it is not her choice," he beamed, allowing his familiar warmth to wash over me, oftentimes a little too garishly. The determination he had to help me to grow roots into this life was evident daily.

Constantly taking me into public, putting me with new instructors, and making me participate in community events. I felt bad about how much I frustrated him, but only slightly.

"Yeah, because that's the way to get someone to be my friend, by force," I jabbed at him sarcastically. He responded by pulling me into his arms.

"Tell me, have you made a negative acquaintance in the whole of your time here?" I soured a bit, knowing his point.

"Maybe not negative, but certainly not positive, or even real." There was a defeated pout in my voice at this.

Pierce had ushered me to countless colorful events, hoping I would connect with people. Each had ended the same way. I was a fun point of gossip, the High God's fated match, basically his fucking accessory. For this alone, I loathed this new life.

"Pierce, I will never be able to grow roots here from your shadow...."

He grabbed my chin as he often did and took a moment to look into my eyes before tilting his head forward and kissing me deeply. "I will never understand the persistence of which you condemn yourself and those around you. I and everyone you have met adore you. Amy is included in that. Maybe she just needs to know you forgive her."

My negative emotions at the prospect of an awkward walk with Amy faded away; hope rose, taking its place.

"Okay, I'll give it another shot. Where do I meet her?"

***

It had been two years since I'd had a direct conversation with Amy. Our last blowout hung heavy in the air between us still. Want be damned, I couldn't seem to cut through it. We were already basically to the division; I had not managed to squeak out a single word.

She had betrayed me. She had been lying to me my entire

life, so in my mind, she should be the one apologizing. Yet, I could barely think of anything else to say to break the silence between us.

Not that I got the chance. We walked the entire path already. Passed through the large golden gates and trudged the full mile of stone path to the shimmering division point.

Amy stepped through first; I followed shortly after. Amy was oblivious to *him*. He had been swaying on a swing not far from us and was now headed in our direction. Something about this guy seemed off, the purposefulness of his walk, the perfect proportions of his body. He looked familiar, but I couldn't place him.

Amy tensed beside me. "Something is wrong," She said, stopping and looking around us, keeping an eye on the stranger approaching. "Act natural, but I'm pretty sure that's Savious's son." Savious had been revealed to me as the man who killed my parents and had tried to kill me.

Jordan was his son, the mysterious ex-ruler of Heaven. Whenever I would ask about him, Pierce struggled to answer, always saying Jordan was a complicated matter and best explained over time.

The only thing I knew for certain was at some point, Jordan was the crowned High God, ruler of all. Thanks in part to his father and Pierce, he was not only dethroned but banished. That, and whenever I asked about him, the subject was promptly and frantically changed. People seemed to fear the mention of his very name.

He had tried to use his power to hide himself. Changing his eyes blue, his hair long and sandy blond with a pale complexion, and cheekbones that were just slightly too high. Amy saw straight through the trickery he wore. Even I noticed, but for different reasons. Mortals didn't carry themselves that way.

Amy positioned herself slightly in front of me and spoke without turning her head, maintaining her focus on him.

"Okay, Christine, here's how we are going to handle this.

I have an emergency signal I can send out in my hand. Once activated, Heaven's shield will go live; he shouldn't be able to get through. No promises, though, 'cause that's by far the most powerful dude alive. We need to be back past the division point. On my count, run. One..."

I looked at Amy and grabbed her hand before confusion could be replaced by fear or anger and pressed the signal.

I grabbed onto the back of Amy's shirt and threw her behind me with more force than intended. She was back in the division point scrambling to get to her feet; confused and more than a little pissed off.

Sure, we hadn't been close since I had been 'relocated,' but she was the only family I had. I always thought eventually we would reconnect. I loved her too much to hold a grudge forever, and I knew she would, at some point, forgive herself and allow me into her life again. But now I would likely never have that chance. She would consider this a show of my lack of faith in her, even if I did manage to survive.

I backed up just to confirm what I already knew. The shield was up. Amy would be safe. I was all he was after anyway.

Pressing my hands against the strange electrical cold current of the clear shield, I could see Amy pounding on it frantically from the other side. Like an impenetrable glass door, it only allowed me to see the safety of the other side without allowing me to be part of it.

"It's okay," I mouthed. For some reason I wasn't afraid. The way Pierce described Jordan, maybe I could reason with him. From what I understood from my approved book on him, unlike his father, he had reason and respected hierarchy.

Granted, he had likely shifted his stance on hierarchy, considering he was no longer at the top of it. I was gambling on the hopes he would spare me. Whereas, I knew he wouldn't have spared Amy when she inevitably got in his way.

Besides, there was no real reason to kill me. Other than to piss off the man who dethroned him.

ADRENALINE IS ONE HELL OF A DRUG

Christine turned back to face him. He was only a few steps away. Looking her up and down, contemplating how to play this out. She tried not to, but she failed and glanced back. Pierce was standing beside Amy now; both hands pressed against the invisible shield, both sets of eyes wide with horror. Seeing the regularly composed Pierce's unblinking panic did nothing to soothe her nerves.

Taking a deep breath, she steadied herself against the slice ripping through her chest at the look on Pierce's face, not knowing if it was guilt at letting him down or fear at seeing actual rage on his features.

'Act strong,' she thought to herself. 'Take control.'

"You can drop the glamor; you don't even remotely pull off being human." He grinned as his features sharpened and tinted. He had short wavy black hair, a sinfully sharp jawline, and the darkest eyes she had ever seen.

Meeting Pierce had been an education on the beauty of angels over mortals, their polished, more symmetrical features making them all look otherworldly and unreal.

Jordan was something else entirely. If he had truly come from Heaven, then Hell must have muted that polish, must have molded him into something significantly more sinful. Energy from deep within her began to run cold, leaping towards him in desperation.

"I didn't quite know what to expect upon meeting you, but I can honestly say I wouldn't have guessed flattery." An amused look stretched across his perfect face. She had to summon every bitch bone in her body to avoid showing the havoc his voice was reaping on her body.

"The whispers I've heard of you don't do you justice." His tone was thick and incredibly alluring. Each word that dripped from his smirking lips sent pinpricks dancing up her spine.

"Cut the act, Jordan, I'm not that stupid or that susceptible to flattery." Her face hardened into a confident scowl.

In the blink of an eye, his chest was obscuring her view. His hands were gripping her arms just tight enough to wordlessly relay a message against attempting to pull free.

Pierce looked on, helpless and in sheer agony. He was trapped inside; the shield wouldn't be down for another ten minutes. Jordan was staring directly at him while sadistically smelling Christine's hair.

This would be Jordan's payback, Pierce assumed, panic growing by the second. Pierce's jaw clenched as he hit the shield with anger, scolding himself for not allowing her to be trained well enough to defend herself at this moment. Their shared history had been reflected in his description of him to her, or lack thereof. Jordan would use all ten minutes to make him suffer for the revolt; it was working.

***

I wasn't naive; I knew I was only a pawn to get payback on Pierce for the moment. Jordan didn't consider me a threat.

That was a mistake; nobody touched me without my permission. Even if the sensation his touch left lingering wasn't unpleasant.

He released an arm to move my hair, but I wasn't interested in this game. I grabbed his hand and twisted it behind his back, forcing him to release my other arm, then pushed him away from me with as much strength as I could summon. He was sent flailing, face first into the moist grass.

"Stronger than I look? Do not touch me; not even the fates know where your hands have been. And leave Pierce out of this. I know your pitiful father has failed to kill me several times. Has he given up and sent his child to do the dirty work?"

I suddenly felt confident and could almost see Pierce's grin behind me. Jordan stood; his cocky smile was gone. I could tell he didn't expect that, and that I had ruined his game, so naturally he was pissed.

"Did you just give me an order? That's adorable and okay; your call. I'll leave him out of this, but that just cut seven minutes off the ten you had left to live." I hadn't thought about that.

'Oops.'

Still feeling surprisingly confident, I decided to push him a little more.

'Why not have a little fun if I'm gonna die anyway.'

"Are you still pissed they gave you the boot alongside your Pops? Well, this is probably a good example as to why. Do you even have any reason to be here other than Daddy said so? Real leaders make their own calls." Something dark flashed in his eyes and I could tell I hit a sore spot.

I should have been panicking; I was about to die. So why did I feel so giddy? Did facing death always make you feel so invincible? Just the irony alone made me laugh.

Jordan was close again, an embarrassed anger bubbling beneath his masculine surface. The gentle wind had stiffened, ants retreated to their hills, the sky seemed to dull away. The nature around us was even perceptive enough to know fleeing in fear was probably a fair reaction to angering this particular being.

Hand gripping my neck, he lifted me from the ground and shoved me against the shield. As my skull bounced off it with damaging force, his eyes snapped open. His grip adjusted; he lowered me quickly back to the ground. One of his hands cupped my face, examining it with a pained and almost disturbed look in his eyes.

"They didn't; they wouldn't...." His whisper came out in a broken hiss as he pressed his fingertips to my forehead and looked me deep in the eyes.

There were black specks in his deep brown eyes that glinted silver when the light hit them. He pulled something from inside me in the same way Pierce had when this all began, back when I thought all he had done was stop a panic attack.

Jordan's face was close, but his eyes were distant as he peered and looked at my soul. My vision was blurring; blood was moistening the back of my neck. There were tears forming in the devil's darkening eyes. Not as an enemy. I couldn't place his expression, but I recognized a vengeful death lingering in the depths of his blackening gaze.

'Fuck you, bastard,' was my last thought. Looking directly at him, I tried burning him with my hate. My gaze locked with his and, unable to look away, my view of him shifted.

A deeper warmth began to radiate where Jordan held my neck. A connection was forming; I didn't know what it meant or what it was, but I knew any fear I previously had of this man was gone. Replaced by a different kind of heightened pulse. He was smiling back at me in the softest way, saying a thousand apologies with just a look.

Images of Pierce flooded my mind, causing me to clench my eyes shut, breaking the connection. Cutting that tie felt like getting punched in the chest as a bomb-like explosion erupted between us, sending me flying back against the shield again.

The world went static. The last thing I heard was Pierce's voice screaming my name.

***

The shield was down. Jordan was looming over her, angry, confused, and betrayed again. Pierce screamed for her, but as he did her eyes closed, and her body went limp. He was behind Jordan, the place he had been trying to transport since the shield was activated, but now Jordan was between him and her.

Jordan stood above her breathing in agitated breaths and seething with bitterness and rage.

"Jordan, refrain from making this personal. I beg you, don't hurt her," Pierce pleaded.

"Hurt her?" he rumbled disbelievingly back at his old friend.

"My throne, the love of my people, my home, I did not take you stealing those from me personally. But how dare you steal her?" Jordan gritted the words past his clenched teeth and made a motion with his hand as something smashed into the back of Pierce's head, sending him to his knees.

The world was spinning. He watched helplessly as Jordan pulled Christine into his arms like a groom about to carry his bride over the threshold to their new home. Pierce tried to move, tried to stop him, but his body wouldn't listen to his commands. Tasting the metallic tang of blood in his mouth, he fell on his hands and knees. Jordan gently cradled Christine against him as if he couldn't hold her tight enough.

"Don't do this...." Pierce reached out, agony eating away at his stomach at the sight of Jordan looking down at Christine with a possessiveness he had never seen in Jordan's eyes before. He fell, fighting and losing against the darkness that was surrounding him.

"Pierce?! He's over there!" Amy's voice was the only thing

that made it through the haze he was drifting in. Several men surrounded him, unfolding a long straight board that they swiftly flipped him onto before a familiar voice warned him.

"Pierce, stay still. It's me; I will be removing the spear. It will hurt," Victor warned.

Two men had jumped into preparations when the signal had flared to life, alerting specific members of the realm. Victor had been the lead advisor under Arcane, Pierce's fathers' rule. He had stepped up to assist Pierce in his unexpected transition to the throne.

The other had moved Amy back away from the scene. After assuring she was unharmed, he bent, silver-tipped wings furled back, and yanked the spear from Pierce's skull. Pierce screamed, going limp. Victor pressed his lips together, making irritated eye contact with the winged man as he pressed his palm to the oozing wound, beginning the healing process.

"Azazel... Your help is appreciated, but a warning would be nice next time. I would have preferred to move him first." Victor attempted to scold.

Being the head of the most coveted and respected of Angelican institutions, The Old Guard, put Azazel in the unique position of fearing no authority. As such, he smiled a small, guiltless smile and shrugged his wide shoulders.

His lower feathers lifted slightly off the ground from his slouched position, and he grinned. The many knifes strapped to his chest glinting light back into Victor's eyes as he responded with an insincere, "Oops."

***

Tense. The first feeling Christine registered while grasping back her consciousness was a tenseness pulling from the back of her skull down to her neck.

She was surrounded by the most alluring mix of soft pressure and downright the most calming scent she had ever experienced. It reminded her of the first minutes of morning, when the dew is still settled and the sun has not yet inflamed the sky. The smell of a peace not yet disturbed by the light of a new day.

Before her brain had the chance to switch back into reality, she bunched her hands and found them full of a thick silky fabric and pulled it to her face. Her mind was soothed to a stillness she had never known as she inhaled deeply, savoring the sweet scent of stillness.

Her eyes snapped open, body uncurling briskly from the tight ball she had been wound in. Fear replacing her calm as quickly as the turn of a coin.

Luckily, there was no light to aggravate her eyes upon opening them, but the darkness was too undisturbed, too still. Something about the lack of light in the air seemed forced, as if someone had taken each little molecule of light between the atoms and punched them down into nothing.

"Good evening, Goddess. You had me worried for a bit there." A restrained and unfamiliar voice filled the room. Stepping near her, he turned on the lamp, illuminating the darkness but not entirely snuffing it out. There was no ridding any room he inhabited of the dark. It didn't so much cling to him as it emanated from him.

Her eyes were brightened with panic. It wasn't the response she should have had to him. Regardless, he grinned down at her, one dimple popping in his olive skin. There was a brief moment he began to bend down to her, seeking to connect to the thrum of her energy.

Jordan returned her panicked look with one of complete dis-alarm. The only photos she had seen of him, he appeared so regal and domineering from his throne. He had looked downright infected with severity.

Before her now was a grinning and comfortable man who seemed completely at ease. Casual wear of loose gray sweatpants and a rumpled black t-shirt did nothing to dampen the sinful effect his gaze spurred deep within her the second their eyes connected.

The weight of the blanket draped across her, mixed with the stiffness of her neck, made rolling to the other side of the bed that much more difficult, fueling her pride at the speed she managed. Falling off the bed onto her hands and knees was not as graceful as she had intended, but distance was distance; she'd take it.

Jumping to her feet, she threw up her fists and worked to steady her swaying legs.

A soft and seductive chuckle rattled his chest as his eyes listed over her graciously, his own arms crossing in front of him.

"Are you..." he asked, suppressing a laugh, "trying to look threatening?"

In her mind's eye, she could only imagine how she looked at this moment. It wasn't far off from the image standing before Jordan now. Hair a wild curly mane sticking in every direction. Her frame was unsteady and very fragile looking.

"Whatever game you're playing, I won't be a pawn..." Her returning strength presented itself in words, faltering only slightly as she reached down, running a hand down her torso and discovering a fabric that had certainly never touched her skin before, and very little of it. "What the fuck am I wearing?"

"I'd be willing to bet you'll enjoy my games." His voice carried with it a stable depth that sank deeply into her very bones. An invisible cord tightened around her, she felt it tug her towards him. "What is wrong with the gown? Not your color?"

Jordan's eyes smoldered with the taunt as he prepared to move around the bed to her. To get closer and strengthen the effect she would feel from their connection. He found her will to be incredible, to know she felt this pull between them and fought it so adamantly.

"If you plan to finish what you started and kill me, then

DELIGHTFULLY DAMNED

just do it." At her words, his advance froze in place, his expression becoming severe and affectionately concerned at the same time, his head tilted to the side.

There was nothing but darkness in the skies of Hell. The God they once relied on for sunlight was long dead. Killed in a war waged against the ancient deities of this realm, a war that had left the land barren.

But at this moment, that darkness found its own form of illumination. A blue, reminiscent of dawn, was peeking through the inky shroud and seeped into his dwelling, reaching for her. He took a deep breath, calming himself and allowing the eternal night to retreat.

Blurred lines and shifting focus distorted her vision, slight pain still ebbing from the back of her skull, but she wavered only slightly.

"To take your life would be to take my own. You must feel this..." He pointed between them while asking.

The gravity of the situation began to sink in.

'I am in hell. Trapped in the personal chambers of the uncontested most powerful being alive, who was thrown from his home by the man who claimed me as his match... I was ready to die by his hand, but not whatever this is.'

"Jordan." A sinful shadow clouded his eyes as she said his name. The hairs on the back of her neck electrified in response to the intensity of his gaze, landing heavily on her.

"I'm not involved in your war. I am no threat to you or your father. You need to let me go. I know this seems like a great way to get payback for everything that has happened, but please, Pierce still regrets what happened with you." Jordan stood, taking a perceivably aggressive stance, squaring himself in her direction.

"He has always been an excellent manipulator. Nothing I can say about him will change your mind. This," he motioned between them, "isn't about him. It's about us. I do not intend to be someone or something I am not with you. You are mine,

57

my dear. And I will treat you like you are mine. You will accept me, and you will find it's easier than you would like." Possessiveness hung in the air of his words, resolute and unwavering.

"That's why you didn't kill me?" The words tasted like a spoonful of thick salt.

'How could this be happening?' She wondered as Jordan stood at the end of the bed facing her.

"I'm not going to kill you, and I don't want to hurt you, but I warn you, I have been waiting a long time for this, and my patience is thin. Come here, sit with me, please." He attempted to lure her in.

She saw a pathway to the door and took it. Jumping on the bed, she slid across the covers, hitting the floor on the other side. She pulled herself up and bolted to the doorway. Ripping the door open she saw, with dismay, Jordan angrily awaiting her on the other side.

"Surprise." He grabbed her neck and forced her back in, smothering her body with his against the wall and slamming the door with his foot. An explosion of pain ricocheted inside her skull, originating from her recent head trauma.

"I'm sorry about your head. You struck a chord. I haven't handled anything as delicate as yourself in a long time."

He composed himself after a regretful twinge, putting an arm on each side of her, and pressing her back against the wall. She was trapped in a cocoon of his body, too close for her comfort, and not liking the way his closeness affected her blood flow. Gasping for air, she summoned an answer.

"You would think an EX High God would have more control over his strength. Delicate in your hands, maybe, but don't think that means I would ever bend to you. Take my advice; you'll want to lock me in a cage before I have the chance to test your own 'delicacy.'" The fire running up her thighs protested the lie.

"I don't have a cage that would suit you. No, I think I'll keep you on silk instead." He chuckled, lifting her chin, and pulling at her bottom lip with his thumb softly. Fire sizzled beneath the touch turning the tips of her face a traitorous red.

"You're fighting a losing battle. I'm not easily swayed." She spat the words at him, refusing to lose her will, regardless of the response her body was having.

He stepped as close as he could, his corded muscles tightening with what she could only assume was anger, and bent, whispering against her neck. "Really? I'm sure I can find some way to sway you."

He wrapped his fingers tightly around the back of her neck, pushing and leading her back to the massive bed. She tried burning his wrists where he held her. It was useless. Being technically mortal, mixed with her powers not being fully her own didn't leave her in the best fighting shape against him, the most powerful immortal alive.

"Let me go!" she screamed at him as he easily tossed her on the bed. She tried to scramble away from him, but with a playful smile, he grabbed her ankle and pulled her back to him. Going for nerves and pressure points did nothing against him. He shook his head at her, grabbed both her wrists and held them above her head, using his legs to restrain hers.

"Get off me!" Her heart pounded as she struggled. Looking up at him, hating the way he looked down at her, causing her thighs to throb and her breath to hitch.

"Done yet? You will only hurt yourself. This pull between us is excruciating; I know you can feel it too. Save your energy," he cooed while lifting the silk nightgown, gingerly pulling it off and exposing her beneath him. She hadn't been naked in front of anyone since she was a toddler, but for some reason, the discomfort she expected to feel never came.

Nothing had felt as inevitable to him as she had right then. He had spent several lifetimes avoiding connecting with people to protect himself from vulnerability. Efforts be damned, fate had decided with this moment; none of it had mattered. He would suffer for an eternity to keep her safe.

This was what it was to meet your fated match, looking into certain doom with a welcoming smile on your face. Their skin felt like a barrier as the tensile thread between them continued to tighten. His shirt began burning away from his skin, falling in charred pieces around her.

His eyes moved around her, drinking her in, adding to the confusing pulse she was feeling for the first time, as if her heart had just now begun to beat fully.

"I know you feel this too. Don't listen to me or the voices of past warnings. Right now, at this moment, what do you want?" She arched into him as he trailed soft kisses up from her belly button to her neck. He stopped to look into her eyes again, thanking fate for sending her.

Her sides were littered with goosebumps in a trail, where he brushed his fingers up and down her gently. She looked deep into his black eyes, hating herself for enjoying the icy shiver he ravaged her with. It was a snap moment of realization that she had begun to fully succumb to him.

This genuine reaction felt like a deep betrayal to Pierce. She tried to refuse the pleasure he was thrusting upon her by pulling her face away and looking to the side.

"You're going to make this difficult on yourself, aren't you, Goddess?" He palmed her jaw, tilting her face to his. "You will learn not to test me. Being mine doesn't have to be torture; in fact, it shouldn't be. You only fight this, this thing I know you want, because of how misled you have been about me. You aren't in danger here. I am not your enemy. I am your greatest of allies. It is natural for you to want me, so let yourself."

Her breath quickened in resentment at the accusation and at herself for proving it to be true as her heart hammered away in her chest, her blood pooling in inappropriate places.

He pulled her face closer, their lips brushing one another. She could feel herself begin to sway in the wrong direction once again, so easily, and decided to act against it as violently as possible, biting his lip as hard as she could manage, drawing blood.

"The only man I 'lust' for is Pierce, and you aren't half the man he is." The lie was so thick she could barely force it from her lips; as she did, the very words tasted like sour milk upon her tongue. But it was all she could think of to dissuade this allusion she assumed he had to be putting forth, thinking it couldn't be her natural reaction, because she had never burned for anyone like this.

His tongue slowly cleared the blood from his lip as his grin dimpled in response to her tenacity, appreciating how inauthentic her lie sounded.

That same devilish grin sent a fleeting wave of dark electricity through her. His fingers moved up her face, sizzling energy ebbing and flowing, seeking its opposite out.

"What are you doing to me?" she asked, half mystified over the brief spits of color she could see dancing between her skin and his fingertips.

The sultry crack in his grin grew as he leaned closer, lips daring hers, "Nothing, yet."

Jordan lifted himself away, becoming entranced. He pressed his palm to her chest. While mumbling a curse into the air, he marked the last place he kissed, just below her collarbone. Her flesh sizzled under his touch, the heat growing with intensity as he chanted something under his breath that she couldn't understand.

She screamed in pain, feeling the mark burn past her skin, etching on to her very soul. A jagged-looking J was etched in the center of his handprint, now forever marking her chest.

"Are you familiar with the marking curse? I perfected it. Back above we marked soldiers with it. That way, if their energies were depleted, more could be sent to them, or if they went missing, they could be easily found...."

He paused, calculating something.

"Three weeks without me, and it could kill you, burning you from the inside out. I can control how much energy you have; I can tell where you are, and it is my mark that will burn on your chest until the end of our days. I will be the first and the only man to truly ever have you in every way. You. Are. Mine. Accept it."

Her face paled while she glowered at him. He brushed long strands of hair back away from her neck, pleased with the shifting look inside her eyes, knowing her internal battle against fate was nearing an end. He grazed the skin of her bare back gently as he pulled her closer to him.

An unfamiliar burning need scrambled every nerve ending in their bodies. He leaned his face to hers, pushing their lips together, softly at first but growing fierce as she reciprocated their kiss. No one had ever felt so good beneath him. When reaching to remove his pants he became impatient, and they, too, began to burn off his body.

Every time she would close her eyes, looking away from him and trying to deny herself this natural feeling, he would cup her face and guide it back to him. He could take his time; the mere dance of energy taking place beneath the skin already in contact was enough to satisfy him.

As much as it may have shamed her, she found herself aching; the heat of wanting him was becoming the only thing she could feel, drowning the rest of her thoughts away.

The bruises forming on her wrists and the pain were adding to the confusing pleasure entrapping her. She had never wanted anyone, but this was more than wanting; her body sizzled beneath him. She felt like she would set fire without him. She had never felt such a strong need for anything the way she did, at this moment, for him.

"I know you want this, but I need you to show me I am correct, or this ends here." He paused and bent to run his nose up hers, only pulling back to pin her with his eyes, hoping she could reach within them and feel his desperation.

"Christine, for the love of all that is right in these realms, show me."

The very core of herself took control as he began to lift

away from her with doubt in his eyes. The doubt was quickly replaced by excited surprise when she hooked his leg with her own and, using a move she had known a very long time, reversed their positions. Pinning him onto his back, putting her in a position to now be the one hovering over him.

She had little experience with men, and she could tell, even if she had, it would not have prepared her for him.

He was the Devil himself, his own species. The desperation in his lips embrace, and the way he knew the perfect ways to hold and handle her made her realize she could have never avoided him. Somehow, she fit him perfectly, as if she were built for his pleasure, as he was built for hers.

Steam rose from between them, lifting from their skin along with her feelings of disgrace and shame.

4

SO, THAT JUST HAPPENED

I woke to find myself disoriented and very, very sore. Looking around the room, I forced myself to accept that I hadn't just had a very shameful dream-nightmare thing but lived it. I kissed him back and held him versus pushing away from him. Good lord, I even climbed on top of him at one point.

My body thrummed contentedly as I tried to stifle the shame-filled thoughts of Pierce discovering how easily I gave myself to Jordan after years of him going at my pace...

Thankfully I woke up alone this time. I tried to take a better inventory of my surroundings and walk myself through what had happened and what I had learned.

'I woke up, confronted Jordan. He proclaimed his dominance over me, I initially tried to fight him, but as soon as he touched me, I completely unraveled. He hurt me; that didn't sway my feelings at all. What the hell is wrong with me?'

Sitting cross-legged in his bed, I tried for a moment to contemplate this and pursed my lips at myself for getting utterly distracted. This place, this bed, kept seducing me with thoughts of the night before.

I had to wonder, was it Jordan that somehow smelled like

first dawn, or was that the normal smell of Hell?

'Hell. I'm in Hell. In the personal bed chamber of the actual fucking Devil. Who wasn't surprised by our connection at all? I am missing something. He said something about me having some sort of calculated ignorance, that Pierce knew this would happen.' I shook the thought off.

Pierce had told me everything I needed to know. The prophecy had been revealed during a show put on by the Fates during the annual Fates festival. That same day the revolt happened. The High God they referenced during the show must have been Jordan and not Pierce.

'That would make sense, 'cause everything I read about the inevitable bonding with a fated match fits perfectly into meeting Jordan. But... Why would Pierce claim a connection if he didn't have one? Put so much work into being patient with me?'

Shame sat, agitated in my stomach for the briefest of moments before my heart stilled in my chest, my blood running cold, as a staggering realization hit me in a new way.

'I'm in Hell.'

'I'm in the realm energy cycles through. The realm that cleanses the energy of the dead.'

'My parents.'

There were so many unknowns, but none of them plagued me now. Whatever my parents became after death was here.

The black, metal handle of the door was fully warmed by the time I summoned the courage to pull it downwards, given the last time I tried to leave this room. A shiver ran through me at the memory of Jordan's rough thumb pulling my lip down and our bodies close after he walked me back into the room. Shoving the invasive thought DEEP down, I crept forward into the gothic hallway.

Taking a deep breath, I knelt on the ground and flattened my hands against the stone floors. One of the earliest things I was taught about my powers was to start by centering myself.

To get a feel for the environment around me, opening up to it and testing what reached back and what didn't. This test would tell me what I could depend on to bend to my will and what would resist.

The response I got was as cold as the tile beneath me; unlike in Heaven, where everything teemed with life and opened itself easily to my influence, here I was blocked. Nothing wanted to act as my eyes; nothing would help guide me. I was surrounded by darkness. The more I tried to connect to the world around me, the darker it got. As if to say it already had a master, the same one as me.

Standing shakily, I propped myself against the wall, irritated. One leg after another, I forced myself to keep moving; it felt like I was walking through buckets of sand, reminding me of a vacation my parents and I had taken to the Sand dunes of Southern Michigan. The ground seemed to give more and more with each step, sucking me deeper down into the exhaustion my legs were battling.

After wandering down what felt like an eternity of hallways that all looked identical, I came across a large doorway. Very castle-like, wooden and embroidered with Iron, not forgetting the big circle handles. I had to reach above my head to reach one, pulling with all my strength; the door, to my surprise, opened.

Heat kissed my face as hot wisps of dry air invaded the cool castle. I dared one foot out the door and then another. I understood I was in Hell, I understood I had no idea how to get out, and if the rumors were true, there was no way out without either having your soul recycled or having the ability to transport, which I did not.

'Getting out will be my next task. First, I need to see that damned river.'

With the heat of the air straining my lungs, I expected it to be blindingly bright out, with sand everywhere, some sort of desert wasteland. What I found was nothing of the sort.

The sky was black with no clouds or stars. It was a moonless rainforest that sat too still, having no wind to encourage the vines and leaves to dance.

Foot by foot, I plopped heavily down each stone step of the grand stairway leading me down and away from the ridiculous monster-sized doors. Thick vines and trees lined a narrow, black cobblestone path that stretched farther than I could see. In my 'Pierce approved' studies, I had learned a common stone here was obsidian. There were many different forms of it, and one of them, although black, radiated a soft light. The path was littered with them, giving off the only light with which someone could make their way.

Luckily, the path leading away from the Castle was a decline, at the bottom of which I could see lights blinking at me encouragingly.

'That could be a city. For fuck's sake, how did the months of lessons on Hell teach me nothing about the geography of this place?'

"Pierce must not have found it necessary," I sneered, a bit of rising bitterness twinging my tongue.

About three miles into my trudge, I noticed I hadn't considered changing before leaving. I was in a nightgown and nothing else. Walking towards a city in Hell, basically naked, wouldn't be a good idea. All the survival skills I had mastered, all for nothing.

With a self-deprecating sigh, I spun on my heels, looking back up the steady hillside to the castle. From this distance I could see the full thing; it made me suppress a laugh despite my current condition. The stone it was crafted of was so dark that the only thing distinguishing it from the inky sky were a few of the same luminous stones speckling the path.

Now, I had a choice. Walk myself back and face Jordan, whose castle seems so small from this distance, or keep pushing forward and hope I get lucky.

'Fuck it, onwards.'

Pushing forward, I finally came across a sign for the strangely dark city.

**Atlantis – Not the lost city, but a city
for those who are lost**

I laughed, appreciating the unexpected humor.

"At least someone finds me funny." I startled, falling to the side at the sudden voice beside me. Hitting the ground hard, I looked up at a slim man with sandy blond hair and dark eyes, eyes that were fixed on me hungrily.

Growling, I kicked his legs out from under him before he had a chance to move any closer to me. Obviously caught off guard, he landed on his side, arm pinned under his body, laughing hysterically.

Still feeling weighed down, I was surprised by how quickly I was able to get up and make a run for it. I felt his fingers slip around my ankle, pulling me back down as he pulled himself up the length of me, covering my body with his.

"What in the three realms are you doing here, peachy?" He was still laughing as he asked the question, standing, then offering me a hand to help me to my feet. I needed help. I needed guidance. I didn't have the luxury of passing up the opportunity to get this man, threat or not, to fill both of those needs.

"I'm looking for my parents. Well... Not really my parents; they were murdered by a resident here, Savious. I never got to say goodbye." Truth was the only thing I had to offer as I grabbed his hand and allowed myself to be yanked to my weary feet by him. As soon as I was up, I pulled my hand from his clammy grasp.

"I hate to tell you this, but if you are a mortal who managed to get through the gates, then you would have passed the river to get to our current location. Seems you overshot your quest..." His pity was dripping with insincerity.

"I never said I was mortal," I responded.

"Well, you certainly aren't one of the locals."

"How do you know?" It was clear I was providing more amusement than he had enjoyed in some time as he laughed back at me.

"You have a couple of dead giveaways, little peach. First thing you should know," he said, shocking me by transporting to the space previously between us, "Is that this entire realm has one group of people, the Givi. They are all deaf, the lot of them, and their skin is hard and very gray." I stepped out of his reach as he tried to run a finger down my face.

"You are pretty vocal and colored yourself," I said, crossing my arms and stepping back again.

"I'm proudly mixed. Dad's Angelican, Mom's a local. I've been stuck here and bored for a bit now. It's nice to meet someone new." There was a tint of threat in his words I didn't miss.

"Is your dad, by any chance, Savious?" His teeth shone through his widening smile at my question.

"Not sure I want to answer that, considering he killed your parents, and that kind of divide can't be a good place to start a friendship." To me, that was a screaming yes.

Jordan had a brother, maybe more siblings. This was interesting, considering I was certain no one in Heaven was aware Savious had continued to reproduce after exile. His family line was a powerful one, and any kids of his, mixed or not, could make some serious waves if they wanted to.

'Great,' I thought. 'Just what the three realms need, more Savious's.'

If he was Jordan's brother, I had to assume he would march me right back to the castle if he discovered who I was. I wasn't ready to give up yet. These last years I have felt emotionally suspended in time. As if my parents were on a long trip and would return at any time.

I needed to see something, anything that would help me

feel like losing them was real.

"Friends help each other. Can you point me in the direction of the river Stx?" I asked.

"What exactly would you do with that information? It isn't close to here, and you won't make it like that." He pointed from my toes to my head in judgment.

"Point the way, and I'll be fine," I assured him.

"I'll do you one better. I'll take you there, on one condition."

"What condition?" His eyes turned predatory as his head cocked.

"I want to taste your skin."

"I'm sorry?" I balked.

"You look soft and sweet and not at all what I am used to. I'll take you for a quick taste." He left me no time to agree or reject his bizarre and creepy request before lurching forward and taking hold of my arms. The heat was gone, replaced by a frigid wind.

I pushed away from him, managing to keep a stable footing on the uneven ground. Before me was the most disheartening sight I could have imagined. I had seen my fair share of rivers; this was no river. I covered my nose, overwhelmed with a scent that reminded me of severely burnt sugar cookies.

An expanse of glowing red liquid stretched as far as the eye could see. It cut itself against the obsidian stone shore we were standing on, illuminating my feet with its eerie red haze. This is how I would imagine radioactive blood would look.

And somewhere within its churning, the energy that once shaped my parents was trapped. Forever being shredded against the jagged salt rocks at its bottom, being purified. Bits of themselves cleansed as their souls prepared to be sent out again. Fresh and ready for their next lives.

With grave intent, I dropped to my knees and shoved my hands deep into the dark rocks. They were small and smooth, welcoming my fingertips within them. I tried to replicate one of the first things I had been taught in Heaven.

Pierce had given me power, gifted me energy that would sustain my life and allow me certain Angelican comforts. Such as feeling life within the world around me in a more direct way.

To search for water, you have to visualize being submerged in it. How does it taste? How does it feel on your skin? What does it smell like? These were the things I was instructed to focus on. If you can imagine something clearly enough, it will reach back out to you, enveloping you with its essence and guiding you to it.

I reached out now, desperate, pining and pulling for my parents. Focusing was proving difficult; the burnt smell smothered my mind as I tried to pull forth what I needed of my parents.

Burnt cookies, this river smelled like one of the worst associations I had with them. My eyes burned now. Not seeing the river any longer, but my mother. She had an apology in her eyes, the blue of which was highlighted by the flour speckling her tanned face as she whispered her very last words to me, ones she had used on many less-horrible occasions, "It's okay, Krissy. Everything will be just fine." Those words were each a blow to me now, followed by the unforgettable crunch of her neck as Savious snapped it, and the thud her body made as she crumpled, lifeless, to the floor.

Her body had fallen beside the rubble my father was buried in, where Savious had thrown him through the support beam in our kitchen, shattering his spine. He had been headed to pull our already burnt Christmas cookies from the oven, a 'kiss the cook' apron tied around his neck, when Savious had attacked.

I had faced Savious with watering eyes from the smoke that came from the oven. My dad forgetting the timer as we bustled about getting the house ready for the holidays, should have been something we would get to make fun of him for.

But instead, the mistake forever cemented the smell of

burning cookies to that night. It plagued me now in a way it had never succeeded in doing in the past. The scent festered, slipping through a growing crack in the reservoir within me I hadn't known was there.

A firm hand wrapped around my arm; I was pulled to my feet. My strange guide was moving his lips, but I couldn't make out the words. The world shimmered around us; then we were standing in front of the Atlantis sign from before.

"Well, I doubt you're mortal, or you'd be dead." His face was close to mine, examining me. This time he didn't allow me to jerk away. "So, if you're not Givi and you aren't mortal, you must be a shiny Angelican. The only reason Angelicans come here is to spy, making you the enemy and fair game." It was clear he was talking to himself more than me.

My energy was still only a wisp inside me. My cheeks felt damp, alerting me to the likelihood that I had finally, for the first time since their death, cried for my parents. I was breathless, lightheaded, and discombobulated.

But I needed to get away from this creep. The motions I had spent years making second nature took over as I slammed a heel down on the arch of his foot. I twisted and sank an elbow into his gut, jarring him enough that he released me, and I was able to make a run for it.

Running didn't do much to help me when this assailant had the obnoxious ability to transport.

'Curse Pierce and Jordan for discovering this specific ability,' I groaned as Savious's son appeared before me, grabbing me again.

This time I tried a new technique. I let out a deep breath and excited the energy within my skin, causing it to heat up.

"Ow, Cute trick. I'm gonna have some fun with you, aren't I? I like a good fight." He hooked his leg behind mine, sending us both to the ground. Now on top of me, he removed his shirt and wrapped it around my arms. Having access to the world around me was the only weapon in my arsenal, and it had failed me. Unlike with Jordan, this wasn't something I had to fight against the want for.

"I held up my end," he said.

"I never agreed, you son of a bitch," I yelled back, head-butting him as hard as I could.

I was seeing stars as a consequence of the headbutt as he ran his tongue up the side of my face. His hot breath seared my throat. His saliva on my cheek felt acidic as my skin sizzled; the smell of his breath was masked by the smell of my burning flesh.

He looked like the California surfer type, tanned skin, sandy blond hair, usually a cute group to be looped in with, yet I had never been more repulsed. A whole world filled with interesting people I hadn't met; an entire population named the Givi, and I was stuck with this fleshy toned jackass.

The trail of saliva on my face still boiled, eating the flesh off my face, the smell of burnt skin invading my nostrils and adding to my nausea.

"Get off me, or you'll regret it." I meant the warning as I said it, but it sounded less than convincing even to my own ears.

"I seriously doubt it, baby; you are too damn delectable. An enemy, walking into my town, a soft little thing like you. You must be a gift straight from Jordan himself, fuck, I've been bored with gray skin."

He leaned in to stick his acid tongue in my mouth, I closed my eyes and turned away. Instead of feeling the burning pain again, I felt his weight lift from my body and the exhaustion I was feeling lift from my brain.

That's when I saw Jordan standing above me, holding the creep by the back of his collar.

"Kielius," Jordan addressed him darkly.

"Christine, are you alright?" I stood while taking in the weird scene around me. Jordan was still glaring at Kielius, whom he was holding like a naughty kitten.

"Considering you found me, no." I crossed my arms shyly, trying to feel less exposed as he glanced at me for the first time; a flash of anger shot through his eyes at the burn mark still blistering my face.

Trying not to make it obvious I was in immense pain, I turned away from them. I tried subtly rubbing my cheek to my shoulder and found myself gagging, disgusted with the feeling of my melting flesh sticking to my bare shoulder. Kielius squirmed and looked at Jordan with pleading and confused eyes.

"What did I do? We had a deal; I take the little spy to the Stx, and in exchange I get a taste of her. It isn't every day something *that* tempting wanders into my town." Jordan shook him while narrowing his eyes in disapproval.

Kielius flinched. "I'm sorry, your town. But you know, the town I watch over."

"Your assumptions have damned you. Remember the last visit we had from an Angelican?" Jordan asked him.

"Yeah... She is more squeaky and less fun," he answered.

"She was right. And that," Jordan motioned his head to me now, "Is Christine. She isn't fated to Pierce. She is fated *to me.*" Kielius went stiff as Jordan shifted his hold of the man to the front of his neck, squeezing, slowly burning him.

"I, I didn't even know that was on the list of possibilities... Come on, honestly, I thought she was just a spy." Kielius whined.

The whole exchange was so strange. The two men were standing out against a backdrop of a low-built city just down a hill from them. One was scolding the other in a tone that resembled a disciplinary more than a brother.

"This sort of behavior is not tolerated in ANY aspect, Clear?"

"Okay, Okay, Clear, for fuck's sake. But like, what is your *fated* woman doing here practically begging *me* to fuck her?"

Jordan lowered him to the ground slowly in response. As

his feet touched the plastic-like pavement, Jordan reached around and ripped the man's ear clean off his head. Blood shot from the open wound; he fell to the ground screaming in pain.

"Spread the word, the cute little mortal, lots of curly hair, dimples, freckles, is Christine. She is Jordan's. As such, she is NOT to be touched, or there will be consequences. Yours is the only warning I will give."

The gravel in his chest was guttural and terrifying; yet it involuntarily warmed me as I remembered the way he claimed me with actions instead of words just hours ago.

I have always been more of the 'calm in the face of danger' type of person, but something about the look in his eyes as he turned towards me sent a chill down my back and froze me in place. I had gotten so far for nothing.

"Come. here." He barked his order at me in a terrifyingly deep vibrato.

"No. I want to go back to the river; I need to try again," was all I could manage to squeak out. Kielius still lay screaming, blood pooling around him between us. The sinfully sharp features of his face softened in knowing.

"You are injured. That river is death. It pulls the energy of the living from both Heaven and Middle Earth towards it; you are included in that. It isn't safe for you..." He offered me his hand.

"I already survived one visit. I'll survive another. I didn't get what I was looking for, but I think I was close. I need to go back."

His eyes were hard. "He already took you?"

"Yes."

He invaded my space at this admission, cupping both hands around my face. His thumbs pressed under my chin as he peered into my eyes and rotated my head back and forth. I gulped, furious with myself for relaxing with his touch.

"How close did you get?" His quietly spoken question was barely audible over his brother's screams.

The silver flecks in his eyes were gleaming at me, waiting for a response. But I didn't know how to answer, I could have sworn we were on the shore, but we could have easily been yards away.

"Not close enough," was the answer I settled on.

The burnt smell was just now lessening. Lessening but not diminishing entirely.

"From the state you're in, you were far too close. I'm not sure how you're alive. You ARE mortal, correct?" "As far as I know," I sighed, stepping from his embrace.

"That river won't show you what you need. It will only kill you," he tried to assure me.

"How do you know? I felt, close."

"Look, you can either come here willingly, or I will take you by force. Either way, this little adventure ends now." He opened his arms to me; an agitating, soft grin spread against the sternness reflected on his face.

My feet were raw and blistered, muscles sore, and I had never felt so small, but there was no way I would willingly walk into his arms.

Shooting him my best fuck you glare, I turned around and began to walk. It took Jordan a solid bit of effort to stop laughing long enough to catch up to me.

"Your strong will is misplaced. Don't get me wrong, it's cute, really, and coming from such a small package will amuse me every time, but you're in no condition to walk. I am taking us back. You will heal slower here in Hell, so walking back will take longer than you have."

I ignored him and kept walking. He sighed and, surprisingly, resigned to follow me. The screams of Kielius were farther behind us now but still bothering me. I stopped and crossed my arms.

"Is it necessary to leave him there like that?" His head tilted in confusion, taking a good second to even register who I was talking about.

"The toad who attacked you?" Jordan asked, flabbergasted with my concern.

"Yes, the guy whose ear you ripped off and left bleeding in the street."

"He will be fine." Now it was my turn to be confused.

"What happened to healing slower here in Hell?" I asked, confused.

"Oh, Goddess, only delicate Angels like yourself heal slowly in Hell. Resident immortals heal just fine." He flashed me a charming smile, complete with perfect teeth.

'What I wouldn't give for a flaw. Any flaw I could focus on would be nice,' I thought.

"I didn't think there were other immortals living in Hell?" Jordan quieted and crossed his arms, appearing annoyed with himself for accidentally letting that piece of information loose. He didn't know Kielius had already announced their relation to me.

"Now isn't the time to interrogate me, keep moving or come here."

"Answer my question," I asserted, wanting to test just how honest he was.

"If I answer your question, will you let me take you home?" I very obviously pretended to deliberate before answering yes.

"Immortal is a false title. The energy that keeps us standing is borrowed and due back to the world once it decides your time is up. The strength of our gifts allows us to retain that energy longer than your kind, that's all. My father, brothers, and I are the only gifted beings to inhabit this realm. That little urchin is, regrettably, my baby brother. As you can tell, we are still working on his manners. He'll be fine. Come here."

He opened his arms again and motioned me forward. I plodded towards him, dumbfounded about him having brothers, plural.

No sooner had his arms enclosed me than I felt the ground beneath me change from stone to carpet. His arms relaxed but didn't drop, hands resting on my hips. I forced myself to stare at his chest and not look up at him. His face lowered into my hair; his chest lifted as he breathed in deeply.

There it was. That flitting warmness I always imagined in romcoms when the love interest makes them blush or does something endearing. Apparently, I was capable of feeling it; I could only pray my face wasn't as pink as it was hot.

"May I take care of you?" I wasn't sure how to handle him asking my permission for anything, so I just nodded. My feet lifted from the ground as he carried me into the bathroom. He sat me gently on the counter, as one would an injured child before giving their scrape a little kiss to make it all better.

"I don't have any bandages or anything. I've never really needed them." His face was close to mine, holding me by the jaw and moving my face up and down, examining the burn his brother left there.

"I should have killed him for this. The infection is already spreading. I need to run to the infirmary and get some supplies. Stay put. His poison is lethal. Try and run, and you won't get very far." He gave me a very hard and authoritative look before disappearing.

I hoped inwardly that the poison would work fast and kill me. Tears stung the wound on my cheek as I realized the only way I was getting out of this was through death. It would take several attempts for me to get away; it seemed more likely I would die trying.

'He thinks I will cave, that I will quit and let him rule me. The time I spent with Pierce in no way prepared me for this type of monster. If anything, it made me soft. Being with Pierce wasn't ever framed as an option; it just "was." With Pierce I could still fully define myself. Here I feel like I am in serious danger of losing myself, which is all I have left.'

I couldn't help but wish Pierce had warned me that Jordan wasn't just evil. Evil, I can handle, I can understand it, I can fight it. Jordan was much more complicated than just evil.

Bath water running alerted me to Jordan being back; I snapped myself from my depressed trance. He was pouring something silver from a bottle into a sleek jacuzzi-style bathtub and mixed it into the water with his hand.

Standing, he looked at me softly and pulled his shirt above his head, dropping it to the floor with abandon and making his way to me. For the first time, I noticed a black smoke-like tattoo wrapping its way up his well-defined left arm.

'Hmm, who knew forearms could be so damn alluring...'

The tattered and dirty nightgown lifted easily from me and drifted slowly to the floor as he carried me to the jacuzzi, gently lowering me into the warm water. My consciousness was fuzzy enough that I mistakenly thought he left me.

I hadn't realized I had lost consciousness until I woke to find myself nestled against his chest, his hands slowly moving up and down my arms, thrumming with energy. As my mind cleared, I stiffened in fear. I would never have expected him to crawl in here with me.

"How do you feel?" It seemed like a stupid question until I realized my face wasn't on fire, and the wounds on my feet didn't seem to sting anymore.

"Violated." My body shook with his laughter at my candid response.

"Cute. I'll let this slide, but next time you pull something like that, the consequences will likely be more severe." I could feel his forehead rest against the back of my head. The intimacy of the moment sparked a bit of fire in me.

"I know for a fact; you do not dislike my company. Why run?" His tone sounded rhetorical, yet I restlessly rubbed my two sore big toes together, formulating a response. I considered myself clever to respond in kind.

"Would you allow yourself to sit stagnant in a similar situation to mine?" I half expected him to respond with a jest about enjoying being trapped by me. Yet, he surprised me. His hands rubbed up my forearms reassuringly.

"You've been lied to. They told you being a Fated match determined your destiny and your value to our realms. Are you okay with the type of life they had planned for you?" Jordan pushed, asking the question he only voiced as a courtesy, knowing the answer.

I jerked forward, causing the water to splash against the tub's adjacent windows. They were able to be adjusted in their tint with a small dial on the wall and were currently completely opaque and allowed our darkened reflections to be cast back at us. This allowed me to see his face was not one of judgment. His dark eyes were pleading with the back of my head in a way he had not allowed me to see previously.

He looked appealing, and I immediately found myself longing to be rested back against him. Because he did not pull me back to him, I did just that.

"I haven't been given a choice to be okay with it or not. Every single person I have been shoved in front of maintains the same story. It is hard to argue a purpose and prophecy so many people assure you is fact." Jordan shook his head at me and I, for the first time, felt how weak those words sounded.

Those couldn't be my words. I couldn't possibly have allowed that sort of logic to poison me. Shaking my head, I felt a shiver run up my legs. Pressing my teeth together tightly, I tried to rid myself of the compliant haze I suddenly was keenly aware was draped around me.

"No," I stuttered out. "NO." My voice was stronger on the second one. I enjoyed the way he smirked at me in the reflection.

"Okay, then I have a question for you. Now that we've become acquainted and you have experienced your true fated connection. How do you interpret its meaning or purpose?"

"I may want you, but I sure as fuck don't belong to you," I said, breathing a bit more steadily, noticing his head tilting down and his shoulder slightly drifting forward as if he were about to pin his arms around me just to prove me wrong.

But he didn't.

"Almost correct," he teased. "You do belong to me." He held a finger up, pleading for a moment.

"Fate is no gift. It's a reality, often, as you know, an unkind one. With matches, it leads two people to the partner they will need. You to me, me to you. We 'belong' to each other, Christine." I slowly digested his words, my eyes shifting, looking for distraction and finding none in the lowly lit room.

"If that's the case, I should be your equal. Not your captive."

"Then allow me to train you to a state of reliant self-protection so that I may free you." This I hadn't expected.

"So, I whoop your ass, and I'm free?"

"I think that should go without saying. You take me down, and you may be free to travel as you please. Though I'd hope you'd come back to me after each trip." I hated the fact that I was enjoying the natural smile breaking itself against my face.

TRAINING TAKES ON A DIFFERENT
SET OF PHYSICAL DISCOMFORT

Christine had spent months avoiding Pierce before agreeing to give him a real chance at Teena's bequest. Several months had passed since then, and although her time had been more enjoyable, she still felt faulty. Pierce was warm and patient with her, but she still couldn't give herself to him.

She was seated yet curled up on her messy bed, a pillow in her lap, a book resting on it regarding fated matches. All night she had been skimming the pages. Eagerly looking for the answer to what was wrong with her.

Ten chapters in and she felt much worse off than when she started. Meeting your fated match was supposed to be resolute; you knew, you just knew. You could feel yourself reaching out to them, feel your soul and energies intertwining. That person becomes an extension of yourself.

"I definitely don't feel this way toward him." She groaned, angrily shutting the book and stuffing it under the bed. An unsettling thought occurred to her, 'did he?' Guilt flared up in her at the thought of how unlucky for him it would be to get

fated to the first known person in history not to reciprocate a fated pairing.

Nearly a year she had been in Heaven. Yet she hadn't even mustered up enough affection to hug him authentically, and although he was good at hiding it, she could sense it was starting to hurt. A soft rap at the door jarred her from her melancholy.

'6am, Right on time,' Christine thought bitterly as the alarm went off. She had yet to go to sleep from the night before. Mornings were garbage. She hated them, especially since Pierce had insisted she switch to tea instead of coffee. He promised she would feel better for it. So far, he was very, very wrong.

"Come on in, Teena, I just need to grab a sweater and I'll be ready to go to his Royal-Sun-shiny-ness's mandatory breakfast," she called. Footsteps approached her from behind as she shuffled through her warmer weather options since it had beautifully frosted over yesterday morning, and she had hoped it would do so again.

"You should wear the purple pullover sweater; it's a good color for you," Pierce said from behind her. "And breakfast is only mandatory because you have a tendency to forget to eat, and then the cooks have to make you something special at night because you're starving, and they won't let royalty eat scraps," he said playfully. She screamed internally.

"Leftovers, not scraps. My God, I was living off popcorn and wine when you found me; microwaving a meal won't kill me," she shot back, grabbing a green zip-up. Pierce's arms were crossed; he was smiling a very warm and amused smile at her as she turned to face him.

"I am your God." He winked at her, to which she rolled her eyes. "And you try telling the kitchen staff that. Besides, we are going out for breakfast this morning."

"Out?"

"Yes, out."

"We can do that?" Christine asked, genuinely excited. People crowded them everywhere they went. This world, like her

home, had sensationalism. The High God's Earthly Fated match made for a good topic. People had even taken to asking for her autograph, which here meant burning a symbol into their picture or whatever thing they wanted signed.

She hadn't figured out how to do that, so it was a frenzy when the 'adorable Earth girl' started a 'brand for herself' by signing out her name with a pen when asked for an autograph. Pierce thought it was adorable. She thought it was annoying he hadn't taught her that just to save her the hassle of signing her name so much her hand cramped every time they left the castle grounds.

"Today we can," he answered plainly.

"I have a surprise for you. Something I have been wanting to show you and finally carved out the time." Eyeing him skeptically, she took his outstretched hand.

When she opened her eyes, she was in an empty restaurant at the top of the Elyon Tower. Not the largest of towers in Castofel, but it had the best views. Floor-to-ceiling windows gave sight to the most breathtaking view she had ever seen. The sun wasn't up yet, but she could see the city just fine. Her lips parted slightly. She raised a hand to her throat and touched the glass, leaning against it.

"I thought," Pierce started, "you would enjoy seeing how mortals were given the impression Heaven rested in the sky. It is a heavy fog we get only here, giving us this unique look...." He joined her at the windows and put an arm around her, his chest contracting warmly at the glow of her awe.

The city's glass buildings and towers were all resting on fluffy white clouds, giving them the appearance of floating, the fog itself shimmering like fresh snow. The way it moved in the reflections of the city gave the impression the city itself was bobbing and drifting.

"Here comes the best part," he whispered, squeezing her hand.

The sun rose in the distance. From within the fog the city

shimmered a warm royal blue before transforming into a deep lipstick red. Then all at once, the 'clouds' burst into an explosion of sunshine yellow and glittered away in the breeze.

For the first time in her life, she was truly speechless.

"Christine," Pierce daringly pulled her face into his hand.

"I have been wanting to show you this because I think it is the best way I can show you how I feel about you. That was nothing compared to the beauty I see in you. The reaction you just had is what I feel every morning when you light up my life with your presence."

And then he kissed her, and with a thawed heart, she kissed him back. She knew he felt stronger, but maybe, just maybe, this warmth she felt would be enough.

***

Pierce stood concentrating on the world around him. Following the channels of energy within the Earth, begging it to allow him access into the realm of Hell, just a glimpse to see if she was still alive. He had requested a meeting with Jordan and the messenger never returned.

The possibility of a connection between Jordan and Christine wasn't something he felt was pertinent for her to know due to its impossibility. The Fates had forecasted a prophecy of a blue-eyed woman wielding the power of a high god, who would be both a great danger and strength to the leader who held her heart.

Initially, he also thought it was about Jordan. That notion evaporated the moment he met her. She may not remember it, but he was the doctor that cared for her after Savious had killed her parents.

He remembered the overwhelming emotional heat radiating off her when he informed her of their demise. He had never seen such a physical reaction to grief before, she experienced a burning sort of nausea before channeling it into the purest and most terrifying form of stoic rage he had ever seen.

Her face had changed at that moment, jaw clenched, eyes setting ablaze, tears streaming down her taut face. As the room began to shake and his ability blockers deteriorated under her escaping rage, he acted, grabbing her face. He pressed his thumbs to her temples and fought against her inner storm.

She was a picture of broken-loose wrath. He hated it; she was terrifying and uncomposed, and he vowed to save her from this in the future. Jordan would never be able to hold her heart; he would only add fuel to that chaotic fire, not help tame it.

Which gave him both hope and fear. He couldn't decide which frightened him more, Jordan wanting Christine or simply using her as a means to an end. One thing he was sure of was Christine was not prepared to face him alone and would not fare well in Hell.

It had been a stroke of uncommon luck that he had heard The Fates disclose her name, and that, at the same moment, her parents had been revealed to him. Keeping an eye on the potential fated match of his greatest threat had simply been a cautious option.

His suspicions of her connection to him instead of Jordan became clear on his last scheduled visit to Middle Earth. Unbeknownst to her, he had played the role of several of her 'therapists' throughout the years. Fated matches were unrecognizable to one another until both had matured.

He would never forget the sheer force of truly seeing her for the first time, standing in a faux office. Her fierce blue eyes were so tired but still so bright.

Now, he would give anything to know how she was being held. All he knew for certain was that their tether hadn't snapped, signaling she was still alive. The world around him was happy to submit to his control, but the underworld blocked him completely. For all he knew, it blocked everyone save Jordan, to whom it opened freely.

The other big fear he had was no longer knowing what Jordan was capable of. The man he knew was calculating and level-headed, could find the humor in any situation and loved a challenge. They hadn't seen each other since the uprising.

All he knew was that Jordan had taken over Hell and become its 'savior.' He had given it order and began strengthening his abilities and testing his limits while repairing the world around him. All while holding a large grudge against Pierce and those who took his future.

Pierce was standing on just his left leg, right foot propped against his inner knee, hands crossed and breathing deeply in the center of one of the many gardens in the training center.

Victor figured he would be in this one as it was Christine's favorite; he hadn't taken any of this well. Pierce had a bad habit of taking too much responsibility for things. Victor, Pierce's right-hand man, called out to him.

"It's of no use, Pierce. I've already tried. We cannot reach within that realm. We are at their mercy on this. Hopefully, he took her only to prove that he could. Try to avoid dwelling on the worst possibilities. If Jordan wants to stay on good terms with the council, he will need to comply with your request for information, at a minimum."

Taking a calming breath, Pierce lowered his foot to the ground and knelt to one knee instead. "I need to try." Victor had known this talk was coming and had been dreading it.

"We can't risk it. Pierce, you aren't powerful enough yet; you don't stand a chance in Hell, you know that. For all we know, this is just a trap. But, if they do not comply, I will arrange for a search party." Victor wasn't aware of the missing messenger Pierce had sent without following the proper channels and procedures.

The council had been formed when Jordan had created himself a throne in Hell, taking over that world and earning the loyalty of all of the residents there. The council kept everyone involved in large decisions and negotiated peace between the two opposing worlds. Jordan had never shown up; he always sent Savious.

Standing up and letting Victor wrap an arm around his shoulder, he filled him in on the missing messenger. Catching a glimpse of expansive black wings tipped with silver caused Pierce to still his tongue.

Azazel landed before them soundlessly, meeting Pierce's eyes with interest. The Old Guard was the only group in the realm that worried him; Azazel was their leader. Pierce may not have been born with all the gifts endowed to a High God, but he was the descendent of the most powerful bloodline ever documented. His disinterest in power earned him loyalty from the people unseen by rulers past.

A loyalty that could only be challenged by Azazel's organization. The loyalty Pierce had earned was a direct result of his looking to help the territories govern and sustain themselves. In doing so, he had completely restructured the governmental systems of the realm for the first time in history.

The Old Guard, however, was an ancient breed of Angelicans who were born destined to protect the people of this world, unquestionably, and without loyalty to any higher power. The people were the higher power to their Guardians. Everyone knew someone whose life had been bettered, if not saved by a Guardian.

They were directly responsible for the thriving peace of this realm; that was something Pierce recognized and did not want to be on the poor end of. Guardians, in an attempt to remain uncorrupted, kept many secrets. The largest of which was their relationship with power. Not frequently using it, but seemingly a bit resistant to it.

Pierce was not the only leader to challenge the status quo. Azazel and he had bonded many years ago over their challenges in getting others to accept change. Both remodeling and adapting ancient organizations and systems to a new and changing world.

The peacekeeper before him looked like an image of war, a contrast Pierce had always appreciated. It was a warm day, and Azazel had chosen, as he often did, to reject the ceremonial robes of his Guard and instead wore black leather pants and no shirt. The metal of the knives gleamed against his chapped skin.

A silver dipped tip of Azazel's wing refracted light into Pierce's eye as the Guardian crossed arms.

"My eyes are up here," Azazel said to Pierce, pointing two fingers from Pierce to himself in a mocking jest the two had completed on numerous occasions.

"Is it my fault to look when you dress so provocatively?" Pierce laughed back without a thought, reaching an arm out and allowing Azazel to grasp it in greeting.

Azazel hadn't seen Pierce following Christine's abduction but could easily decipher the physical differences in the man before him beneath the glamor. He wasn't sleeping; that much was clear.

"I was on my way to visit a buddy of mine, Pete, at the gates. When he confided in me the happy coincidence that he was actually on the way to visit you." Azazel said, keeping his tone as airy as the breezes of Castofel, his home, Heaven's great city in the sky.

"The realm of Hell responded to your summons. They will be here tomorrow at noon per request." The realm took great interest in Christine's return. Everyone there felt, in a way, responsible for her, given the precarious nature of which she had been forced into this life.

Where the citizens adored her, the Guardians truly loved her. Initially, Pierce had allowed them to assist with her training. The whole group of active members had taken a liking to Christine's unpolished ways.

Azazel had told Pierce it was her growling and tenacity during training that had won them over. Unfortunately, there was a disagreement regarding the extent and nature of the training she was receiving. In response, Pierce privatized her instruction.

Azazel was the first guardian she had met. He would always remember the confused look on her face as she asked him why the 'birdmen,' who obviously flew, would think wearing robes was a good idea. Lost in memory, he hadn't noticed Pierce staring expectantly at him.

"Sorry to hover, friend. Since Christine is a citizen of this realm, I consider it my duty, and the duty of my men, to be involved in all facets of her recovery. Including this meeting," Azazel advised his old sparring partner, trying not to sound as forceful as he felt.

"I'll allow it. However, it needs to be a silent observation." With a nod, Azazel unfurled his large wings and took to the sky. Holding back a snarky comment about the fact he hadn't been asking permission.

***

Sitting in a large marble-accented room, Pierce tried not to appear desperate as the large marble doors opened. In walked Savious, and Savious alone.

"Where is He?" Pierce gritted out, rising to his feet as the devil's father approached.

"Not sure. He doesn't share his schedule with me. I was told you wished to speak with one of us, so I'm here. What do you want?" Savious took in the room. It had been a long time since he had seen so many Angels in one place. They were really attached to this girl.

He could tell Pierce was attempting to keep his composure but was failing miserably. Council members sat in their chairs against the walls, rigid, and ready to jump in should anything get too heated. They thought they were negotiating Peace.

They were clueless to think Jordan was honestly participating. Savious was only there to give them the impression they were still at a point where negotiations were possible.

"Savious, we are here to demand Christine be released back to us. She has been chosen to rule beside me and was taken by your son after he attacked her and one of her guardians on a routine trip back to Middle Earth."

Savious feigned surprise at the accusation.

"That's strange. I wonder what would compel him to do such a thing? He has never been one to show interest in *other* people's toys." Pierce took in the hidden taunt.

"Please, I can't help but take this attack personally. Jordan must return her to me. Only then can we move past this." Savious weighed his response carefully.

"I'm sorry to tell you, but I haven't seen your princess. But if I do, I'll let Jordan know you asked for her return. That's the best I can do, aside from offering you any information I happen to come upon. I have no sway over him. He has always surpassed my abilities tenfold and, as you know, runs the show." Nearly sashaying away, Savious paused briefly to glance at Pierce before making his exit.

"I'd bid you good luck, but if you're planning on taking anything else from my son, you will need a hell of a lot more than luck." The eye contact held a higher understanding, lost to the rest of the room. A communication Victor noted. In a blink, Savious disappeared, leaving a quick swirl of silver skating along the white marble floor.

He looked to Victor. It was as if the crinkled-eyed man could read his mind. Pierce didn't even give him the time to shake his head at Pierce's terrible idea.

The world exploded in a red world of pain around Pierce. He had attempted to transport into Hell.

His attempt was unsuccessful, to say the least. Instead of his matter phasing through the mysterious realm as it should have, he hit a wall that turned electric. Screaming, he opened his eyes to the courtroom he hadn't left to see people surrounding him from above, concerned looks in their eyes.

"What just happened? I failed to transport into Hell..."

"I would say that is fortunate for you. Making it into Hell would be suicide," Azazel retorted. "You looked at Victor and then started convulsing and fell to the ground. If I had to guess, Jordan blocked it off. But I'm assuming it's a shield that he generates himself, unlike the one we had engineered here."

Pierce couldn't help but notice a slight hint of mockery in Azazel's tone at this.

"How long do you think he can sustain it?" Pierce asked.

"No way to tell. But if you try again, it could kill you. That wall was meant for you if it did that much of a shock to your system." Azazel offered a hand to Pierce and helped him from the ground, gripping his hand a bit harder than Pierce considered necessary.

"Come with me. We will put a plan in place for a search and rescue. We will need to gather information first, though, and that will take time. Jordan has done a solid job in securing Hell, and we'll have our work cut out for us, but she is a citizen of this realm, and if you consider her in danger, she is our responsibility," Azazel said, walking beside Pierce out of the room and towards the war chambers.

***

Jordan was sitting at his desk outlining some plans for another medical center to be built outside the city of Atlantis to cut down on wait times between the residents' visits when he felt it. They had a group of seven more people nearly trained up enough to start seeing patients.

His eyes flicked to Christine as he felt Pierce's attempted entry into his world. She hadn't stirred; her form lay motionless on his bed, one of his favorite sights.

It amused him that Pierce hadn't taken the time to consider he would have blocked off entry. He got the message that Pierce had wanted to meet. Unfortunately for him, Jordan couldn't give less of a fuck about what Pierce wanted.

He knew Pierce would demand he give Christine back, as if she were a toy he had borrowed without permission. Earlier that evening, Savious had made a reasonable point that had he appeared before the council, they would likely side with him.

Especially if the hickey was still present on his neck during that appearance. But that would insinuate he felt subject to their laws and outrageous overreach, which he did not.

They were content to play pretend. Like they had the power needed to hold him accountable or even the judgment to determine his guilt or innocence.

He had now spent countless mortal lifespans attempting to rehabilitate a previously God-dependent world after its annihilation. He would be damned if he allowed the same tragedy to fall upon the realm of Heaven because of Pierce's ignorance. And they were headed in that direction if he couldn't relieve some of the strain he felt, managing the needs of both.

Contrary to popular belief, his favorite of the realms was Middle Earth. His love for Middle Earth, he long suspected, was driven by its lack of dependency on him. The energy of that realm dispersed itself. It was incredible how advanced the realm could function while the residents remained rather stunted.

'If they want to come try and take her, let them. She was done being their plaything.'

Reaching out with his senses, he called forth the energy within her and felt its diminished strength attempting to respond. After confirming she was still sleeping, he put the paperwork down and made his way back to the bed.

He didn't enter it, just stood against the wall at the foot and took the sight in, trying to think. It wouldn't be long until she tried to run again, and the scar from her last attempt was still healing. Even with him giving her excess energy, she was completely drained from fighting the infection.

It was unsafe to wait for her trust in him to build enough

that she wouldn't set herself loose upon this world again. She had no idea what the realm contained, the dangers that hid in plain view. Running into Kielius had been a bit of luck for her.

The Givi people tended to enjoy the disgusting games he played, their hardened skin appreciating the exfoliation Kielius's acid provided. Christine may not know it, but there were much greater threats here than his brothers. He was now tasked with attempting to keep her safe as she fought against him.

He threw his head back and tried to imagine Pierce writhing in pain after hitting his shield and being thrown back to wherever the fuck he tried to come from. More would come, and soon.

They would have no idea where to look for her. He doubted they would be aware that he would be able to sense their presence the moment they breached his realm. They may prove useful, though. Provided they can fill in some of the blanks regarding the scrappy little Goddess currently curled up in his sheets.

Giving in to distraction, he decided to celebrate his private victory over Pierce and crawled into bed. Pulling Christine against him, he hoped to get some sleep before the inevitable information scouts began to invade his home away from home.

***

She slept hard, her body too hot to be comfortable, fighting off an infection she felt she received far too easily. Dreams came and went. Many were agitating ones of Pierce.

They prompted a recently ignited fear she had that had resulted in her asking a brave question while eating dinner in bed with Jordan.

"Based on the plans on your desk, I assume you are planning to try and take back your throne." Jordan looked up from her bowl of gray slop, the only common food here, with a rare entertained light in his eyes.

"You are correct."

"Is gaining more power really worth the bloodshed it would cause?" she asked. He took her food from her and sat both their bowls on the bedside table.

"Are you concerned about bloodshed or me spilling Pierce's blood specifically?" she crossed her arms.

"He is a good leader," Jordan only scoffed at her.

"No. He isn't. That being said, I held no joy while planning his death." Taken aback by the bluntness of his tone and the surety of his statement, she paused.

"What makes you think you CAN kill him? I think you underestimate him." Jordan just smiled at her, gently grabbing a wrist and pulling it to him before lightly brushing his lips on the soft skin.

"This is something that has been in motion for a long time. You were an unfactored risk. A lot of planning has gone into my reclaiming my throne and my home. And one variable never changes. Pierce dies."

Pierce was so good at what he did. She could see the way the people greeted him in public, openly running up and hugging him. Not being afraid to ask him for anything, with everything he did to better the lives of those around him and beyond. All the people who relied on him, with the gentle goodness he spread to the world, a universe without him seemed dark in comparison.

"Nothing to say? You aren't going to beg me to let him live?" Jordan said mockingly.

"It wouldn't help. You have your plan." With that she continued to think, trying to imagine what she could do to disrupt his plans more. It was like he said; she was the unknown variable.

He could tell she was plotting his demise; there was no talking her out of it. He didn't need to explain himself; therefore, neither did she. Her training would start today, regardless of her defiance, and regardless of her still wanting to escape; keeping her abilities capped could only result in her hurting herself.

"Well then, Goddess, are you ready to start learning what it is you can actually do?"

"What?"

"The training you have had thus far is pathetic. I will always come for you if you are in danger, but you should be able to defend yourself as well." Confusion was evident on her face as she looked up at him.

"You should know, if you are going to train me. If it becomes necessary, I will kill you myself before letting you shed blood for selfish reasons." He knew what she didn't, that she was perfectly capable of it. Yet he couldn't bring himself to fear her. Grinning a savage grin, he tackled her and kissed her deeply before jumping up from the bed and pulling her with him.

"Bring it on, baby." With a wink, he disappeared into the closet, emerging in a black button-down shirt tucked into dark black pants. It continued to stagger her how attractive he was and the effect he had on her.

She wanted to hate him, and yet, she couldn't help wanting him while watching him roll his sleeves up his defined arms. A flush of vanity encouraged his prideful grin as he caught her sneaking a peek at him. He tossed her training gear with a flirty smile.

"Don't look at me like that right now. I need to train you, but if you turn those eyes to me like that again, we may just need to wait another day." Her cheeks went hot as she grabbed the clothes, turning to run to the massive walk-in closet to go change.

"What do you think you're doing?"

"I'm going to change." She kept her eyes forward, not wanting to invite his advances, as she continued towards privacy. Suddenly his hand wrapped around her wrist and turned her to face him.

"You," he said, running a hand down her arm, "have not earned the luxury of privacy after that last little stunt."

"You can't be serious." Goosebumps were forming up and down her arms where he touched her.

"Dead serious. After all, if you plan to kill me, I should have my fun now, right?" He chuckled while pulling the nightgown above her head, touching every part of her sides on the way up, all while keeping eye contact.

Although her mind was on alarm, her thighs were tingling, and butterflies danced across her spine. He watched her squirm and took a second to revel in it before offering her a stack of clothes. Embarrassed by the disappointment, she snatched them from him.

"I don't need to be undressed like a child." He grinned at her as she finished dressing.

"You will need this too, but it's only for training; hair like that deserves to be down and on display. It's the only one I have as well, so try not to break it." He held out an elastic ribbon. She had almost forgotten how good it felt to pull her hair into a ponytail and have it off her shoulders.

Pulling the door open, he motioned her ahead of him, "After you, Goddess."

"Since you're taking me out of this room, anyway, could I get a tour?"

"Don't push your luck." He grabbed her hand and escorted her hastily down the corridors of his home to a large auditorium.

He smiled at the intensity on her face as she tried to memorize how many steps she was taking and look for any identifying features on the walls around them. It wouldn't do her any good. Beneath the wallpaper he had engraved Enochian symbols that caused anyone without a special pendant to experience disorientation, guaranteeing they would get lost.

Her eyes widened when they entered the large room; the

lights turned on immediately. The room hummed to life, doors opening to weapons and training obstacles. It was as if the room came to life once Jordan entered it.

"I'll warn you, little one. I won't pull my punches with you. Because an enemy of mine, or yours, will not hesitate to kill you. With how far behind you are on your training, I need to assess just how damaged your progress is. What exactly can you do other than attempt to make your skin really hot?"

"Nothing here. Hell doesn't let me in." Jordan smiled a pitying smile.

"Did you try getting Hell to guide your escape? Goddess, this is my realm, and it is fully aware you are right where I want you. First lesson, a world is a mixture of different converging energies, just like us. Capable of loyalty and scorn. Hell has been wronged by its people on a much larger scale than both the other realms combined. It will not easily open to anyone without someone investing in it first. But that being said, this specific building isn't in Hell."

Looking around and seeing nothing out of the ordinary, she assumed they must be in a Bridge room. She had been told of them. They had been used by those who couldn't transport to travel between the worlds.

"But Hell doesn't have any bridges." He shrugged at her incorrect statement.

"This is a great example of the differences between me and everyone else. This room can be used to leave Hell but not enter it unless specifically blessed by me. We are technically in Heaven right now. When I got evicted, I found myself occasionally homesick and used this a bit to meditate and reconnect with my stolen home. Creating a pathway like this isn't something just anyone can do."

On his last syllable, she made for the door, surprising herself when she reached it and pulled to rip it open. It didn't budge. Jordan stood with his arms crossed, looking at her feeble attempt and shaking his head.

"Tell me, did you really think I would bring you here if this room were unsecured?" Her hand lifted and pressed against the door in longing, to be so close and still so trapped. Taking a deep breath, she turned around to face him.

"I didn't expect anything. The intense urge to get away from you got the better of my rationale." Her snappy response amused him.

"Well, better suppress the urge, baby, because it's not happening anytime soon. Now come here; we need to at least get you some basic defense skills."

"Those I know already."

"Really? Then how can I do this?" He transported to her, forcing a hard kiss on her with his inked hand knotted in her hair. Then he pulled away abruptly with a challenging gleam in his eyes.

Gasping still from the kiss, she muttered the only response she could think of, "You are literally the most powerful being alive. Not really a fair comparison." He warmed at the effect he had on her; he brought her close enough that his lips grazed hers softly as he answered in a seductive tone that sent fire through her.

"Well, I guess you're just fucked then, aren't you." Entrapping her in another kiss, he was grateful to find her tongue anxious to meet his. He tested his restraint by pulling away with a reluctant growl and transporting to the other side of the room, trying to train the fire inside him.

"I will slowly come at you from the front. As I approach, put your hands up, palms facing me. And when I say, flex your palms as hard as you can and think of density, try to feel the very idea of mass and density."

With that he transported to the other side of the room and began slowly making his way towards her. Doing as he said, she raised her hands, palms out, and began focusing. Nothing happened; he quickened his pace.

Feeling heat accumulate on her palms, she opened her

eyes. The room was distorted as if she was looking around through water, the light not quite reflecting right. Jordan's image was blurred but still progressing toward her. Jordan's mass pushed through the haze only slightly slower.

"Okay. Not bad. That may work against someone less endowed than myself. Now," He transported to her again and repositioned her, pushing her shoulders back and widening her stance.

"I assume you know how to punch, correct?" To demonstrate, she punched at him with perfect form. Without any effort on his part, he caught her fist, turned her and pulled her back against him roughly.

He couldn't remember before or after Hell an instance where he had enjoyed himself this much. Feeling her body against his, her quick wit keeping him on his toes. He would need to find someone else to assist in training her because this was going to be far too much fun for him to actually be productive.

He chuckled and lightly pecked a kiss on her neck.

"Try that again, but this time, focus less on your form and more on your body. Feel what it is telling you. Feel the evenly distributed strength throughout it, and then try and focus that strength into the force of your punch." After spinning her away from him, he crouched and put his hands up, playfully anticipating the next hit.

Looking unsure of where to start, he gave her some more coaching, reminding himself this was no novice to combat. One of the most attractive things about her was the intensity at which she took to her interests.

Based on her ravenous hunger for worldly education, he couldn't even imagine the effort she put into training on Middle Earth when she thought her life could be on the line.

"Ground yourself, make sure you feel stable, breathe deeply and feel the power running through your veins. I'm going to come at you again; aim for my center of gravity. Come on. You have put me on my ass before, do it again." He pointed to his chest and then started for her again.

Doing as instructed, she found her center of gravity and remembering to breathe, she punched forward while focusing her energy in the same direction. She made contact and he fell back onto the ground. A proud smile stretched across his face as he sat, legs splayed out in front of him on the ground.

"Good job. From those two techniques you can learn to do a lot. But keep in mind, these won't have nearly the same effect in Hell as they do here." Remembrance of where they currently were forced her shoulders to slacken a little.

"Okay, Goddess, we are going to do those on repeat until I think you have it down."

"Why does it matter if these won't even work in Hell?" While walking away from her, he paused and flinched as if she had asked a question he didn't want to answer. Letting out a sigh and making eye contact, he answered her with a hard expression,

"Hell isn't the only place you need to be able to protect yourself from enemies." The accusation was clear to her.

"No one in Heaven would do anything to hurt me like this."

"You weren't properly prepared for what could happen before; I won't do that to you. There may come a time when you are no longer seen as my victim but as their enemy, and you need to be prepared for that." Doubt settled on her face.

"They care about me." His face softened at her with an aching understanding.

"They cared about me once too." He was right; she knew that. They did; Pierce admitted to being his best friend, just like Amy had been to her before she suddenly wasn't.

After training for several hours, until he felt she had the formations correct, he escorted her back to his room and ushered her towards the shower. Ignoring the worry she felt in this familiarity, he playfully removed her clothes as they went.

He was so unlike what she had expected. He pushed her,

ALLYSON KUEPFER

but she could see a hesitation within each push. There were times when he would be forceful with her, but he always left that last, split-second decision in her hands.

The connection he had was rooted deep within her, even before he marked her. That was her biggest source of fuel for defiance, for reminding herself why she needed to stay alert, reminding herself that this wasn't a vacation but imprisonment.

Jordan stood behind her, water cascading between them in the large glass shower. Black tiles were always the center of her focus there. Keeping her eyes down was her only chance of escaping these moments without falling into them. She knew if she were to take in the playfulness of his antagonizing smile or the smolder of the heat behind his eyes, she would give in.

Her hair was pulled across her shoulder in the front, cascading in a thick, black halo, accenting the innocence of her features. Remembering the look of confusion in her eyes at the mere suggestion that she may need to defend herself somewhere other than Hell worried him.

The amount of damage they had caused her mentally equal parts annoyed and impressed him. Trust was something he assumed this particular woman should struggle with, but for some reason, she threw it around freely. Coming clean and telling her everything, throwing her 'friends' in an unflattering light would do nothing but isolate her more from him, which was not safe for either one of them.

What worried him more was the thought of Pierce getting his hands on her again. The calm and collected pretense he put on for everyone else could snap at any time. He wasn't sure how Pierce would handle her rejection after all these years, which was inevitable. After being with a true partner, she wouldn't be able to continue the facade of their 'relationship' or whatever they called it.

The last time Jordan saw Pierce lose it, he lost his home and his purpose in life, but that would be nothing compared to losing Christine. She was home now; she was his purpose. She ignited a passion he had long since forgotten.

'Going home' had entirely new meanings now. Taking her home and regaining dominion over Heaven would mean he unilaterally ran all three dimensions, which was necessary to ensure peace and uniformity. He had grown up shouldering that pressure as his purpose, until that was, he walked away from it.

"What are you thinking about?" Concern was clear on Christine's face, and he noticed her eyeing the water evaporating off the skin of his chest.

"I'm thinking about the struggles of the near future, and how you will be worth the extra effort it takes to overcome them."

"Why do you do that?" she asked.

"Do what?"

"Care about me. You aren't supposed to be like this..." He reached around her, grabbing the shampoo and applying far too generous of an amount to his palm before pulling her hair in between his hands and lathering the soap into it, contemplating the best response.

She enjoyed the feeling of him pulling her hair through his fingers enough to ignore how wrong he was doing it.

"Everyone has their own version of evil. To many, I am the face of that evil. That doesn't mean I need to be yours." He rinsed her hair and respected her silence, grateful she didn't have a follow-up line of questions. There was a new energy thrumming within her now that captured his attention, something that wasn't gifted from Pierce or himself.

After cleaning them both thoroughly, he took a towel and wrapped it around her. It caught her by surprise when he stopped her and bunched her wet hair in his hands, grabbing and releasing it in clumps of dried curls.

"Neat trick," she jousted at him before testing her rope and walking away.

6

WELL FUCK

I woke to my bottom lip being gently pulled into a kiss and Jordan searching for a sign of life in my eyes. Since coming here, he'd put me on a loose and simple schedule.

He would manifest in the morning above me, waking me with gentle caresses and kisses. Then he would leave me, heading out to do whatever it was a High God did, allowing me time for self-study.

Throughout the day, he made a game of appearing at random, hoping to catch me off guard. Sneaking up on me had earned him several reflexive elbows to the stomach. Bruises he would laugh off after begging me to "kiss them better." He would hand over the reason for his appearance, providing me with whatever resource I had requested if he had found it.

I was allowed to wander the castle and the grounds, read, and use his computer for research, which I took great advantage of. One of my favorite discoveries had been that there was no actual electricity in the realm other than generators Jordan himself had sourced from Middle Earth.

So, the majority of the light in the cities was from naturally occurring minerals or moss the people had repurposed, making the most enchanting-looking towns I had ever seen. Spirals of glowing brick and patterned moss growths up the sides of buildings, forever illuminating the shiny, black paved streets.

Upon returning each evening, I was at his disposal, it seemed. I often wondered if we would ever tire of one another, or at least need to slow down a little. Logically, I should have wanted that, but the truth was, I didn't.

Every time he so much as touched me, a fire burned in me that only he could cool, and as much as it annoyed me, I looked forward to each encounter.

Refusing him wasn't even something I had honestly tried, and I had no intention to.

'Why should I? I am comfortable with him. I am enjoying him, and I don't want to give up the one comfortable thing I have experienced since my parents died.'

His long, strong fingers wrapped gently around my neck as I felt his lips on my forehead.

"No. It can't be morning yet. I refuse," I groaned at him, pulling the covers over my head and trying to burrow back into the serenity of sleep.

There was a deep purr of his amusement as he joined me in my burrowed fortress, to my surprise, fully clothed. While pulling me against him, I could feel he was wearing a fitted button-down and a silky vest. He was going somewhere. I could feel the spark within me return. A reminder of my forgotten zest at the possibility of an opportunity.

"No, Goddess, it isn't morning, not even close. But I have some urgent business I need to take care of. I'll be gone for longer than normal." His arms tightened around me and gently squeezed. A new feeling began to agitate my stomach.

"Only two days, but I wanted to let you know, lay down some ground rules, and prepare you." He gently pulled the blanket down away from us, lifting me with him to a sitting position and pulling my face to his in a new type of kiss. I could almost taste his worry.

"What the fuck's going on, Jordan?" His eyes were closed, his forehead resting against mine, his hand tangled in my hair. Had he not been holding me in place, it would have been a romantic and warm embrace.

'No sweet moments when you're preparing me for bad news. I am NOT that easy,' I thought bitterly, possibly a bit more irritable than normal due to being woken up. No one had ever accused me of being a morning person.

"It will start to hurt. And for that, I am sorry. I wouldn't be going anywhere unless it was urgent, I promise you I will never lie to you, but there will be things I may need to keep from you, for now, for your own protection."

The embrace we were in was officially too affectionate, and that was a problem for me after his statement, but instead of fighting it I calmed down and let myself think.

A realization hit me so hard it threw me off balance. I was more concerned with him leaving for two days because I would miss him than I was about needing him to placate the scar he burned on my chest.

'This is Stockholm syndrome, I'm a literal textbook case and have been allowing myself to be. I don't fucking think so, not anymore.' I disconnected myself from him abruptly and started to reorient my thinking.

"When do you leave?" Attempting to not sound concerned, my words came out as flat and icy as I felt. He flinched, and I could tell he had forgotten the sting of my understanding reality.

"That was a quick change, Goddess. Why are you upset? Afraid of the scar or of the fact that you'll miss me?" Grin firmly back in place, he lifted himself from the bed and grabbed a black jacket off his office chair, throwing it on and buttoning the front.

Seeing him in a full suit caused a feeling of heat to pool between my legs, and the way my heart constricted in the cavity beneath my breasts did nothing to help me regain any sense of pride that I had only just noticed I'd abandoned.

He was the literal God of Hell, and he looked the part. Jawline sharp enough to cut through any sort of modesty one may hold, the fabric of his jacket tensing perfectly around his sculpted arms, and the way his tailored vest accentuated the perfect shape of his body.

His thick wavy hair was pushed back and was almost as perfect as his freshly styled and very intentional stubble beard. All I knew was that I was far too mortal to deal with his physique, so hopefully, with him being gone, I would be able to think clearly and get out while I still had the sense to want to.

Something seemed different about him, his composure seemed unsteady compared to his usual perfectly put-together self. His jaw muscles were constricting as if he was having an internal debate, walking around the room gathering random things and putting them into a bag.

"I can tell you're concerned about something, and it bothers me. From what I've gathered, you aren't one who worries about much. I am also confused about how and why someone as obnoxiously adept at transporting would be packing a bag and not returning for two days."

His back was to me, facing the wall where he was punching something into a box near the door, he often used to communicate with his people downstairs, mostly telling them which directions to take when someone got lost.

"Is this some kind of test, to see if you have me whipped by now, to see how I'll try to escape without being under the 'almighty's' watchful gaze?" As soon as the words left my mouth, a menacing stillness fell over him and the world around us. The very molecules floating around in the room, stilled in fear, afraid to move or multiply at the ominous way he turned to face me.

His eyes were almost entirely black. The strongest sense of primal fear I had ever felt was at that moment. Before I could even exhale the breath that stuck in my lungs, he had me pinned to the bed, full body weight atop me, lips brushing my ear with a warning.

"I assure you if you so much as attempt to leave this room over the course of the next two days, being whipped will be the last of your worries." Fueling my desire to want to hate him, I decided to push him some more, give me some good lasting reminders of the reason I needed out, regardless of how much I was enjoying his heat mixing with mine.

"What was it you said to me before training the first day? Bring it on, baby." Grip tightening against my wrists, I could tell I snapped some sort of resolve in him. I had pushed him into whatever he had been holding back from since he woke me up. He sat slightly grabbing my face not so gently beneath the chin, forcing me to look him in the eyes.

"Contrary to your brainwashed belief, I truly am keeping you here for your protection. I had thought your last little venture would have shown just how serious I was about that."

"Oh, you mean when *your* brother attacked me? Good point. Then save me the trouble and drop me off back at home. If you really don't want to kill me, then there is no reason I can't go back to my real home, where I belong to only myself, where I am no one's responsibility but my own. The only reason I got scooped up in the first place is because your stupid fucking father thought I was some kind of threat to you, and Pierce believed him; everyone knows that's not the case now. Neither of you has any reason to hold me. Just let me go."

For the first time, I thought I caught a glimpse of genuine pity flash across his eyes.

"You are much more of a threat than you know. In truth, you are much more of a threat than anyone but myself and the fates know. Pierce was attempting to figure out why or how, by taking you. They were trying to figure out how to use you to protect themselves. And my dear, you have to stay here because they failed to figure it out, regardless of what they told you."

"I'll bite, so say they did concoct the whole story they told me. How can you be so damn certain they didn't figure out whatever your little secret is while I was up there? They tested my blood, my abilities, everything. So really, how can you tell they don't know?" A new hardness had taken over his features, and a seriousness showed in his eyes.

"I know they didn't figure it out because you're still alive. I plan to keep you that way, so for now, you stay here."

"That excuse got old the first time someone used it against me. I'm sick of being the rope in your childish game of tug and war."

"Are you really going to make me motivate you in other ways to stay here?"

"I'm not sure such motivation exists."

"Wanna bet?"

My heart was pumping in my ears, my palms were hot and slick, and I could practically smell his want. I needed his heat in a way I had never known.

His lips met mine with an unrelenting passion, pulling the finely tailored suit from his body with a predatory-like grace as he kissed his way down my body, settling himself between my legs, pulling me onto his mouth and baring his arms around my thighs so I couldn't escape him as he devoured me. He flipped me over and pinned my arms to my back, pressing me against him and down to the bed at the same time until he growled and released himself in me.

I came back into my own mind in panic at the possible repercussions of what just happened, as I did every time. Frozen, I stayed completely still, not that he would have let me move anyway; he always took several minutes to release me, only after admiring the state he left me in.

This time was no different. He ran his hands up my sides, down the back of my thighs, grabbing my arms. He pulled me up and against him, barring one arm around my waist and wrapping a hand around my neck.

"I can feel your panic. It may be wrong, but I sort of enjoy it. You have no need to worry though, Goddess. I assure you, a pregnancy isn't possible yet," he whispered into my hair as my panic was replaced with curiosity before he reminded me of a fact I had learned back in Heaven. After particularly enjoyable moments like this, damn near everything left my mind.

"We are not yet bonded. That is an honor awaiting us on the other side of this war."

Marriage in these realms was to literally bond yourself to another person. It was basically a declaration of "Hey! Look at us; we are gonna try to have kids together!" It was nuts to me that conception wasn't even possible until after the ceremony was completed.

"How do you manage to distract me like this? I am going to be so late. Now about your motivation." He kissed my neck briskly before jumping off the bed and dressing himself hastily, not looking quite as put together as he had before, but much happier.

"I need to be able to go and not worry about you trying to escape without me being here to get you out of whatever disaster you get yourself into, but I also need you to start trusting me, so I'm making the decision to trust you first as a show of good faith. I could drain you of all your energy and leave you passed out for two days, but I won't. Also, if I return and find you incident free, I will answer any of your questions, anything you want to know."

"And if I'm not 'incident free?'" He leaned against the bed rail at the bottom of the bed and made himself eye-level with me. His knuckles became frosted in anger as he caught the implication. Lying was never a skill set of mine, and I wasn't even going to try.

"If you decide to make poor choices, I will take you to Earth myself." A spark of hope flurried in my chest for the brief second that I forgot he was the Devil. "And kill the first person we come across," he said, expression clearly gauging my reaction.

"AH, yes, because nothing makes me feel trusted more than being threatened into submission. I never bought into the rumor regarding your attitude toward mortals, but wow. You really value their lives so little?"

The wood from the bedpost was stressed as he shifted against it, adding pressure like he was trying to push himself back from me.

"It isn't that mortal lives mean nothing to me, it's that your life means everything, Christine, and we have not gotten to a place where I can trust you not to put your life in danger. Do not think for one moment that I value anything over your life, including your comfort or happiness with me. Don't make me do something YOU will regret. Are we clear?" I looked away from him, feeling exasperated.

"Fine."

Frustration washed over me in waves, mixed with bitter resentment. Not just at Jordan, but at Pierce, Victor, Amy, fucking Savious, everyone. I went from being completely isolated and self-dependent in life to having no say over my life in any aspect. That was the real enemy I was fighting. The real objective I was fighting for, independence, or at least a semblance of self-propriety.

"Christine, hey, hey, Look at me." I hadn't realized I had begun crying in frustration until he wiped the escaped tears away with his thumb.

"For what it's worth, I am sorry. Not about having you here; I'm admittedly far too selfish for that. But I am sorry about the frustration you are feeling and my large part in it. I have been so content simply with having found you that I haven't thought about doing anything to make you more comfortable. Obviously, you need some more freedom. As soon as I'm back I will have a better idea of what that looks like, and the adjustments we can make. I give you my word."

"You do see the irony here, right? Two minutes ago, you were threatening to kill somebody if I 'so much as think about leaving this room,' and now you are kissing my hand, promising me freedoms and comforts." My tears had stilled, and I could feel myself calming again.

"True enough. Look…" I could tell he had more to say, but a buzz from the intercom interrupted him.

"This conversation isn't over; I'll be back in two days. I am asking you not to do anything reckless while I'm gone, please." He grabbed my hand and pulled me into him, kissing me with pleading passion before grabbing his bag and disappearing from the room.

It took me a solid two minutes after he had left to call his bluff. There was a lot at stake, but at the end of the day, he had nothing to gain in my eyes by going through with his promises. Killing someone would turn me from him permanently; he had to know that.

Unfortunately, I had no fucking clue how I planned to actually get out. I had been out with an escort on several occasions, but the way to the exit seemed to change every time, and after a few attempts, I stopped trying to memorize the floor plan.

If what Jordan said was true, if I really could do everything he could with training, then, in theory, I should be able to transport. The thought of failing to transport and how badly that could go sent a shudder down my spine. This time around, that isn't the option. Also, I doubt I'll get him to teach me how to use that particular ability, ever.

Sauntering into the closet, I decided to be more prepared than my last outing. Slipping on black tactical pants and a tight windbreaker, I tried to inventory what I had learned of the landscape since being here, from being out and about with Jordan and from the research he had allowed me to do.

Feeling pretty confident I could eventually find my way out of the castle itself, at least within two days, and still I knew there was no way to get out from any of the outer villages. And I could only get to them undetected after making it through the dense, un-growing forests of the underworld.

Unlike Heaven, where you can walk to the gates, there was no such passage here. Those who came here weren't meant to be able to leave of their own volition, or enter for that matter.

My best bet would be the training room that served as a bridge. Knowing Jordan, there would be a way to open that door; there had to be.

Everything he did had a reason; he wouldn't create a door that had no use. It wasn't his style, and one thing Jordan had in spades was style. From his clothes sending a message of what could be expected of him to the way he went about every situation, the man was resolute and also endearingly dramatic.

He got a kick out of adding a bit of style to every move he showed me; there was the formal way to concentrate energy, and then there was Jordan's way, an extra flick of the wrist, and light variations appear, serving no other purpose than looking cool.

Before pulling the door open, half expecting him to be on the other side, I glanced back at my cage. As far as cages went, it wasn't terrible. Everything I could ever need was taken care of.

There was a lavish kitchen with all the trimmings, an elegant and luxurious master bathroom, and a small gym area. Even a small balcony overlooking the forever nighttime sky. But as wonderful as it seemed, the cost of being there was too high. I may not hate Jordan, or his company, but I would never be okay with belonging to someone this way.

Getting out no longer meant going back to Pierce either; there was no way I could face him after this. Lying to him wouldn't be an option either. He never pushed or pressured me, and I respected him and held some trust for him on that premise, but it never felt real with him.

A large part of me never bought his story of us being destined together. I always felt like a prisoner there but accepted my fate in an attempt to lessen the discomfort of my own uneasy existence. But I didn't know what else I wanted;

this strength they gave me would make training impossible without hurting someone.

My clients and others like them, the people who needed someone, anyone to throw them a damn life raft, as Amy and Evan had done for me, were worth fighting for. Were worth the coming challenges if it meant I would be able to get back to actually doing something to help this world.

Even if that fight was this uphill battle.

Getting out isn't my only problem; this curse is. His distance, as warned, caused me serious continual discomfort. Even flaring extra every now and again, reminding me to hate him. Helping me fight the annoying sensation beneath that heat in my chest of missing him.

My hope was that being in middle Earth would weaken the intensity of the pain, in the same way being in the underworld weakened my abilities. That would be the next problem I would work on. For now, I needed to focus on this one step at a time.

Step 1, manage to get out of his labyrinth. Step 2, find the bridge room. Step 3, Sneak through Heaven to the gates. Step 4, convince whoever was on guard to let me through the gates without alerting Pierce. Step 5, Hide and hope Jordan was full of shit and this curse doesn't burn me alive.

'What could possibly go wrong?'

***

Jordan decided to take the time to walk the streets in preference to transporting. He enjoyed walking; it gave him time to sort his thoughts. Whereas Atlantis was governed by Kielius, Kronos was watched over by the only family member Jordan trusted, Thad. Kronos was much bigger and far more important to the growing infrastructure of the underworld.

The residents here needed structure, schools, education, roads, homes, and food. They needed reform and a leader willing to take the time to provide these things.

Walking along the lowly lit cobblestone paths, he admired the work he and Thad had already accomplished. Fully erect buildings lined the streets with enough luminous stone and growth harvested to light the path ahead. Things were clean and unbroken. Nearby a worker painted over some fresh graffiti, whistling, enjoying having work to do, a purpose.

Jordan preferred Kronos to Atlantis due to its similarity to Heaven. Christine had once told him it was like Europe but plunged into an eternal and starless night. A fitting description, he had agreed. He fondly reminisced, embracing the memory of walking down this same street, hand and hand.

He wondered if she was already trying to get out of the Castle. As much as he hoped she wouldn't, he had no doubt she would, which is why he glamoured the castle and removed all the windows and doors, which should keep her busy for at least a few days.

He smiled, imagining how annoyed she was to be finding herself upset at the thought of being away from him. There were times he debated telling her everything, she wouldn't even remotely believe him, but there were times like this when the physical evidence may be enough to help convince her.

She needed to come to the correct conclusion herself, to know she couldn't resist him, that they were meant for each other. Once she accepted that, her world would open to far more truth than just their inevitable lifetime of entanglement.

He was well aware of her guilt regarding Pierce, another check against his life in Jordan's mind. Confusing her like that. Making her feel guilty for not wanting him and naturally falling into the right man.

Approaching a street that was entirely taped off, he knew he was getting close. This was their current project, and Thad had been leading the development of this center for some time now. The surviving residents of this realm, named the Givi, were more at ease with him.

Thad was half Angelican and half Givi, but genetically he looked Givi, which meant a great deal to the people. Jordan felt like it meant even more, negatively that the people knew of his natural appearance, considering Thad consistently used glamor to look like one of the 'Savious's.' Jordan couldn't fault him for that, though. They were isolated here but still in power, and he was the only one who looked like one of the people instead of a member of the ruling family.

Glamor or not, Thad was the shortest of the brothers, and the bulkiest. His natural skin was dense and a mute gray. His eyes were a sandy gold, like Kielius's. However, Thad's shone in the dark and allowed him to navigate easily within it.

Grinning mischievously, knowing his Givi brother couldn't hear him crunching through the gravel, Jordan picked up a small piece of rubble and underhanded it. It plopped perfectly in between Thad's shoulder blades, violently breaking him from his work trance and causing him to squawk in fear as he jumped around to face his 'attacker.'

"We really need to work on how you respond to a threat," Jordan laughed, forming the words in the local sign language his deaf brother had grown up on. Jordan had spent years helping his brother master verbal inflection, and now Thad helped him keep up with any shifts within the sign language of the world he may have missed out on due to his interaction with the people.

"You really aren't funny," Thad perfectly articulated while working to get his breathing steadied. "Did Christine agree to behave while we're gone?" he asked.

Jordan responded by raising his brows in a wordless, "what do you think?"

"Shocking." Thad's mastery of monotone annoyance was really a feat that would always impress him. "If you did what I warned, and filled in the gaps of her knowledge, maybe she would," he added.

Jordan broke out in a grin, thinking of the angry scrunch

of Christine's nose and the fire she gets in her eyes when he orders her to do anything.

"What fun would that be?" Jordan signed back with a laugh.

Thad rolled his eyes and shoved his dense brother's shoulder in jest, knowing the hole he was digging for himself. "Where are we going?" he asked.

"It's a surprise," Jordan signed, eyes radiant with pernicious intent.

"Wonderful," Thad snipped while simultaneously grabbing his bag with one hand and Jordan's shoulder with the other. Once he had a firm grasp, they transported to Middle Earth.

* * *

With a black pen, Christine marked the end of each hallway as she left it behind, trying to make sure she didn't backtrack at least. Nearly dropping the pen, mid-X, a sting of heat enveloped her, starting from her chest. She sat against the wall, sliding down slowly, clutching her chest, and trying to breathe through it.

Breathing became difficult and very painful. She needed to force herself to breathe in and out in the angriest form of meditation to ever take place.

'Breathe in... That motherfucker.'

'Breathe out... fuck. Fuck. FUCK.'

'Breathe in... Him. Him. Him.'

'Breathe out... fuuuuuuuuuck.'

She had no idea how long she had sat against that wall. Sweating and trying to breathe through the crushing waves of heat, but her mind cleared as her skin cooled.

'Well, that completely sucked. I'm assuming he just left Hell. I reeeeally hope I am right about this dulling when I get to middle Earth. Fuck.'

Pushing against the wall, she leveraged her weight against

it making sure her legs were steady before continuing, knowing she needed to be at full strength for this venture. There was a lot of ground to cover.

People working in the castle paid her no attention. By now, they were used to seeing her and knew she had zero likelihood of getting out. As long as they made no move to assist her in escaping, they wouldn't be held responsible for whatever mischief she managed.

7

A SURPRISE GUEST

It had been twelve hours since I had begun my foolish quest. And five since I started hating myself for attempting it. He must have taken precautions I hadn't expected, glamoring more of the castle than I assumed he would, or maybe finding the bridge room was more difficult than finding my way out. I couldn't help but be impressed that he was able to maintain such an elaborate glamor from a different world. Guilt swelled in my throat in response to the slight pride I felt toward him.

"Ready to give up, little peach?" My cheek fizzled in recognition of the voice behind me.

I turned to face Kielius, squaring my shoulders. He smiled at me with a crooked grin that was a sad, watered-down version of Jordan's. My confidence had risen since our last encounter, and I almost hoped he would give me a reason to flatten him.

"Calm down, I'm here to babysit. No fun allowed. As much as I would enjoy having some fun with you while my hot-headed brother is gone, I would prefer to stay alive, and Jordan is a bit touchy about you, so I'll pass."

"Babysit?"

"Not for a single fucking second did any of us think you would actually behave yourself. You aren't the type. You are the type that gets herself killed simply because she is too proud to allow someone to protect her, so in simple words, you are stupid, like a child and require a babysitter." I was not in the mood for this, but I had a hunch that revealing himself meant I must be getting close.

"So now what?" I feigned defeat, dramatically leaning against the wall, making my eyes big, and sticking my bottom lip out in a pout. Too quickly his gaze went from inconvenienced to all too interested.

***

"What do you mean missing?" Pierce demanded, frustrated that his people were nowhere to be found.

"Exactly what I said, we sent out an emergency signal to all of the scouts, including Amy, and no one has responded. I personally went to a few homes of random scouts, and there were obvious signs of a struggle, but they were nowhere to be found."

Victor was just as frustrated as Pierce but was trying to keep his composure. Being one of Pierce's only real friends meant he knew how dangerous his temper could be, and his stress had been mounting since the moment Christine was taken.

"Alert the territories," Pierce demanded Teena, who had been standing aside, awaiting orders.

She hurriedly shuffled from the room to send out a mass communication as he stood from his chair and walked to the balcony. Victor had been standing aside, unsure of what to say. He approached Pierce as the door clicked closed behind her.

Joining him to look out at the kingdom as it was and may never be again, Victor felt a reminder of the agony he felt the day he lost his wife. He quickly adjusted himself, trying to avoid overwhelming Pierce.

"You realize, of course," Victor said. "If Jordan is attacking, I doubt it is because taking Christine proved useless. This timing cannot be coincidental."

Pierce looked to the sky, exasperated.

"We aren't going down that rabbit hole again. I told you we need to focus on bringing her home. But unfortunately, due to the unknown circumstances and the fact that we have people missing, that will have to wait. She would be furious if she found out I had put her life ahead of others. Which would not do me any favors in winning her." Victor's eyes scrunched together in judgment of the phrasing of Pierce's priorities.

"Okay, fine. But if I know Christine, she would want to be taken out if it were possible she was a threat to innocent lives, and she very well may be." As Victor struck the last syllable, the room filled with muffled gasping and moans. Turning to face the noise, Pierce and Victor were met with the most ominous sight either had ever seen.

Jordan stood in the center of the room, arms outstretched, surrounded by thirty or so grown men and women, all on their knees, physically wounded and gagged, black tendrils of power inching off them before vanishing.

The missing scouts. Victor didn't know which worried him more, the fact that Jordan could transport into Heaven while the defenses were up or that he did it with thirty people in tow.

"I'm almost insulted, you have me to worry about, and you are wasting time framing Christine as a threat; it's just sad, really." Pierce's fists and his jaw clenched simultaneously with Jordan's taunt.

Jordan lowered his arms and rolled his neck, casually walking over to a whiskey decanter Pierce kept for special occasions in the corner and poured two glasses offering one to Pierce, then sat in his chair, tipping back and forth between the two of them once.

"You and I need to talk."

***

Kielius inched his way closer to Christine, testing the waters. "Did Jordan tell you innocence is one of my kinks? There is nothing hotter to me than a big-eyed, innocent, helpless little girl or woman. So, don't play with me, little peach. I don't want Jordan to kill me, but I may not be clear-headed enough to stop myself if you keep up the act." He took another step forward.

Christine settled herself against the wall, trying to look as upset and little as possible. She thought of her parents, the night at dinner before their murders. The way it grossed her out that they still held hands during half of dinner and flirted so openly.

So lucky in love, two people who should have had a long and happy life together, but instead, they had a daughter who would lead them to their deaths. A tear rolled down her cheek as her eyes watered in memory.

'That'll just about do it,' she thought triumphantly to herself.

"Playing you? I am a mortal who was abducted by Angels, and now your crazy brother. Trapped in this strange place, lost, being attacked by an immortal who already dominated me once, I think my fear is warranted." She forced her voice to occasionally break and come out soft and shaky. Kielius was practically salivating on himself by the end of her little act.

"Well, I may be able to help you, baby, but it comes with a price...." He pinned her to the wall and leaned in.

"Will this suffice?" she asked, focusing all the energy she could into her knee and thrusting it upward into his erection.

As he stumbled back, she grabbed his arm and pulled it up and behind him while rolling herself off his back and using the momentum to leverage him into a throw into the wall so hard he broke through it, revealing the bridge room.

She stepped over Kielius's unconscious body and walked

into the bridge room, unable to stop herself from jumping around and dancing excitedly at managing to make it this far.

***

Pierce accepted the glass from Jordan and glanced uninterestedly at the whiskey before setting it down. He tried to take inventory of everyone present and to watch what he was saying in front of his people, but it was hard to take his eyes away from Jordan.

He had known Jordan better than anyone at one point in time. But he barely recognized the man before him. A seriousness had replaced a once flippant humor. Physically he was larger than he had been, and he had let his hair grow, no longer sporting a clean-cut look. As much as he didn't want to be intimated, he couldn't help it. Jordan's powers greatly surpassed his own; he had counted on fighting a battle with a mounted defense, not one on one. It was Victor who broke the silence.

"What is the meaning of this, Jordan? An act of war, simply a show of strength, what exactly are you hoping to accomplish?"

"This." Jordan used his glass to gesture to the room.

"Is a favor. Until their intentions can be vetted, anyone who served under you is henceforth suspended. I figured I'd save you the trouble of recalling them all and give them a lift home. And while I am being generous, I thought I would personally deliver the news that your time filling in for me is no longer required. You have two months to step down publicly. If you fail to comply, I will be forced to assist you in your resignation. Any questions?"

Jordan abruptly stood back up, making Pierce involuntarily flinch. He let his statement hang in the air as he walked to the whiskey decanter and poured himself another glass.

"You've been without the sun too long if you think I'm going to simply step down. I do have one question, though, when are you returning Christine to me?" Thad audibly sucked in air, failing to slide under the radar as Jordan's composure broke for half a second. A tint of death was dancing in shadows through his eyes.

***

Christine checked to make sure Kielius was unconscious before walking around the huge room, and she took her time to inspect every piece of it in an attempt to find anything hidden. She felt the crevices of the wall, feeling for anything that could be hidden via a glamor. After successfully locating the light switch, she was able to illuminate the auditorium. She pulled one of the many cabinets along the walls open and pulled out some rope.

It had been a while since she had hogtied a man and hoped these ropes would be strong enough to hold someone like him. She fully inspected the entire room twice before the defeat started to rise in her throat. There was no skulking back to Jordan's suite without him knowing she tried to escape.

Even if she could somehow hide the gaping hole in the wall, there was the matter of Kielius still snoring, face first, into the floor. Yet, her biggest problem was that the agonizing fire engulfing her chest had become almost unbearable, telling her time was almost up.

"Well fuck, now what am I gonna do?" she hissed, picking up a solid metal chair and beating it angrily against the door that wouldn't open.

Mid-swing, something miraculous happened, and the door jutted and creaked open inwards toward her. Still holding the chair above her, her head cocked to the side in confusion as someone stepped through it.

***

"Two months. That is the time you have to bow out gracefully and alive. I'll pop by again soon. Have fun packing," Jordan said the reminder flatly, tempering his cool. He shot Thad a disapproving look before grabbing him and transporting them both back to Hell.

Pierce stood amongst his tied-up people, more intimidated than ever, yet as he worked to untie each of the scouts, he felt more resolute. Each one of them was in bad shape after getting the beating of their lives from Jordan. In Pierce's eyes, these people were innocent and not deserving of Jordan's brutality.

But he had to admit, as far as intimidation tactics went, he couldn't imagine anything more effective. It boggled his mind that Jordan had just transported this many people without breaking a sweat. He had known Jordan was good at continually strengthening his gifts by pushing his limits and training as rigorously as he does, but this show of power went above anything he could have fathomed.

Victor returned to the room, followed by Medics, who quickly took to assessing the injuries of the scouts.

"I will need to speak with each of you individually once you're up for it. Please follow the medics back to the ward. I will find each of you to schedule a debriefing," Pierce announced to the room. He got a responding unison of black and bloodied faces nodding back at him as they shuffled from the room.

"Victor, he just transported an entire room of people, without touching them, in-between worlds. I didn't think that was possible. We are going to have to get very clever very quickly to think of some way to combat him." Victor leaned against Pierce's desk, face scrunched in question.

"What I want to know," Victor said. "Is who was with him?" Pierce stilled. He hadn't thought of that. There was a shorter man with Jordan who wasn't a captive; someone Pierce had never seen before.

"That's a good question. Honestly, Savious likely had a few

more kids. I wouldn't be surprised if Jordan had several siblings running around in Hell, based on Savious's reputation. But their bloodlines would be diluted, so at least we don't have to worry about them reaching the same threat level as Jordan. Besides, we need to figure out how we deal with Jordan before worrying about any less powerful siblings he may or may not have."

"That's a fair point. You're going to want to change. Sorry to tell you, but your little 'rescue mission' is going to need to be put on hold. We are officially at war, and we cannot afford to let Jordan get the drop on us again."

"I think you're right, we need to prepare an offensive strategy, but that may need to include a trip to Hell. Having her standing beside us may make the only difference that will matter," Victor looked at Pierce in disbelief.

"Are you hoping she will stand with us, or with you?" Pierce couldn't help but smile.

He thought back to that last day with her, the wind chime nature of her voice as she flirted with him, her hair feeling like silk between his fingers as he held the back of her head while they kissed. Pierce missed the taste and feel of her lips and felt a deep ache respond in him at the memory. He looked at Victor and answered as honestly as he could, deep down unsure of the future.

"I have faith that she will stand beside me to defend us."

8

A MOTHER'S GRIT

I stood, mouth agape, staring at the completely out-of-place woman in front of me. Amy's eyes widened fretfully as she rushed inside and, to my further surprise, hastily shut the door behind her.

"Dude, what exactly was your plan? 'Cause this is just sad," Amy asked, glancing at the chair still above me. I slowly and cautiously set the chair down, facing and bracing myself to confront my old friend.

"Amy? What the fuck? How did you find me?" I felt annoyed with myself for not feeling the excitement or relief I thought I would have from someone rescuing me. Instead, I felt apprehensive, confirming how badly I didn't want to return to Heaven.

"I'm not looking to get rescued if that's why you're here. I have no interest in being ripped from one prison just to be thrown into another." I crossed my arms, waiting for her to say anything.

She masked a face I remembered well. Whenever she was trying to explain something complicated, she seemed to chew her words first, almost like she was trying to taste the way they would sound.

"Well, I can understand that. So, why then are you trying so adamantly to get out of here? Or do you just really not like that chair?" I squinted at her in confusion.

Amy always was someone who needed to be coaxed to get to the point. She liked to dance around a question before giving an answer, and she was the type of person to tell you what you wanted to hear versus what you needed to hear. It was always something that drove me crazy.

"Amy, seriously, what are you doing here? What's going on?"

"Jordan told me that he agreed to give you some answers. That is, if you didn't do anything stupid while he was gone. He thought some of those may be received a bit easier if I was here to corroborate."

Guilt singed through me at the thought of Jordan kidnapping her, at the fear she must be feeling. "I am so sorry. I'll make sure he takes you home as soon as he gets back. I can't believe he did this. That rotten bastard...." Mid rampage, she cut me off.

"No, Christine. I'm no victim. But I may be once you kill me because I do work for him. I have for a while now. You weren't supposed to be here, in this room, like this, right now. Jordan was supposed to meet me here so we could go over how to tell you."

Without time to process the fact that my best friend had conspired with my kidnapper, Jordan and another man appeared suddenly in the room. The pain I had been in lifted from me, and I felt myself shrink in shame at the mess around me.

Until I saw his posture shrink, his weight falling against the man beside him. Jordan looked around the room in confusion. His eyes met mine, and he grinned, a half laugh escaping him before he completely crumpled to the floor.

I ran to him, practically shoving the stranger out of the

way, completely forgetting about Amy's presence or the threat he had made to me. He was cold to the touch and covered in sweat. A set of thick hands gripped my shoulders and pulled me away from him.

"I am Thad. Jordan's brother. He will be okay," the man said, pulling at me again, ignoring me as I snapped at him to tell me what was wrong.

He turned me to face him, but I couldn't bring myself to look away from Jordan. Not even as he took my hand to shake it.

"What did he do?" I asked. Again, he didn't answer. He didn't bother to respond until I acknowledged him by looking him in the eyes and asking again.

"He transported thirty people from Middle Earth into Heaven. Simultaneously." I blinked back at him in shock. His words were crisp and almost overly clear, so I knew I couldn't have misheard him.

"He transported thirty people at the same time?" He scoffed at my bewilderment while lifting Jordan from the ground.

"Follow me. I will get us help," he said.

"Sure, I guess...." I was surprised that he assumed I would take care of Jordan, and even more surprised at myself for proving his accusation to be correct. In the distance I could hear Kielius moan, finally waking up.

"Oh good, you didn't kill my idiot brother. I'm sure he deserved the beating. Only wish I could have seen it." Thad made a point of stepping directly on Kielius as we passed.

I didn't look at Kielius or Amy as we left. I had a lot to process and couldn't take any more. I was going to get Jordan healthy and, come hell or high water, get him to tell me what was really going on and how specifically it involved me.

It irritated me profusely how easily Thad was finding his way around the castle I had just spent days failing to navigate. We walked into Jordan's suite and Thad, not too delicately, dropped him onto the bed.

"We will resume your training in the morning. I know he cares about you, and regardless of if you plan to fight against us or with us, you should be able to use the gifts you have. It's your right." Unlike his brothers, Thad seemed humble and unthreatening, but very stiff.

"Okay. Thank you, I guess."

Reaching the door on his way out, Thad turned back to me, sporting a softer version of the snarky grin Jordan frequented and threatened me. "He forgets that his immortality doesn't make him impervious to death. If you wanted to kill him, now would be easiest."

That softness stoned over as he added a pointed threat. "He trusts you, and therefore so must I. Anything happens to him; remember you are in a world of people who would take great joy in making you pay for it."

The door clicked shut, leaving me standing beside the bed, wondering what I was supposed to do now. I had never taken care of anyone in my life; I could barely take care of myself.

I looked down at him, enjoying being able to inspect him like this. Jordan was a morning person and was always up and about by the time I awoke. Part of me suspected he did this on purpose in an attempt to avoid me catching him in a vulnerable position. Seeing him like this, so pale, was unbalancing. Generally, he had the complexion of a Spanish model.

I wondered what had kept him so busy he hadn't had the time to shave. The stubble that normally peppered his jawline had grown out into a beard in the last few days. A short one, but seeing it was fun, nonetheless.

I enjoyed that it had multiple subtle colors, appreciative of the stray rust and russet strands that were peeking out among the rest of his black hair. It softened him somehow, smoothed out the sharp angles of his jaw that was currently clenching and unclenching.

Realizing I was creepily hovering over his face, I pulled away, brainstorming how in all the three worlds I was going to get him out of this sweaty suit. Jordan was not light, and I was questioning Thad's decision-making skills leaving Jordan in my care.

'Thad can threaten me all he wants, but if Jordan dies from something as human as pneumonia, I'll kill him for just dumping him and dipping out.'

A knock at the door was a relief to hear after a good ten minutes of attempting to roll Jordan over enough to get his suit jacket off. I opened it, sweaty and overwhelmed, to reveal an elder-looking and lopsided woman hauling buckets.

One had dark blue liquid, and the other was stuffed with rags, the liquid side was weighing her down heavily. She had crow's feet, and a gray complexion, unlike anything I had ever seen before.

"Could you move out of the way? This shit is heavy." The authority in her tone was at complete odds with her maid-like attire.

I opened the door wide, stepping out of the way to let her in. She pushed past me, grabbing a tray from the kitchen and setting it softly on the bed beside Jordan. On it was a pair of scissors and a bowl of ice. I took one cursory glance down the hall, contemplating running for it while Jordan was incapacitated. The thought stung enough that I shut the door and joined her at Jordan's bedside.

"Did Thad send you? He didn't say he would be sending help," I asked her, trying to start some sort of rhetoric between us. She looked up at me through a pair of bottle-thick glasses; her face settled into a seemingly permanent state of annoyance.

"Look, girl. This idiot is the only thing keeping this place running. Without him our infrastructure crumbles, I lose my job, and I'm back to living in a wasteland. His brother may not be too concerned about him because he happens to pull this stunt every few years, but it is my ass that keeps saving his arrogant life. SO, you can either shut up and come over here so I can show you how it's done, so you can do this next time or get out of my way."

I realized then she was talking. Verbally.

"You can speak?" I asked.

"Some people where you're from can vocalize, and others can't, correct?" Her rhetorical response silenced me. My babysitter growing up was crass and mean like this. I remembered being afraid of her as a child before she passed away, but my mother taught me that everyone shows love differently.

Sometimes, even though it's not right, people lash out because they care. If that was the case here, this woman obviously cared a lot about Jordan. Which wasn't something I was accustomed to seeing, so regardless of her apparent disdain for me, I couldn't help but take an immediate liking to her.

"Jeesh, Okay, ya crotchety old witch. Just tell me what to do and I'll do it," I retorted; my tone was much softer than my words.

Her face brightened a little, and I could tell she was trying not to smirk at me. Waving me over, she handed me the scissors and instructed that I start by removing his clothes while she began to soak half of the rags in the blue liquid. As I was cutting through his Obsidian black suit, I noticed that he had started to tremble slightly.

He was getting worse and not healing as expected. I asked her if cutting his suit up was really necessary, and she responded by letting me attempt to lift him up on my own, which I had discovered was damn near impossible before she had even got here.

That was my cue to just shut up and do whatever this strange woman told me. Luckily, we only needed to remove his coat and shirt. Accordingly, to her, the damage to him would be centralized around his chest and abdomen.

The damage was much more visible than I had expected. Peeling his shirt off revealed black pooling under his skin. It looked like someone had savagely beaten him with a baseball bat. His broad chest was lifting and falling at an uneven pace, and the dark pools were spreading.

"Here, take these and start laying them across the dark spots." She thrust a wad of blue-soaked rags into my hands and ran back to the kitchen. Internal bleeding, the devil was laying in front of me with internal bleeding. I could probably restrain this old woman, and my capturer would die.

'Why don't I want to do that? I should want to do that. God, what I wouldn't do for a large disciplinary glass of wine.' I internally chastised.

Looking over Jordan and seeing the life drain from his features didn't bring me the satisfaction I wanted it to.

He threatened to kill a mortal if I didn't stay locked in my cage. I should want him dead. I even tried convincing myself I had Stockholm syndrome or something else that made sense.

But as his life drained from him, I felt something dying inside me. Before I had a chance to talk myself out of it, I had covered all the pooling black spots with dripping rags. Beads of the liquid dripped and ran in streaks down his sides from the excess.

"Fucking Jordan, can't just leave the one fucking thing I tell him not to touch alone," the older woman grumbled. She shuffled her way back into the room angrily.

"There was a heat lamp in there four months ago. Where is it?" she barked at me.

"I have no idea. I've never noticed a heat lamp. Jordan can create heat and fire itself. Why would he own a heat lamp?"

"That's just great for him, but I can't exactly create heat from my hands, and his dumb ass needs heat to activate the healing properties in the water." She had started opening and closing all of the drawers in the closet now as if he had stashed her heat lamp in there.

"I can. How hot do they need to get?" She paused and looked at me quizzically.

"You have gifts? I thought you were supposed to be mortal." She made her way back to the bed beside me, the accusatory squint never leaving her eyes.

"Honestly, I don't know what I am. These fuckers have enjoyed keeping me guessing." I shrugged my shoulders and felt a small amount of pride as she laughed at me.

"I guess…" she said hesitantly, throwing a warning squint at me before continuing with her instruction.

"We need these to get very hot for them to work. If you think it's hot enough to burn him, go a bit hotter, and that should be enough." As instructed, I rubbed my hands together and concentrated my energy into my palms, taking deep breaths as I went.

My hands were throbbing as I moved them above the wet clothes slowly. As the tattered rags warmed, they lost their color, and the water turned clear.

"What is this, and why is the color fading? Am I doing something wrong?" She had walked away and had begun tidying up the mess she had made in the kitchen while searching for the heat lamp and returned to inspect my work at my question. Lifting one of the now completely white rags from Jordan's chest, she examined it and let out a relieved sigh.

"It's working. This is water from the Phlegethon river; it has magical properties. Jordan, being the only God this world has allowed to rule over it, is nourished by that magic. That was enough to stop the bleeding. He should be able to heal up the rest on his own. This one was close. You tell him I said his immortal ass is lucky to be alive, and I want a raise." She grabbed her buckets and made for the door.

"Hey, wait. It would be easier to drop your name while scolding him if I actually knew it," I called after her.

She paused, looked back, and answered me, "Tell him, Chacha said," and with that she was gone.

'Her name is Chacha? Interesting,' I thought to myself while removing the leftover rags and putting them by the bedside table.

Where the pools of black had once been, bruises remained in their stead. I let my hand wander while sitting on the bed beside him, tracing up and down his abdomen and onto his chest, feeling for any abrasions or irregularities. My heart nearly stopped as his hand grabbed mine.

"I could wake up to this every day for an eternity, and it wouldn't be enough," he murmured, then lifted my hand to his lips, kissed it and promptly passed back out, leaving me blushing in embarrassment. It threw me off to hear something so sweet come out of his mouth without it being smeared with sarcasm.

I decided I should probably take him out of his sweat-soaked clothes and wished I had some humiliating outfit to put him in as payback for when I woke up here and he had changed me.

Digging through the closet, I started to feel exhaustion setting in. Wandering through a castle for two full days and kicking the devil's brother's ass apparently was enough to completely drain me. It's not like he wore anything while he slept normally, anyway.

Taking his pants off wasn't as easy of a task as I had thought it would be. With every yank of his pants, I gained a new level of respect for long-term care workers and people who have to do this every day.

It took some time, but I managed to get him stripped and clean enough that I felt comfortable throwing a blanket over him and then attending to myself.

After my failed attempt at escape, my stomach was cramping from lack of food, and you could snap my hair off with how thick it was with grime. There was always an abundant amount of food available in both the cupboards and the refrigerator, but neither seemed to hold anything I could summon interest in. Most of it was the same, colorless 'sustenance' this world depended on.

I grabbed a dark gray bar from one of the containers and

forced myself to ingest its sandy texture. Then I downed several tall glasses of water.

'Hell's food has a long way to go.'

Showering alone was a commodity I hadn't noticed I had been missing since being brought to Hell, and I couldn't help but relish it. Jordan liked his showers cold. So, I turned it to the hottest setting, allowing myself to stand in it as long as my legs would allow.

Reaching to turn the water off, I felt the hairs on the back of my neck electrify, feeling the presence of someone behind me.

"Showering without me, Goddess?"

Letting out a frightened squeak, I jumped around to see Jordan leaning against the doorway, one arm wrapped around his midsection.

His hair may have been seductively disheveled, but the discoloration and bruising patterning his midsection replaced my initial appeal with concern. Yet his eyes were full of life, staring back at me vibrantly. A relieved smile invaded my face at the sight of him up and lucid.

"I figured I would savor some alone time while it was available to me. I'm glad you're up, though; I've been looking forward to you answering all my questions," I retorted, stepping out of the shower and wrapping a towel around myself. He shook his head at my tease, his grin returning.

"Good try. That scene I came home to was anything but behaved. Although, I am impressed you found the bridge room. That was unexpected. I'm not sure if I'm more impressed with you or annoyed." His voice was missing the strength of its usual dark timbre, and it was clear even the simple act of holding himself up was exhausting right now.

"I have no idea what you mean. You must have been hallucinating. I've been completely behaved. Regardless, I'm pretty sure I could take you right now. So, I'm thinking now is the time to get my answers," I said, making sure to bat my eyes at him.

"Beautiful Goddess, you can take me anytime." His dimple popped as he threw a wink at me. Trying to move forward, he lost his balance and I found myself catching him with my full body and walking him back to bed.

After laying him down, I went to walk away when he grabbed my hand, and with a sheepish look, asked me to stay. I curled up against him, his arm around me.

I was starting to understand why he never took my threats seriously. There was no way I could move forward with any of them.

"Chacha says you were lucky she was able to save you this time. Oh, and she wants a raise." Eyes remaining closed, he tilted his head towards me and burrowed his face into my wet hair, letting out a small laugh.

"She told you her name was Chacha? That sounds like her, and don't worry about me. I know my limits. As long as you are alive, I won't push them too far," he reassured me.

"Her name isn't Chacha? What is it then?" I asked.

"When I came here, she didn't have a name. Had no need for one. She was starving and vicious and was the first soul I rehabilitated as well as the only Givi I have gifted with immortality. She gave me my introduction to Hell, and I took care of her. She runs this household and takes care of everything. Everyone calls her Mother, which she hates."

Real endearment was evident in his tone, and a part of me warmed further to him in response to seeing him so fond of the bitter old woman. I could sense he was drifting back into unconsciousness and fought the urge to ask him more questions while he was still in such a seemingly compliant state.

"Christine," he said, using my real name for once. "I can almost hear the hundreds of questions bouncing around that beautiful head of yours. I want to answer them, but you have in no way earned the trust that would take. Get some sleep, Thad will be here early to take you to train, and I'm assuming you haven't slept in days."

And just like that, he was back to ordering me around.

"I'm not tired anymore," I pouted and began trying to push off him feeling his arm stiffen around me. "Jordan, let me up, god damn it." A tired smile stretched across his face at my irritation.

"You can either calm down and go to sleep, or I will drain the energy from you, so you have no choice. Your decision, Goddess."

Resigning to my fate, I curled up against him, shooting a glare at him before closing my eyes, irritated that even in this state, I couldn't break free of him. He responded with a kiss on my forehead, relaxing further into the mattress and allowing himself to drift back asleep.

I woke up feeling Jordan's arm still beneath me, my back stiff from being in this position for far too long. We couldn't have been asleep for more than a few hours, but I was restless, and the anxious ball of fire in my stomach was stronger than my exhaustion.

There were so many things adding to my unease. My punishment, Amy being here in Hell, Jordan almost dying, Jordan being alive, Jordan being strong enough to transport that many people between worlds, and the response Pierce would have to his display of power.

The biggest question I had was at the center of it all. What did I have to do with any of it? I pulled myself out of bed and curled my toes in the black shag carpet, grounding myself as much as possible before reluctantly standing and making my way to the kitchen to make myself a cup of coffee.

The smell lifted my mood in the way only fresh coffee could. Coffee was the first thing I had asked Jordan for other than being let go. He insisted I should drink some of the tea he already had. 'It's stronger and tastes better anyway,' he had insisted.

Angelicans had coffee. But most only drank it as a novelty. It was very much a Middle Earth thing.

I always wondered where the little produce he had came from, considering nothing grew in Hell, but I had never really bothered to ask. Pulling the French vanilla creamer from the fridge, I felt a pang of guilt at the thought of Jordan getting me this stuff himself. He even had the brand I liked, which I was so used to seeing I had never really thought about it before.

In heaven, because they have the gate and easy accessibility to Earth, it wasn't difficult to have produce purchased from Middle Earth; there was a thriving business for it even.

Earth was considered a tourist destination, and people fell in love with food from different countries on their travels; eventually, some Angels took notice of this and started an Earth produce delivery service. But the likelihood of that sort of thing in Hell was unlikely.

I poured the creamer in and took my time wrapping my hands around the mug, closing my eyes and breathing in the rich, earthy smell of the dark roast coffee, trying to let it loosen a bit of the knot in my stomach to no avail.

Jordan had a wonderful balcony from his room that looked out over the cascades of Hell, the city of Atlantis twinkling in the distance of eternal night. There was a chaotic and untamed beauty to the uninhabited forests surrounding the palace I couldn't deny, and I enjoyed having my morning coffee here most mornings before anyone, but Jordan, was awake.

I suspected he abused my energy via my mark to keep me from fully noticing his comings and goings in the night. Most mornings he would allow me this time to myself; since being brought here, a few things had been added to the balcony.

There was now a small Spanish-tiled coffee table, bursting in so many colors that even Hell couldn't dull them. There was also a Large egg-shaped chair that swung from a hook and was large enough I could curl up in it.

I enjoyed swinging back and forth while looking out over the landscape before Jordan would inevitably come and lure me back inside, usually to bed with him.

Leaning against the railing, I caught myself missing him sneaking up behind me, wrapping his arms around my waist and pulling me back into my cage. It was as if I were a bird he feared I would fly away upon seeing the window left open.

There was a soft knock at the door, and I realized Thad must be here for training. I was in a small nighty and Jordan was still turning in a hot and restless sleep. I left my mug on the tiny Spanish table and ran across the room on tip-toes before Thad had the chance to let himself in and see me like this.

I reached the door as it creaked open and stopped it with my foot, peeking through the slit before telling him I would be five minutes.

He looked humorously accosted as I briskly shut it in his face.

I tied my hair up on the way out of the closet after changing into training gear. I hated the way the rough fabric felt on my skin; I missed stretchy jeans and t-shirts and oversized sweaters. I kissed Jordan softly before leaving, a pang of sadness catching in my throat at the look on his face.

He was still in a lot of pain, and there was nothing I could do to help him. As much as I wanted to be free, to have my own life, I had to admit there was a connection between us and seeing him in pain drove that knowledge deeper with each wince.

9

PUSHING BOUNDARIES

Thad was tired himself but needed Christine to go a bit farther, and it was abundantly clear she wasn't aware he couldn't hear her.

"Okay. Harder now. Your abilities are like – a muscle. Working it in patterns makes it stronger. Overwork it, and you may strain or hurt yourself, but you learn your limits. Jordan is strong from this. Training harder and longer than anyone else has been willing. Get up and STOP me from knocking you down."

Christine lay on the ground against the floor where Thad had blasted her moments ago. She hurt everywhere but had no desire to stop.

"You're so full of shit. Jordan has the power he does because he was born a High God," she mumbled.

Training with Thad felt productive. He trained her with a less-than-gentle approach she appreciated. There's more motivation to block if a fist will actually smash into your face, and Thad's had several times now.

It took her back to training in her gym with her business partner Evan. The base of the self-defense moves she displayed in her classes, she had learned from him, and he had never pulled his punches.

Thad backed away slightly and couldn't help but feel a bit unimpressed with her. The movements didn't come naturally to her, and her instincts were far more defensive than he expected, given her strong personality. To truly push her limits, she would need to tap into her deepest inner strengths and connect with her core. Unfortunately for her, that meant he needed to beat her down to her breaking point. It also meant risking his brother's wrath.

She pulled herself up from the floor, clutching her abdomen, before putting her hand in front of her in the same stance he had shown her hours ago.

Thad threw both hands together, condensing energy into his clasp and blasting it toward her. He shifted his hands back and forth, creating friction, and in the same second, set the energy blast ablaze as it was hurled towards her.

His instruction had been to condense a shield around herself. Angling it to deflect the blast back at him, he had added the flames to assess how she'd handle a surprise scenario. Considering a practiced one was clearly not her strong suit.

With one foot on the ground and the other against the wall behind her, she pressed her open palms together while crouching. As the flaming energy blast approached her, she launched herself off the wall. Her arms were extended, hands flatly pressed against one another. This created a wedge, cutting through the blast. She reached Thad, and her whole body smashed into his abdomen, knocking him to the ground.

"What was that?" Thad grunted, not bothering to hide his annoyance as he shoved her roughly off him.

"I don't know. The stupid technique you're showing me doesn't work. So, I tried something different. I fucking hurt everywhere and kinda just went on default," she huffed out defensively. He pulled himself up off the ground and offered a hand to her, noticing her eyes had changed from blue to a light purple. The usual ring in the center now a much deeper green.

It was time to stop for the day.

"Remember how you feel at this moment. This is your current limit," he said to her. An annoying sense of anxiety rose in him at the thought of Jordan seeing her like this.

"What do you mean? How do you know? Maybe I'm ready for another round?" she fired back at him defensively.

"Have you ever wondered about Jordan's eyes turning completely black?" This got her attention. She had, in fact, wondered about this, but she learned long ago that asking questions was a waste of time.

"They reflect a slip in control and the limit your body can sustain your power. Jordan's power is not easily contained," he gulped, envisioning the shade of nightly death that would be inhabiting his brother's eyes when Jordan came for him later before continuing.

"All empowered Angelicans have this tell. Kielius's turn yellow, Jordan's turn black, and yours, apparently, turn green and purple." Looking in the large mirror on the wall, she didn't recognize the reflection.

The clothes, the softness her lack of training had caused her body, and now, otherworldly eyes. They were a thick lavender where the whites had been, and her irises sparkled emerald green in stark contrast. Her reflection did not mirror her mind's image of herself, and she wasn't sure yet if that was good or bad.

"What about Savious? Or Pierce?" she asked, finding it curious that she had somehow never seen either of them do this before. His back was turned to her, and he had started leaving the room.

"You've earned yourself a break. Come, I'll give you a local's dining experience," he said, waving her to follow.

"So, you're gonna ignore my questions, cool," she griped, following him anyway.

"Use a guest room to get cleaned up first, though, so you don't wake Jordan up. I'll find Mother to see if she has any clothes that'll fit you."

Fully annoyed now, she jabbed him in the back with her finger, and he turned to face her. It was clear he was just as spent as she was, so she decided to drop the issue.

"She told me her name was Chacha," Christine said with a conspiratorial smile.

He grinned back. "Good to know."

Christine had experienced meals in the grand hall before, but being with Jordan had made her other meals a very different experience. When Jordan had brought her, everyone seemed to clear out. He had told her it was one way they communicated their appreciation to him, as the people here coveted privacy and personal space.

Tonight, there was an entirely different energy. People bustled around the massive room. There was a cacophony of clinking and clacking as people ate, unaware of the noise their utensils made when coming in contact with the dishes.

Men and women of varying shades of gray ushered children around, everyone seemingly sharing the responsibilities of the young ones around them. Movement was everywhere as families and friends used their hands to yell, joke, admonish, and tell stories. This meal added resolve to her desire to begin learning the language during her daily self-study.

Making eye contact with Thad, Christine spoke loudly above the noise of laughing children, "It's so loud in here. I love it." He cocked his head in a private joke.

"I hadn't noticed," he responded before turning his attention back to his food.

Christine knew there were also souls in Hell as well and was happy she wouldn't see them here. Jordan devoted many paid bounty hunters to keep the souls in the Stx river. It filtered their energies and prepared them to be reborn in one of the three dimensions.

The more negative energy you put out into the world that you inhabited, the lighter your soul would be at your body's end. The more positive energy you put out, the heavier. Heavier souls required less time in the river before rebirth as the minerals at the bottom of the river cleansed your soul and allowed its energy to be sent to its next life.

The lighter souls stayed near the top, and over time, as they were cleansed, began to sink toward rebirth. Although occasionally, they were light enough to climb out of the river and wander, usually causing trouble.

There were probably a few people in the dining room with them right now employed to watch the river for escapees. Christine found it all fascinating and adored learning about it, but also feared approaching the river. The thought of seeing her parents' essences floating amongst the other dead kept her far from the river.

This castle was more of a sanctuary to them than the overlord's home, it appeared from this perspective. Thad explained people come from all over to stay at Castle Jordan, where they are taught skills that they could, in turn, take back to their homes and help heal their lands. Food and shelter were provided, and the unspoken rule was that in exchange, Jordan had their loyalty.

The food may have been free, but it was also extremely bland. Jordan created this place as a refuge for the gentle inhabitants of the realm and found the only food sources that grew naturally were able to be combined into a hearty dish. It was sustaining and would keep the people healthy, but it tasted the way you would expect a gray blob to taste. Christine poked at the slop in front of her, feeling guilty about her special creamer.

Motioning with her fork, Christine asked, "What exactly does Jordan plan on doing with this purchased loyalty?" Thad's eyebrows scrunched together in judgment.

"You are really determined to convince yourself he's evil, aren't you?" He jabbed his spoon angrily into the goop. "Twisting everything he does into its worst light doesn't undo the good. Yes, he is earning their loyalty. No, it isn't for 'nefarious purposes.' These people needed a leader, a protector. Someone to establish some sort of order. A place like this, where souls find themselves lost, needs guidance. Jordan is rehabilitating them, but we won't be able to fully heal this world without the resources we would have if Jordan were still sitting on his rightful throne."

A familiar face rounded the corner just then, her frown lines ever prominent, people parting for her as if they could feel her scorn without even making eye contact with her. She was carrying a large basket filled with dirty dishes on her hip and heading directly for them. She tapped Thad on the shoulder, gaining his attention.

The dishes clattered violently as she dropped the box to the table and began signing to Thad.

Her eyes darted around Christine's bruises and landed on her eyes. Chacha added something in her communication that caused Thad to shrug and respond in sign himself.

"You're fucked, buddy," Chacha's sneer echoed against the rough stone tables as she verbalized again.

He signed to her in a frustrated flurry of movements before setting his plate and cup in a basket at the end of the table filled with other dirty dishes.

"I CAN blame you. Look at her; you're an idiot. Yeah, I'll take her back. It's not like I have anything else to do." Chacha's radio scratch voice was lighter this time as she turned away with a grin.

"Thanks, 'Chaa - chaa,'" Thad called as he left. Slightly over accentuating the A's in her name.

Chacha's grin faded, and she pointed her crinkled daggers at Christine. Standing up and ignoring Chacha's tapping foot, she sauntered to the end of the nearest table and started stacking abandoned dishes in the baskets that were left on the end of each.

"What do you think you are doing?" She suppressed a smile

at how ridiculous Christine looked, glowing purple irises, hair in a messy bun and wrapped in a gray dress that drowned her frame, gathering crusty plates from the large obsidian tables like a commoner, looking nothing like the Queen she was.

"Well, Chacha, I am helping you with the dishes from the lunch rush." Chacha huffed out a laugh at her, grabbed the basket from her and put it on the receiving counter that was within a square cut in the wall that connected to the kitchen.

"What makes you think I'm doing them? I run the estate and the grounds. I don't have time for shit like this. I supervise and make sure the work is getting done, and getting done right. Now let's get you home before Jordan burns the place down in frustration," Chacha said, leading her down one of the many halls.

With how dire Jordan's health had sounded in Chacha's last diagnoses, it warmed the knot of anxiety in Christine's soul to hear Chacha speak of Jordan without making him sound like he was on his deathbed.

"Thanks, Chacha," Christine said as they approached the now recognizable door to her and Jordan's suite, thanks to the little X on the doorframe Christine had drawn with a marker during her escape. Chacha stalled before walking away, forehead wrinkles bunching in annoyance.

"I know Jordan told you that isn't my actual name," Chacha snapped.

Pulling the door open, Christine shot her a wink and jabbed her with, "It is now," before closing the door on her. Through the thick wooden door, she could hear Chacha huff and shuffle away.

She turned to walk into the room, meeting complete disorientation, meeting the black wall that was Jordan's Chest. Fire ran up her spine as he grabbed her arms and thrust her back up against the door. He gently brushed the side of his face against hers, grabbing her ear for a split second with his teeth before scooping under her thighs and completely lifting her from the ground. The all-consuming nature of his kiss diminishing the rest of the world around them.

She lost herself in him, wrapping her legs around him, her excitement growing as he lifted her from the door and carried her to the bed. He lowered her gently down, his mouth never leaving hers, the clothes burning from his body. He pulled away just enough to look at her, sliding his hands into her shirt to lift it from her body before freezing in place.

Her eyes greedily made their way up his body, appreciating the sculpted figure appearing between the holes of charred clothing until she met his eyes. If there was a look of death, he had it at that moment.

Jaw muscles knotted; his completely blackened eyes fixed on her. He cupped her face, pulling her closer for inspection, tilting her face this way and that. By the intensity of his gaze, she couldn't help but think, 'this is why people think he is evil. With this expression, he looks like murder personified.'

The sound that formed his words was less of a voice and more of a growl as he sent a demand into the space between them, one not meant for her.

"What. Was. He. Thinking?" Through the anger, a pained whisper escaped him. "Purple..."

Something ancient and assured surfaced within her, and looking past the inky appearance of Jordan's eyes she saw what was really there. His nature was telling him that he had failed to provide her with protection, and the primal urge he felt to correct that was consuming him, manifesting itself so purely that even the flecks of silver normally present in his eyes were eclipsed.

Any fear that had initially presented itself at his composure was replaced with a sense of security one can't understand until they live without it.

This man would burn the world down for her. Not just burn the world down to have her. His eyes, his look, it told her more than his words ever could. And as a woman who had spent most of her life feeling afraid or uncomfortable, there was nothing more endearing than being necessary to someone.

He was her first choice, and she was still deciding if she was happy or concerned about being his.

"Jordan," she said softly, reaching up at him. "He was thinking the same thing you have been thinking. If, and that is a big if, in my opinion, I needed to defend myself right now, I'd be fucked." She had his full attention.

"He fears what would happen to you if I died because I was denied training that you could have given me. I don't want to wait until I'm as dangerous as you. I need my freedom, and according to you, I may have to fight for it." Reason softened his sneer. "These marks are proof that I'm working towards the ability to do so. Something I did back home, and now am doing again."

The black slowly drained from his eyes as she pulled him back into a kiss.

Jordan lay atop her, pinching the bottom of a strand of curls playfully. Pulling it down until it straightened, and he released it, allowing it to bounce back into place. She watched as his contemplative expression dissolved, and his mischievous grin took its place.

"That was the best distraction technique I think anyone has ever used on me. Touché, you cunning Goddess," he said, kissing her softly.

"But I'm still going to have words with my brother. If you are going to push your limits, I need to be there. Understood?" There was concern behind the demand in his voice, and instead of pushing against it, she accepted it. Only because his concern carried weight as the reigning expert on pushing one's limits.

"Fine, while I learn to identify my limitations, I won't overexert myself unless you are there, ya drama queen," she jousted.

"Did you really just burn your clothes off?" He pulled himself off the bed and walked to the closet.

"You're lucky I didn't burn your clothes off. I'm an impatient man when it comes to you." She glanced at the shredded clothes she had previously been wearing and huffed out a light laugh at his so-called restraint. When he returned to the room, he was carrying an unmarked gift bag and had managed to fully dress himself and comb his hair back in what seemed like a matter of seconds.

"I picked something up for you, other than coffee and creamer, that is." She suddenly felt overly exposed, him handing her a gift while she lay naked in his bed. Christine sat up, wrapping the blanket up around herself, to Jordan's amusement.

"Cover yourself up all you like; there isn't an inch of you I haven't committed to memory. Here, open it up."

The plastic material of the bag felt cool and foreign in her hands. Discomfort and heat started gnawing at her stomach lining.

Jordan noticed her shifting eyes and took it back from her. He placed it to the side, taking both of her hands in his and kneeling in front of her.

"I can practically taste your panic. Are you okay? If you don't like presents, that's fine. After this one, I'll take that into consideration." She stared dumbly back at his response, never having seen someone have this empathetic a reaction before.

Gifts meant pressure or that someone wanted something from you. She already felt the guilt of not reacting the perfect way to said gift. Looking back at him now, it was clear she could spit on the gift and throw it in his face, and his ego wouldn't be damaged.

"Please say something. You look like I hit you." She shook her head and laughed sheepishly, the pressure she had felt deflating.

"Sorry about that. I'm not very good with getting gifts. In my experience, gifts are more for the other person than me." He pressed his forehead to hers knowingly.

"Open it, and you will see there is literally nothing for me to gain in giving you this. I promise."

Trusting him, she grabbed the bag and pulled out a pair of stretchy fabric Jeans and a soft graphic t-shirt printed with bold words on it.

If you can read this, you're too close to me.

Absolute gratitude filled her heart and reflected in her laughter. Jordan had never seen anything more beautiful than the sparkle in her eyes while she laughed.

"You, the lord of the underworld, King of Darkness, Heir to the throne of Heaven, walked into a store and bought this outfit?" she asked, still trying to picture this terrifying God with a grocery cart.

"I shop in stores all the time to keep up with your coffee addiction. Target is great. I figure the weird looks I get are a small price to pay for your comfort."

Imagining Jordan perusing the aisles of Target made her laugh harder, to the point of tears. Feeling lighter than she had felt in years, she tossed the outfit aside and grabbed him, pulling him back into the bed with her.

BY ANY MEANS NECESSARY

"Are you sure this is the only solution? It's risky; if word gets out, we could lose the support of the people." It was a redundant question, but Victor felt it needed to be asked regardless.

"Yes. I don't have the time or born gifts to match Jordan's raw strength. I always thought that when this war came, I would be able to leverage the army against him to even the odds. This is no longer just about the war, though; this has gotten personal. Christine is mine, and I will get her back, and to do that, I need to be able to take him on. Me having heightened strength can only benefit our people." Pierce said the words the same way he had many times before to himself, trying to justify what he was doing.

"The problem we are going to have is finding useful candidates. Those willing to give up their abilities will be those whose gifts aren't worth hanging onto. And even once you have fully acclimated to their gifts, they take some getting used to. Additionally, what do we do if the transfer is incompatible and the Gifter dies? We are dealing with practices that haven't been used in a long time for good reasons," Victor reasoned. Pierce rolled his eyes at him.

"My friend, we both know wars have collateral damage. And the only reason the transference of gifts is no longer practiced is because the 'almighty' Jordan forbade it out of fear someone would surpass his abilities. I think our best bet is to petition the scouts. Most of them are looking for retirement anyway after the savage beat-down Jordan gave them," Pierce said casually while flipping through the files of possible candidates on his desk. After circling a few possibilities, he handed the files to Victor, who took them reluctantly.

"You know I support you. I just remember a time when you were still adamant that it didn't matter if your strength matched his because you were backed by the people, and that was enough. I can't help but feel this is about playing tug of war over Christine more than winning the war. I don't want to see you lose everything over a woman who may not even want you." Victor placed his hand on Pierce's shoulder, trying to give his words time to sink in before leaving the room to gather the approved recruits.

Pierce sat at his desk trying to focus on the plans in front of him, all of which needed his tweaking and approval. Everything from security perimeters to militia training, but he couldn't seem to take in the words in front of him. He tried to read, and her voice filled his mind along with images of her. He could see her clearly. Her dimpled cheeks and the sway of her prominent hips as she walked toward him, her eyes shining.

"What is wrong with you?" he hissed to himself, clenching his fingers in his hair and walking away from the desk, accepting he wasn't getting anything done.

'If I could just get her back. Knowing she was safe with me, I'd be able to focus again. Everything would go back to normal.'

Looking around the room, he decided a change of scenery was needed. She was everywhere here. From the sweater he kept to remind him of her scent to photos of them together on their 'little adventures' as she had called them. Adventures with her while showing her around the world she would someday be queen of.

It was almost time for dinner, and thinking it would be a good idea to make an appearance, he decided to join his people in the great hall for dinner since it had been a while. He could hear laughter and conversation booming well before reaching the giant room. Pushing the massive doors open, he was met by hundreds of pleasantly surprised faces as he entered the room. Upon seeing him, the conversations had halted, and a stillness sat over the room. Pierce smiled, never tiring of the effect this position gave him over people.

"Please don't let me disrupt your meals, friends. I've come to join the revelry, not dampen it." His voice boomed out over the audience, bouncing off the rows of tables and high walls. The muddled conversations continued, and those in his path rose to shake his hand and pass along a friendly greeting. He made his way around the room, making conversation and reassuring his people that they were prepared for the coming war.

He encountered a familiar face while moving from table to table. A woman Jordan used to date casually when he had first ascended to the throne. "Nacentra, is that you?" he asked, taking her hand and helping her to stand before pulling her into a friendly hug, which she stiffly reciprocated.

"Hello, Pierce. How are you?" He noticed a cold tone in her voice and a disinterested expression on her face. Pierce's keenest ability had always been that he could feel people's emotions and see glimpses into their minds, sometimes, even change them. Nacentra was one of the few people who were privy to this knowledge, as Empaths were not widely or warmly accepted.

People didn't enjoy the possibility of someone being able to reach into them like that, so it was a skill he carefully kept hidden. He hoped her icy behavior was simply because she knew he was trying to read her, and that would make anyone uncomfortable.

"I've honestly been better, as I'm sure you've heard. But I remain optimistic in righting the current wrongs very shortly. Your ex hasn't dropped in to see you, has he?" Pierce asked. A glint of amusement betrayed her.

"We both know Jordan isn't really my ex-anything, other than a friend. He hasn't paid me a visit, but I did hear he paid you one. Any news on Christine? I truly pity any girl trapped in a war between you two." There was more than indifference in the emotions he was picking up from her now but genuine sympathy. For whom though he couldn't tell, Christine or himself.

"No, he came to declare war. I couldn't get him to tell me what he has done with my Queen. Rest assured, I intend to find her soon, and she is strong. I have faith she will be okay." Doubt colored her face at his words.

"There isn't a woman strong enough in any world to fend off Jordan. Trust me; if he wants her, he likely has already had her, my Lord." She didn't bother to hide her mocking tone, sending a wave of anger through him. He took a menacing step towards her; jaw clenched, before stopping himself. Plastering on a wide smile, he masked his anger in overt friendliness.

"Well, that's how you know you haven't met Christine. If you'll excuse me." He shook her hand again, dismissing himself.

After hours of repeated reassurances and adjusting several worried souls into a much more optimistic attitude, he decided it was safe to call it a night for now.

Walking down the torch-lit alley and taking in the stars, he was able to discover a little peace and clarity. Jordan had once banned him from using his abilities, saying it was wrong to force people to feel a certain way. But what Jordan hadn't understood is that emotional manipulation was a force for good.

He could calm the agitated, soothe the worried, and, as

proven with Christine, make the endangered secure. He considered being a slave to your own emotions to be a terrible burden. One he was destined to save those around him from.

Breathing in the cool night air, he remembered back to the first time he saved Christine after discovering their bond. She had run directly into him on the street and, upon seeing him, began to panic. He had offered her his hand, and as they touched for the first time, he pulled that worry from her.

"Pierce, I'm sorry to disrupt what looks like your first moment of peace in quite a while, but I have gathered a few recruits for you to speak with as you asked." Victor's voice broke him out of his daydream and pulled him back into the present.

"No apologies necessary. I'll head right over. We don't have any time to waste."

***

Christine lay on her side facing him, deep asleep, exhausted from thanking him so vigorously. After that night, he knew he would need to make a change for her. Keeping her locked up here would increase her attempts to 'escape,' which would be more dangerous than anything.

He brushed her stray baby hairs back gently, trying to remember how he had lived before she came into his life.

He needed to speak with his brother. Thad must have lost his damn mind to get that rough with her. It wasn't just her eyes proving that he had pushed it too far, but she was covered in marks. It was normal to get bruised during training, but the amount she had was unacceptable.

He didn't bother to drain her energy, knowing she wouldn't bolt with the questions she planned to hammer him with. As convenient a method it had been to ensure her safety, leaving her asleep in his bed, it also distanced him from earning her trust. After dressing himself for the second time that night and pressing a gentle kiss to Christine's lips, he transported to Kronos.

It was gnawing at him, knowing she had seen Amy. Even with Amy by his side explaining things, it would be very hard to explain that betrayal away.

Clearing his mind, he approached Thad's house. Jordan figured he would make a grand entrance and toy with his baby brother a smidge before beating him to a pulp.

Jordan kicked Thad's doors open hard enough, they shook the house and announced his presence. Letting himself in, he surveyed the room while rolling up his sleeves, flexing the stiff mark Hell had branded him with.

"Thad, I need to talk to you...." He knew his brother wouldn't hear the taunting words, so he focused on the appearance of the house, cloaking any color within it in darkness to provide a visible notice of arrival.

Thad had a small two-bedroom home filled with thick plants and gaudy art, the only thing in Thad's home that made any sense to Jordan was the fully reinforced bunker he had in the basement that they occasionally used for training.

Thad's voice responded from downstairs in the training room. "I'm down here. Take a deep breath before coming down, will you?" Each step Jordan took landed heavier than the last, hoping the force was enough to send vibrations to Thad. Entering the now-darkened cement room, he tried not to laugh.

Thad was sitting on a stool in the corner; one leg draped over the other with a glass of red wine in his hand.

"Sitting in the corner and I haven't even put you in time out yet?" Jordan signed. Thad sank in his chair before chugging the entire glass of wine.

"Punch my teeth out, and I will be unable to disclose my discovery."

Jordan slowed his advance, narrowing his eyes and signing back, "You, baby brother, don't need your mouth to speak."

Jordan continued aloud, letting his brother read his lips. "Given your new-found stance on testing one's limits, it is high time we evaluate yours."

Resigning to his fate, Thad rose and took a firm stance, preparing for the first blow. With a low sweep kick, Jordan blasted Thad's feet out from under him, sending him crashing to the ground. Jordan transported to the spot Thad fell and grabbed a fistful of his shirt, lining up a solid punch.

"Christine is Angelican," Thad blurted out, throwing his arms up in surrender. With a contemplative furrow of his brow, Jordan slowly rose, keeping eye contact with Thad.

"I'm aware," he mouthed.

"How?"

"I don't just sense the energy flowing through the realms, but the energy that fuels its inhabitants as well. After the first day of training her, I sensed something within her that wasn't mine or Pierce's." Thad watched his brother run through countless scenarios in his mind before his shirt was released.

"Is that a bad thing?" Thad asked, smoothing the chest of his button-down, checking it for damage.

"I have no idea who she is. Not to mention, both Pierce and I gifted her abilities without knowing if she was compatible with them. We could have killed her, Thad," Jordan explained, Thad nodding in understanding.

"Now," Jordan signed. "Face or gut?" he asked.

Dropping his arms in exasperation, Thad pointed to his face, knowing his stomach was much more prone to long-term bruising. Jordan cracked his knuckles before punching Thad hard in the gut.

After giving him a second to catch his breath, he looked at his brother and warned, "Ease up on her, or we'll test your limits next. Savious is too much of a menace for her to fear you too." Thad could now understand his anger and nodded back to his brother as he was helped from the ground.

***

Visiting the fates would require an unexpected trip to Middle Earth. When Jordan was dethroned, they fled and had been under his protection ever since. Initially, they lived in Hell with him, but they never adapted to living in a world without sun or decent food. So, he set them up in a city of their choice with handlers.

They were not fans of being supervised constantly, but unlike Christine, they knew better than to waste their time trying to argue with him. Taking Christine home was something he had been considering; after all he had a promise to keep. He just had hoped to do so after Pierce's deadline and after removing him as a threat. New York was even more of a problem. So many passing faces, but it needed to be done.

He transported into the entryway of their suite, which was shadowed just enough for him to go unnoticed. Leaning against the wall he had trapped her against their first night together, he took a moment to savor the sight in front of him.

Christine was only wearing the T-shirt he had gotten her and underwear, laying on her stomach, feet in the air and kicking to whatever music was blasting from the headset she was using.

Pleased that she was clicking away at the laptop he had recently given her, he couldn't help but wonder what she was looking at. When it came to research he tried not to pry too much. When he had presented it to her, she had such a hard time grasping that he hadn't placed any restrictions on it.

The thought of Pierce filtering their shared history and scolding her for looking for her own answers into the world they had dragged her into infuriated him. Treating her like a child. Granted, Jordan could understand why he had done so.

Christine was intelligent enough to figure out just how gray history really was, and Pierce wouldn't be able to continue his made-up 'chosen bride' story after she had access to any information regarding his rule or the public prophecy that had started this whole mess, and there wasn't enough censoring in the world to keep all related information about either from her.

With a mischievous grin, he decided her vacation started now. He transported to the bedside. While she was mid-key-stroke, he grabbed her feet and pulled her legs around his waist.

He reveled in the frightened squeak that escaped her. Bending forward, he kissed the back of her head, chuckling while removing the headphones. She buried her face in the bedspread, trying to hide her shame at letting him sneak up on her.

He ran his hands up the back of her thighs, enjoying the way his hands were able to cause her skin to flush and raise goosebumps along their trail. With one hand, he pulled the cheeky underwear down and pushed his fingers into her hair. She got onto her hands and knees, simultaneously turning her head back to look at him.

"I've told you before, delectable Goddess, there's no hiding from me." Desire and playfulness dripped from his tone.

As confused as she felt about her part in all of this, she was constantly feeling more sure of him. Regardless of being the good or bad guy, she could feel herself becoming assured that he was her guy. She fit too comfortably with him, too quickly to 'belong' to anyone else.

After roughly enjoying each other, Jordan lost to his own curiosity, pulling the edge of the laptop closer and clicking a key to awaken the screen. He sat straight up, seeing Enochian symbols glowing back at them, blinking in brief disbelief.

"What made you look this up?" he asked. Still in a disoriented haze, she looked from him to the screen deciding there was no harm in answering honestly.

"A grudge." He cocked his head at her. "A show I loved back home touched on Enochian, and I got excited when I saw some familiar symbols etched into some old buildings. Pierce told me it was a dead language and not important enough to learn about. Then changed the topic as quickly as possible every time I brought it up."

That didn't surprise Jordan in the slightest.

"And what do you think of it so far?" he prompted.

"Personally, I was raised to believe words are powerful. Language and communication is powerful. I just wish I could find more on this one," she answered dismissively. Her statement could not have been more perfect.

"Well, you won't find anything on this," Jordan explained, clicking the lid shut. "Arcane's father, Pierce's grandfather, outlawed the language in the first few years of his reign. It was never used for verbal communication. If it really interests you, I can dig up some material on it."

"Yeah, sure, sounds great," she said, waving him off and flopping back down, covering herself in the blankets again.

Only after he delighted in watching her burrow down into his sheets did he pop up from bed. She watched as he disappeared within the closet. Appreciating his form and wondering again about the tattoo up his forearm again as he walked away.

Christine tried to gather her thoughts and composure. She was still reeling from him and felt envious of how quickly he was able to get his mind straight.

The research she had done wasn't helping clear anything up. The Internet was a mess and not at all what she had been used to.

The internet she was given access to was also a special connection for Jordan. It had access to Middle Earth's information as well as Heaven's. Magic, she decided, was confusing but amazing for being able to manipulate science like this.

Hell may not have joined the world of technology yet, but Angelicans had, and they were not shy about posting what they thought they knew about the realm.

The lore she found, written in Heaven and Middle Earth, was all over the place and completely useless. Honestly, the

Enochian search was just a fun break she needed from frustration.

One thing she had learned while searching was that the 'events' of history were documented depending on the perspective of the individual's writing and financing of the publication. Heaven and Hell were no exception to this rule.

She was determined to make heads or tails of the two men that had forced themselves into her life. She decided the best she could do was take in both sides and try to find an unbiased story, which she figured lay somewhere in the middle.

A bag thumped next to her, breaking her from her train of thought. Jordan stood in front of her with a wide grin, fully dressed in dark Jeans and a black cashmere sweater. Like normal, he appeared completely poised while she still sat rather ruffled and completely exposed.

"Come on, Goddess, we don't have all day. We are going on a field trip, and you have about five minutes before I change my mind," he said, grinning from the entryway to the closet. Looking back and forth from her to the clothes he had perched atop the duffel bag expectantly.

She stared back at him in disinterest, assuming he was making her go on another bleak tour of Hell. She hated being carted around like a princess, her hand always inside his, tight as a vice, as if he were afraid someone might try to take her from him.

It always darkened her heart to see so many people in disarray that she couldn't help. And god forbid they see a wandering soul like the last time. She would never forget the sight of the poor translucent man being tackled and hauled off by Jordan's men to be thrown in the river to be recycled back to Earth. Each trip helped remind her that not only was she helpless in her own life, but she was unable to help others as well.

Seeing a gloom beginning to darken her eyes, Jordan sighed and rolled his eyes at her.

"Well, I thought you wanted to go home. But if you prefer

not to go, it saves me the logistical nightmare of keeping you safe while also attempting to make you happy, if that's even possible," he said, grabbing the bag and heading back toward the closet.

"Wait!" Christine yelled. She lunged from the bed, grabbed the clothes from the bag, and thrust them on as quickly as possible.

"Did you say home? Like, you're letting me go?" The hopeful glee in her expression as she peered up at him made him feel a little guilty as he firmly explained that although he would be taking her home, he was in no way 'letting her go.' Her shoulders dropped slightly, though he couldn't tell if it was from disappointment or relief.

"Besides," he stated, "I have a promise to live up to. You need to know I am a man of my word."

He suppressed a twinge at how still she suddenly became. With that, he grabbed her shoulders from behind and kissed the side of her neck. He loved the way a rosy blush appeared on her neck wherever he kissed her while transporting them both to Middle Earth.

CHANGING PERSPECTIVES

The iridescent light invaded her eyes, shaking her loose from the memory she had been trapped in.

"Can you hear me?" Jordan's voice soothed her like cold water against the throbbing sting in her brain.

Feeling like she was made of rusted-over steel, she tried to move to make sure her extremities were still made of flesh. As clarity repossessed her, it became apparent that she was standing up and was pinned tightly to Jordan's solid form. His hand held the side of her head as he inspected her ashen face.

"Unfortunately," she responded with a small smirk. His body loosened with the exhale of what she assumed was a long-held breath.

"Don't do that to me, Christine, fuck," Jordan said, exasperated, placing her firmly on her feet. Stepping back, he kept his hands on her shoulders, steadying her.

"Are you stable?" he asked. The room wasn't spinning anymore, and her eyes were able to open fully without the feeling that they would be pulled apart in every direction. She nodded yes. Unlatching his fingers slowly, he trusted her to stay upright on her feet.

"Well, Goddess, bad news, you are one of the few unlucky individuals out there with a slight incompatibility to transport. The farther the distance, the more severe the reaction. You had a reaction with us jumping worlds. If someone less experienced than I was to try and take you somewhere, it could kill you. Keep that in mind." She rolled her eyes, mentally adding yet another thing life decided to weigh against her to the 'what is likely to kill me' list.

The room she found herself in was a spacious loft-style suite with a modernist look. Similar to Jordan's quarters back home. She thought the word home and immediately struck it out and replaced it with Hell before continuing. Lots of black against white, very sterile and masculine looking.

"Your taste doesn't have much range, does it?" she mocked. He shot a dangerous smile at her.

"Are you mocking my decor?" he challenged her.

"Yes. Look at this place. You're so cliche." He feigned hurt at her words; the rest of the tension he had been harboring left his body.

Noticing his uncharacteristic nervousness, she walked to one of the glass walls overlooking the cityscape, trying to figure out if she were to ask him what was wrong, would she even want the answer and decided to ponder this while appreciating the view of the city she once considered her refuge.

Jordan approached from behind and wrapped his arms around her, trying to soothe whatever anxiety was causing her nose to crinkle slightly and her lips to purse.

"It's hard. Being away from home for so long, isn't it?" he asked, tone laced with a thick longing.

Home. When she thought of home, she didn't see New York. She saw a small house in desperate need of a new paint job, the white wooden side shingles chipping from the harsh winters of Northern Michigan. The windows were the four-pane kind, and during the holidays were always illuminated with lit-up Santa or reindeer window decorations, regardless of whether Christmas was over or not.

She could practically feel the worn carpet curling between her toes and the smell of vanilla and cinnamon boiling on the stove.

"New York isn't my home. I moved here with Amy after your dad destroyed my life. She was moving with her parents anyway, and they convinced the foster system to move me here with them to help me escape some of the trauma. I love New York, but home to me was a small town in the Upper Peninsula of Michigan, Escanaba."

She wasn't sure why she was telling him. The word home and being back on the same plane brought out a nostalgia in her.

Despite the cynic inside her, she found comfort in sharing something so personal with Jordan. Thinking about it, she had never really talked about home with Pierce.

Pierce had been to her real home and saved her life there, but she had never really talked about it with him. When they spoke, it usually centered around the future, current dangers, or their 'relationship.'

"Would you like to visit Escanaba while we are here?" he asked, chin resting on the top of her head.

"No." A ghost of sorrow swept through her. "Any joys one gets from visiting home were robbed from me. Being home just pushes their faces into my mind, and not them smiling on a weekend morning, but what it looked like when they were murdered." Ice began to form over her again, and she stepped out of Jordan's embrace, the knowledge of who his father was forever frigid in her brain.

"Have you ever tried visiting home? Now that time has passed?" he asked.

"No. I didn't really have the funds to fly back to Michigan, and I couldn't drive my non-existent car. Besides, I never wanted to."

"Christine, you miss your parents, your life with them.

Obviously, they gave you something worth missing. I'm assuming your childhood had memories that may be worth revisiting, even if it means confronting the painful ones as well." He stepped closer again.

"Don't do that," she warned icily.

"Do what?"

"Act like you have any idea what I'm talking about. Give me hollow advice based on an outsider's perspective." She walked to her bag, giving herself more space, and picked it up to begin searching for the bedroom. Before she could fully get out of the room, Jordan's response stopped her.

"You are not the only person alive who has been through trauma, Christine, and it would benefit you in this life to remember it," he said simply and without scorn.

"RIGHT. Right, I forgot, your life has sucked too, that makes my trauma and anger invalid, I forgot," she snapped at him.

He looked out the window, eyes downcast, refraining from speaking and angering her further. A churning heat built in her stomach, torn between ironic irritation at the prospect of the son of her parents' murderer giving her grief advice and remorse for belittling the solace of someone she knew was not attempting to measure scars.

"Sorry... For biting your head off. But, think of it this way, would you be able to take advice from you, given the same circumstances as me?" Jordan nodded, agreeing, crossing his arms and leaning against the window, facing her.

"I have lived the years of many lives and, as such, will not belittle what you have gone through by pretending to understand how you feel." She scoffed and threw her arms frustratedly in the air before spinning on her heels, prepared to aptly storm away.

He transported himself into her path, cupping her face, lifting it in encouragement to meet his eyes, an encouragement she rejected. Her eyes focusing on anything and everything in the room but him.

"My stubborn woman, I am not finished." Her eyes met his then, daring him to repent. "I do not need to understand your feelings in order to respect them. I am sorry. Truly." He pulled her face to meet his, hoping to apologize with more than words, but she put a hand to his lips, stopping him and stepping from his embrace.

"Admitting my reaction is valid, and apologizing doesn't just magically fix everything. I'm still mad at you." Although she was rejecting him, her words held a new warmth, and although he knew it would infuriate her, he couldn't help the triumphant grin that broke across his face.

Turning quickly enough for her curls to flop against him, she hastily began a retreat to the bedroom. She paused, rushed back to him, pecked him on the lips, then completed her rush of storming from the room and slamming the bedroom door.

PESKY EMOTIONS

Pierce woke up feeling dirty and unsatisfied. He rolled out of bed to go for his morning run. Routine was his saving grace. Taking on additional abilities was overloading his system and leaving him exhausted, and honing them was leaving him in a constant state of physical pain.

Some god groupie named Evangeline lay in his bed, infecting his sheets with the wrong woman's scent, furthering his feeling of grime. He had often kept discreet company while allowing Christine to adapt to her new world and give her the opportunity to come to him. But it had never made him feel so self-contemptuous.

He was hoping a woman's company may help warm the frosted chunk of his soul Jordan ripped out when he took Christine. He had closed his eyes and imagined it was Christine writhing beneath him just to finish, but he was still completely unsatisfied, now with a sour taste in the back of his throat of regret.

He would transport her home to avoid anyone seeing her leave to avoid any issues. The whole world knew he was betrothed to Christine, and his people didn't take kindly to adultery. It also wouldn't help that they worshiped her. His favor had been fleeting until Savious had made a move against her and given him the opportunity to bring her home.

His rule came with more guidance and regulations for the people to better protect them, but it also meant the crime rates were going up since there were now more laws to break.

Heaven, contrary to popular belief, was just another world. It was filled with both good and evil, but here they had more complicated forms of both, being the average citizen was empowered. To the people, she was relatable, kind, spunky, and sweet.

The kind of person you could sit and talk to for hours and also the kind of person who would do anything to help you. The people were thrilled with him selecting her as their queen, and losing her was losing any headway he had gained in public faith.

Pierce looked in the mirror while pulling his hands back through his hair attempting to straighten it. There was a time when Jordan and himself were children together learning about Middle Earth's popular bedtime stories and literature, and came across a story about a woman thief who broke into a bear's home.

After reading it, Jordan had called him Goldilocks up until the Revolution. He could almost hear the taunt every time he looked in the mirror, and sometimes found himself missing his friend.

Shaking the thought off, he threw on some sweatpants and running shoes and debated waking Evangeline to take her home. He really didn't want her deciding to leave while he was gone. Not that he realistically expected her to wake up. He had spent hours using her body, and the sun wasn't even up yet. Still, he thought, better safe than sorry.

"Hey, wake up. I need to take you home," he gently whispered to her. She blinked big brown eyes at him in confusion until she remembered where she was and that she was well informed this was a one-time thing. He gave her space to collect her things and went to brush his teeth.

The poor girl looked pitiful as she slumped around, gathering her clothes. She wasn't the first to sleep with him in hopes that he would change his mind about Christine being the one. He tried to be as clear as possible right up front. They were a means to an end, temporary company in his lowest moments of missing her.

After finding her last sock under the bed, Evangeline looked over her shoulder to steal a secret peek at him. She was so proud to have shared his bed. She had been a fan of his since long before he took the Helm, back when Jordan was still running things.

And sure, Jordan was a beautiful man, but he was completely unreachable; he never even hinted at having serious interest in anyone. Whereas Pierce was known to be warm, fun and incredibly chivalrous with the women he took home. His only problem was he was the casual type, and after bringing Christine here, he limited his female companionship even more and made it super hush-hush.

"Are you ready?" he asked, emerging from the other side of the room. The light blue walls brought out the fierceness of the aqua in his eyes, and she could barely sigh out a yes after noticing how eager he seemed to get rid of her.

He grabbed her upper arm, and within a blink, she was standing in front of her apartment building. The green lawn on either side of the door looked a little too perky, contrasting with her sour mood. Pierce noticed this might turn into a pleading fit for another night together and let out an apologetic sigh in response to her turning pouty eyes up at him.

"Evangeline. Last night was fun. But it would be wrong for me to let you think this could ever be more than it is. You know the story. I'm fully devoted to another, and before she was able to make the same commitment I did, she was stolen from me. I am only lonely for now. I'll be retrieving my true partner soon, at which point she will be the only woman I'll have any interest in." His tone came out a bit more condescending than normal, and he inwardly scolded himself for it. She squinted back at him, her lips pinching at the rejection.

"Last time she was here you kept company. Why should this time be any different?" she sneered at him. Jaw clicking, he tried to temper his patience.

"Where did you hear that?" The question was more of a demand, but he asked it calmly.

"Girls talk. The people from here think Christine is fine. But seriously, what kind of prude could push YOU away? Like, she isn't worth your begging; she should be grateful you wanted her." Evangeline felt like she was in control of this conversation and had gained confidence, grabbing her keys and making her way to the front door.

"I don't think you quite understand. I mean, specifically, where did you hear that? I'm not asking as your *company* last night, Evangeline. I'm demanding an answer as your Ruler." A hint of threat lingered behind his words, and her spine stiffened slightly. Her confidence seemed to leach out of her body as fear rose.

"It's an online chat group. It's called Christine's shadows. I can send you the link?" The words spilled out of her. She didn't know why she was being so complacent; it wasn't like her to back down like this.

"No, send it to Victor. You should be able to find his information. I don't have an online presence, intentionally," he said. Her shoulders were pinched together as if she were mid-flinch, and he noticed he may have gone a little far in the amount of fear he was forcing on her. If he didn't act more carefully, someone would figure out he was an Empath. Taking a deep breath, he released her from his emotional hold.

"One last thing, if I catch wind of Christine's name leaving your lips dripping with anything but praise again, I will be back, and it will not be a pleasant visit. Are we clear?" No manipulation was needed this time around. She nodded eagerly, and with one last threatening glance, he left her there.

Standing on her stoop, practically shivering and sweating at the same time.

Pierce had only transported to the other side of her building, needing to be out of sight of her, and took a few deep breaths to calm himself down. Hearing anyone bad mouth Christine brought out an anger in him he had a hard time controlling. Evangeline's building was in the center of town and was a good fifteen miles from the Palace grounds where he normally did his running. He figured running back amongst some new scenery would help clear his mind before proceeding with the work that needed to be done that day.

Work that he was dreading more and more every day. Life had become monotonous. Dense vibrations rippled underfoot, pad by pad as he ran, dreading the oncoming monotony of the day ahead of him. He had gotten very good at adapting to various new abilities, and training them had become more natural. Taking on new abilities reminded him of stretching; his range grew easily as long as he consistently stretched the right muscles. But it also meant he was in a constant state of discomfort trying to expand his previous reach.

It irritated him to think about the necessity of his struggle. The whole purpose of dethroning Jordan was to give the people the right to govern themselves, to live and fail on their own terms, and yet, they seemed to have no interest in solving their own problems.

Mist dusted his face, astray from a plant's irrigation system, along with various greenery hanging from buildings around him. Stride by stride, he passed his reflection in the city glass as he approached the royal estate. It was a large castle-like structure nestled on a hill that was surrounded by the gleaming city. The walls surrounding the Main building were made from the same mix of chunky red and gray mixed stones.

The structure Gates opened wide upon his approach. Victor stood, arms crossed, at the main door. "Do we really need to have this talk? I am meant to be your advisor, not your babysitter." Pierce rolled his eyes as he slowed to a jog and then a full stop. Victor had stood directly in his path, chest raised, clearly looking to pick a fight.

"You're more agitated than normal. What's really wrong?" Pierce probed. It didn't take an Empath to know Victor was upset about more than Pierce having a one-night stand.

"I need reassurance."

"Get to the point," Pierce snapped. Gardeners working on the surrounding landscaping glanced their way.

Leafy brush under fingertips seemed to also turn in observation of the rare sight. Pierce didn't lose his cool often; seeing it added to the building intensity felt by the onlookers knowing something was coming. "Not here." Pierce led Victor away from the gate and towards his floor in the upper wing of the main house.

Pierce felt as if all eyes were hanging on him longer than normal in quiet judgment as he led the way through the estate. The cotton shirt felt like burlap stretching against his back under Victor's agitated glare.

These were the moments being an Empath felt like more of a curse rather than a blessing. To feel the tension spread off him and onto his people as he made his way through the halls added to his feeling of unease.

He was supposed to calm his people, help them feel secure, not spread his agitation onto them, but in moments like this it was hard to contain, and leapt from him, latching onto anyone who happened to cross his path.

Slowing his breathing, he focused on the white and gray lines smeared along the marble floors, light from the endless windows casting illumination through the building. Generally, it made for a beautiful lit space that felt open, bright and airy. Today, however, the light felt aggressive in nature, attacking his senses, and heightening his irritation.

It wasn't until reaching to turn the doorknob to his Suite

that Pierce realized his fists had been clenched. Any sort of relaxation he had gotten from the long morning run was completely gone. There was a level of comfort Pierce felt with Victor that he no longer had with anyone else.

He hesitated once he reached his suite, deciding to send Victor ahead of him. This would give him time to take a shower and change, with the added benefit of Victor having time to simmer down.

"Are you planning on assisting me shower, or did you want to meet me in my office?" Pierce glanced back at Victor with a sarcastic smirk.

"If you heard what I had to say, you would agree it cannot wait. I will not be berated later because you wanted a shower." Concerned by his urgency Pierce paused. This was a different type of urgency. There was something personal in the eagerness of Victor's voice.

"Okay, come on in."

Pierce had no more than shut the door behind them when Victor demanded, "How long have you been working with Savious?"

Pierce looked away from him. "What leads you to that assumption?" he asked.

Victor responded by smacking him upside the back of the head, to which Pierce only laughed. "Sit down and stop seething. Let me take a shower. I'll be right out.

***

Christine and Jordan had both completed the small amount of needed unpacking. Their earlier heavy talk hung heavily in the room, thickening the air with unspoken words. He was trying not to overstep the progress he had made with her. While she was trying to push that progress aside.

"Are you planning to tell me why we are here? I would think being in Middle Earth would be a logistical nightmare for you," Christine asked, breaking through the tension.

She was sitting in long, fuzzy socks and a large sweater against a ceiling-to-floor length window.

Looking up from his desk at the other side of the room, a smile pulled one side of his mouth up at the sight of her, glowing skin already recovering from the time in Hell, this world's abundance of energy feeding her without her even knowing it.

"I already told you why we are here, but I would be lying if I said I am looking forward to it. I have this suspicion you are not going to be as cordial with me after making good on my earlier promise." His heart contracted watching her glow lessen, real fear in her eyes.

"That's why we have been here a day and haven't gone anywhere? Because you really are going to murder someone in cold blood just to prove a point? Are you fucking kidding me?"

The email he had been working on to send out to the current executor of his Earthly estate would have to wait; he decided as Christine marched toward him, the green in her eyes ablaze, already fighting to save some random mortal she didn't even know.

"Christine, this isn't something that is up for debate. It is important you know my threats are not idle. In the coming days, I need you to trust me when I tell you to stay put," Jordan said in a straight tone, closing his laptop.

Her head tilted in a way he had come to recognize meant he had said something she found utterly ridiculous. Her mouth opened, stilled, and suddenly, the blaze in her eyes lessened. With a deep breath, she took a step forward.

"I'm not sure if you've noticed, so I will explain things to you very clearly." His brows raised at her diminutive tone.

"I am a fighter, Jordan. You present me with a challenge, and I am going to try and beat it. When someone backs you into a corner, do you kneel in surrender, or do you start looking around for a calculated way out, even if that means you start swinging?" She crossed her arms, her eyes prodding him, demanding an answer. He knew the point she was making and that it was a good one, but it infuriated him.

"It does not matter how I would respond to things. I am a High God. No one in their right mind is going to corner me because they wouldn't live to tell about it. You are not me."

She unfurled her arms and let out a sound of exasperation. "You aren't hearing me."

"I am hearing you fine. You just don't like that I'm not backing down. Your actions have consequences." He stood up; irritation apparent. She noticed this and let him stew for a second before responding in a collected tone.

"Actions do have consequences; for me and you. You kill an innocent man to strong-arm me into fearing you, to force me to submit to your 'authority,' and I will never be able to be your equal. You say I'm your destined match, that you are doing this to get me to trust you. But rest assured, you murder someone in cold blood, and all that will do is prove to me that your arrogance and pride are more important to you than I am. You do this, and it will mean losing me."

It surprised her how much just saying those words hurt her, but she knew they were true, and based on the tightness of his clenched jaw and the dark clouds in his eyes, he knew it too.

"I'll be back later. Stay here," Jordan demanded cleanly, not meeting her eyes and leaving through the door, locking it behind him.

"Seriously?!" she yelled in the empty room. "GAAAH," she screamed, storming to the closet and pulling on pants and sneakers.

Disappearing had been her specialty on Earth, and maybe she could do it well enough that none of them could find her. The threat of the curse didn't scare her like it used to. Jordan may be controlling, and though she could see him killing someone else to control her, she was willing to stake her life on the fact that he wouldn't do anything that could result in ending hers.

The lock to the door broke easily when she twisted it, popping her head out first to check it out, to her surprise no one was there. Closing the door behind her, she entered the elevator, pulse racing, and hit the lobby button.

Walking alone through the streets of New York at night used to be something she feared. Luckily, since training with Jordan, she had discovered she was much stronger than she thought, and if anyone tried to mess with her it would end poorly for them. In all honesty, she was hoping someone would try something so she could blow off some steam.

The air was dry and dusty. The recent lack of rain made the streets and the bricks of the building look dirtier than normal. Hood up over her face, hands in her pockets, fidgeting with the cash she took out of the cabinet of Jordan's closet, she hadn't noticed where she had been walking; until she looked up and saw a sad, condemned building with a gaping hole in the side of it.

She hadn't been here in years. But it was in this apartment, her sanctuary, that her life was turned upside down. Thoughts raced through her mind, bouncing off each other and splitting into new ones.

'Was anyone hurt in the explosion? Is my stuff still up there? What happened to the other people that used to live here?'

A bit of guilt nestled in her stomach thinking about the number of lives uprooted because of her living here, people who couldn't afford to just relocate, having their homes blown up.

The door had been boarded over, and a condemned sign hung up on it, along with a picture of the new building coming. A company named Novis Initiis construction had purchased the building and land and was starting construction on a new project soon. She thought it was weird anyone would bother buying land or real estate in this area but shrugged it off and crawled through one of the broken windows.

Landing with an ungraceful thud into someone's obviously deserted apartment, she quickly made her way to the hall, feeling like she was violating someone else's memory, another displaced soul's past. After climbing up three flights of unlit, littered stairs, she stood outside apartment 3A, torn between entering or not.

'What am I really expecting to find?' she scolded herself, pushing the door open cautiously.

Everything was as she left it, just weathered by the years and the hole in the wall. A small, sad laugh escaped her at the pot in front of the stove, a few stray kernels still visible. Her hand pulled along the back of the first piece of furniture she ever purchased herself as she walked past it.

Amy had been so annoyed that she bought a couch that couldn't be delivered as they struggled to get it up the stairs with just the two of them and a dolly. A shiver of fear made its way up her spine as it dawned on her that this was probably the least safe place in the whole world for her to be, and she picked up her pace, rushing to the closet where she had left the mementos of her parents.

It was unsurprising that the textbooks were gone, but her breath caught in her throat as she saw the box sitting on the floor where she left it. Waterlogged and gray.

Slowly approaching it, as if time could heal the damage it had caused, she looked into it, and confusion replaced her sorrow as she saw it was completely empty. She didn't know how long she had stared at the box when she suddenly heard a floorboard creak behind her.

Without thinking, she clapped her hands together and pulled them apart, quickly generating heat the way Thad had shown her. Jordan stood behind her goodwill couch, looking at her regretfully.

"This was where your human life ended, wasn't it?" he

asked, looking around curiously as if the ceiling tiles may hold the answer to the riddle that was Christine.

"Yes. I should have known you'd follow me." Her fight was gone for the night, and in truth, she was grateful he was there to see for himself proof that she had a life before them.

"I went to calm down when I sensed you left. I figured I would give you space, but after you came in here, I figured it was well... I mean, it isn't glamorous, but I can understand why you mourn it, Christine. It isn't the place; it's what this place represents. Your independence, your claiming your life as your own, and your connection to me ruined that. For that, I am sorry." There was a warm sincerity in his voice, and it dawned on her that if anyone could relate to homesickness, it was Jordan.

"What was in the box?" he asked, looking from her to the wilted cardboard in front of her.

"The only things here that really mattered. It was everything I had left of my parents. It's all gone, though; I expected as much," she said, fighting tears and forcing a smile.

"I just had to be sure and to get out of your condo and away from you, which obviously failed."

"How many times do I have to tell you? There is no getting away from me," he said with a light humor in his tone. It wasn't fear in her eyes at this, but something disconnected that worried him more. He was losing her, and in turn, she was losing herself. He let a frustrated sigh escape.

"Look, I am just as new to this as you. I tried taking the easy and sure route by threatening you into submission because the stakes we are playing with are very real. I cannot live in a world where you don't exist if anything happens to you...." He leaned against the doorway, shoulders slumping.

"So, show me I can trust you instead of making me fear you," Christine said simply. One of his rare full-flash smiles hit her, prompting her to walk over to him and let him fold her into his arms.

"I'll do my best," he whispered into her hair, still looking around the room at the squalor she used to live in, for the first time realizing how important her independence was to her.

She rested in his embrace for quite some time, grieving her life in a way she hadn't realized she needed. Letting the emotions wash over her, breathing them in and letting their sting free from her soul with each exhale.

He stood with his body wrapped around hers, holding her up as she cried, finally accepting there was no getting her old life back. Even if he wanted to fix this, he couldn't. She had been gone for too long, her world had moved on without her, and she needed to accept it to be able to finally start to heal and move on. As she shuddered against him in a final sob, he gave her one last reassuring squeeze before briefly pulling back to lift her face up to him.

"Is there anything you would like to take with you, or have me move to storage?" he asked.

"No, anything worth anything to me here is gone. Let's go," she answered, grabbing his hand and pulling him towards the door.

Once they were down the street a bit, he noticed they weren't headed toward his condo and slowed them both. "Where are we going?" he asked.

"There is someone I need to see," she answered honestly, avoiding his inquiring gaze.

"Someone from your previous life?" Her eyes squinted in response, a confrontation brewing within her.

'Oh, here it comes,' he thought, knowing that look all too well.

"Previous? I am still alive. I didn't die for real. Pierce abducted me, then you abducted me, and now I'm here, and I left things messy, to say the least." Guilt hung over her at the amount of debt that must have fallen in Evans' lap when she disappeared because of her poor business practices fueled by her bleeding heart.

"I hate to break it to you, but I'm not about to let you put yourself at risk by engaging with someone from your life here. Not. Happening." He had brought them to a dead halt. They were no longer off the side streets, and the tension between them was thick enough that passersby were beginning to stop and notice.

"Aren't you all-powerful?" her question threw him off. It wasn't at all what he was expecting to come out of her mouth.

"What?"

"You heard me. Aren't you 'all-powerful'? The great High God, Mr. Untouchable? Am I not babysat at ALL times because I'm the only thing that could hurt you?" Jordan crossed his arms and wondered what trap she was walking him into.

"Yes, and?"

"WELL, if you're so powerful, I'm just not seeing how taking you to meet my previous business partner, who is human, is putting me at risk. You will be right there with me. So, explain." She nodded at him triumphantly, prompting him to think of a reason.

"Drawing attention to your presence here is dangerous. Word getting out that a woman who mysteriously disappeared years ago after an explosion has suddenly reappeared would most certainly draw attention." The retort was weak, and he knew it, but it was all he had.

"Evan will be at the gym alone this time of night if he even still owns it. I left him in debt, and he has spent his life teaching people how to defend themselves. If I tell him it's important that he doesn't mention me to anyone, he won't."

It wasn't Evan that concerned him. Evan, he had already checked out, and he knew she was right. The man would die before giving up anyone he protected, and he was one of the few out there, maybe the only one, who believed Christine was still alive.

"I'm going on record as saying this is a bad idea, but I can't argue your logic." She went to walk past him triumphantly, his fingers wrapped around her wrist before she could do so, though, and he roughly pulled her back to him and kissed her. His words had been playful, but his kiss was heavy with worry.

They had walked the city streets in silence, usually Christine would protest to his arm being draped around her possessively, but not tonight. She was frustrated with him still, but also confident in her assessment that his current mood was a direct result of her being in some kind of real danger. Being here made her an easier target, and whether or not she believed anyone would use her as one or not, Jordan seemed confident they would.

If their roles had been reversed and she was holding his safety in her hands, she had to wonder if she would be confident walking around so brazenly, just to make him happy. The thought led to her subconsciously melting into him a little; a small smile warmed his previously scrunched face in response.

Jordan scanned the empty streets as they walked through them, making mental notes. In ten blocks, they had seen five homeless men, seven empty beer cans collecting towards the drainage holes after the earlier rain, and several other pedestrians had passed.

Mortals tended to take notice of him when he was here, and he was trying to gauge if Christine was drawing the same attention. A picture posted to the internet in any context could flag enough attention to alert Pierce to her presence, and he couldn't afford that.

Earlier that day, he had visited the Fates to lay down some ground rules before bringing Christine to meet them. The last thing he needed was them ruining the work he had done in letting her craft her own opinions about things, about him, and he knew they would try to talk him up to her if given the chance.

They were loyal and kind, but she knew that, and it would come across as a manipulation. Good friends that they were, they sensed his concern and started looking a bit more deeply into Christine's background based on his hunch. What he learned may have proven him right, but it also cemented a deep, settled panic in him at the threat Pierce would be if he were to get ahold of her again.

Lost in thought, she hadn't registered they had stopped moving. Daily, for years, she had walked to this spot before running across the road to the welcoming building in which she had built her life. It was small in contrast to the condos surrounding it. Light still beamed from the large windows in front, the ones that never had their shades open.

The first suggestion she had given Evan while they had set everything up after buying the building. Privacy was important to people who felt vulnerable, and most people working out or learning how to defend themselves felt just that, as she knew from firsthand experience. Nothing was more terrifying to most of the women she trained than the threat of being discovered, even if by happenstance. So, the shades remained closed, as they were now.

Jordan watched in amusement as Christine gulped nervously. He remembered when they had first met and the fierceness with which she confronted him. A fight didn't scare her as much as the emotion of this reunion, and yet, she had insisted upon it. Rolling his eyes at her, he pushed the door open and dragged her in behind him.

Christine noticed the snapped-off lock fall from the bolt as Jordan dragged her into the room and made a mental note; they would need to fix that. She wondered if he had even noticed he'd just busted through the deadlock. The small, one-room fitness studio was mostly the same as she had remembered it.

The solid red floor was now covered in the mats Evan had always wanted to buy, but Christine had protested.

'When getting thrown around in real life, they won't have a mat to dig their heels and toes into or to break their fall.' Had been her argument, that, and the fact that it would cost money to fill the place with mats.

Evan had caved, as he did on most things, knowing her

well enough to not waste his breath arguing. His big concern had been liability insurance, a requirement for renting out the building. There were also larger mirrors hung along the entire wall, floor-to-ceiling, new ones. The ones here when she left had started to show their age, with black creeping in around their corners.

Looking in the mirrors now, she could see why so many people stopped to stare at Jordan as they had walked down the street; he looked absolutely menacing. His eyes were dark, and his expression was one of tight, festering rage, his lips in a tight line. While he basically held her to him.

She looked small and frightened, and just like the kidnap victim she technically was. The door opened behind them, and all she could see, squinting at the figure in the mirror, was a tire iron coming down fast toward Jordan's skull.

With swift ease Jordan turned while pulling Christine closer and lifting her while he spun, catching the tire iron in midair. The mortal wielding it didn't release it but tried frantically to pull it back from him. Jordan looked to Christine for some guidance, and recognition of the man sparked across her face. He reluctantly allowed her to step out of his embrace. It was Evan.

"Evan, he's with me." Her cool, calming voice struck him hard.

It had been years since he had heard her voice, and he had accepted the fact he never would again. And yet, here she was, with the most intimidating man he'd ever seen. Evan wasn't sure what it was about the guy he feared; his appearance wasn't overly rugged, he wasn't even the biggest guy he'd ever gone up against, but he could feel the threat coming off him in waves.

Evan released the tire iron and eyed Jordan skeptically before turning to Christine and lifting her up in a bear hug. Jordan tensed, watching another man wrap his arms around her, but he tried to behave himself for Christine's sake.

Once her feet were back on the ground, Jordan stepped to her side again, wrapping a protective arm around her. At this, she elbowed him and stepped toward Evan and away from him. Jordan narrowly resisted the urge to reach out and pull her back to him.

"Where the Hell have you been? What happened to you? Are you back?" The questions were coming out of Evan in his thick Latino accent faster than Christine could answer. Evan registered the shift in the brooding man's stance as he pulled Christine into another hug. Once back on the ground again, she summoned what she could as an answer.

"Remember the guy everyone told me not to worry about?" she asked Evan rhetorically. They had many late-night deep conversations about it over wine and dinner, sitting on this very floor.

"No way, he had to have been ancient," Evan said, confused.

"Very ancient, yes. Anyway, turns out his son is an even bigger problem. But after some time away, I've managed my way back, and I think I'll be okay."

Jordan snorted at her little jab. Evan noticed the intentional holes in her explanation and didn't push, but he did stare at her softly, taking her in as if she may disappear. She felt the heat in her mark flare a little and realized she had never introduced Jordan. Moving slightly to the side, she gestured in Jordan's direction.

"Evan, this is Jordan. He's my.... Well..." She wasn't sure what to call him, and at this Jordan cracked a grin and extended a hand to him.

"I'm the reason she's able to be here today, safely, that is." Seeing what Jordan thought might be hope rising in Evans' eyes, he hoped Christine would allude to their personal relationship and crush that hope before it grew too strong. But that would need to be her choice.

"So, you're what? Bodyguard, witness protection...?" Evan

prodded. Christine stepped into Jordan then, wrapping her arm around him.

"He saved me, and we fell for each other. You're the first person I've seen, so we haven't really had to label it yet. But I guess he's my... boyfriend." Jordan flinched at the word boyfriend, and Christine shrugged.

"We have a lot to catch up on, and it's late. I just got to the city today and needed to see you. Will you be around tomorrow?" Jordan felt only slightly guilty for enjoying watching the spark of hope in Evans' eyes fizzle and die at her claiming him, but had to admit, the term boyfriend sounded juvenile, and he would need to correct that.

"Doubt I'll sleep now, but yeah. I'll be around all tomorrow. Ey, the remnants of your students have a class with me tomorrow, the last one of the day is at 7pm. Bring the boyfriend, and maybe we can show him a few moves." Jordan didn't react at all to the joke, earning him another elbow to the side.

"I'll see you then. Oh, and please don't tell anyone you saw me. I'm not out of the woods yet." Evan nodded in response as Jordan practically dragged her out the door.

Halfway down the street, she pulled free. "Slow down. My God, what is your problem?" He grabbed her arm again and continued to hasten down the street.

"Something is wrong, and I don't know what. But we need to get back right now, and to do that, we need to be out of lover-boys' eyesight." She rolled her eyes but matched his brisk pace until they turned the corner, and he abruptly pushed her against the wall. Arms on each side of her, blocking her from an outsider's view.

The cool brick pressed into her back, and he dipped his head to kiss her, nose brushing his up hers before their lips met. When he pulled away, it was only a few centimeters, and he spoke on her lips.

"I love you, Christine." Her eyes went wide at the unexpected declaration, earning a smile from him.

"Don't say anything right now. I think, after tomorrow, you'll have a better idea about how you feel. Wait. Until you're sure. Words are powerful things. I just needed to say it because something is about to happen, and you needed to hear me say the words before whatever that is. And honestly, I needed to say them too." Pulling her into an embrace, he transported them to his New York loft.

His forehead was pressed against hers as they arrived at the same moment chuckling echoed throughout the loft. Jordan's eyes rolled in response. "What are you doing here?" Jordan groaned, annoyed and ready to call it a night. Kielius and Thad were sitting on the large black sofa, snickering. Kielius answered.

"We are here to clean up your mess. Where is the body?" Jordan shot him a suspicious glance.

"I thought I made it clear you were not to set foot in this world for another fifty years?" Jordan said, pointing to a cross-armed Thad. "And since when do you volunteer for anything?" he added, redirecting his pointed glare to Kielius. Christine retreated to the bedroom.

"So, where's the body?" Kielius reiterated the question playfully.

"What body?" Jordan asked aloud while also signing.

"The mortal you were gonna kill if Christine didn't obey your orders." He clarified. Instantly Jordan regretted telling Thad about that.

"There is no body. Now get out and go home." Jordan dismissed, sitting at his desk and opening his laptop. Kielius's mouth dropped in shock, and Thad's smile grew wide.

"Pay up." Thad motioned to Kielius. From his pocket, Kielius produced a folded piece of paper and heartily slapped it into Thad's hand.

"I can't believe it." Kielius shook his head in bewilderment. The shadows misting Jordan's eyes reflected his thin patience. He and Christine needed some time alone. Today had been emotional for her, and he didn't want Kielius's presence add-ing weight to the slump of her shoulders.

"Is something amusing?" Christine asked Thad. He had been snickering and leaning against the wall when she re-en-tered the room in her light gray pajamas and hair up in a very loose messy bun.

She could feel Thad's disapproval of her as his amused and relaxed posture faded. His spine straightening and arms crossing.

"She asked you a question," Jordan reminded him, briefly shooting him a 'you-better-fucking-respect-her-with-an-an-swer' glance. Thad rolled his eyes.

"I bet Kielius that Jordan wouldn't risk your wrath by kill-ing a random mortal, and he underestimated your sway over him," Thad explained with a smile in his voice.

"You, of all people... That is too good." Kielius laughed, his shock breaking. Now it was Jordan's turn to roll his eyes as his brothers laughed. Christine regretted asking.

Jordan shook his head at them with slight amusement; he couldn't fault the humor they found in the situation. There was no way in Heaven or Hell he would have backed down in the past from going through with a threat. Truth was, he didn't mind the sway Christine had over him, so their taunts didn't bother him.

Until he looked up and saw Christine curled up on the couch with her headphones on now. He cringed, seeing her rub her cheek against her shoulder when looking at Kielius. Following her gaze, he saw the hungry look in his brother's eyes. He stood, closing the laptop.

"You got me. You're right; I didn't end up killing a mortal as previously threatened. Christine and I agreed that since she tossed Kielius through a wall and knocked him out cold, she proved she was capable of taking care of herself. Therefore, she doesn't need to be threatened into submission," Jordan ex-plained curtly. Both Christine and Thad grinned, and Kielius's smile dropped flat. "So, what did you win?" he asked Thad.

Thad approached him and handed him a folded-up piece of paper. Unfurling it, Jordan read it, shooting Thad a denunciatory look.

"Kielius, what have I told you about betting things that aren't yours to lose," he admonished, maintaining disapproving eye contact with Thad, who just smiled innocently back at him. Kielius flinched at Jordan's tone.

"Well...." Kielius stuttered, "I just had such faith in your unwavering masculinity I never thought you would bend to the will of your bed warmer." Thad didn't hold the highest regard for his brother Kielius, but he had to admit that was undoubtedly the ballsiest sentence he had ever heard.

Looking back and forth between them in astonishment and excitement, Thad waited for Jordan to pummel Kielius. Unfortunately for Thad, Jordan hadn't stopped staring directly at him. Ignoring their brash little brother.

"Kielius, Christine may be immune to my threats, but you are not. Disrespect her again, and I will rip the tongue from your mouth here on Earth, where you will heal at the same pace as a mortal," Jordan said in a dark warning.

From the couch he could hear Christine whisper under her breath. "That would be an improvement." This quirked his lips, and the reaction sent a bit of fear through Thad, who hadn't heard her.

Kielius heard it, though. He shot Christine a threatening glare but bit his tongue. Wisely deciding he had pushed enough limits today.

"You're dismissed," Jordan declared. Kielius glanced around the room and, much like a toddler being sent to bed early, stomped out.

Thad went to follow, grinning again when Jordan stopped him.

"I expect more from you. Putting you in charge of Atlantis would be a waste; it damn near takes care of itself. I need you where the work is. Kielius can't handle Kronos, and you know it. I need you there to finish setting up infrastructure so that when I have reclaimed my throne, it will be ready to receive Heaven's vendors and volunteers." Thad barely blinked.

"You have no faith in me, do you? We didn't trade. The bet was he would relinquish any command of Atlantis he has to me if I am right, giving me control of not only the ghetto of Hell but also a functioning city as a reprieve, and if he was right, I let him take over one of my training sessions with Christine without telling you." Darkness flared in Jordan's eyes. Christine stiffened on the couch, and Thad shrugged nonchalantly.

"Calm down. She can hold own against the little worm. Besides, I have been in love. So, I was certain there was no chance you would risk her hating you forever." Thad shot him a knowing smile and patted Jordan's shoulder. "I'm not technically supposed to be here anyway, so I'll make sure our little toad makes his way home." With a wink he exited the room.

Christine removed the headphones she hadn't even turned on and looked to Jordan for some kind of explanation. Trying to shrug it off, he raised his shoulders. "Brothers, what can I say?" Her brows scrunched together in disapproval.

"No, not gonna let me off the hook on that one?" Her scrunched brows raised slightly, still waiting. Letting out a sigh and running his hand through his hair, he relented. "Fine." He said, sitting next to her on the couch he took her hands.

"Questions?"

"So many. Maybe start at the top?" she suggested.

"Be gentle with me; it's been a long day. I need specific questions," he said with a smile in his voice.

"You're just trying to gauge what I picked up on to avoid disclosing more than necessary, aren't you?"

"Busted." He chuckled, rubbing her hands in his after noticing they were a bit chilled.

"To clarify the best I can... My brothers don't have much in the way of entertainment and often make bets on how I will approach a situation." He paused, mulling his words over. "It's usually related to how I will manage my father, but now, you are the more interesting topic." After a quick scoff, he squeezed her upper arms again before continuing his explanation.

"Kielius gave up his title and responsibilities. I'll need to find something to keep him busy. Thad will be able to unite the two cities of Hell as he has been wanting to, by now overseeing them both." She nodded in understanding. "Had Thad lost, you would not have been subjected to any contact with Kielius. I would have known as soon as you arrived for training and saw him because your scare would have alerted me to you being in danger, not that you can't handle him, but you shouldn't have to. Did I miss anything?" They were sitting closer now, and she was pleased he was openly filling her in.

"At some point, I would love a bit more of a breakdown as to what 'infrastructure' you are referring to and what taking Heaven back has to do with it," Jordan tensed slightly.

"But, right now, I'm honestly more curious about Thad. He was in love? He just seems so frigid... I struggle to imagine him being with anyone." Looking up into Jordan's face she could see a remorse she hadn't expected. He sighed and looked her in the eyes, holding her there, appreciating the moment.

"I have been waiting for him to get over the past for a long time, but now, after being with you, I know it will never happen." He kissed both her cheekbones, the tip of her nose, and her forehead before continuing.

"Thad used to be different. He was married to a mortal man named Alyk. Other mortals took Alyk's life, in no small part, because of their marriage. It isn't my business to tell you this, as Thad is not fully healed. Someday, ask him about it."

Christine's eyes shimmered with tears. "I can't imagine. At least now I understand his problem with me."

"What do you mean?" Jordan asked, unaware she had sensed Thad's distaste for her.

"He is afraid I will inevitably be the cause of you experiencing the same pain he went through because we are going into a war, and he thinks I will end up a casualty." Jordan couldn't meet her eyes.

"I'll have to whine less now when training with him," she said curtly. Catching his half smirk and warming where his hands had been running up and down her legs where he had pulled them across his lap, she decided they needed to end the day happy and not so morose. There would be time for more questions later, and some she could research to find the answers to.

She pulled herself off the couch and grabbed both of Jordan's hands, proceeding to lead him to the bedroom. "It's been a very emotional day. I don't know about you, but I'm done talking and can think of much more pleasant ways to wind down for bed." His devious half grin responded in approval while tipping her onto her back and climbing atop her.

The day's stresses poured out of them as they gave themselves to each other. Slowly, each touch resolute and deliberate as they savored this feeling of closeness, both finding comfort in the ease of existing in each other's arms like this.

TO BE OR NOT TO BE

Pierce looked out around the garden grounds, scanning them for his love. He knew she liked to roam the castle grounds helping the gardeners in any way she could. She had told him once it would do him some good to "get some dirt under his fingernails every once in a while."

The thought made him smile. Truth be told, he enjoyed having to fight for her, to win her affections. He enjoyed the chase and didn't have much practice at it, even if she shouldn't be able to resist their fated connection. He smashed that thought down quickly.

"Pierce, you're running late again." Victor's voice broke through Pierce's daydream, his black leather shoes tapping impatiently on the white marble floors.

"I'm sorry, I got distracted. Let's go," Pierce said wistfully.

"You are incorrigible; you know that, right?" Victor joked in a playful tone.

"Come now, transport us over there." They had a long council meeting regarding the allocation of resources during some of the harsher seasons coming up, and Pierce did his duty nodding and occasionally throwing in a few suggestions on which territory should partner with another to help pick up the slack.

Mostly, he was distracted by Christine trying and failing to fly under the radar sitting in the grass, pretending to fuss with a lilac bush so she could listen in on the meeting. He smiled when she tugged too hard on a branch while zoning out and cut herself. He could tell by the form of her lips that Victor wouldn't approve of the word she had mumbled to herself angrily.

"Excuse me," Pierce cut into Hinto and Astor's collaboration.

"My attention is needed elsewhere." Hinto glanced at Christine, still sucking her finger from the cut and forced a smile. Astor just looked confused; usually Pierce was more engaged in these meetings than he had been of late.

"Go on; we are almost finished anyway," Hinto said, shooting her an appreciative look and trotted over to Christine, feeling the eyes of the council on his back as he walked away.

Christine looked up at him sheepishly as he approached her with a gleaming smile. "I didn't mean to pull you away; I just wanted to listen. The different territories fascinate me," she gibbered out apologetically. He dropped to a crouch and gently took her hand, inspecting the small cut on her finger.

Her comfort had grown over the past few months. After that first meal together, she had put effort into not flinching away from him. Upon touching her, he adjusted her hormones slightly, calming her, trying to help her feel safe and content with him, with his general closeness. He would prefer not to need to interfere, and he hoped, over time, these small adjustments wouldn't be needed.

"How about you join me at the next meeting?" Surprise widened her eyes at the offer.

"Really?"

"Why are you so surprised?"

"Maybe because you constantly restrict the information

I'm allowed access to...." she retorted bitterly. His brows arched, and his eyes hardened. This argument was one he had told her not to bring up again, they had discussed it at length, and it poisoned both their moods. A regretful look swept across her face, hiding the defiant rage she was building regarding the subject. "I'm sorry, I know I tend to dwell... I would adore attending the next meeting. It means a lot to me that you would be willing to allow me to sit in."

His features softened again, and he exhaled a breath he hadn't realized he had been holding. He didn't want to ruin her mood by enforcing his education plan with her again, but he wouldn't relent either.

"How did you find the subject today?" he asked, holding out a hand and helping her to a standing position. Each day she spent three hours with various scholars learning about Pierce-approved topics.

Today was one he had been fearing as it was the first day she would finally learn something about Jordan's reign. As such, he had set Amy up to deliver today's lesson, hoping she would report any strange reactions Christine may have to the lesson, as she was constantly attempting to regain the favor she lost in failing to keep Christine safe on Middle Earth.

She flushed at his question remembering the photo of Jordan, and the intense effect it had on her when she had seen him. He felt a flare of heat go through her, causing the muscles in his jaw to tick.

"Umm..." she struggled.

"It was unexpected." She shifted uncomfortably. They were hand in hand, walking through the vast gardens. Bushes and trees were alight with different white flours, all patterning from above to create Pierce's mark.

When she didn't elaborate, he prompted her.

"Unexpected?" The question was smooth and light, and he intertwined her fingers in his as they walked along, using the connection to her as an anchor to dim the fire rising in her.

Once she had cooled down a bit, she gathered enough steel to answer levelly.

"I don't know exactly. He just looked more to me like someone tasked with great burdens versus someone who enjoyed the position he was born to," she said, recalling the body language he exhibited in the photo she saw. In it, he was contemplating a request from one of the council members, standing with his arms crossed and a hand rubbing his Jaw contemplatively.

From what she could see, he looked to be in heavy debate, not at all the flippant attitude she would expect from a dictator who didn't care about the wants of those making requests.

"But," she added, seeing the displeased look on Pierce's face, "it was only one picture, and I tend to make a lot of assumptions...."

His grip loosened slightly, and she felt him relax a fraction. "You do tend to make quick assumptions. Hopefully, soon, you will rule by my side. Once that happens, you will need to be more mindful of reserving judgment until you can base them on facts," he gently chided, grinning at her gritting teeth. He didn't know why, but he drew intense amusement in watching her struggle to hold in her retorts.

"You're right. I guess," she conceded. Trying to gain points in response to her having such a strong reaction to Jordan's photo, he let the issue drop.

"How do you feel practice is going? I plan to stop in later today to observe your progress." She stiffened at his question. He knew she hated working with trainers on developing her abilities, but he had hoped she would start presenting greater ability and similar abilities to the ones he had gifted her. But she hadn't. He initially teetered between having the trainers push her to progress faster and having them slow up to prevent her from getting hurt, even if it was a challenge she had wanted.

Her martial arts on Middle Earth were nothing compared to what she was learning now, and he didn't want her getting hurt because she overestimated herself. It was his assumption that she was already maxed out on capabilities anyway since she was born simply to be his wife; all she needed was immortality to be able to exist here with him and, hopefully, one day give him a family.

"It's the same as it is every day. I feel like I can do more, but no one I have worked with will let me try anything else because they fear ramifications from you if I get hurt."

"As they should." He cut her off, pulling her to a stop and grabbing her chin, looking her in the eyes with a demanding expression as he often did when she got testy with his commands.

"You have no need for further advancement. You are not meant for fighting. Your trainers know this." Her mouth pinched unapprovingly, but she didn't bother to defend her case again. At least, not with him.

He dropped her off with Tevin, her most recent trainer and likely her last. In Pierce's opinion, she knew what was needed. Tevin disagreed but knew better than to fight with Pierce about it. When it came to Christine, he had a short and unwavering fuse.

Tevin could sense there was more within Christine than Pierce thought and wanted to explore it with her, but also didn't want to be cast out of Pierce's good graces, as much as Christine attempted to get him to break the rules. Had he not been warned off, Tevin could easily see himself developing a decent friendship with her.

She was feisty and surprisingly resilient, with a sharp tongue hidden behind her innocent features. It hadn't taken long for Tevin to decide Pierce's over-protection was warranted. To love that passionately was a gift, and he could understand Pierce not wanting that at risk.

Not to mention fated matches were notorious for being incredibly possessive of each other. Which was natural, con-

sidering they relied on that one other person for any sort of happiness.

"Salutations, dimples! Prepared for today's instructions?" Tevin called to her in his gravel-like voice as she entered the training Hall. It had high ceilings, the walls lined with ropes and various different climbing apparatuses. There were also composites of different minerals available for ability enhancement training, such as Christine's. She shot him a sardonic smile, and he let out a laugh.

"Oh, come now, you have yet to master fire touch. You are not allowed to be upset with me for not advancing your training if you have not yet earned it, can you?" he said and immediately regretted his choice of words.

She couldn't help but love listening to Tevin speak. He hadn't adapted to more current patterns of speech as most people had and still retained a more rigid countenance.

"So, IF I can conjure enough heat from fire touch to dissuade you from further contact, will you teach me an offensive skill?"

"You twist my meaning, friend...."

"That's what I heard...."

"Christine..." he groaned. She made her eyes big and stuck a bottom lip out, being comically overdramatic. Suppressing a laugh, he mulled it over.

"I concede. If you can manage fire touch, I shall teach you one small offensive skill. But it must remain between us. Are we in agreement?" he asked lightly, not really concerned because she had been working on this skill for three months with no progress.

"It's a deal," she said, a wolfish grin spreading across her normally angelic face. Worry shuddered down his spine at her confidence.

"Let's do this." Her voice was laced with challenge as she waved him towards her.

He rushed her from the front, reaching out to grab her

arm, but he was too slow. She managed to grab his wrist, her thumb pushing painfully into a soft spot at the bottom of his palm as she thrust downward. Physical defense he knew she was comfortable with from her years of teaching it on Middle Earth. She had even taught him several moves. Although a mortal would be otherwise incapacitated by her arm barring him, this wasn't combat training; it was ability enhancement with a focus on defense.

He let out a deep and slow breath, rolling his head and willing the matter around him to reflect light harshly back at her, causing mirror-like flashes to disrupt her vision, disorienting her enough to cause her to let go. Reaching for her again, he missed as she ducked and rolled behind him, kicking him hard in the back of the knees and sending him crumbling to the ground. As he fell, he thrust his hands up and into fists, the ground around her slightly absorbing one of her feet that had been newly replanted to the ground in a fighter stance.

He grabbed her wrist, pulling himself off from the ground, feeling with dismay her skin was warm, with the heat growing. Usually, she lost heat and focus by training to resort to other combat moves, but today she stilled, focusing in on her skin, and soon the touch was unbearable as the stinging heat caused him to release his hold.

"You cheated me," he complained, panting.

"You fell for it," she said, shrugging her shoulders innocently. He threw his head back in defeat as she did a little victory dance.

Prepared for the day, she would talk him into teaching her something that wasn't strictly defense; he had the move ready. It was the same type of energy manipulation as fire touch, so it should be easily adaptable.

"Well, let's get on with it before Pierce arrives and berates us both. This is called the push. Focus the energy the same way you did on your skin. Think friction and heat, but focus it in your mind with growing pressure to a single point on your palm. Let that energy build, and on my say, let the built-up energy release outward in a focused blast."

Her eyes were wide and excited, and he couldn't help but laugh at her excitement. She had started to feel like the little sister he never had. They had been training together for a year, and before this he was a teacher. Pierce pulled him from his class one day and assigned him as a tutor. Initially, Tevin hated the job. He felt like a glorified babysitter, but he had grown close to Christine and found she was much easier to be around than he expected the future High Goddess to be.

A deep thundering sound snapped him from his thoughts, a worried look on Christine's ashen face. Her eyes were darker than he had ever seen them.

"Christine, pull back; something's wrong," he guided, but she didn't hear him. Her hand was still held up, and the focused look in her eyes had gone, replaced by pain.

"Christine," he called louder.

"Let go. Release the energy. Let it dissipate."

An explosion erupted from her shaking hand, tossing him back into the roped wall and knocking a bowl of water over. He almost laughed until he noticed the blast had imploded as well as she was soaring through the air, towards climbing bars protruding from the walls. In that realization, he noticed Pierce standing in the doorway, glaring at him.

Pierce transported from the doorway to the tightening space in between Christine and the bars, the force slamming her hard enough into Pierce's solid frame to knock her flat out.

Pierce scooped her into his arms and walked slowly towards Tevin when he stopped suddenly, death in his eyes. Tevin shivered at the expression on Pierce's face as Pierce looked him up and down, then turned briskly and walked away, leaving Tevin confused and unbalanced.

***

She looked around the decaying home of her childhood. After a quick breakfast and a bit of schmoozing, Jordan had finally convinced her to visit her childhood home. He promised to stay with her and that if it overwhelmed her, they could leave. To her surprise, it wasn't.

Everything was as she had last seen it. A time capsule of the life she had lived, in peace with her parents, before her life had crumbled around her. The remnants of the destruction of that day were still present around her in the large room. She was almost impressed the house hadn't collapsed with the support beam snapped as it was.

After recovering at the hospital, she had been brought back here to get a bag of her things and one box to take with her to New York. She had packed in a frenzy and ran out of the house, not wanting to linger too long in her stolen past.

She had never known what would be done with the house, and at the time, she hadn't cared. She already had filed for emancipation with the help of Amy's parents, both Lawyers.

They had been surprisingly okay with her wanting to file for emancipation and assisting her with it. Although now she knew that Pierce had been involved in the entire process. Through some digging, Jordan discovered *Novis Initiis construction* had owned her parents' mortgage and had not done anything with the property since its vacancy.

Jordan explained to her that the same corporation that had purchased her apartment complex owned this house and the land it was on. It was one of many corporations The high throne kept on Middle Earth for emergency funds and to stay relevant in this world if any sort of intervention here was necessary.

Jordan speculated that Pierce must have purchased this land with one of their many real estate companies under a large conglomerate. What he didn't understand was why Pierce had his people retain both properties. Jordan made it clear to Christine that it was a bit strange for the home to be left here like a time capsule.

Her first real bit of anger settled in towards Pierce; he never told her he bought her childhood home or offered to let her come see if there was anything of her parents she may want.

Leaning in the bent door frame, Jordan's dark presence seemed so out of place and pulled forth the memory of what his father had looked like standing here, in her home, only moments before ending the only life she had known. Noticing her shudder, he stood a bit straighter and made his way to her, stepping around debris.

He stood behind her and wrapped his arms around her, bending slightly and placing his chin on the top of her head. He didn't ask if she was okay. He knew better.

"You know, part of me wishes I had known, that I had paid attention and looked for you like Pierce had. Maybe even that I had kept a closer eye on my father and what he had been up to. But I can't help but be glad I met you as a grown woman, the thought of discovering you as a child creeped me out." At this, she managed a small smile.

"What? Grooming isn't your thing? Would you have even been able to tell for sure?" she poked and prodded.

"I have a lot of kinks, but that definitely doesn't make the list, and no. There is a chemical reaction that occurs, and it is only possible *after* puberty." He kissed the back of her head and pulled away from her, something on the dusty counter catching his eye.

It was a lumpy orange crystal that her mom had used as a paperweight and occasionally a nutcracker. Jordan picked it up hastily, holding it to his face and examining it intensely.

"That," Christine drew out dramatically, "is called a crystal. They are found in mountains or caves all over the world," she said as if she were talking to a five-year-old. He narrowed his eyes, glanced at her, then snapped it in half.

"No. It isn't," he responded gravely.

"Where are your parents' things? Where would they store

stuff they didn't want you going through?" There was a sharp urgency to his tone.

"My parents were open books. Honestly, I was welcome to 'go through' any of their stuff. Why?" He disregarded her statement and started examining the room more closely.

He teleported all over the house, causing dust and loose papers to fly into the air, going through all the drawers and shelves. Once he landed in front of her parents' bedroom door, she'd had enough.

"Jordan!" He stilled as he reached for the handle and flinched. Looking at her and seeing the face of a girl who just watched her childhood home get ransacked, that look of utter violation sent regret down his throat.

"What are you looking for?" she demanded, even throwing in a little, unintentional foot stamp.

"I'm not sure. I'll know it when I find it. That 'crystal' is Angelican Deminite; it's created by Angelican children when they are practicing mineral creation," he said and pushed the door open, keeping his eyes connected with her. "Let me check one more place, please." She crossed her arms in annoyance as he made his way into her parents' bedroom, not waiting for the permission he had asked for.

The room was small and just off the kitchen. Her parents shared a queen-sized bed, and the hand-knitted quilt she remembered watching her mom stitch still lay across it, the dust so thick atop it the pattern was indistinguishable.

There were two windows on the far wall and a large dresser on the opposite. They didn't have their own bathroom; they shared the house's one bathroom with Christine on the other side of the kitchen, connected to her small room. Only hesitating slightly, Jordan pushed the bed all the way to one side of the room.

Beneath it was a small door Christine hadn't noticed before, with a small round handle, it looked like it could belong to an old-timey saloon door.

"Christine, come here really quick." Curiosity had completely replaced her annoyance as she joined him, kneeling next to the small door.

"Here," he said, gently grabbing her hand.

"If I've assumed correctly, this will only open for you." He guided her hand, his fingers atop hers as they curled around the smooth handle and pulled. She thought it was strange that the medal didn't feel cold as she would have expected, but it seemed to thrum with warmth at her touch.

The door swung open easily, sending another wave of dust through the air. Jordan's jaw dropped as he lifted a strange-looking medallion. The symbol on it looked like a wave, peaking just before breaking into a whitecap.

Looking slightly panicked, he tossed it aside and started pulling files from the small, square hole the door had been protecting. Christine assumed it must have been some sort of safe or storage.

What she didn't understand was why Jordan was reacting this way. Most people had a safe. Her dad had even shown her that medal once, he told her he had won it in his youth at a surfing competition; water had always been where he was most at peace.

The color drained from his face as he opened one of the files. Inside was a relocation rejection letter, and at the bottom was unmistakably, Jordan's signature and corresponding stamp. With a sharp intake of breath, he slammed the folder shut, grabbed the box of hidden papers with the medal, and disappeared for a split second, only to reappear in the same place empty-handed. Before she could process what was happening, he had hoisted her up by her arm and transported her back to their loft.

She looked at him expectantly as he walked away from her, throwing his jacket off and pacing around the room. His hand ruffled his usually neat hair, his eyebrows were furrowed in confusion, and he was mumbling to himself in a language she didn't recognize.

"You practically dragged me through my childhood trauma, only to thrust me out of it because my mom had a weird rock as a nutcracker? What is wrong with you?"

Finally looking at her, he crossed his arms, looking confrontational.

"There is no way they could have kept this a secret. Are you really going to pretend not to know?" There was a suspicion in the squint of his gaze.

"Know what?"

The confrontational stance he had been sporting relaxed, and an expression she hated much more invaded his eyes, pity. Transporting to her he took her hands in his, his thumbs tracing small calming circles on the tops of her hands, on the soft spots near the crook of the thumb.

He pulled a chair from the extravagant, maple wood kitchen table to her and forced her to sit. Kneeling in front of her, he delicately dropped a bombshell on her.

"You aren't Mortal. What I mean to say is, you are no Earthling; you're Angelican." Shock widened her eyes, and she pulled away from him.

"What are you talking about?" she demanded.

Reclaiming her hands, he explained, "I knew your father. He was a general of mine, a good one. He fell in love with a healer, your mother, and they asked to be reassigned together as scouts. I denied the request, not wanting to lose his service. During the unrest, they disappeared. I hadn't put much thought into where they had gone, but now it seems they moved to Middle Earth and had a daughter...." His words were cautious. In response, her forehead crinkled as her eyebrows rose and her head tilted, her mind chewing the words before digesting them.

"My Dad was a geek with back problems, and my mother was a mechanic who constantly had cuts and bruises she got at work. There is no way they were Angelicans," she retorted weakly.

"Glamor is a pretty elementary trick, especially if you're just trying to fool mortals. Your parents had received licensing to become scouts on Earth, which requires passing a series of tests showing that you can fit in amongst the natural residents of Middle Earth." They sat in brief silence as she continued to try and take it in.

"No, I saw your father murder them," she said resolutely.

"He snapped my mother's neck, Jordan. Killed my dad by throwing him through a support beam; Angelicans wouldn't have died so easily." This gave him pause, but only slightly.

"Christine, my father is among some of the most powerful people out there. Not many would slow him down; he could honestly hold his own against me," he clarified and then quietly asked, "Did you identify your parents after they were killed?"

"No." The question seemed out of place to her, but she elaborated anyway. "I was in a coma for a bit; my parents were already cremated by the time I woke up."

He seemed to mull this over, but when he spoke, it was about something else entirely. "I could have killed you. The fates.... They said you would be born amongst mortals; we just assumed that meant you would be mortal. Such a big over-sight." He ran his hand over his face nervously.

"How exactly?" She had known both Pierce and Jordan had gifted her abilities, which is what they previously had thought was necessary for her to exist amongst them, but she didn't understand how that could have killed her.

"Your abilities are as much a part of your anatomy as your blood, and there is certain compatibility needed between different power types. In Heaven, to gift abilities to another person, you undergo testing beforehand to make sure the new ability will be a compatible match; if it isn't, it can cause your system to reject the new energy and kill you. At least this par-tially explains your eyes."

He went on to explain that if the only abilities you have are gifted, you shouldn't have an inclination or core ability because none of your powers will be rooted strongly enough in you to cause that kind of physical reaction.

"Well, my eyes turned purple... I read about inclinations and the meanings of the different colors, and that the more vibrant the color, the more powerful the ability is, so what exactly is purple? I don't remember seeing purple, or black for that matter, in any of the material I've read," she asked, raising her eyebrows at him expectantly.

"I'm not sure what your inclination is. I need to confer with the fates. Mine, on the other hand, used to be blue, which symbolizes great strength in many abilities. All the High Gods have been blue," he said, pulling her into his arms and taking her with him to the couch, where he pulled a blanket over them, tracing the lines of her face as they settled in.

"But, they're black now...." she prompted. He smiled back at her softly.

"They changed when I gave part of myself to Hell's domain. It was an exchange, Hell gave me unique and incredibly strong powers, but I committed myself to it as well. That's why I am the only one with black eyes. When my eyes turn black, it is because the very domain of Hell is reacting within me, fueling me." She looked at him in fascination.

"You seem to really suit being the ruler of Hell. I see the pride on your face as you survey all that you've built and restored. I know part of revitalizing that land requires Heaven, but have you ever considered alliance versus war with Pierce?" He stiffened under her and closed his eyes while breathing out a long, rigid breath.

"No. I plan to rule both, primarily from Hell. He was never meant to lead, and the people are suffering because of it."

"I didn't see a whole lot of people suffering. From what I saw, people loved him, and he worked tirelessly to help them in any way he could. They wanted independence, and he gave it to them." She thought he would pull away from her as she defended Pierce, but instead, he somehow managed to pull her harder against him.

"Everything you saw was a facade. Pierce crafts himself into who he needs to be to meet whatever goal he has with you. I doubt you ever had a conversation with the real Pierce. Honestly, sometimes I doubt if the core of himself is even still there or if his constant flux of personality has caused him to lose all sense of who he ever was. He will say exactly what he needs to line you up for the perfect response. What I fear most in this world is you have to discover, as I did, what happens when Pierce discovers you have seen the man behind the curtain, when he feels like that facade is no longer necessary."

He shuddered slightly at the thought but pushed it away.

"Well, I am needed at some meetings, and you promised your friend a visit. I plan to reclaim my Earthly holdings today, which should really piss Pierce off, so today will likely be our last day here."

He went to leave, but she grabbed his fingertips gently, "Do I have to go?" The pleading in her eyes almost broke him.

"I thought we would see a few places around the world first, but ultimately, we need to get back home. In light of the new information, I am even more convinced I need to keep you as far away from Pierce as possible. We are just too exposed here."

"I understand, but I feel like we have come so far; I don't want to be locked in a black cage again. Staying here, I could teach classes and help people again... To train, maybe you could lift your ban off Thad, and he could train me and keep an eye on me."

"That is a lot of exposure, my love. I don't know."

"I need freedom. I need to make my own choices, even if those choices end up being mistakes. They should be mine to make." He looked up at her, unconvinced.

"Being fated to the most powerful being alive comes with the added benefit of being protected from making stupid mistakes," he responded playfully, taking her face between his hands and running the tip of his nose along hers before kissing her.

"Jordan...." she pleaded. He sighed in exasperation.

"Fine, but if you stay, you need to listen to Thad, regardless of how ridiculous his demands may sound and the instant he says there is danger, you summon me." His face was hard and very stern.

"I can summon you? What are you gonna give me a little bell to ring?" A smile crept over his face at the little giggle that escaped her with that question.

"I may have bluffed a little about that," he indicated to the mark on her chest.

"The burning is a warning that the effects are fading; being separated for too long will do that, and because your healing capabilities are lessened in Hell, the feeling was more intense than it should have been. I can control your energy levels, and as you grow stronger, you will be able to control mine. It isn't really meant as a form of control, more of a way to give the person you mark a boost when needed, or lull them to sleep when they are in pain... You are also able to summon me, just run your finger down it from top to bottom and then tap it once quickly back at the top." He traced the pattern himself showing her.

"So... I can just make you appear. Anytime? Like you're my own personal genie or something?" She laughed again at the absurdity.

His grin widened. "You summoning me makes me feel the same burning you feel after I've been away from you for too long in my chest; that feeling pulls me to you. Once we have an idea of what inclination you are, we will be able to complete the connection. Once you're stronger and in control, you will be able to do everything to me that I can do to you. Your hold on me through this mark is only as strong as your power. See?"

He held his hand out to her, and she traced a very faint patch of discoloration on his thumb pad, the lines were fuzzy, but it almost looked like a star with eight points.

IGNORANCE IS BLISS

Pierce's blue eyes blazed from behind an old wooden door. At thirteen years old, it invigorated him to think that he and his best friend Jordan had just invented a new ability. One they had quickly adapted into a game. He closed the door a bit more so he was peering through the tiniest crack at the sound of quick, attempted tip-toes approaching. He stifled a laugh at how horrible Jordan was at being sneaky.

The game was simple. They had adapted a game Jordan knew from his time on Middle Earth called hide and seek with another called tag, except with their new ability, it made tagging the other person much more difficult, and you got tired way faster because it took so much energy, so you had to be strategic. Pierce couldn't help but feel a bit of pride in the fact that it was the first ability he had shown more aptitude towards than Jordan.

Ever since the day Pierce's father, the High God of Heaven, had dropped the news to him that he was going to be the break in his family's chain of successors in the role and that it was Jordan who would take over one day, he had pretended to be sad for his father's sake.

In reality, he couldn't be more relieved. Not only did he have the literal weight of a world taken off his shoulders, but they had moved Jordan into the castle, and it was like overnight he went from being an isolated royal kid to having a brother and friend to play and train with that was his own age. According to his father, they even shared a birthday, which they both thought was awesome.

The footsteps had stopped, and Pierce went on red alert. He thought he had a pretty good hiding place, this building wasn't on any of the blueprints he had stolen from his dad's office, and it was far enough away from the rest of the buildings that there was no way Jordan had been in it yet, meaning he couldn't teleport behind him and into the room. They could only teleport to places they could see, something they were working very hard on.

Too late, he noticed fingers enter the doorway down by the floor, followed by a skinny arm. He was knocked just slightly, but just enough, by Jordan ramming his shoulders in between the door and frame to wiggle his way in. He had stealthily crawled from one corner of the building over and leapt with all his might in an attempt to get enough of a hold on Pierce for it to count as being tagged.

It was all so sudden and unexpected that it caught Pierce by surprise, and he screamed as he fell back from the resistance of Jordan holding his leg. They lay on the ground laughing at one another for what seemed to them like hours. Jordan at Pierce's high-pitched scream and Pierce at Jordan's crumpled and obviously injured frame in the doorway from thrusting himself inward so hard. Jordan only knew how to do things with 120 percent of his capabilities, something Pierce vowed to help him break the habit of.

"I don't know how, but I know you cheated," Pierce said in between laughs.

"I'm sorry, I didn't understand you; I think you mis-artic-ulated 'I suck at this game.' I can help you with your English if *you need," Jordan jabbed back, pulling himself off the ground with a sly grin and helping his still-laughing friend from the ground. "I don't understand how you can be so much better at this and still so much worse at the same time. It's impressive," Jordan added, elbowing him. In the distance, the Castle bells rang four times, signaling they needed to head to the main hall for lunch.*

"We better head back before my dad comes looking for us. But hey, what do you think of this place? No one really knows it's here. I figured we could use this to come up with new applications of our abilities and stuff," Pierce said excitedly. Jordan and him breaking into a slow jog.

"I think it's genius. We can call it Fort Goldilocks, in honor of its founder."

Jordan laughed mischievously, then tripped over Pierce's outstretched leg. Pierce raced ahead, his long blond curls falling into his face while laughing triumphantly and looking back at his grinning friend. Jordan now had a nice grass stain on his forehead and was no doubt planning his revenge. The thought made Pierce smile, feeling more hopeful for the future than he ever had. Maybe existence would be fun now that he had at least one friend to share it with.

***

Pierce stood with Victor outside the abandoned building he and Jordan had used as children for their hideout. The echoes of their childhood laughter and ignorance chiming in his refreshed memory, adding to his irritation. He hadn't been there in years. It was the last place he had seen Jordan on the day of the revolution, the last place he approached Jordan as his friend, and he had avoided it for that reason.

"What are we doing here?" Pierce finally asked.

Victor stared back at him, annoyed. "Pierce, you are brighter than this; come on." He kicked against the old wooden door that Pierce had once peeked out of looking for Jordan, and despite the obvious decay on it, it didn't budge. "This room meant something to you two, didn't it?" Victor asked in a demanding tone.

"Yes, it did. Why?" Pierce asked, confused and having no interest in sticking around. He would need to have this site demolished soon.

"During your..." Victor stopped himself before saying father to avoid furthering Pierce's already sour mood and continued with a safer approach.

"Predecessor's reign, bridgeways between the worlds were much more commonly used and closing them was incredibly difficult, which is why most of them were disguised. I thought if anyone would know about one of these bridges, or even find a way to make one of them, it would be Jordan. So, I started searching the grounds looking at old bridge sites and possible new ones. While reviewing schematics, this building didn't show up, and I have yet to be able to find a way in. It is fortified, but why?" Victor asked intriguing Pierce's curiosity.

Pierce looked from Victor to the door and approached it cautiously, thinking it would be a poetic place for Jordan to set a deadly trap for him. He smoothed his hands out over the door and reached out to the life force around him.

What responded both inside and out was purely Angelican and nothing sentient. Figuring that was as good of a sign as any, he pushed the door as hard as he could while attempting to turn the knob, but it didn't so much as quiver against the godly strength he was using on it. Again, he heard Jordan's childhood laughter in the back of his mind, mocking.

"This is very good news; thank you, Victor. I needed this today," he said to a very conflicted-looking Victor, struggling to decide between taking the win or questioning how it was a win.

To put him out of his misery, Pierce elaborated.

"This door may not open for us, but it is enchanted to open

for someone from the outside, and I'll bet that someone is the key to more than one of my problems...."

***

Jordan was pulling shiny metallic parts out of a large box when Christine woke up and made her way into the kitchen. The floor-to-ceiling blinds were still closed, darkening the room. She stopped to admire his thoughtful face before making her presence known.

Her mark flared, and a devilish grin stretched across his face. "You trying to sneak up on me?" he asked, still concentrating on the task in front of him.

"Nah, it's too early for games," she yawned. He transported behind her then and kissed a little mark on her neck he had left the night before, a gravelly chuckle vibrating his chest.

"It's never too early for games."

He kissed up her neck to her ear, and reaching around, he playfully squeezed both of her breasts before transporting back to his project, chuckling. Shaking her head, she made her way to the kitchen with an amused grin playing on her lips.

"Are you an immortal God, or a fifteen-year-old?" she asked, sitting at the counter and inspecting his project. "I am THE immortal God, but I am also a man, and it is my strong belief that all of us are capable of reverting back to our fifteen-year-old selves when given the right temptation." He wiggled his eyebrows at her, earning a laugh. She reached out and turned the box to see a picture of what the random silver mechanisms would become.

With a drop of her jaw, she looked at the photo of a full-scale espresso maker/steamer. "Why are you putting this together?" she was dumbfounded.

"Well, last I checked, things work better once they have been assembled, and I thought you may want one this morning. You're up earlier than your usual 11am, so now I must work faster." He smiled back at her still confused expression.

"This is by far the most fantastical thing anyone has ever purchased me, but I meant, why are you assembling it here? Why not wait to put it back together when we get home." The word 'home' slipped out faster than she could take it back, and though she saw his flash of a full smile, she was grateful he didn't comment.

"I thought you made it clear yesterday that you were staying here?" he said casually. She dropped the manual she had swiped and had started perusing.

"You're letting me stay?"

"Let me be clear. Staying is a mistake. But you were right. It's your mistake to make." Before she could thank him, he held up a hand.

"You are *never* to be alone. You need to agree to this, or I won't be able to give you this freedom." The thought of spending that much one-on-one time with Thad wasn't really appealing, but she figured it was worth it.

"Deal. Do I need to sign somewhere? I always wondered if deals with the devil came with an actual contract...." He looked back at her, that devilish smile back again and leaned on the counter before answering.

"They usually do, but considering they are normally written in blood, I'll save you the trouble and take you at your word." He winked and started assembling the machine in front of him without glancing at the instructions as a ringing blasted through the Highrise. "Could you get that? That would be your new shadow coming to 'brief' you on your approved activities."

'Thank Christ I already got dressed,' she thought, then after glancing back at Jordan, internally confused herself.

'Or praise who or whatever, I guess? I'll need to ask Jordan. Everyone in Heaven always says, "Praise Pierce," but there is no chance I'll ever use that one,' Christine was thinking as she pulled the door open, expecting to see Thad's glare on the other side, but instead was greeted by a nervous Amy. She was bouncing up and down with her hands collapsed in front of her. Confused, Christine shut the door in her face, then opened it again to make sure it was real.

The nervous composure was gone this time, and Amy's hand was sitting on her hip feistily. "Are you gonna let me in or not?" she snapped. Any sleepy fog Christine had felt lifted abruptly.

"Um, yeah, I guess," Christine muttered, moving aside and letting her in.

"You guess?" Jordan laughed from the kitchen. "If you want to stay here you better let her in and be nice. She talked me into this." Christine's eyebrows pinched in confusion as she followed Amy into the kitchen. The bewildered look on her face wasn't lessened by Amy's comfort within the Condo.

Christine took a seat at the counter and watched Amy with piqued curiosity. Amy was weirdly at ease. She had breezed into the kitchen and placed a friendly hand on Jordan's shoulder. He nodded at her in acknowledgment as she grabbed a mug from the upper cabinets.

Catching the skeptic glances Christine was shooting at Amy, Jordan twisted the last piece of the steamer onto the espresso machine and grinned triumphantly.

"You should probably refrain from glaring at people until we have an idea of what inclination you are; the last thing we need is you burning a literal hole in the back of my best informant's head."

He leaned on his elbows in front of her, lifting his eyebrows in a playful scold. Amy ignored them while pouring milk into a cup and pressing some coffee grounds into the espresso device.

Jordan and Christine volleyed glances at each other while the machine whirred. His were of encouragement and hers of annoyance. Amy pulled the mug away from the machine and leaned next to Jordan, pushing the mug to Christine.

"Well, I guess that solves that once and for all," Amy stated, looking back and forth between their non-verbal conversation. Jordan laughed and straightened, grabbing Christine's mug and taking a sip.

"You were right; this stuff is amazing," he said to Amy while walking around the counter to Christine. He placed the mug back down in front of her, kissing her forehead.

"Amy is in charge, that is if you want to stay here past today. I need to meet with Thad. Do not kill her or run off." He shot a pitying grin at Amy, wished her luck and disappeared.

"Yuck," Amy said, sticking another mug under the espresso machine.

"Super weird to see you like this. I've... I've never seen you lean into someone's affection. It's gonna take some getting used to. So, now that we are unmonitored, are you actually okay?" Amy said the words in a pinched voice, just a bit more nasal in tone than normal.

She always sounded this way when she was trying not to cry. Christine could remember the same tone in her voice as she said she 'really wasn't crying' during the movie Ted, when the dirty-mouthed stuffed bear got ripped open.

"I'm... better. I do really enjoy being around Jordan; there is none of the discomfort I felt with Pierce. And I have tried and failed to hate him. What I want to know is how you fit into everything. Who do you actually work for? Why did you vanish from my life?" Christine rambled out.

Amy took a long drink of her coffee, set the mug down, intertwined her fingers, and then made real honest eye contact for the first time since walking in the door.

"My parents are some of the most diehard Pierce loyalists alive. Thanks to that, I was chosen when you were born, and suspicion arose that you were the girl from the Fates' prediction, to watch over you and influence you into becoming someone suitable to the throne of Heaven. Since I was raised with this job, it was my normal." She took a deep breath before continuing her rapid fire.

"It wasn't until that day. That you pushed me down, where I could tell you would much rather hurt Pierce than fall into his arms that I started doubting everything. I confronted him about it, and he assured me you just were fighting it due to all the trauma you had endured. After that, he blocked me from seeing you at every turn, until that last day anyway." Amy paused and took another drink.

"Influence me?" Christine asked. Amy tapped her fingers together nervously.

"Well, I tried to influence you." She laughed nervously. "It didn't really work. There are certain personality traits I was supposed to encourage as your only friend. Ones I was told would make a good Queen. Anytime I interjected it didn't make any difference, though. I think the only thing I really influenced was when you wanted to dye your hair green, and I convinced you not to by guilting you based on if your parents could afford it. Pierce wanted you 'pure.' Looking back, it's kinda creepy, but it was all I knew. I'm sorry."

Tears were streaming down Amy's face in guilt, ruining the sharp lines of her eyeliner and adding to the weight of regret on her features.

Christine got up, set her coffee down, walked to the other side of the counter and pulled her friend into a hug. They stayed there for several minutes, and when Amy's breathing calmed to normal and her sobs stopped, Christine released her.

"Did you tell Jordan I would be walking with you that day? And if so, how could you just offer me up like that?" Pink shame had settled in Amy's cheeks, and the flush darkened at Christine's last question.

"I was mad at Pierce. All the research I had done showed me that technically Jordan was the High God when the fates made their prediction, so I thought it was reasonable that HE was your real fated match, and if HE was your fated match, he couldn't be evil, because you wouldn't allow it. Fated matches are rare, and I have never known a set, but everything I have heard and read says you can't harm your own fated match, so I thought you would be safe."

"Till he cracked my skull open...." Christine snarked.

"YEAH, and then he took you! He wasn't supposed to take you. Just meet you, and then we would all go talk together. But you blew that up when you hit the friggen signal. I was lucky Pierce was unconscious. To get a hold of Jordan the first time, I had basically camped out at the old gates to Hell, screaming and trying to break in. Then he sent Thad to scare me away, but it's Thad, so that failed miserably...." Amy's face softened, and it was apparent she was fond of Thad, which was so perplexing to Christine that she zoned out, missing part of Amy's rant.

She tuned back in, "and then he showed me this place and told me if I was ever on the run from being discovered as giving him information, I could hide out here. I've been staying here, though, just to get away from my parents on my days on Earth. Luckily, no one expects anything. I trashed this place the day Jordan took you. Sat here angry, crisscrossed on the floor for like a week until he came and filled me in. Now I am playing double spy, and I hate it. Honestly, the stress is killing me. I think I'm losing hair; is it thinning?"

Amy's face was tight with anxiety and panic as she tilted her head and ran her fingers through it. There was no thinning that Christine could see, and she felt lighter hearing Amy revert back to her machine gun way of delivering information. Wild and rapid but her own form of normal.

Noticing her own rambling, Amy took a breath and then asked, "You are, though, right? Fated together?" The question in her eyes was desperate.

Christine let her fester for a moment before answering 'yes.' Amy relinquished a large sigh. Christine went on without prompting, feeling a surprising amount of relief to have someone to share with.

"He's demanding, hotheaded, abrupt, overprotective, high-handed, and irritating as all fuck. But I can't get enough of him. He seems to know me better than anyone ever has, without me having to tell him he just knows what I need. He told me he loved me, and I almost said it back. I feel like an idiot. I'm technically his captive...."

The stark contrast between the Amy standing in front of her compared to the one that initially walked through the door was impressive. A stranger would have thought they were different women.

"Not anymore, you're not," Amy corrected. "I told Jordan you would never be able to find yourself if you continued to be told your existence is solely to belong to someone else. And he agreed."

"You emotionally strong-armed the Devil?"

"YUP," Amy said proudly, crossing her arms and straightening her spine.

"Impressive." Christine's head bobbed admiringly at her friend.

***

Amy took Christine to a small diner a few blocks away from the condo for breakfast, and they sat and ate, drinking coffee for two hours, filling each other in on their lives since that fateful day at the gate. Amy told Christine about Pierce reassigning her full-time to Earth to look for any mortal sightings of her or Jordan. She also delicately explained that Pierce wasn't taking her absence well. He was noticeably aching for Christine, and the people were suffering right along with him.

Although they suffered, no one blamed him. Everyone in Heaven believed Jordan had taken her as an appalling first strike against the high throne, signaling a coming war and adding to tensions.

'I wonder how they would feel about him if they knew Jordan was the one I wanted?' Christine wondered.

"You have a long day ahead of you. Being a free woman doesn't mean you don't have certain responsibilities." Christine's head was spinning by the time Amy had finished listing off her lengthy schedule.

"Wait." Christine stopped Amy from getting up and then laughed. "You're training me? Since when can you fight?" she snorted.

"For your information, I have been training since I was two. And I mastered my inclination by the time I was thirteen. I am perfectly capable of teaching you, regardless of how hopeless Thad thinks you are."

"WAIT. What's your inclination?" Christine's eyes were round with fascinated wonder, and it reminded Amy how new all this still was to her.

"It's nothing crazy. And honestly, I am not all that strong. But I have the power of persuasion. I can whisper suggestions that people can't help but reeeeally want to follow. But I have to be touching them, and you can build an immunity to me specifically. You did, so did my parents. I have to be very careful, though. Messing with people's free will puts you in a bad light with the fates, and that is never good, so I super-duper make sure I don't cross any lines. Here watch..."

Casually Amy reached out and touched the waitress's hand while taking the check and made eye contact. "I overheard that poor woman at table three saying her kids couldn't order juice because they couldn't afford it. It would be real nice of you to give each of the kids a milkshake and comp their meal," Amy recommended, sweetly. The waitress's face went from confused to downright copacetic.

"You know what? That's a wonderful idea." The twiggy waitress disappeared through the kitchen doors and re-emerged with Oreo milkshakes and a friendly smile on her lips. Amy watched proudly as Christine's jaw dropped.

"That was epic," Christine praised. Amy mock bowed from her seat.

"It can be dangerous, though. It has a lasting effect. If I sway someone to do something kind, they will stay in an agreeable mood for a while, complimenting people, waving, and smiling at strangers, etc...."

"Spreading kindness is rarely dangerous," Christine pointed out, downing the rest of her coffee and shoving the last piece of jelly-covered toast in her mouth.

'Fuck, I missed real food,' she thought in pure pleasure at the texture of something other than gray slop.

"True, but I have the same effect if I have someone do something harmful, selfish, or dangerous. It's a tricky inclination, but it's mine." Amy shrugged, taking out her wallet and throwing some bills on the table.

"Have you passed your limit; do you know what color your identifiers are?" Christine asked, still interested. Inclinations were a subject that fascinated her.

Amy gawked. "Of course not. Most people don't even have one. Even if I was powerful enough for that, I would have to be trying to convince someone to do something super crazy to get enough resistance to push me that far. I guess I could probably push my limits with matter manipulations too, but I just haven't been in a position to take that risk. According to the big book of identifiers, they would be sage colored, though."

"Did you happen to see purple ones in that big book?" Christine asked casually. She had told Amy earlier that she had pushed her limits in training with Thad but not that she had an inclination or what color they were.

"Purple? I've never heard of anyone having purple identifiers. Is that what color yours were? Hmm, probably because of the rando pieces of abilities you have on top of whatever your natural inclination would have been. Friggen idiots."

Amy had called both Pierce and Jordan idiots earlier, too, when Christine explained that they discovered that her parents weren't mortal. According to Amy, part of her parent's job was to find out as much as possible about Christine's lineage and as far as they could tell, she had none. They even told Pierce they couldn't, with 100 percent certainty, confirm that they were, in fact, mortals.

Christine smiled, watching the two young boys in tattered clothes devour their milkshakes. Amy considered it was no big deal, but to those kids, it meant the world. It was then she noticed she recognized the mom and noticed the sunglasses indoors, scarf still on and the nervously tapping foot.

'Oh no, she didn't,' Christine thought angrily, getting up from the table and leaving Amy halfway through a sentence of words Christine didn't even remotely catch as she marched aggressively toward an old friend.

IMPULSE CONTROL PROBLEMS

I marched my way to Gabi's table furiously. Her kids had grown so much since I had last seen them, and I didn't know which emotion was driving me forward faster, anger, disappointment or concern.

"After all the work we did. After everything we accomplished, please tell me I'm wrong?" I begged, now standing at the side of their table.

"Christine?" Gabi asked after sucking in a breath of pure shock. "But I heard you were dead." Her hands were trembling, and her kids were looking at me, and I could tell by their tight little faces they lived a harsh reality filled with tense situations like this and had adapted a common survival technique of freezing in place. The mindset that if I just don't move, they won't explode, they won't see me, they won't hurt me. Seeing that, I forced my stance to relax a little.

"Gabi. I see the 'I fell down the stairs' attire. Tell me you have a migraine, and show me there are no bruises under that scarf, please." Rage was boiling in the pit of my stomach as I tried not to rip the scarf right off her.

The last time I saw her, she was moving into her own

apartment. She had full custody of her kids, and I had gotten her in touch with a grant that would pay her living expenses while she went back to school for nursing.

All because her abusive, garbage husband, Lus, had tried to burn the kids and her alive. He hadn't known she had taken a survival class with me that showed her how to get out of ropes.

She had managed to free herself before the flames could reach her or the boys, tied up in the living room. They escaped out of a main floor window, and she ran, carrying both her sons, to the center of the street, collapsing in the center of onlookers, many of whom were recording on their phones.

A tear rolled down her cheek as she took the sunglasses off, exposing a nasty black eye. "He went to counseling, and he got sober. I thought it would last."

"It never lasts with a man like that, Gabi, for fuck's sake. I'm back, and I have much better resources now. I can get you out. And I mean out. A new start in any country you want." I knew I was being a forceful bitch and very much inserting myself into something that was technically not my business. But she wasn't just endangering herself, she was risking her boys, and that was unacceptable.

Hope started to smooth Gabi's expression, only to dissipate when the little bell above the diner door chimed, and in walked Lus. Amy was standing beside me now. Gabi had made the news when everything had gone down, as had my involvement, so Amy recognized her and matched my defensive stance, shielding the boys.

'Here we go,' I thought, itching for a fight. The last time I had seen Lus, he had tried to jump me after class for 'fucking with his wife's head,' and I had broken his nose and left him bleeding in the parking lot.

His mouth opened, and the smell of sour vodka assaulted my senses. "So, you're back in town. Still trying to break up families. Or did you find something that pays better? I'll be thankin ya to step away from ma-familiee." His words were slurred, and he was obviously drunk.

'Jesus fuck dude, it isn't even 10am,' I judged silently, although I would bet my facial expression spoke plenty.

"Actually, you're spot on. I AM still breaking up families, only the ones with drunken assholes who can't keep their hands to themselves," I judged much less silently.

"Except this time, she won't take you back; you 'burned' that bridge. Yes, pun intended." He lunged at me wildly, causing one of his sons to break his statue-like composure and flinch.

Effortlessly, I grabbed Lus's swinging arm and twisted violently, shoving him face down on the nearest empty table. He was a stocky man, but he was also drunk and slow. He was no match for me before I had tapped into my strength, so subduing him now wasn't even satisfying. It was so easy.

"I'll take them back to Jordan's place," Amy said, grinning at the wiggling man I had firmly pinned. Both the boys looked at me like I was some kind of superhero.

'Not a whole lot of worry for Daddy,' I thought, unsurprised. Gabi's face was marred with exhaustion and defeat as Amy ushered them out the door, and I found myself disgusted at the way she had checked out on them.

Releasing him in an ungentle manner and stepping away, I taunted him with an arrogant 'have a nice life' smile before turning around to leave. My mistake was getting cocky. I was strong, and now I could confidently use my abilities, but unlike Jordan, I was not impenetrable; this was a good lesson on that.

A flare of heat shot up me, causing me to turn around, too late, as Lus jabbed a serrated steak knife, hilt deep, into my side. I felt a gush of breath leave me, and my mark burned and began to glow.

'You son-of-a-bitch,' was the last thing I remember thinking before something overtook me. I wasn't sure what, instincts, anger, hatred, maybe?

I reached out and clamped my hands around Lus's dense, ugly neck without thinking and burned right through it with my bare hands. The flesh melted and charred in an instant between my fingers, like hot kinetic sand. His head, a look of shocked terror, still frozen on his face, fell backward off his body. Jordan appeared then, his expression and eyes as black as death.

***

Pierce sat in a chair that was much too small for his large frame at a table packed with small Angelicans, all under the age of ten, all watching him in fascination as he used matter manipulation to create a swirl of light dancing back and forth between his hands.

Victor stood in the doorway to the cafeteria of the Castle's orphan wing watching Pierce with relief. He had been worried about him. But finding the bridge had given him hope, and that hope had lightened him back into being the bright light of a leader everyone counted on. This wing had been empty when Pierce had claimed his birthright to the throne after usurping Jordan, and it had been Pierce's idea to open it up to 'less likely to be adopted' orphans.

Heaven is an accommodating enough place to live that the number of orphans in the entire realm were able to be comfortably housed within this one wing of the castle, but circumstances of unwanted children were bound to happen anywhere people could reproduce. Housing them in the castle had given Pierce the opportunity to help fill the gap the kids were all scarred with due to abandonment, and it gave him a chance to use his abilities to provide reassurance to them when needed.

Looking into the awed faces of the kids he had taken in, most of them since they were infants, Pierce felt the familiar ache of longing that was always festering in him for Christine.

Finding her had meant he was supposed to be able to start his own family and continue the royal bloodline, but now all that was on hold.

He may have been the break in the chain for inheriting the abilities of a High God, but he doubted his son would be. Being here and spending time with the kids helped calm the ache in him. One of the most admiring looks Christine had ever given him was when he had introduced her to this group and explained what this wing was for.

Noticing Victor in the doorway, Pierce dramatically sighed and slapped his hand onto the table.

"Sorry guys, fun time is over for me; the boss is here, which means I must have work to do," he said, standing. In unison, the twelve kids rang out with an adorable "awhhh" at their ruined fun.

"Next time I come to hang out, I want to see each one of you create light streaks. Once you all can, I have a game I can teach you with them," he encouraged. At the prospect of a new game, they all started rubbing their fingers together, attempting to produce the light filaments that grew from sparks as Pierce had. He approached Victor, still chuckling at their hyper-focused expressions.

"One of them is going to set something on fire, and Annie won't thank you for it. Can't you ever teach them something that isn't dangerous?" Victor asked, remembering the incident where Pierce had taught them how to freeze existing water so they could make their own ice slides in the back gardens during winter.

Only they didn't tell anyone, so it resulted in a bit of a disaster when the kitchen staff attempted to cut through there with pots of food for an event on the other side of the castle, resulting in a large mess and several lightly burned cooks.

"Come now old man, what is childhood without a little danger?" he said, winking and remembering Jordan and him inventing transporting for the purpose of a game, passing out several times in the attempt. The memory dampened his previously playful attitude.

They walked down one of the large corridors, the sound of Christine's airy laugh came from a nearby TV in one of the rooms, and Pierce shot Victor a knowing glance.

"Why are we running Christine's bio-clip again?" Pierce asked. They had created a short video about who she was and her life on Earth, as well as her abduction when she had first been taken. Victor saw it as a way to gain favor with the people as well as alleviate some of the inbound demands for information from the public. They usually only ran it when they had an update to give. The first time Pierce watched it, he laughed, knowing how much Christine would despise the very idea of it.

"Honestly, your favor is down with the people, and we always see an increase of good faith after they run. It is hard for people to have faith in a leader that is separated from their fated match," Victor said the term fated match with his usual disdain.

"I don't like spreading propaganda to the people. I shouldn't need to gain favor via sympathy. Is the door still monitored?" Victor assured him it was.

"Good. For now, I will turn my focus back to the people. I'll visit the different territories and offer my services where applicable and make emotional adjustments where needed, now that I feel I have regained enough control of myself to do so again."

With each confident word, Victor was reminded of the faith he had for Pierce, and he couldn't help but swell with pride at his bounce back. When faced with a comparable situation, Victor had fallen to pieces and stayed that way for a long time. Pierce had given him purpose and saved his life, and now it was his turn to repay the favor.

***

"Christine…" The deep sound that escaped Jordan's lips seemed to form my name, but I couldn't be sure.

My vision started to blur as I listened to the people around me in the cafe screaming, although I wasn't sure at what.

'Was it from me burning a guy's head off his body or fear of the look Jordan was giving Lus's corpse? I killed someone. Lus. His kids. I know his kids, Brock and Ben. She is never going to forgive me; they will fear me. I killed someone. I murdered someone.'

The black never faded from Jordan's eyes, but his expression softened when it landed on me. Staggering, my hand explored the sharp pain in my side, being careful not to touch the knife. I could feel the warmth of blood on my fingers but didn't dare look.

Thad appeared beside Jordan, mouth dropping open with interested shock as he took in the room. The confusion in his expression turned into amusement as he shot me a mocking thumbs up and mouthed a sarcastic 'nice job.'

Disoriented as I was, I hadn't noticed that Jordan had been mumbling the entire time. The room was filling with a silvery fog, and the screaming had stopped.

Jordan's lips stilled, and his hands dropped, running for me as my legs jellied and I fell to my knees. I stared in horror at the remains of the man in front of me. The familiar sensation of Jordan's hands sent relief through me as he pulled me gently into his arms.

Stubbornly, I remained conscious, if not entirely coherent, as he transported me back to his condo. We stepped into the foyer, and I registered the sound of Amy ushering our guests into a different room and briskly shutting the door.

"Come on, Christine, how did you manage to get stabbed fighting that idiot?" she chastised, her worry showing in the form of irritation. Jordan shooed her away with the task of getting water and a medical kit.

"I'm putting you under to have the knife removed, don't

fight it. Trust me; you won't want to be awake for this." He was looking at the knife in my side with dread, having already ripped my destroyed shirt off. My mark started to heat up, and I allowed myself to be wrapped in a calming blanket of his black warmth and drifted off.

***

"What. Happened?" Jordan didn't look up from the blood he was washing from his hands as he asked the question in clipped words. Thad sat drinking an espresso, looking entertained as Amy fidgeted with her shirt end.

"I'm not sure." She shrugged. His eyes met hers, demanding elaboration. She did her best, "Christine saw one of her old students. Went to say hi, I think. Things got heated fast, and she seemed to have Lus handled, so I brought Gabi and the boys here because Christine said she would relocate them to get away from Lus." She avoided his eyes.

"She DID have him handled," Thad chuckled but quickly withered under Jordan's glare, which was almost immediately redirected back to Amy.

"You brought mortals into my home. Leaving Christine with a known violent man. Your one job was to keep her safe. For Heaven's sake, Amy, you know we don't interfere with mortals, Christine is still learning, but you have no excuse."

Not a fan of conflict, Amy slumped and sat down at the counter next to Thad, who threw a supportive arm around her. They had hit it off from their first encounter outside Hell's gate, and he didn't like Jordan's obvious double standard.

"Be kind. She grew up here too, and she is just as young," Thad said, playfully shaking her a little.

"Now, what am I supposed to do with them?" Jordan said, motioning to the closed door of the guest room the young family was stashed in. "I doubt the wife, battered or not, is not going to be pleased to discover Christine killed her husband."

Amy dropped Thad's cup that she had been stealing a sip from. "She killed him!?"

Thad was approvingly nodding his head up and down. "She burned his head clean off his body after he stabbed her. A bit jarring for the mortals in the room. Jordan took care of them, though. They'll all be fuzzy on the details."

Amy touched her own neck in shock.

"It's fine, Amy; all-powerful gods and goddesses have a mortal body count from when they were still figuring out their strengths. We are just lucky Christine's was just an act of self-defense and that Lus got a knife in her side before she erupted and leveled the building."

She relaxed for a lovely small second before processing the intentional hard shut of a door, seeing Gabi fuming with rage. Jordan responded to her rage with complete disinterest.

"We are not ready for you yet; this is a private conversation," he said, crossing his arms in a way that only Jordan could, both authoritative and aloof at the same time.

"A private conversation that very much involves me and my family. You people are crazy. I've heard every word. Where is my husband? What did she do to him?" Gabi demanded, stomping her foot and jabbing a finger at him.

Jordan's head dropped and rolled to the side to shoot Amy an annoyed glance, as if looking at a cat who had just dropped a mouse at his feet and then ran off, leaving him to deal with the mess. Amy shrunk farther into Thad. Rolling his head back to Gabi, Jordan started cleaning the sink out while speaking to her.

"I'm not entirely sure what happened to your husband," Jordan lied, grabbing the now clean knife from the sink and inspecting it closely. Sharp light glinted off it menacingly as he rotated it back and forth. Due to the trick of the light, Gabi could have sworn she saw his eyes darkening. "What I do know is that whatever fate he has met, it was kinder than he deserved." The air around them became chalky and stale.

"He relapsed last night and was still drying out. It was none of her business. If that bitch so much as...." She didn't get the chance to finish her sentence. Jordan transported to the spot in front of her causing the breath to catch in her throat.

"That *Goddess* almost died attempting to save you from your own poor choices. You should be praising her. If not for her infuriating persistence, you and your sons would have died in that fire years ago, and how do you thank her, by running back to the bastard that locked you in that house to die?" His eyes ever-so-slightly continued to darken and Thad, seeing this, slowly rose from his seat, taking the knife from Jordan's hand.

"Sorry. He is very protective of the woman your husband stabbed. Tread carefully. As you can see, we aren't normal, and neither is she. That is good because if she were normal, she would be dead, and he," Thad motioned to brooding Jordan with his head, "would become very violent. So please, calm down, have some coffee, and work with Amy."

Jordan had regained his composure and backed away a bit, loosening his stance. His eyes remained a shade darker than any brown or blue Gabi had ever seen.

Gabi cautiously walked to Amy, who was holding out a glass of water for her.

"He isn't all bad," Gabi snipped defensively, raising the shaking glass to her lips and drinking. Jordan narrowed his eyes at her before slowly turning and leaving the room.

"He *wasn't* all bad," Amy corrected softly.

Gabi choked on her sip of water and stared at her with wavering defiance.

"Christine killed him in self-defense. And she did it in a way that no one will understand, strangers won't believe, and scientists will want to study. I'm so sorry, Gabi, but you have a chance now to start over, free of financial burdens and beatings. Take it."

Gabi felt the sting of so many losses at that moment. Her

children, sleeping soundly in a stranger's bed, had lost their recovering father. Lus and her and been through so much together, divorce, abuse, recovery, and even a blissful year of sobriety.

The last year he had been the husband he had always promised he could be, attentive and warm, until the bender that ended his life. And now he was gone; there was no more recovering, no more warm morning kisses, and laughing goodnight tickles.

Now, with him gone, she couldn't even remember the pain of busted lips and black eyes. Of tearful nights up alone, waiting for him to stumble home, or evenings of watching her children flinch against his harsh words, followed by hiding in their rooms, terrified they may end up being the recipient of his drunken wrath.

She would make sure her children remembered their father at his best in hopes that he would be the man they grew up to replicate.

WHAT'S A GIRL TO DO?

Not wanting to disturb her, Jordan sat at his desk, thumbing through the information gathered from Christine's childhood home. One piece of information kept resurfacing in his thoughts. There was an Angelican picture, one that could move due to the abilities of the photographer.

It was of Christine's parents and a menacing-looking young man. He was strapped with knives and uniformed like a member of the Old Guard, but Jordan had never seen him.

What bothered him was the resemblance between Nett, Christine's father and this young man. Same eyes, nose and, most noticeably, the same rare black, silver-tipped wings. The back of the photograph said:

Initiation Day 103JR
Left: Gaire
Right: Nett
Middle: Azazel

Jordan was certain if Christine had a brother or possibly uncle in Heaven, he would have made himself known to her.

From what she told him, the people looked at her like a celebrity; there was even a documentary they had made about her and played on one of the top channels once a week. Surely, a family member, one with enough sense of honor to be in the Old Guard, would have seen this young girl alone in a new world and reached out?

Christine began to stir. He had checked her wound just an hour ago. It was healing nicely; a few more hours and she would be out of the woods. Her increased training had encouraged her powers to flow more freely throughout her body, giving her more resilience. Had he kept her on Pierce's schedule, she would be dead.

Jordan sat beside Christine, running his fingers along her bone structure, not quite touching her but reassuringly feeling her energy, loving the way their energies seemed to pull to one another. To him, it felt like a constant thrum of pushing and pulling electricity, as if their souls were dancing.

With time, he knew Christine would begin to feel it too, once she figured out how to connect with her center, that is. He looked over the darkness under her eyes and the sharp edge to her breathing and felt his rage boil again. It was torture not having anyone to take it out on.

"Hi…" Christine groaned, not quite opening her eyes. He could sense she was stable an hour ago, but the sound of her voice felt like a cooling balm to his agitated soul.

"Hi." He smiled with a sigh, delicately wrapping his hand around her neck before lightly pecking both sides of her mouth until she caught his in a real kiss.

Once he had tasted her long enough to fully lift the stress from his muscles, he lifted his face and was met with guilt-laden eyes.

"What is it?" he asked, still running his fingers through her hair. She was generously bundled in blankets, but beneath them, she laid bare. Jordan put effort into staying soft with her by staying above her cocoon of nude warmth.

There was a gnawing in her stomach at the thought of Lus's face and of facing Gabi and the kids. But on top of that was this unfamiliar feeling she was having of self-disappointment for letting Jordan down. He had given her freedom, and within two hours she had killed someone and almost died. She was trying to form the words to apologize, to say anything, but couldn't.

"It's okay to be upset, Christine." His gentle words broke her.

Her chest constricted, her breathing came in gasps, and she felt heat begin to build behind her eyes, in her stomach, and on her palms; needle-like pinpricks were amassing an army behind her eyes and nose and all at once, all that pressure broke loose into a fury of sobs and tears and unattractive gasps for breath.

Stunned by her response, he hesitated, not well practiced in the art of consoling others, before pulling the blankets off her, and pulling her into the safety of his arms.

"Shh, I'm here. Breathe slower and deeper, good girl, that's it...."

"Please, make it stop," she begged between sobs and tapped her temples. The hand that had been stroking her hair stilled, and he went rigid as an alarming realization chimed in the back of his mind.

"I can't." He barely gritted the words out and was thankful she didn't seem to notice. Kissing her forehead, he pulled her flush against him, letting her work through the pain in her own time and being the only type of support he could be.

"I'm - I'm s-sorry for the m-meltdown."

He shook his head at her unnecessary apology and gently shushed her, pulling her back against his chest, smoothing her hair and reiterating reassurances for a good fifteen minutes before she calmed and pulled a bit away from him.

An embarrassed huff escaped her as she felt the need to explain herself. "I don't know what got into me, I mean, I feel awful about everything, but his face it just, I just, my Dad had a similar expression and... I've been angry and sad about everything before, but this was, is different."

"How is it different?" he asked delicately.

"This, it's less of a sharp pain and more of a deep ache. It's like before, when I would remember, I would get panic attacks, and it was awful, but it was quick and when it was over, it really was over, and I would be fine after that," she said looking away, overflow still visible on her waterline. "This is an ache. Like something in me has been burnt, it isn't going away; it's just dulled, kind of."

"You've never 'ached' like this?"

"No." He blinked back at her in surprise, a hint of anger in his eyes, and she flinched seeing it.

"Did Pierce ever 'fix it' when you would start to feel like this?" He was clenching and unclenching his fist as he asked.

"Yeah... He said something about him putting up mental blocks and them being damaged or something, and that was what caused the attacks, but I haven't had one until now." Jordan took a deep breath to soothe his own, vastly different type of emotional attack. He took her face in both of his hands and gave her a serious expression, one of hard lines, worry and authority.

"That's your grief, Christine, needing to be acknowledged, wanting to be felt. In a misguided way, Pierce thought he was helping you by stopping you from feeling this. This is what it is to mourn someone. Not just miss them or be mad at the world for taking them. Truly mourning them is much more torturous, and I am so sorry to tell you a part of that feeling will always be there."

One of his hands remained cupped to the side of her face, and he gave her a reassuring look before continuing.

"In a way, that feeling is a tether, a reminder of the love you had. Feeling this honors them. I'm just sorry that you have had to wait to mourn them until now, compounded with this new trauma."

Her eyes were bloodshot and swollen, her hair knotted, and she still had bloodstains in various places on her skin. But as she leaned her face into his hand, the thought occurred to him that she may have never been more beautiful than she was at that moment. He was seeing her become whole, and thankfully he was the one there to help her find these scattered pieces.

"Sorry you got fated to such a mess," she mused, trying to break some of the tension. He wiped the tears from both of her cheeks, sensing her need to move on from this for now, and smiled back.

"And I'm sorry my bastard father is the reason that you're such a mess." This won a laugh from her.

"That is a very good point." She smiled at him, but it was a shadow of the smile he had come to know.

"What happens now? I need to apologize to Gabi and set them up to be able to build some kind of lives... I can't believe I snapped like that. I didn't even think about it. I just did it." He had gotten up to grab her a glass of water, first wrapping her back into the blankets.

"A mortal stabbed you, and you reacted. It happens," Jordan said with a dismissive wave of his hand.

"Jordan, I killed a man. That doesn't just happen," she protested from her fluffy fortress.

"You didn't kill him. He killed himself the second he wielded a knife at you." She recognized the darker shade of his eyes and knew exactly what he meant but had a hard time imagining his malice as he handed her a glass of water and curled back up to her.

"Our next steps are to leave as soon as it is safe for you to make the trip due to the exposure this caused. Speaking to the wife is unnecessary. You have done her enough favors." She pushed away from him and got out of the bed, head pounding, shooting pain in her side still, and a finally realized weight in her chest. Jordan pouted after her.

"And you don't hate mortals?" she accused, looking at herself in the standing mirror, poking the red scar with her finger, amazed that it was a closed wound and that there were no stitches. Being injured or broken wasn't entirely new for her but healing this quickly definitely was.

"As a whole, no," Jordan said. "This one was certainly not worthy of my hate." He glimpsed her curious reflection in the mirror while enjoying the sight of her on full display. Part of him warmed at the thought of her gaining comfort around him.

"The more you use your abilities and accept your nature, the more invulnerable you'll be, just like the rest of us Angelicans. Your swift healing is a direct result of your increased training and the active power running through your veins." This irritated her, another thing to be added to the list of things she should know but didn't.

"Ah, so you mean all my childhood scraped knees were for naught? Or that time you nearly smashed my skull in, damn. Wish my parents had filled me in on that little nugget." She meant the words as a joke, but there was an unmistakable edge to them. Jordan winced at the barb.

"You plan to hold that against me forever, don't you?" he asked, poking a finger to the tip of her nose with a suspicious squint in his eyes.

"The world's worst first impression? Oh, absolutely." She stuck her tongue out at him playfully, but the glint in her eyes faded, and with an exhausted sigh she looked out the windows, and her weight relaxed into him.

"Why do you think they hid all this from me?" He wasn't sure if she was asking him or her own reflection in the large windows, but he could sense her wheezing soul, straining in unchecked grief.

"We may never really know. But I have faith that their decisions were made with nothing but love driving their intentions. Your father was a good man. He spent his life protecting the innocent." It made him smile to recognize the curious fire flare back to life in her eyes.

***

Pierce leaned expectantly against an open wall in one of the larger training rooms. His curly blond hair was falling around his young face, and his eyes swam with uncertainty as Jordan appeared in the room, looking around, presumably for him.

They had invented Transporting together a few years back, and Pierce's father and Jordan's mentor, Arcane, had instructed them to teach the skill to select others looking to learn.

With their competitive nature, they had both chosen one person to teach at a time and decided to make it a race. The first trainee to successfully do a full-body transport won. The loser would be the one to request money and accommodations to spend a small vacation on Middle Earth from Arcane.

"Eager today, huh, Goldilocks? I don't remember you ever beating me to training," Jordan barbed with a light-hearted smile. They were only twenty-four, but Jordan had already taken on several trainees in other areas of combat; this would be Pierce's first time instructing.

"Training seems more entertaining at the prospect of giving the orders and not having to take them," he shot back. Jordan laughed, and the large mahogany doors opened as their two trainees made their way into the room. Strategically the two chosen to learn this skill first were a married couple, known to be incredibly competitive with one another and both high-ranking members of different areas of government.

Alexie was a slender and quick man with caramel skin and an unmatched air of intelligence about him that accented his angular features well. He complimented his wife Satrai perfectly. She was thick, curvy, and ambitiously energetic, with dark eyes and a sweet face. Their arms were looped together in a cutesy way that had Jordan rolling his eyes.

"Good morning, boys!" they called in unison. Many people in the upper circles still referred to them as Arcane's boys; knowing them since they were children, it was a hard habit to kick. Satrai pecked Alexie on the cheek and broke apart from him, making her way to Pierce's corner of the gym but not before warning Jordan to speak slowly so that her hubby could keep up, scuffling away with mischievous laughter. Alexie just shook his head after her and handed a portable coffee cup to Jordan.

"What's this?" Jordan asked. He was not a fan of coffee in the slightest.

"Oh," explained Alexie, "that is black tea and honey. We ran into Nacentra in the hall, and she mentioned you didn't have time to finish at her place this morning, so she sent it over with us." Jordan flushed at Nacentra's forwardness. Pierce fake coughed across the room, obviously overhearing the exchange, and wiggled his eyebrows jokingly at Jordan.

"If you had a late night, we would understand if you needed to wait a day to start training. I am sure it wouldn't give us that much of a head start. Right, Satrai?" Pierce's laugh was light and playful, and Jordan couldn't help but crack a grin at him.

Nacentra was Jordan's current attempt to sate his loneliness, and she was making their relationship a little too well known. She wasn't his future; as much as he had hoped it would be possible she would be, he still felt the same gnawing emptiness with her as he had with anyone. Great sex or not, he wanted more. A fact he had vented to Pierce about on several different occasions.

"Ha. Ha. You are hysterical. Truly, maybe the calling you're looking for is in comedy," Jordan responded in such a deadpan manner that neither Satrai or Alexie could tell if he was joking until Pierce started laughing and shaking his head in response.

"Thank you for the advice, great future ruler of ours," Pierce added with a wink knowing how uncomfortable Jordan *still was with the idea that one day he would be in charge of literally everything. Pierce liked to joke that Jordan would need to bulk up his chicken arms if he planned to start carrying the weight of three worlds on his shoulders.*

"To begin, we should have them start with transporting an apple to get a feel for the molecular displacement. Then we will test on mice, and once they are confident enough, they can try to transport themselves. Did you have an instruction plan in mind for Satrai, or would you like to borrow mine?"

Pierce debated his answer, sure that Jordan's lesson plan would have much more structure since he had experience with training. But he was resolute in the fact that they invented the skill based on feel, and he could teach it the same way.

"Thank you, but I have my own methods of instruction," Pierce responded.

"I'm sure you do," Jordan huffed.

"Good luck Satrai. Meet back here in six hours?" Alexie and Satrai laughed, and everyone nodded in agreement.

Both instructors had very different teaching methods. Pierce explained the feeling behind transporting and then had Satrai start working with the apple, getting a feel for the molecular structure of it, and then they hopped right into trying to transport it, he would demonstrate, and she would try to replicate.

On Jordan's side of the gym, Alexie was given the history of how they had discovered the skill, a mapped-out diagram of the phases of broken-down transporting that Jordan had studied and mapped, and key focus points to use to assist in concentration while attempting to transport.

Satrai had already been trying to move her apple for four hours by the time Alexie was even given his, but after only twenty minutes of guidance and adjustments made by Jordan, Alexie had done it. Sweat beaded his forehead at the effort expended, and Jordan rewarded him with a ten-minute break and watched from a distance as Pierce became frustrated with Sa-

trai and watched her become frustrated with him in response.

Jordan made his way over to them, "Satrai, your husband is on a break. Why don't you join him and recenter yourself." She took off without question.

"She is too stressed out to move anything, Pierce. I think a hands-on approach is a good one for her, compared to her analytical husband, but she needs to be reassured and calmed to succeed with this. Not pushed." Pierce shook his head, taking in the advice.

"It just comes so easy to us that it is hard to imagine what she is doing wrong." They both chuckled at his sarcasm. Jordan had stunned himself the first time he transported, and Pierce had lost an eyebrow.

When the couple returned, they were both flushed and looked a bit guilty. Satrai's hair was a bit ruffled in the back, and Alexie looked equal parts guilty and sated. Jordan met him at their table on their side of the gym, grinning.

"Help your wife destress?" he asked, causing Alexie to choke on the water he had been drinking.

"What can I say? I take my husbandly responsibilities very seriously," he answered with an earnest shrug. Jordan smiled and patted him on the back.

"As you should, you may also spend the night on the couch, considering we are moving on to mice, and she has yet to move her apple. So it's smart to get what you can now." Alexie nodded in agreement.

Transporting was proving to be an easy skill for Alexie to complete. His natural inclination was a weak and common one; he was good with nature, growing, moving or manipulating anything organic. He couldn't create new life, but he could manipulate and assist anything that already was. Although a common inclination, Alexie wielded it with more skill than most, which helped him rise in the ranks quickly, overseeing the agriculture committee under Arcane's rule.

"So," he asked in between teleporting a confused mouse

from one end of their table to the other, "Nacentra, huh? Any chance she may be our queen one day?" Jordan considered the question. Nacentra would make a wonderful queen, but he couldn't begin to imagine her sitting by his side.

"I don't claim to be gifted like the fates in regards to the secrets of the future. But, Nacentra would be a wonderful queen, just not my queen."

Alexie grinned and nodded knowingly. "Poor girl."

"Nah," Jordan appeased, "She's getting off easy. I'm a handful."

"Now that, I believe." They both chuckled.

With an hour left of their day, Jordan gave him approval to begin attempting to transport himself. He readied a bucket of water and warned him of signs to be aware of. Spikes of heat were common, but if he felt ice in his veins, he needed to slowly release the attempt. Jordan demonstrated a few times. Alexie's goal was to transport one foot and land on a red-taped line on the floor.

Mid-way through instruction, they glanced over at cheering from Pierce and Satrai's side of the room; she teleported the apple. Alexie ran over and kissed her passionately as Jordan applauded, sitting on the table he had used for his lesson plan.

It lifted Jordan's spirit to see the pride in Pierce's eyes. He had been struggling to step out of Jordan's and his father's shadow, and this was an opportunity to shine of his own accord. Transporting was a skill Pierce had not only invented but was one he was best at, and Jordan hoped this would be something he could share with his people, something to be proud of.

Gleaming with unabashed pride, Alexie returned, rubbing his hands together determinedly.

"Okay," he huffed.

"So, to recap, focus on everything. What I'm moving, where I'm moving it to, while also thinking of nothing. Matriculate an energy grasp on me, condense, and then release with intent." He clapped nervously.

"Yup, easy, right?" Alexie huffed back at Jordan's nonchalant response.

"Don't forget, if you feel cold, back down," Jordan concluded.

Nodding his head, Alexie closed his eyes and stilled, breathing deep and focusing. Jordan watched the energy around him shift and dance around his skin, slowly expanding out. He thought it was a shame that no one else seemed to notice the appearance of energy like he did.

Mid thought Alexie's energy snapped inwardly, and he vanished, reappearing on the taped goal line in front of Jordan. They both threw their hands in the air, mouths open to yell in excitement, when a blood-curdling scream cut the legs off their joy and drowned their victory.

Arms slowly lowering to their sides, heads snapped over to Pierce, whose hands were covering his mouth, eyes wide with horror. Jordan acted instantly, teleporting to the other side of the room to inspect Satrai.

Her eyes were missing, and thick blood ran like tears of death from the haunting emptiness where amber eyes used to sparkle. Blood then began to run from her nose and ears. Her mouth hung open as she gasped against the blood blocking the screams clawing their way for release.

Jordan dropped to his knees in front of her and placed a hand on each side of her head, closing his eyes to assess the damage. He knew at once there was nothing they could do; her brain had mostly liquefied. They could never have imagined this could happen. Teleporting back to an ashen Alexie, he grabbed him by both shoulders.

"She has seconds. I think she can hear you, say your goodbyes. I've blocked her pain receptors, and she can't feel anything. She will be confused and needs to hear your voice to make her go a peaceful one. Are you up for it?" The back of Jordan's eyes burned at the way Alexie's soul cracked before him. Arcane had taught him to be a pillar of strength, *'We don't feel*

their pain, we carry it with us, we allow them weakness, but weakness is something we cannot afford.' Arcane had told him.

Alexie pulled his wife's terrified and broken body into his lap, sitting on the ground, wiping her hair from where her eyes used to be. Jordan pulled Pierce away from the two to give them a private goodbye.

Pierce looked at him, tears streaming down his face, still welling in his arctic eyes. "What happened?" Jordan whispered to his friend.

"I would like to know the answer to that myself." A thick voice boomed around the room. Arcane knelt beside the weeping Alexie; Satrai's body had gone still, and Arcane's hand was on Alexie's shoulder. "Congratulations on your success today, and I am sorry for your loss. Follow my people, and they will give you a more private place to grieve." Uniformed medics made their way into the room and carefully lifted Satrai's body onto a stretcher, covering her. Alexie held the railing of the bed as it left the room, never glancing back at them.

"Jordan, respectable job blocking her pain. I cannot fathom the discomfort you saved that poor girl." Arcane was a large, uncompromising man. He felt every mistake was an opportunity to assign blame. Blame that usually fell to Pierce. "So, what happened?" he prompted, puffing out his chest and placing a hand on each hip as if he had caught them stealing sweets and not walked in on the death of a trainee.

Jordan spoke up as Pierce shrank away, still not done processing what he had just seen. "Alexie took to transporting much more easily. It is my suspicion this ability will be one where compatibility plays a large role. Satrai reacted in a way we could not have expected." Arcane nodded his head.

"Who was training her?" he asked the inevitable question, and Pierce flinched. "Ah, I see." Arcane blew out a long breath.

"She was working with me," Pierce said, stepping forward. Jordan didn't back down, wanting to lend strength to his friend.

"Was she displaying any struggle to suggest this ability

would not be one she could complete?" Arcane's question was harsh, but his tone was flat and inquisitive.

"She was struggling with the first exercise but completed the second easily. She was confident and wanted to try." Pierce was in no place to answer questions. He was shaken and ashamed. He lost someone he felt responsible for, and Jordan had lost trainees too. Messing with magic was dangerous, but Pierce didn't need to be grilled.

"Arcane," Jordan interceded. "This ability is one not even you know how to do. It is experimental. Pierce just lost his first trainee; he will have more constructive answers if given some time to process. We will write up a report and get it to you soon. For now, please release us for the day." Arcane nodded in agreement and slight pride at the straight tone of Jordan's voice.

"Yes, you have a point. But do not go too easily on him. The failure of the student is the burden of the teacher. This will be his burden to carry; you cannot carry this weight for him. Pierce, this will help prepare you for greatness; tragedy is inevitable on any great man's path. Right?" Pierce nodded, not meeting his father's eyes. Arcane turned from them and left the room, and Pierce fell to his knees, releasing the tears he had held in his father's presence.

"Cold bastard," Jordan said, pulling his friend into a hug. "Shit happens, Pierce. This wasn't your fault." Pierce pushed off Jordan, hands on each shoulder, when a force pushed itself into Jordan, a force filled with grief and shame. The emotions ebbed from Pierce's hands, and Jordan pulled away, startled.

"What just happened?" Pierce's eyes were wide as he regarded his own hands and Jordan's shocked composure.

"Pierce. I-I think you're an Empath." They stared at each other wide-eyed. Empathic abilities had been outlawed by Arcane. He thought the gifts were invasive and unnatural.

"Don't tell Arcane," they said in unison, both gulping and feeling some relief that they were on the same page.

"If these abilities are manifesting, they will need some work. I will tell Arcane we are taking a holiday and we can go to Middle Earth, and you can practice on Mortals. I'll help you." Jordan placed a reassuring hand on Pierce's shoulder.

"What if Father denies our vacation request?"

"He is always telling me I need to take charge and act more like a leader. Well, leaders don't ask permission for a break; they advise of their upcoming absence."

***

Jordan had Christine propped up on the counter as he inspected the mark indicating where the knife wound had been. The skin was healed over, and he could sense that internally it was healing nicely. Amy sat, fingers on her lips, impatiently waiting for the verdict.

"She is fine." He squeezed her sides and kissed her forehead. Amy let out a long-held sigh.

"Yay, I live to see another day!" Amy exclaimed with a half-kidding smile.

"Why does my healing stab wound mean you get to keep on living?" Christine asked. Amy's eyes darted to a distracted Jordan who was punching something into his phone.

"Jordan knows better than to hurt you. I'd come back from the dead just to smite him." Jordan just laughed at her threat.

A full day and night had passed since Christine was stabbed. She spent most of it in and out of consciousness as she healed, and Amy spent most of yesterday assisting in the family's relocation to Germany.

"If we are going back to Hell, can I at least say goodbye to Evan this time? I kinda blew him off yesterday. He is probably assuming I'm dead."

"No, he isn't. Amy let him know you couldn't make it. We need to help a few friends pack up before moving anyway. You could meet him tomorrow evening after we spend the day with them." Amy and Christine stared at him blankly.

"You have friends?"

He feigned hurt. "Yes, I have friends. And it will be safer for them in Hell for a while. They aren't thrilled about it, but have been begging me to meet you, so you are my way of softening the blow." Christine and Amy exchanged confused looks, seeing if the other was keeping up at all.

"Who? Mortals?" Jordan raised his brows at the stupidity of the question.

"Cyx and Fritz have been on Earth for a while. They prefer the comforts of the mortal realm." Christine jumped excitedly from the counter and clapped her hands together.

"I have read about them! The fates? We are going to help the Fates pack? This is so cool!" She was dancing around excitedly as Amy looked on with jealousy. Christine paused, "Wait, just Cyx and Fritz? I thought they had a brother.... Uh, what was his name? NO. Wait, don't tell me, I know this... Elix!"

"Does Elix live on his own?" Amy asked.

"No, Elix doesn't live on his own. And don't ask his sisters about him. They will get upset, and we have too much to do for that."

Christine fiddled with her hair. "Why would they want to meet me? Don't they kinda hate Pierce for taking their abilities away?" Christine asked.

She had several lessons on the Fates. They had once been burdened with a life in service to the fates of all Mortals, assisting in predicting large-scale events and helping determine the best way to negate them. When they fled with Jordan, Pierce had taken their ability to manipulate Fate in penance for abandoning the people. Christine figured they wouldn't be her biggest fans since, as far as anyone knew, she was tied to Pierce.

"They do hate him. But not for the reasons you think. To manipulate fate and pull forth large-scale premonitions, all three siblings had to work together. On the day of the uprising, Pierce killed Elix. He stole their brother from them; that is why they hate him." His words lacked venom, and telling them seemed to drain him. Christine could tell Elix's loss was one Jordan felt responsible for based on the slump of his shoulders and the raw tone of his voice.

"I won't bring it up," she reassured him. "But can Amy come?" Jordan looked at a very still Amy.

"Fiiiine." The two women jabbered excitedly at the prospect of meeting some of the most influential people who had ever lived, and Jordan enjoyed their enthusiasm. The Fates were two of his favorite people, and he looked forward to introducing them to Christine, the woman they had all worked together so many years ago to empower and protect, blindly putting her in more danger.

"If all that is happening tomorrow, what is on the agenda for today?" Christine asked.

"Well, you are well enough to train, so you will spend a good chunk of your day working with me on glamor and enhancing your offensive strategy. Then we will spend the evening together."

"What happened to Amy training me?"

"Well, you may be healing well, but I have not gotten to a place where I am comfortable having you out of my sight, and I have other work for her." He glanced at Amy, who had a coffee-soaked donut hanging above her mouth and was not paying attention. Both Jordan and Christine smirked at her.

Amy caught their glances, her cheeks puffed out like a hamster, and she swallowed her treat self-consciously.

"What? They don't have Krispy Kreme's back home, and I love them; besides, I need the calories. I've bumped my three-mile morning run to five to combat some of this double spy stress."

Her arms crossed, and she jutted out a proud chin, and she found it both unsettling and adorable when Jordan and Christine both put their arms up in surrender; Christine shot hers down upon noticing their mirrored reactions.

"So 'Jordano,' what work am I in for today?" Amy asked, standing from her stool and stretching. Both Christine and Jordan were giving her questioning looks.

"Jordano?" they asked in unison.

"Yeah. I feel like you need a nickname. Jordan is so rigid. What, Jordano not doin' it for ya? Hmm, How about J-man? J-dog? No, that's too 90s rapper. Skipper? I don't know; I'll workshop it." Jordan rubbed his temples as Christine cackled.

"Skipper. Yup, that's the one!" Christine laughed, slapping her thighs. Amy shrugged her shoulders at Jordan's unamused expression. "Could be worse, she calls Evan 'Hombre,'" Christine warned.

"Anyways," he said, changing the subject.

"Do you think you can get these to the different council members? It may be tricky with them being scattered around the different territories, but there should be a summit soon. I've enchanted the training room, so you should be able to enter it as a bridge from Heaven into Hell. Thad can meet you there to bring you in on some other projects if you're interested."

Amy beamed at the trust he was instilling in her.

"Very interested. I haven't been able to spend much time in Hell, and the people there fascinate me. I'm happy to use my unique position to help you gather info, but anything to get me away from this double-edged sword I'm walking on would be much appreciated."

"I figured. This should be the last thing I need you to do. I want you stationed in Hell while this all goes down. You will be safest there." Holding out a manilla envelope to her, he held onto it as she tried to take it. "It will be best if they don't know these came from you. So, deliver them and get out. We'll see you tomorrow." With a confirmation nod, he released the envelope.

The easy air in the room had hardened with the serious timbre to Jordan's voice. This job was risky enough that he was concerned, which raised the anxiety of both the women in the room with him.

Christine wasn't afraid that Amy was in any physical danger, but she did know that, technically speaking, this would be an act of treason. If caught, she would be imprisoned and stand trial, where Pierce would be the Judge and Jury.

"Well, I better get this out of the way. I'll see you both tomorrow." Amy ran and hugged Christine goodbye, then hastily left. She had never liked goodbyes, but the look they exchanged before she closed the door said more than words ever could.

***

Jordan and Christine spent hours sitting at the countertop drinking coffee, laughing, and working on glamor techniques. The more they worked on it, the more she was surprised that she hadn't started her training with this, even if just to boost her confidence. Compared to the other things she had been taught, this felt easy.

He started her on small stuff first. One of his favorites was color manipulation, and he had a great idea for her first task.

She sat impatiently, shifting around on the bar stool as he disappeared and reappeared a few times, setting up lights, mirrors, and an array of paint sample slips with various colors before landing behind her and kissing the back of her head.

He pushed her hair so that it draped in front of her shoulders and then selected a mint green color pallet and placed it in front of her.

"When you were growing up and wanted to dye your hair green, what color were you thinking?"

Realization dawned on her slowly. Reaching out, she picked up the pallet, and the soft widening of her smile hit him from the reflection, nearly melting him. Once he had stopped admiring her lips, he met her questioning gaze.

"Amy told you about that?"

"She did. Once I learned what her placement in your life had been, I asked for any corrections to you Pierce had requested. I got more than I bargained for by asking her. She rambled out everything within one breath. I had to tell her to slow down a good three times to get any actual coherent information from her. I made a mental note to show you this trick first."

'Heh, sounds like Amy,' she thought, laughing in her head at the scene playing out in her imagination.

"This one," she said, pointing to a bright green sherbet-like chunk in the strips of green on the sample resting in front of her.

"Subtle tastes, I see," he joked, raising a brow.

"Now, this should come easy to you. The key to this is not overthinking it. Simply imagine you are looking in a mirror, like these," he said, motioning to the random assortment of little vanity mirrors he had set up in front of her.

"Feel free to use them. We will take them away once you get the color right and see if you can hold the illusion. Focus on the energy surrounding the area you want to change; for this exercise, your beautiful hair. Then picture it turning into this color and hold that image in your mind. Ready?" She nodded yes.

Squinting into the mirror, she tried to feel the air around her until she could feel the buzzing of the world warping around her. Once her grasp on the buzzing was firm, she focused on that feeling on the energy wrapping around, in, and all throughout the strands of her hair. While looking in the mirror, she imagined the color change starting at the root and squeaked, jumping in shock when the roots of her hair sparked green.

Jordan was enjoying everything about this. From her hyper-focused eyes, scrunched nose, the excited little hop off her seat she did when her hair had begun changing. He especially loved the way she scooted closer to the mirror, concentrating harder when she lost the illusion in her excitement and was trying to call the color back.

"Look, I did it!" She shook her now sherbet-green hair and ran her fingers through it. "It looks terrible! I love it!" she exclaimed, laughing and kicking her feet back, attempting to throw herself against the back of her chair.

Forgetting, of course, that she was sitting on a counter stool that had no back, sending herself flailing toward the ground. Jordan transported underneath her, catching her with his body, and they both lay in a tangle laughing for a few minutes.

Her hair was back to its normal brown mess of waves and curls, and she had a sparkle in her eyes that he wanted to chase, catch and bottle to get high on later.

He helped her up and flipped the mirrors, having her replicate the task, which she accomplished easily. Then moved on to skin, nail, and eye color distortion, which she again mastered quickly.

With each test, he gained unnerving confidence that his alarming theory on her inclination was accurate. They would know soon enough. He planned to ask the fates for their opinion, desperately hoping he remembered wrong and she wasn't what he thought she was.

Facial reconfiguration was a bit more challenging, as it was for everyone. She noticed quickly how much easier it was to change color or add to her features, such as lengthening her nose or hair, but taking away from them was an entirely different challenge. After successfully evening her skin tone to remove the appearance of freckles, she chuckled, stating how useful this skill would have been during puberty, earning a laugh from Jordan too.

"You have a firm grasp on glamor. I think it's time we work on your offensive skills," he said, popping up here and there, returning the mirrors to their original location in the two bathrooms on each side of the large penthouse.

"Here?" The thought of doing any kind of ability-based

sparring in his super fancy penthouse seemed like a terrible idea.

"Yeah, this will be fine. We aren't really using any abilities today. What I want you to work on is being more attuned with your opponent, reading the way they move, their body language, so that you know the best way to strike."

This intrigued her. She had spent so much energy and time working on defense and what she was doing that it had been a while since she had fought with that sort of mindset.

"Even so, I don't want to break anything in here," she said, cocking a hip.

She shot him curious glances as he pushed one of the large couches out of the way. Shoving it against the wall, then grabbing a remote from in between one of the cushions. Christine glanced, confused, to the TV stand, where the actual remote for it rested.

Shooting her a devilish grin, he hit the power button. A languid music vibrated through the penthouse.

Jordan extended a hand to her. Her initial response was a very unattractive and exasperated groan.

"Nope. No. Absolutely not," she said, waving her hand and backing away. "You are not actually asking me to dance. I strongly prefer fighting."

"That doesn't surprise me in the least, but nothing will help you understand reading an opponent's movements and energies like dancing, so get over here," he said, curling his fingers and motioning her over.

"Seriously, no. My only attempts at dancing have been awkward and ended in many a bruised toe." She crossed her arms stubbornly.

"Probably because you haven't found a partner you are comfortable enough with to allow them to lead." He teleported behind her and slowly slid his hands down her crossed arms, lowering his head to whisper in her ear.

"Trust me, Goddess." She relaxed a little and let him lead

her to the open space of the cleared-out living room. "You need to loosen up. Here, let's try something a bit less formal." He hit another button; the song changed to one more uptempo by one of her favorite bands.

Jordan grinned and grabbed each of her hands. Pulling one forward at a time, he swayed her to the quick beat. Her shy smile spread to its full power; he could tell she was responding to him without thinking about it. He spun her back against him, swaying with her back pushed against his torso.

"See. You can feel my energy. Almost sense how I'm going to move before I do, right?" Then he kissed her neck and spun her back away from him, wiggling his shoulders playfully.

"I do see. How did I never know this?" Jordan shrugged. He wasn't sure if this was a well-known thing.

"Now, keep this feeling and see if you can guess what I'm going to do." He spun as she continued to move with him; she could feel his energy shifting to transport. She twirled to wrap her arms around him as he appeared behind her. "Perfect. You're a quick study," he said.

"Or you're just one Hell of a teacher," she said, grinning at her own pun. He cupped her smiling face in his hands. Both thumbs grazed her visible dimples; his smile had never been more comfortable as he bent to taste the lingering sweetness of laughter on her lips. They both reveled in the peace of the moment and all it promised of the future.

After pulling away, she saw that his smile had turned mischievous. He scooped her into his arms and carried her to their bedroom, thinking he had the perfect test to see if she had really learned how to predict his movements.

Several hours later, they lay in bed, her head resting on his. She wasn't sure where the words came from or why her mind was suddenly pulled from this wonderful moment. Perhaps it was the fact that she was feeling nothing but bliss while knowing Pierce was likely suffering at their separation.

It wasn't long ago she was going to marry Pierce, and now,

she felt completely at home in Jordan's arms. Before she could think better of it, a completely out-of-place question escaped her still-tingling lips.

"Are you still going to murder Pierce? Do you need to dethrone him? Is this not enough?" Jordan's wistful state turned to stone; he pulled away from her to look down into her eyes.

Taking a deep breath and giving her one of his more resolute looks, he answered a plain and simple "Yes."

She pulled off the bed and stomped over to the window, letting go a frustrated sigh and crossing her arms over her chest. Jordan took a second to appreciate how beautiful she looked standing there.

The moonlight was casting an incandescent glow across her speckle-patterned skin. Her hair was loosely bound in a big messy bun, allowing curls to dangle around her face. All she wore was one of his black shirts; it flattered her full figure like a little black dress. Too soon, that second was over as she turned the fire in her eyes in his direction.

"Stop looking at me like that," he said lightly. "Your perception of him is more than a little skewed. I know him better than you, and I know how serious of a threat he poses if left alive. This is a war. One he started, and I'll remind you, in war, there is always death."

Christine took a deep breath and exhaled through her nose. Hoping that calming herself would allow her to better articulate why what he was saying was asinine.

"The consequences of War are determined by the individuals leading it. You are making a choice to kill a good man, a kind leader, and justifying it by acting like there is no choice. It IS a choice, one that YOU get to make." Jordan's jaw set.

"You have no idea what kind of man or leader he is, Christine. All you have seen of him is what he wanted you to see, the image of himself he crafted specifically for you. It was all a manipulation. He is such a poor ruler that the leaders of his people have reached out to me asking for help; they are dying.

Under my reign, do you know how many people died during a given year from natural disasters? None. How many do you think they have averaged since Pierce inserted himself into the role? Thousands." He sounded desperate as he continued on, pleading with her to heed his warning.

"Furthermore, what kind of good man could hold you hostage? Knowing full well you were uncomfortable with him while manipulating you into thinking you were rightfully his and had no say in the matter?!" His voice was raised now, his control slipping, the anger he felt with Pierce bubbling over.

Christine knew he wasn't speaking directly to her, but that only chafed her irritation. He approached these arguments as if she were a pawn in Pierce's scheme and not a person.

Her voice was soft and very, very dangerous. "Manipulate me? How did he manipulate me? Did he scar my chest in order to literally control my energy levels and deter me from running away or face excruciating pain? Did he threaten me into submission with an innocent's life? No. That was you. Pierce was consistently kind, patient, and gentle with me. Can you say the same?"

Through narrowed eyes, he measured his next words. "I have always been, and always will be authentically me with you; faults and all. Pierce worked very hard to craft an image of who he thought you wanted him to be, and it worked. It was a strategy. It is what he does. The minute he discovers that strategy isn't enough, it will change. I desperately hope I have the chance to anger you before he does in that scenario. Because I choose your anger at me over you discovering just how twisted the real Pierce is when he accepts his current manipulation will not get him what he wants." The tired look under his eyes took the wind out of her sails.

She suspected he may be correct, but she wanted him to be wrong for so many reasons. He truly had been patient and kind with her. Having access to information now started to add suspicion towards Pierce, though she couldn't deny it.

Too many times he spoke publicly about their 'relationship' in far too gracious a manner. She had even read a current article that Pierce had been overheard telling someone he had proposed to her, and that she had accepted, before Jordan stole her away to Hell. But tabloids could be fictitious in any world; she felt she owed Pierce the benefit of the doubt.

"Part of me wants to tell you to shove it," she sighed, sauntering towards him. "But the other part appreciates your concern for me. I'm not used to someone trying to convince me of their argument. Thank you for fighting with me instead of dismissing my concern," she finished, pushing his sitting frame back onto the bed and crawling on top of him.

With a disbelieving shake of his head and a widening smile, she could see the irritation leave Jordan as he caressed her hips with his hands, pulling her closer to him.

"Debating is not really fighting," he whispered into her neck, playfully biting the soft skin. "Fighting is when you are trying to hurt the other. You used your different perspective and hard truths to attempt to make me see things the way you do... You failed. But, it was a good try, and I'll never retain malice towards you for defending your beliefs." His nose traced up to her earlobe, and electricity shot up her legs at the feeling of his breath in her ear.

She giggled as his hand reached up the back of her shirt and grazed the skin tickling her softly.

"Well, I think you're wrong. But, if ever in the situation where I have to make the choice, I will tread carefully for you." Warmth filled him. Pulling back, he searched her face for any hint of deceit; he didn't want her simply appeasing him, not with this.

Finding none, he cupped her face and ran a thumb appreciatively along her dimpled cheek before pulling her into a heated kiss, sliding her below him, and showing her his appreciation the best way he knew how.

17

EARLY BIRD BENEFITS

"Good morning!" Amy's voice pinged off the marble in the penthouse like a bouncy ball, ricocheting dangerously off each surface as Jordan groaned from bed, Christine curled up against him, one of her arms hugging his chest. He was overly warm, and she clung to him like a frightened cat, occasionally digging her nails into him, but he didn't have the heart to push her away.

Their bed was large and luxurious; it satisfied him to know that he now had an actual use for it. Before Christine came into his life, he considered sleep optional. He could easily go days without it, but once he passed a certain limit, he became agitated, and his powers would become unreliable. So, he averaged around three or four hours a night.

Now though, he had her. And one of his greatest pleasures in life was being curled up in any of their beds, with her either on, below, or beside him. There was nothing more soothing than feeling her warmth mixing with his in the way only resting bodies did.

He glanced at the door to their room and moved his head, causing it to swing shut to avoid Amy walking in on them. Neither of them had any clothes on, and he wanted to attempt to wake Christine gently, which was not always possible because she was not a morning person.

He usually had no qualms about letting her rest until her natural clock woke her up. She was a night soul, but today she had a lot happening; she wouldn't want to miss any of it.

"Goddess, Amy is here." He slowly turned to her, breaking her hold on him. Her eyes squeezed shut tighter; he felt his heart constrict a little as she burrowed into his side to hide from the fate of morning.

Chuckling, he moved her hair out of her face and ran a hand down the length of her body. He pecked her nose, eyes, cheeks, and each side of her mouth with a kiss before whispering to her again.

"It is time to rise, stubborn, little Goddess. Come on; you're breaking my heart." He kissed her again.

She flipped around, grabbed the covers and buried herself in them, twirling like a little hurricane of silk. He smiled, pulling the covers away. "You get to meet the fates today," he cooed. With that, her eyes shot open; she almost smashed her forehead into his as she sat up so quickly.

"Guys, wake the fudge up already; I have coffee!" Amy called from the kitchen. Christine moved to get out of bed after smiling sweetly at him. He met that sweet smile with a mischievous one as he grabbed her arm, pulling her back to bed and beneath him.

"She can wait. I don't even know how she got in here. I took her key away when we moved in. I already know she completed the task I gave her," he said, running his nose up her neck, "Come on, I spent all night missing you; we need to get reacquainted. We can try something new, try to be quiet..." He appreciated the way her blush ran from her chest up her neck as giggles escaped her.

The path that blush took was a shadow engulfing the freckles of her cheeks. He leaned forward, intent on tasting the heat of that trail and encouraging it. To his amusement, she placed a hand on his chest, halting him.

"Jordan... You can go one morning without me; I need coffee if I'm gonna be up this early," she said, not really having the conviction to go further in stopping him.

"Hmm, you are *my* preferred morning drink, darling. Is it fair that I go without?" She laughed against his soft kisses and opened to him, wrapping her arms around his neck and happily reciprocating his kiss.

Body going still, he pulled away from her, listening intently. The muscles of his jaw strained. Unease dripped down her spine at his change in demeanor.

"Everything's fine. Just more than Amy has shown up uninvited this morning. Get dressed; I will be right back." He transported off her to the closet, dressing quickly in a suit with no jacket. As he tightened his tie, he warned her she may want to stay in the bedroom.

Her immediate assumption was that Kielius must have shown up. But something didn't sit well with that. If he was here, it was more than likely Thad was as well; Jordan wouldn't be interrupted if Thad were here to contain whatever problem had popped up.

Since he didn't specifically order her to stay put, she decided the waiting expresso was worth the discomfort of whoever had come to visit that had Jordan so frazzled. Negating makeup since she was severely out of the practice of wearing any, she decided to attempt to hold glamor for a while today to practice instead, focusing on imagining subtle eyeliner, eyeshadow, mascara, and a rosy lip shade.

Since being back on Middle Earth, Jordan had given her free reign over her wardrobe, with a few things he had picked out sprinkled in as options but not requirements. She couldn't deny he had excellent taste.

She pulled on a pair of tight dark skinny jeans and a purple V-neck that flattered her waist and made her very average chest seem a bit bigger. Everything she was wearing were things he had picked out. She decided it would be great payback for him getting her excited this morning only to leave her.

Using long hair pins that resembled fancy chopsticks, she twirled her hair up and off her shoulders. Little strands of curls were escaping and highlighting her neck and face.

She had always loved these things. It made her feel like she was in one of the old kung-fu action movies she loved. She liked to imagine herself taking them out and using them as weapons and told Jordan as much.

He had looked at her like she was terrifying, crazy, and the sexiest thing he had ever seen when she told him it was a dream of hers to have some made that concealed daggers.

Feeling triumphant in crafting a look that would torture her devil, she strode from the bedroom feeling ready to face the day and show Jordan he didn't need to protect her from unwanted guests; she could handle them herself.

She barely got to register Jordan's satisfying reaction to her appearance upon entering the kitchen. Her confidence died in her throat as she met Savious's sharp eyes, slicing her with their very gaze.

Her lungs filled with ice, frozen in place, facing the kitchen. Her mom's empty eyes and the deafening crack of her neck flashed through her mind, along with the sight of her dad's body sprawled against a broken support beam.

It's okay, Krissy, everything will be just fine...

Jordan winced at the painful shock in Christine's eyes. Knowing now that all of Christine's emotions regarding the trauma his father had caused her had been repressed. Thus, to her, the trauma was fresh, real and raw. He had demanded his father stay away, for Christine's sake, but today Savious had decided to push his luck.

"There are other people in the building below us, so try and keep a lid on it," Amy whispered. It was enough to jar Christine from her frozen shock.

Amy handed her a steaming cappuccino in a fancy cup that

was made for specialty coffee. She must have brought these with her as a surprise.

Savious wasn't the only unexpected member of Jordan's family in attendance this morning as Thad stood on one side of Savious and Jordan on the other. Neither of Savious's sons seemed comfortable with his presence. Christine's hand shook; some of the coffee spilt, causing her to curse and Amy to take the cup back from her.

Savious glanced at her shaking hands, sliding his eyes up her body, hesitating on the visible mark, then meeting her eyes again, grinning. His grin was one the love of her life often wore, but his was dripping with malice; she wanted to cut it off his face.

"What are you doing here?" Christine demanded, snatching her coffee back and walking to sit at the table with Amy. She tried to sound indifferent but failed miserably as the words came out so bitter she could taste the spite.

"Don't." Jordan raised a hand, halting Savious's response. "You have no right to speak with her. Leave now, or I will escort you home myself."

She didn't know why but this annoyed her. This slime ball killed her parents; she wanted him to know she didn't fear him anymore. She needed him to know he couldn't shake her, even if her hands were literally shaking.

"Jordan, please. I asked him a question; I want an answer from him. You don't need to protect me from him. I managed to protect myself just fine, even when I thought I was mortal. Remember?" Savious's grin fell, and Thad snorted.

"I'll ask again. What are you doing here?"

Savious tilted his head and leaned back against the counter, assessing her as Jordan crossed his arms and nodded at him as if giving him permission to speak.

"I was here to see my son and touch base on a few things about a war he seems to have forgotten has started. I can understand the distraction. You have always been a cute little thing, but power suits you. Have you taught her your good tricks yet?"

The compliment buried in his words was said in a way that was meant to sound like an insult, and it worked. Jordan's eyes narrowed dangerously, making it clear to Christine that Savious was hinting at something Jordan didn't want her to know. She made a mental note to ask him later.

"We will finish this discussion tonight when I come home for our pre-scheduled meeting. Now leave," Jordan demanded. In response Savious stood, flashing her a toothy smile that practically dripped with animosity.

"I also thought I would let you know I spoke with poor Pierce. You left that boy in shambles; you could at least let him know you don't want to be found," Savious said as he transported from the room, leaving a plume of black smoke.

Everyone in the room knew the smoke was not a natural occurrence with transporting, but like his son, Savious had a flair for the dramatic. Jordan walked to where Christine sat at the long dining table they hadn't yet used and stood behind her, placing his hands on her shoulders and rubbing them softly.

"Well, that was interesting," Thad mentioned, pouring himself some cereal and leaning against the counter. "When are we supposed to be at your ladies' house?" he asked Jordan.

"They are going to be annoyed with me regardless of when we show up, so there is no rush. Moving is a quick process when I am assisting," Jordan answered, teleporting to where Thad stood.

He grabbed Thad's bowl of cereal and his spoon before teleporting back to the table. Leaning over, he kissed the side of Christine's head, making eye contact with Thad and putting a large spoonful of cereal in his mouth. Thad just glared back at him as he got another bowl and spoon and pulled the milk back out of the fridge.

A timer rang out; Jordan dropped his spoon into the now

empty bowl and transported to the sink, depositing it. Then he pulled a little pan off the stovetop, pouring it into a new bowl with dried cranberries and sliced banana.

He grabbed a new spoon and walked back to the table, setting it down in front of Christine. She had been staring at her hands, resting on the tabletop ever since Savious had departed; Amy stared at her tensely as if waiting for her to snap.

She snapped out of it and looked around a little, grabbing the hand Jordan had placed on her shoulder and squeezing it. He knew she didn't like cereal in the morning.

She found it sweet that he had made a point of having groceries delivered to accommodate her preferences without making a big show of it. There was no "Did you see what I got for you?" or any sort of expected praise, he was thoughtful just for the sake of being thoughtful; she loved it.

Amy was smiling at them while Thad looked like he had swallowed a pill that had broken in his mouth, the bitter medicine coating his tongue.

"Any chance I can help them pack boxes and NOT have to transport anything to Hell?" Thad's question was innocent, but Jordan's sardonic reaction told them there was something more to this than they knew.

"You need the practice. Just don't freak yourself out, and you'll be fine," Jordan said, struggling to suppress a laugh. The women in the room glanced at each other and then back and forth between the brothers questioningly.

"Do you have something against transporting?" Amy asked after signaling down Thad.

"It is not something I do unless I need to. Unlike Jordan over here, it isn't something that I naturally thrive at, and it's dangerous. Not to mention, not all of us are so showy."

Jordan's smile was pinched; his restraint in holding back his amusement was evident as he responded. "If you were incompatible, you would have died. No need to get *short* with me," Thad's face reddened.

"It isn't funny."

Both Christine and Amy looked at Jordan, who was focused on Thad, prompting him with his eyes to explain.

"Training can be dangerous, and some skills are riskier than others. Transporting being at the top of that list. I had an incident while Jordan trained me, and I have tried to limit my need to transport as much as possible as a result," Thad explained plainly, taking a sip of his coffee. "Shouldn't we be on our way?"

"Wait, what was the 'incident'? Pierce told me about him and Jordan creating the skill. If his recollection is correct, Jordan stunned himself so badly the first time he couldn't talk or breathe for like a minute. Like someone had taken a bat to your stomach," Christine teased, poking him in the ribs lightly.

"Ah, did he leave out that he managed to lose an eyebrow," Jordan added. Amy and Christine started cracking up at this.

"How long did it take it to grow back?!" asked Amy in between her laughs, imagining appearance-obsessed Pierce missing an eyebrow and how crazed that would have made him.

"Last I knew, it didn't. He's constantly glamoring the appearance of the missing one," Jordan said, snickering; even Thad had forgotten his irritation and grinned until the laughter slowed. The woman looked back to him, smiles wide and expectant.

"Fine!" he exclaimed, setting his cup down a little too hard. "I was doing well in training. The first part of my jump went smoothly; I reappeared correctly. Somehow, I lost three inches." He waved his hand dismissively in the air.

"Three inches off what?!" Amy asked, looking downright remorseful.

Jordan had just taken a swig of his coffee; it shot down the wrong tube in his throat at that question, causing him to go into a coughing/laughing fit. He failed to regain his composure and began hitting his hand against the table, covering his face with the other.

Thad's face turned a sickly shade of green as he registered the meaning behind her question. Christine was patting Jordan's back since he was half choking on the coffee, half laughing still and shook her head at him, trying to distract herself to avoid laughing at Thad too.

"My height, Amy. My height! I wouldn't tell any of you if I had lost inches elsewhere. For the love of the Gods on high, how did your mind go *there*?" He shifted uncomfortably, looking positively disturbed.

"Really, though, you got shorter. How does that even happen?" Amy asked incredulously.

"No idea. Magic isn't science. I lost focus, and that was enough for me to become the shortest brother," Thad said, looking to the distance dramatically, as if remembering back to a better time.

"You were never taller than me." Jordan's brows raised in response to Thad's drama as he tidied up the kitchen and adjusted his sleeves. He shot Christine an appreciative wink when he caught her admiring his forearms in the process. Amy caught the moment and warmed, watching her friend wriggle girlishly at being caught.

It made Amy feel like the risk she was taking was worth it. Seeing Christine exist outside of a state of fear and dread gave her mission a personal purpose; even if Pierce isn't a bad guy, Jordan has definitely done more to coax the real Christine back to life in these last few months than Pierce had in years.

"Maybe not, but I wasn't shorter than our little toad." Jordan nodded his head agreeing.

"Okay, ladies, ready to go?" Jordan held out the travel mug to Christine.

He pulled her to him instead of allowing her to take the mug and hugged her with one arm, pressing a soft kiss to her forehead.

Only after enjoying the peaceful moment, he extended an

arm to Amy. "Would you also like a lift?" he asked her.

"Since I have no idea where we are going, yes," she said, locking arms with him.

"How about you?" Amy asked Thad jokingly. Thad looked at his brother and took in the sight. It was weird and pleasant at the same time.

His rigid, often cold brother was chuckling and smiling with an angel on each arm. He never thought he would see a sight like this, but it gave him solace to see Jordan enjoying his own life while working so hard to improve everyone else's.

"As he said, I need practice," Thad snarked, and with that, he vanished. The three chuckled as they followed suit, transporting to the Fates' estate.

***

Pierce had paid a visit to each of the territories of Heaven in the last few days. Apologizing for his absence and making a point of being as candid as possible regarding the effect Christine's loss was having on him. The only one of his representatives that didn't seem to exude any empathy towards him in this matter was Hinto.

Hinto had delicate and elf-like qualities to her features. They daintily rested on a beautiful complexion of night-colored skin that was starred with white freckles along her cheekbones. To many, she was considered the most beautiful amongst the Angelicans, and she knew it.

This fact deepened her irritation at Pierce's consistent rejection of her advances. She had loved Pierce long before Christine had even been born and didn't appreciate how unfair the situation was.

The people loved her. She was a strong voice for them in all ways. Due to Pierce's recent distraction, she had the opportunity to step up and lead council meetings, giving her territory a leg up in any needed supplies and a higher sense of priority than the others.

The territory she represented, Asmal, was Pierce's least favorite to visit. He found the heat overwhelming and considered the deserts and tropical beaches to be useless land. It didn't provide anything; therefore he did not see its value.

That aside, Pierce knew he was alone in his distaste for the tropical as when asked, the other council members often voted to have any needed summits in one of the more tropical regions of Asmal so that they could bring their families and make a vacation out of it; relaxing and enjoying time in the sun and the warmth.

It was possible, Pierce considered, that in itself was the reason he disliked the territory so much. It reminded him of a life he lived unburdened by the needs of others. When his life was his own and he trusted his friend to rule the people fairly and with honor.

This summit was no different. At the end of Pierce's circulation of the territories, he called a summit to gather and discuss findings and new structures. The representatives had chosen the summit to take place in Murcia, Asmal. A luxurious beach city with sweltering heat and crystal-clear water that Pierce didn't have time to cool off in.

The meeting had been, by all appearances, a success. Everyone had their best face on. Everyone acted as if all was well. Unfortunately for Pierce, he was an Empath and unable to delight in the false platitudes. Every one of the representatives was on edge. They were nervous. More alarmingly, each of them brought with them the weighted mist of guilt.

It had been a long time since he had struggled to keep others' emotions at bay. After discovering his abilities, he had traveled for years amongst the mortals of Middle Earth practicing and returned home to search for others like him in hopes of learning more. He found the help he needed. All it had cost him was his way of life, his father, and his closest friend.

Currently, he blamed Jordan for his lack of control. Taking Christine was effective in unbalancing him. The longer they were separated, the more Pierce felt like he was losing his mind. He had never known a worse torture than this particular unknown. If he could go back and smack some sense into himself, he would.

"Warn her about him. Warn her," he would scream the words in his own face if he could; in fact, he had in the mirror on several separate occasions.

A breathy feminine voice pulled Pierce from his unpleasant reverie. "I remember the boy who loved this city. Loved its taverns, its women, and its lack of modern technology, allowing him to escape the demands of his father," Hinto chimed, putting a thin arm around his waist, leaning on the balcony next to him, her gaze of the ocean joining his.

"I would fail to recognize that boy even if you dropped him in front of me equipped with a name tag," Pierce chuckled, gently removing her arm from his person, hating the way it made his skin go cold. It was like his body longed for Christine the same way his mind did and was punishing him for the time apart.

"I liked that boy," she pouted.

"That boy liked you. If I didn't love her so much, I would apologize that the man that boy grew into was bewitched in body and soul by another. But I wouldn't trade our intertwined fates for anything." He turned from the ocean and looked sincerely at Hinto.

She was unaware that he could feel the sting of his rejection radiating off her in sharp pinpricks. For a quick moment, he debated intervening to lessen her feeling of slight refrain, knowing she needed to feel these things in order to move on from them.

The emotion that truly interested him was the guilt she was drowning in. It was a delicate situation he often found himself in with his abilities. Knowing what someone was feeling without always knowing why could be difficult as a leader when you couldn't just ask without exposing yourself to being something people feared.

Today he found this problem even more grating. He needed to know what was causing everyone to feel this unbearable guilt in his presence.

'Were they planning to rebel? Did they know something they are keeping from me?' Worried thoughts bombarded him.

It was lucky in times like these that he had Victor. Victor had been his father's right hand and universally retained the respect of not only the people of this world but the leaders. Pierce had discovered in the early years of his rule that one of Victor's specialties was gathering as well as utilizing intel.

Often Pierce considered the only commodity of real value left from his father's reign was his right-hand man. Victor had practically raised him, and it felt like he saved his life on a daily basis with his invaluable guidance.

Jordan had received training and grooming to take over in private, so at the end of the day, Pierce had no idea what he was doing when he took over. No one would have been able to guess that, though, thanks to Victor.

"Has Jordan made any other moves against you?" Hinto asked, abruptly and intentionally changing the tone of the conversation.

"No."

She seemed to be waiting for elaboration, but he didn't have more to offer and felt no need to soften the response.

"How are you handling everything?" He shot her a look that said, 'did you really just ask that?' and she laughed.

"Seeing Jordan after all this time must have been difficult. No longer a friend or the man you dethroned, but a real enemy. I, for obvious reasons, have never been the most invested person in your relationship with Christine, but I was there to witness your friendship with Jordan. If you ask me, that was the real loss. You two had something special."

An annoying ache sprang up in his chest; he crushed it

down and stepped further away from her.

She took the opportunity to flip her long red hair over her shoulder, trading the spray of the Ocean for Pierce's dry disinterest by facing him directly.

Pierce tried to find the words to respond, but nothing he could muster would come out as anything but bitter, so he remained silent. She smiled triumphantly as if they were playing a game and she had just pulled the winning number.

"Pierce, do you have a moment?"

'Saved by Victor again.' He thought as his mentor poked his head out of the balcony door towards them.

"Excuse us, Hinto. Thank you for your concern; truly, you are a good friend," Pierce said, noting the feel of her guilt swelling as he said the words.

"Consider me your loyal friend and subject, my Lord," she said, curtseying and leaving the balcony, closing the door behind her.

"What did you find out?" Pierce asked, assuming Victor's presence wasn't just to save him from Hinto's advances.

"There has been activity with the doorway." Pierce stood up straighter, looking at Victor, hope rising in his eyes.

THE FATES

My breath caught in my throat at the sight we materialized in front of. I felt myself lean into Jordan, shaking him to make sure he was seeing what I was seeing. For some unknown reason, I had made the incorrect assumption that the fates lived in New York and was expecting to arrive in a condo similar to Jordan's. I could not have been more wrong.

We were standing in the most magnificent driveway I had ever seen on what looked like pressed red chalk. The stark brick color drew attention only slightly away from the rainbow assortment of colors lining the driveway, blocking the chalky substance from the perfectly manicured greenery beyond its borders. The large estate house in front of us was a mass of beautiful gray stone and wood accents, two storys high and complete with a large grand doorway resting in the middle.

Amy's voice pulled me from my gawking as she asked Jordan where we were. He shocked us both by disclosing we were in England at the Fates' primary and oldest Estate. For some reason, my nerves had begun to rise at the prospect of meeting the Fates.

While studying in Heaven, I had been so disappointed to

learn that they had fled with Jordan. After my lessons one day where I had discovered the Fates were real people, I had gotten it in my head that I would find a way to meet them; they could answer all my questions about the prophecy they had forecast.

I had practiced little conversations with them in my head. It had always seemed to me that meeting them would be a chance to get solid and unbiased answers. What the actual prophecy was, and why me? They may not have been the ones to weave my Fate, but they had foreseen enough of it to forecast my life to the people of Heaven and land me in this mess, so they had to know something that could help me make sense of it all.

Before having a chance to back out of possibly the most important first meeting of my life, the grand oak doors swung open. Two screaming middle-aged women came bursting through them. You would think they were being chased by a murderer with an ax by the way they were howling, but they bee lined to me immediately. It was only after they plowed me over and peppered me with kisses and hugs that I noticed Jordan had abandoned me, leaving me to the affectionate wolves.

Once the two of them came up for air, they continued to completely ignore Jordan and Amy and clasped hands together, the side of their heads resting together and admiring me like I was their long-lost puppy, who had finally wandered home to them after many years away.

There were no photos or matching descriptions of them that I could find while studying them in Heaven, thanks to Jordan, so I was truly seeing them for the first time. Both women were utterly eerie with profound beauty. Both had flawless midnight complexions and dazzling smiles, but that was where the similarities ended.

One sister stood at an average height and was rocking a shaved head that had white tattoos curling up her neck onto her scalp with long light silver chains hanging from the many piercings up her ears. She was decorated in every way but none of that distracted from the alarming liquid gold quality of her hard eyes.

In contrast, the other was at least 6'5" with dark forest green eyes and long straight hair cascading around her like a midnight version of one of the elves from Lord of the Rings. She seemed to have a softer way about her. There was an air of gracefulness that befell her I immediately admired.

"Christine..." they simultaneously sighed out my name with such reverence that the all too familiar discomfort of un-earned admiration crept up the back of my arms. Their tones were breathy and relaxed, like my name carried a sense of relief with it. I was already planning my apologies for being a total disappointment.

'How could they think I was anything special if they knew what was and what could be? I was literally almost just offed by a mortal with a diner steak knife.'

"We are being incredibly rude. I am so sorry, dear. I'm Cyx, and this is my sister Fritz. We have been looking forward to meeting you. You have been a subject of our premonitions since long before even Jordan was born, so please excuse our inappropriate leering."

'So the taller one is Cyx,' I noted. Not knowing a better response, I awkwardly waved and fumbled out a strained greeting. "Hiya, um, thanks, and it's nice to meet you?"

The two exchanged a look as if suppressing laughter at some inside joke. A tightness expanded into my chest caused by extreme discomfort with attention like this. Jordan, taking notice, appeared beside me and wrapped an arm around my waist in a demonstration of support and protection.

The two's grins grew wider.

"Okay, stand down, boy..." Fritz giggled jokingly, waving her hands at him and then patting his head lightly like he was an errant dog, turning his scowl into a look of exasperation.

"Please come in. We have so much to ask you, and words flow faster from sated lips. We can have tea and coffee brought in," Cyx appeased.

Jordan's head tilted forward with pinched, disapproving eyes.

"Ladies, we are not here for a tea party. You had better be packed."

They gave each other and then him non-committal glances that glinted with mischief in a way that had me smirking as we headed inside.

'At least I'm not the only one who likes to push his buttons.'

Not dropping his arm from around me, I got to enjoy the casual feel of him walking with me like this. Jordan led us inside and whispered loud enough that he knew the Fates would hear him.

"I know they are a bit *eccentric*, but they'll grow on you."

The inside of the mansion was no less gaudily extravagant than the outside had been. It looked like it had been furnished by a bored thirteenth-century housewife trying to prove her family's wealth and status. Before losing my parents, I had dreamed of traveling to Europe and touring places like this.

A dream I had forgotten until now; being here and seeing this, I couldn't help but think how much my mom would love the excess dripping from the very walls while my dad would be resisting the urge to touch everything.

The beautiful women motioned to a group of high-backed chairs that were red and decorated with elaborate blue patterns and gold trimming. The backs were taller than even Jordan sat; the tops of them were shaped like the outline of a crown.

I had the impression I would be swallowed up by one if I sat in it, not to mention sitting up that rigidly straight was a source of discomfort thanks to the stab wound still internally healing. They could not have looked less appealing.

Jordan's chair turned black as he sat down. Amy and I looked at each other, confirming we were both trying not to laugh at him. Forever the showman. The Fates watched me like I was some crazy and exotic creature as I stretched a little, then promptly sat on the ground to the side of Jordan, my legs splayed in front of me, resting back on my hands.

"What?" I asked at the amused looks I was getting. It was Cyx who responded.

"Oh, nothing. You are just too perfect for one another. Neither was compelled to stay within the bounds of what normal society would consider polite. One of you blatantly insults our taste in design by changing it, and the other sits on the floor. Adorable."

Cyx's words weren't laced in an admonishing tone, but I sat up a bit straighter anyway, a bit embarrassed. I was met with the feeling of Jordan's strong fingers landing on my shoulder, keeping me in place. A silent communication to me that in his world, I was to adjust for no one.

"Ladies. We both know you didn't design these; you found them. I also know you are snippy simply because we missed your lunch yesterday, but you can calm down. We didn't brush you off. Christine was stabbed."

Both Fates lowered the tea they had been sipping from mismatched porcelain cups and, with wide eyes, turned their hurt glares into worried shock as they pointed them at me, eyes examining me.

"She is still healing, and sitting up rigid, like these chairs would demand, causes her pain. Besides, I enjoy having her on the floor in front of me."

'Jackass,' I thought. He threw the last part in just for me, and in response, I willed the shoulder he had been softly gripping to sting him with heat; his mischievous grin told me he felt my retort, even if he didn't let go.

"Jordan, how could you allow her to be injured?" Fritz asked in an icy tone. I was suddenly bereft of Jordan's touch as his hand balled into a fist. He leaned forward, putting his elbows on his knees, expelling a long and seemingly painful breath.

You would think with how often people discussed me like I wasn't in the room, I would be used to it, but it still irritated me to no end. I ignored Amy and Jordan's amused glances as they read my expression, both knowing me well enough to know this was a trigger of mine.

"Well, 'her' is sitting right here, and contrary to everyone's beliefs, my mistakes are my own to make. Besides, you're a Fate; shouldn't you already know what happened?" I bit back, temporarily finding it difficult to understand why Jordan adored these two so much. Amy lit up, obviously just as curious about the Fates as I was. I grew a bit concerned and slightly guilty when their posture sagged in response to my question.

"Why would us being Fate's mean we would know how you managed to get stabbed while on Middle Earth? Has Pierce found you? If so, you shouldn't have come here you need to go home, where he cannot get ahold of you. YOU," Fritz directed the conversation back to Jordan. "Should know that." He nodded in agreement, accepting the scolding to Amy's immense surprise but not mine.

I knew this was a conversation he already had with himself. He felt very responsible for me. That was my biggest regret about the whole ordeal, making him think he failed me by giving me the freedom I had begged for.

"You're the Fates. Isn't your whole thing knowing the past, present, and future? Like, I know you used to be able to weave fate, so it's an easy assumption that you could tell what happened to me so recently," I explained, regretting each word as they came out of my mouth by the gloomy expressions fogging their features.

"We could. A long time ago. But we are shadows of our previous selves," Cyx said gently, placing a calming hand on her sister's rigid knee. They exchanged a look that held eons of struggle and loss that made me feel terrible for making assumptions about them.

"To answer your previous question, Christine ran into someone she used to know, and there was a confrontation. He surprised her by stabbing her, and she killed him," Amy said, chiming in for the first time.

Both the Fates nodded, content with the information and an awkward silence fell over the four of them while Jordan and the Fates were having a stare-down, like each of them was waiting for someone else to break first, none blinking.

After a few minutes of looking between them, I decided to intervene and clapped my hands loudly, startling the Fates. Jordan's nerves were obnoxiously sound; he didn't even flinch but did grin at me for making both the Fates jump.

"Fine. No, Jordan, we have not packed," Cyx said, crossing her arms.

"We decided there is no reason for us to leave," Fritz added, mirroring her sisters' crossed arms.

"Relocating isn't a request. You can either pack your own belongings, or I will have them packed for you. I am going to war, and you two are, whether you like it or not, mistaken for two of my largest assets." Neither woman backed down. Fritz's eyes sharpened with her annoyance.

"Listen here, child. We love you dearly, but do not begin operating under the illusion we are ignorant of war. Your first day of strife with him cost us everything. The only reason we have even agreed to relocate is that you agreed to prioritize balance by removing Pierce permanently from the scales."

Shock tore through me. Jordan had told me that he planned to kill Pierce, but I hadn't known it was a promise he had made to the fates.

"How does killing a kind leader whose people love him restore balance? And for that matter, who decides what is balanced?" I looked at Amy. Her lips pinched a little as her head nodded, showing her agreement with the confusion I was feeling. Jordan, however, looked to the fates desperately.

"They haven't told me what balance will and can be thrown

off. They have only advised that Pierce is a large threat to the balance of universal power and that you could play a part in that," Jordan said, filling the air left empty by the Fates' lack of response. He was having an entire conversation with them that I couldn't decipher with just his eyes.

"Jordan," Cyx said.

"You know how," Fritz finished, both lifting their tea to their lips and drinking without breaking eye contact with him. Black flashed across Jordan's eyes. He stilled, going completely rigid before taking a deep breath, and while releasing it, seemed to force himself to loosen his composure, nodding at them in some sort of unspoken agreement. I looked at Amy, who thankfully looked as perplexed as I did.

"I am taking her home tomorrow, and I am taking you as well," he stated resolutely. The look he shot Amy and I closed that topic of discussion, and any follow-up questions were dead in our throats.

Fritz stood up, spilling a small amount of tea and placed her cup down hard on the table before storming past me to the parlor doors. Slamming them, she revealed a large world map pasted to the back adorned with notes. She looked Jordan dead in the eyes, gestured to it, and stomped.

"That's what this is all about? For the love of all the Gods that came before me," Jordan grumbled, throwing his head back and shaking it in disbelief.

Amy and I looked around the room and noticed, for the first time, the number of strange trinkets scattered and piled up everywhere. Large chests and old-looking wood pieces, with gold-accented everything.

"Wanna address the class?" I asked Jordan, amused, regardless of having no idea what was going on because I knew that this, for once, had absolutely nothing to do with me.

"My ladies here," he gestured to the beautiful but seething women, "are on a hunt and are annoyed about being delayed in their discovery," he said in a bemused tone.

"A hunt?" Amy asked.

"Yes. We are close to uncovering the resting spot of the Knights Templar treasure," Fritz answered, crossing her arms defensively.

Amy and I both lost our eyebrows in our hairlines as it sank in.

"You're... Treasure hunters?" The words came out slowly as I struggled to say the absurd words.

"We are history acquisition specialists," Cyx advised softly, standing up gracefully and moving to one of the chests at the sides of the room, opening it to reveal heaps of gold and silver coins.

"This is some of the first technical currency ever used in this realm. I am able to sense the past of whatever I touch. Fritz is able to process time at a slower speed in the present and predict the outcome of now and how certain changes affect things on a short-term basis. Our readings work on people, places, and populations. We use them and our knowledge from living through these centuries to locate lost history and return it to the right people." Cyx explained almost regally.

"Most of it," Fritz added in.

"So, yes. They are treasure hunters," Jordan said lightly, earning warning squints in both the Fates' eyes before they relented and made their way back to their seats.

"Besides, we relish the thought of a confrontation with Pierce," Fritz said, a sinister smile breaking her regularly gloomy expression.

"So why make us go back to the very dull existence of Hell?" Cyx asked, elaborating.

"Christine is going to need training, and you two are the only ones who have any idea how to best help her. The way you once helped me when no one else could. You just said yourselves I cannot let Pierce get his hands on her again, so trips here to you are not possible. Please?" His pleading question hung stiffly in the air for a moment while they appeared to be debating a response.

"Only until he is no longer a threat?" Cyx asked.

"Yes," Jordan confirmed.

Both women sighed and agreed with the unanimous nod of their heads.

"We will leave most of our belongings here, and it will only take us a few hours to complete packing, so there is no need for you or Thaddius, who is already upstairs rummaging through our stuff, to bother yourselves," snapped Fritz in response to a large banging that sounded above us, no doubt caused by Thad accidentally knocking something over.

"He is just securing the house. With the value in these walls, it is wise to board the place up if you will be gone for any length of time," Jordan said and seemed pleased by their apparent acceptance of his explanation.

By this point, I was about to explode. These were the women who told the prophecy that had gotten me into this mess. The two people who could tell me word for word what was said, which would be nice considering even Pierce heard it second hand and even then, it could be interpreted more than one way.

My outstretched foot was kicking impatiently as I sat, agitation waiting for a moment to bring it up when, to my relief, Amy snapped first, and the Fates got their first taste of Amy's 'delicate' way of asking things.

"What were you thinking? Subjecting some random girl to such a vague and heavy public prophecy? And is there a reason you couldn't be more specific, like, I don't know, maybe using Jordan's actual friggen name to save Christine years of discomfort at Pierce's hands?" The last sentence hit the Fates hard. They both became grave as they looked from each other to me.

"What is she talking about?" Cyx's question was directed to Jordan, but I answered.

"At the Fates festival, the day of the uprising, Pierce was

told of your public prophecy regarding the 'Fated Match to the God on High, born of Middle Earth with power enough to not only match the God she is fated to, but rival him.' Pierce assumed that since he was the God on High when I was born, you were talking about him."

I wanted to chastise them for making me a folktale, for basically subjecting me to everything I had dealt with over the more difficult course of my life, but the questions in my head were swirling around so violently I couldn't seem to get a firm hold on one in particular.

Jordan spoke, "When all three Fates were still able to join together, they could summon visions at will. They were also able to focus on someone to pull their specific fate forward. During my reign, I freed them from eternal servitude and, in doing so, unleashed cosmic Fate to play out naturally." He paused with a sigh. It was only as he lifted my chin, causing our eyes to meet, that I realized I had been looking down.

"They told me they had looked into my future and had a vision about me, picked out to share with the people for the festival's display. One that would make a good show and also humanize me. At the time, my image desperately needed it. So I gave them approval to use you, my future match, as their show."

I contemplated this as the Fates avoided looking at me, hesitantly sipping their tea. I supposed it wasn't entirely their fault my life got blown up. They just told a piece they had plucked of my fate; they hadn't altered it. Jordan wouldn't have allowed them to do so, but I needed to hear him say it.

"They only displayed a prediction; they didn't thread anything into my Fate, right?" Jordan smiled from his seat back at me. It was a reassuring smile that cooled the unease itching beneath my skin.

"Not even. The Fates see a lot of information when they pull forth the future. What they used to put on display at the festival was only ever a summary; more for entertainment than anything else. Their actual visions are in their minds. They used allusions to make the experience more fun for everyone else," Jordan explained.

Cyx chipped in while Fritz glared angrily at the elaborate ceiling art. I felt bad for the blond, harp-wielding baby she had fixed her malice on and was grateful it wasn't directed at me.

"The display we wove about you two was full of ice, laughter, and flashes of purple. Neither Jordan or Pierce witnessed the display. They were up at the castle, meeting with Arcane when we put on our show, and turmoil broke loose. We explained it to Jordan. Pierce made his own assumptions after hearing the ramblings of a rioter." Pierce's name left her lips in a sneer that was so strong I could almost feel the venom meant for him stinging me.

"Yeeah, no. Pierce saw a video copy later. After the initial report from one of his men had been delivered to him. Before the information blackout caused by Jordan breaking in and destroying a bunch of information about a year after the uprising," Amy filled in.

"I've never gotten to see what your shows looked like," I said in longing. I had heard the stories, but the videos had been destroyed by Jordan to protect the Fates.

"Me either," Amy added with a bit too-sorrowful twinge in her voice, clearly hoping we could guilt them into putting on a show for us. Jordan grinned at us while Fritz and Cyx looked at each other, playful grins growing.

"Before Pierce stripped us of our divine purpose, we could channel the future, all possible futures. We could channel it, but things also used to appear to us at fate's will. There is one glimpse we may be able to show you, though," Cyx offered. Amy and I mirrored each other in excited bounces. Jordan's thumb was stroking my shoulder, no doubt admiring my interest.

"Please?" I asked, holding my hands up in a begging motion. "As payment for telling the whole world I would be the first person fated to a high god, causing riots and ultimately ruining my life."

A guilty look passed between them before they rose to their feet, standing directly in front of each other. Cyx and Fritz closed their eyes as they reached for the sister in front of them. Their arms were raised shoulder height, fingers pointed to the ceiling while their fingertips pressed against each other's opposite hands. With a single breath, they clapped their hands together and abruptly pulled them apart.

It was then I understood the lore of the Fates weaving people's fates in threads. It was the most beautiful thing I had ever seen. Glimmering frost-like threads connected their fingertips from a distance as they weaved a moving image before us of sparkling white tendrils. After only a few seconds, the fuzzy picture started to clear; I became visible in the icy image.

I was an image of frost, but even so I could see this version of me was an older one. The assured looking ice-me stood at a podium, a crowd of shrouded people stretched out before me, their features indistinguishable with the lack of color. My hands were waving with a currently unfound conviction as I spoke to the masses.

The Fates wove a moving image of a smaller me, my little crystal fingertips splayed towards the sky; a large Enochian symbol appeared above me. Their hands were moving so fast I couldn't tell them apart as they weaved tiny purple eyes into all the people before me, matching mine.

The blast of energized fire sizzling in the symbol above my hands looked like dripping diamonds in this display. The symbol disappeared as the purple in the image faded.

The Fates clapped their hands together, breaking the display and practically punching Amy and me out of a trance as they sat back down and began casually sipping their tea as if they hadn't just put on a beautifully crafted show.

"That specific vision of you will make more sense in time," Fritz said.

Amy had a whimsical smile on her face, but Jordan was being uncharacteristically quiet. I reached a hand up to him, resting it on his thigh. I didn't know what was bothering him, but I wanted to lend him some of the strength he was always lending me. I smiled as he took my hand in his and squeezed.

"In all the time I spent in Heaven, no one told me about your gifts from this perspective. With so much of it being a show, I don't get why everything about me was taken so seriously."

"We are sorry," they said in unison.

"We need to know, though, has he hurt you?" Cyx cautiously asked the words. The way Fritz's eyes snapped to me and the burning intensity coming off both women told me if he had, these two women would enjoy making him pay for it.

"He would never hurt me. I spent two years with him coddling me and pampering me in attempts to win me. He failed. But he was very sweet in his attempts." I'm not sure what idiot part of my brain was strong enough to take over and say my next words, but it's by far my least favorite part of my brain,

"I know he made mistakes when trying to keep you from aligning with Jordan, but Pierce is a good man and leader. I've seen it. I trust him."

Fury I could have handled. Annoyance would have been understandable. Instead, I saw two vastly different emotions reflected in their distinct faces. Cyx looked like she was so terrified that it was making her ill. Her eyes were wide, and mouth agape, failing to take in air.

Fritz was toying with the gage in her earlobe, looking at me with an expression I completely understood after spending so much time with Thad. It expressed that she thought I was the dumbest creature to walk this planet. So ignorant and pathetic that she may have even felt sorry for me. Both reactions pissed me off.

"My God, you two are ridiculous. Jordan once told me that

good and evil are all about perspective, that my evil isn't necessarily someone else's evil." I stood up in the middle of my rant and crossed my arms as I angrily paced back and forth, ignoring the dark tint of Jordan's eyes.

"Or something better articulated with the same meaning. I'm just saying to you two he may be the face of your evil because he stole your brother from you, but he isn't mine. He saved my life and cared for me for years."

Cyx and Fritz had composed themselves and started looking at each other in what looked like another non-verbal communication, as if debating telling me something. Cyx's head swayed back and forth, weighing some kind of internal decision before she relented a verbal "FINE" at her sister.

Fritz stood in a snappy motion, placing her spilt tea down, and walked to meet me, planting a firm hand on each of my shoulders.

"We swore an oath, on our freedom, not to tamper with Fate. That means not disclosing seen futures to those whom we have seen. I cannot give you details. But please know, our hatred for Pierce is not simply because he killed Elix; it is because we care about Jordan and about you." My mouth fell open; Jordan's brows knitted together in confusion.

"What does that mean?" he asked. Fritz pinched her lips shut, and Cyx was bouncing her leg and looking at the ceiling.

"We can't say more. Just please; heed the warnings you have been given. I know you are operating under the impression that we *think* Pierce is a specific type of person, but my dear, we are the Fates. We don't 'think' things. We *know* them." With that, her hands dropped away. She sauntered to one of their large, heavily marked maps, turning her full attention to it.

A clap sounded through the room; all eyes went to Jordan. He continued in a dramatically slow applause. "Great show. Now, what are the two of you hiding?"

Clearly, they were going to ignore his question.

"We need to speak privately. Thad and I need to run a theory by the two of you." On cue, Thad appeared beside Jordan. I had to stifle a laugh as he ran his hands all over his body, making sure everything appeared with him as Fritz ushered Amy and me out the door, clicking it closed behind us.

***

After a good five minutes of politely waiting for Jordan, Thad and the Fates to wrap up their obnoxiously secret meeting, Amy and I snapped. Admittedly, we knew it was rude to explore someone else's home and go through their stuff, but we figured the Fates knowing more about me than I did meant boundaries just didn't apply.

Besides, these bitches had been tracking down lost treasure. There was no way Amy and I should have been trusted to have the discipline not to snoop around the place looking for treasures. The breach of social contract was completely worth it, and we hadn't even needed to leave the parlor room.

Upon our initial entrance, I had been so enamored by the intricate gold designs on the walls I had missed the neatly arranged cabinets and chests lining the halls. The first one I managed to break open was plenty to engage both Amy's and my interest for the entire night, let alone the thirty minutes we ended up having. It wasn't treasure we had discovered, though.

It was a chest of old photo albums and mementos of the Fates' lives on Earth through the ages. I grabbed the album that had 'Enacting our Civic Duty' labeled on it in woven stitching across the thick fabric binding in red. Civic duty couldn't be something that was too personal.

The polaroid picture stunned me with its brutal display. The fates, all smiles, were posed as you would with a shot deer. Though it wasn't a buck they had slain, it was a man. His eyes were open; he stared lifelessly at me. Fritz was knelt behind him and holding his head up with a handful of his hair. Blood was streaked in a wild splatter across Cyx's triumphant features. The picture sat in the middle of the photo album page, surrounded by dates accompanied by symbols I didn't recognize.

"Christine, you look sick. What are you looking at?" Amy asked from the other side of the room, closing the door to a cabinet she had been rummaging through. Amy's footsteps matched the hastened speed at which Christine flew through the pages, intrigue pinking her cheeks.

"Every page is a new dead person," she said, tilting the book and her head as if the angle would provide a new perspective.

Now standing in front of Christine, Amy took a second to appreciate the newly returned sparkle in Christine's eyes. As kids, Amy had always admired her friend's spark. If you looked close enough at the right time, Amy could have sworn you could see the glittering coals behind Christine's eyes sparking, daring you to fan the flame and face the heat.

Bending over the time-worn pages, Amy allowed herself a better look. Her stomach lurched at the sight of the Fates holding a stranger's head up, their eyes empty as they snapped the selfie with a polaroid camera.

Simultaneously, Amy and Christine yelped in surprise, chucking the book away from them at the sound of Thad's unexpected voice. They had been so engrossed in the haunting photos they hadn't heard or noticed Thad joining them.

"Jordan told them to get rid of those years ago. I swear those two have a dangerous hoarding problem. You should see upstairs; I arrived up there when I transported in and nearly buried myself alive," he said flatly.

Both women stared at him expectantly. Waiting. The air stiffened after a few seconds of him communicating with his eyes that he was unsure of what they were expecting.

"That's it. That's all you're gonna give us on the Charles

Manson book?" Christine asked, motioning to the album still lying on the floor where she tossed it.

"Oh, I assumed you knew. I'm surprised this isn't studied in schools... Interesting. Well, the Fates can sense past actions and the current actions being contemplated by a person just by touching them. For a while, before Jordan ended the hobby, they would follow anyone with ill intent that crossed their paths and remove them from the future's complex equation."

"So, they killed anyone they determined was negatively tipping the scales?" Amy said, voice barely above a whisper.

Thad grinned at the large eyes staring back at him. Growing up in the mortal world had given them a different view of death than how he had been raised. He knew mortal lives had their own form of immortality. He considered theirs the better deal; being reborn, living many different lives, their energy recycling back onto Earth. He had seen the process; it was unjustly beautiful.

Living one life. Living in the prison of a singular soul, in his opinion, was no better than eternal damnation. The purpose his brother gave him was his only reason for continuing his eternal trudge. Had he been mortal or Angelican and had that option of a clean slate, essence preserved, he would have ended things for himself when Alyk was stolen from him.

Christine saw a flicker of hollow pain shadow Thad's eyes. She debated asking him about it for half a second before the doors dramatically burst open, Jordan angrily leaving the Fates behind him. Christine had lightly touched Thad's arm, giving him a look that wordlessly offered an ear if needed.

"We are leaving. Thad, ensure Amy gets home safely." The darkness of his voice was a tint of severity she had only heard one other time; when he had seen her body covered in bruises.

Thad, who had been looking at Christine, didn't hear him.

"Oh, Jordan. Don't overreact. Please, you have to understand it was our duty. It has been our sacred destiny since before you were born. Give us time; let's talk this out?" Cyx begged, her hands together as she trailed behind his storming figure. He wrapped his arms around Christine protectively.

Fritz watched, unlike her sister, calm and content with the goings-on.

"Christine, please, calm him. Anger is muddling his thoughts. We only wanted to help," Cyx pleaded.

"You should be saying thank you. We did nothing wrong," Fritz stated strictly, crossing her arms in impatience.

Jordan squared himself in front of Christine, somehow managing to block everyone else out. Desperation was clouding his eyes as his fingers brushed across her cheek, his thumb landing under her chin and pushing her face up towards him.

He looked so worried, so contrite, and so very much like the dramatic Jordan she had come to know. Regardless of not knowing what had him so riled up, she smiled softly up at him. She pressed his palm more firmly to her cheek by leaning into him.

The muscles in his jaw popped at the motion. She wasn't sure if he was angry or sad by the confusion of emotions playing across his face. As his gaze moved from her to the Fates, the storm stilled, and his features smoothed as his eyes iced over.

"You are on your own," Jordan clipped the words at the Fates, then looked to Thad and motioned with his head to Amy.

"Get her home safely. Christine and I need to talk alone." With that, Jordan pulled Christine tightly into his arms, burrowing her face into his chest and transported from the room. Leaving Thad and Amy looking at the watery-eyed Fates, expecting an explanation.

FACING ONE'S DEMON

I patiently, well, patiently for me anyway, waited a good hour after Jordan had transported us back to his place before slipping into agitation. Something the Fates had told him had worried him. Considering he couldn't meet my eyes, I couldn't help but jump to the assumption it was about me.

Was I aware that Jordan was likely thinking of ways to talk me out of going? Yes, yes, I was.

Did that stop me from changing into my sparring gear, hand wraps included, and trying to duck out the door before he noticed? No, no, it didn't.

Not that it mattered. The second I tried to pull the door open, he appeared around me. His palms were outstretched on each side of me. I awkwardly shuffled around to face him. Had I been given the space, I would have crossed my arms. He probably stood so close to prevent me from doing just that.

"Leaving without saying goodbye?" he mocked, but I could hear the strain in his voice and knew he was trying to force a lightness he didn't feel.

"OH, so you CAN talk to me?" I asked rhetorically and with much sass. We had been back for hours; he had been brooding ever since.

"Please, Goddess, I just got some very... heavy news. I need some time to process it before sharing." His words wrapped tenderly around me.

"You know, I prefer poor communication over no communication. Whatever 'heavy' news you just found out involves me. Instead of ignoring me, we should be troubleshooting together," I said, making sure he registered my words with some tight eye contact. "That's how love works. Both parties need to be willing to share their..." Famished lips seized mine, cutting my words off and gently distracting my tongue from the scolding it had been delivering.

"Did you just say love?" he asked breathlessly against my lips. My cheeks warmed, and my stomach twisted in the best way.

"Yes. I'm not sure I'm happy about it, but I do love you. It may be Stockholm syndrome love, the jury's still out on that, but it's love." His grin wasn't full, but it was something. I would take it knowing I had at least somewhat lightened the burden he was shouldering. Selfishly, I was also celebrating saying the words and meaning them.

"Are you ready to talk about it?" I asked gently.

"Not yet. But tonight, I promise. You go. Enjoy teaching again; say goodbye to Evan this time. We will talk when you get home." He kissed me again, softer this time. "The gym is only a few blocks away. But it will make me feel better knowing you will summon me if you need me; show me?"

I rolled my eyes but still smiled up at him while tracing down the mark on my chest before tapping the top of it. He sighed, lifted my hand to his heart and held it there. I felt the heat of the pull I had initiated grow beneath my fingertips as that warmth spread through his chest.

After what seemed like too brief a moment, he curled my fingers in his hand, kissed them and closed the door behind me. I felt ridiculous as I walked breathlessly down the hall, fingertips hovering above the mark in lingering memory of the feeling of heat rushing through Jordan's chest.

After I got two blocks down the street, my curiosity got the better of me. After confirming no one was around, I traced the J on my chest and tapped the top. Jordan appeared in front of me, a hand on his hip and a playful grin on his face.

"I just knew you wouldn't be able to help yourself from testing me." He kissed me lightly again, renewing his scent in my hair as he ran his fingers through it. "Have a nice class; come directly home." With a kiss to the forehead, he was gone again before I could protest his last demand.

If there is one thing New York does not have as much of, as movies would make you believe, it is screens. Every movie and show has a moment where a character sees some important news broadcast in a store window, and it's a big, important moment.

Christine and Amy had spent a ridiculous amount of time watching films and shows and all those cheesy moments popped into her brain now. She had managed to stumble upon a store literally selling TVs only. Several were sitting in the display window, a reel looping of a large typhoon that was headed towards the Philippines.

People were rightfully in a panic. Natural disasters happened in Heaven as well, but the difference was the people there had the power to make such things trivial. Jordan wanted to unite the three realms; looking at this, she felt herself sway slightly more to his side of that belief.

***

Jordan hadn't returned to the penthouse after sending Christine off but instead had gone to Hell. His temporary elation was immediately doused by his new company.

Savious, Thad and Kielius sat in a war room, diagrams pulled up on large screens and press releases printed out and scattered among the tables. Savious was glaring angrily at the door, obviously waiting for Jordan to arrive to pierce him with it, while his brothers were wadding paper up and flicking the little balls at one another.

Thad, along with Amy, had been filled in by the Fates after Jordan's abrupt departure from their estate on what was causing his current panic.

"Jordan. This isn't that dire. Christine is safe. We have Amy shadowing her; Pierce will not get her." Thad signed without verbalizing, much to the annoyance of their father. Jordan's responding laugh came out crooked.

"For the first time since I put all of this in motion, we have learned information that basically proves your reservations regarding Christine correct, and you have the nerve to tell me she is safe? She will never be safe. I'm going to have to get used to that."

Jordan stood up taller and tipped his head to one side, cracking his very stiff neck as he signed his response to the room. Knowing the entire party could speak it and that it irritated Savious to use it. But right now, he needed a small win.

"Want to fill in the rest of the class?" Kielius asked, deciding to both verbalize and sign. Jordan held a hand up to stop Thad from responding.

"Savious, I am not sure your presence is necessary," Jordan advised coolly.

"Don't start with me, boy. This is my fight too. Whatever our differences, we are on the same side," Savious responded, pointedly refusing to sign.

"I have your loyalty, then?" Jordan asked, signing only.

"You always have," Savious signed back stiffly.

Jordan considered for a moment, took a deep breath, and exhaled it as he looked at his family. The men leading his army, plotting the reclaiming of his throne, and hoped they would not soon become his enemies.

"Christine is a Creationist."

Thad braced, buckled against his father's fury and related

to the way Kielius's jaw practically hit the table. His had nearly done the same when the fates told him and Amy only hours ago.

Creationists had ceased to exist long before any of them were born. The first Angelicans did not all possess abilities. In the beginning, only one out of a hundred or so of the population was a Creationist. They generated power so intensely that many of the first known to carry the gift died from not being able to channel it properly.

It was the Creationists who began gifting abilities to others. Abilities that would later be discovered to be hereditary. As time passed, so many gifts had been passed down to the children and grandchildren of those originally blessed by a creationist that having abilities ceased to be a novelty but a way of life.

And where there are those who have tasted power, there are those who find an insatiable thirst for it. The Creationists' history was dark and short due to the enslavement and mistreatment they experienced through the years, leading to their eventual extinction.

"And that means what exactly?" Kielius asked, cutting off his father's rants about 'being right' and 'should have let me take care of this earlier.'

"Do you know the most notable abilities an Empath possesses?" Thad signed to Kielius.

"They fuck with your hormones and are incredible at manipulation," Kielus answered confidently.

"They also," Jordan filled in. "Have the ability to take another's power without consent. The Creationists were wiped out due to the subsequent enslavement they experienced at the hands of Empaths, who used this ability to continually compound their abilities by draining these people against their will and amassing incredible power in the process."

"If they gained such power, how is it that none of them ever took over?" Kielius asked.

"Because the God on High killed them before they got the chance," Jordan clipped irritably, his signed communication mirroring his agitation. The room quieted, all attendees knowing the discussion of Empaths was a sore subject for Jordan.

"Do you think Pierce knows?" Thad asked with slow and cautious motions.

"No," Jordan answered too quickly, touching the center of his chest in the signed motion. His eyes shot to Savious, looking to gauge his reaction as he repeated the sign. The man seemed to have aged with the sheer declaration of Christine's power. The gray tendrils of his beard stood starkly against his tanned skin. His frown lines seemed deeper; his eyes were burrowing into Jordan with a sharp disapproval.

"He doesn't yet. He kept himself in the dark by suppressing her training. We opened the door to her abilities; they have begun to grow. It shouldn't impact our plans as she will be safe in Hell during the possibility of any battle."

Savious scoffed. "Yes. Because she is a sweet type that does what she is told."

"She has strong capabilities, yes. But she has no idea how to use them. She won't be able to join us in Heaven even if she wants to." Even as he said the words, he doubted them. Her power manifested differently; he had no idea what she would be capable of.

"That is even if things become physical. Pierce cannot face me. He is strong, but he knows, especially now, that he can't physically stand his ground against me. He will voluntarily step down, and the appearance of his 'support' to my return will make the transition much easier and a lot less bloody."

"Son. You cannot have both. You will need to kill one of them. Those two together have the ability to overpower you. Regardless of if she is willing to assist him or not. The Fates told you this would happen, and now we know how." Jordan ran a hand through his hair, agitated at the very thought of Christine being put in that position.

"The plan holds. The only adjustment is Christine's safety is no longer solely my concern but all of ours. She not only could be used against me, but if our end goal is to unify the different worlds, she could very well be the key to that. Being able to offer a level ground to the people of all worlds gives us a new method of unification we haven't even considered."

Savious stormed from the room without another word. Jordan motioned with his head for Kielius to keep an eye on him, knowing his mortal-hating father would disapprove strongly at the notion of empowering the mortals in order to unify the worlds.

***

"CHRISTINE!" Warmth and recognition filled me as four of my previous students embraced me in a hug. Taking turns asking questions and filling me in on little tidbits of their lives. Thanks to Jordan's distractions, I failed to arrive before class had started, but Evan, leaning against the wall on the other side of the room, just smiled as he watched the reunion.

Class went by far too quickly. After a brief time of catching up during our initial stretching, we moved into some bag rounds. The new stability of the business had allowed Evan the funds needed to get bags that were shaped like people. Creepy, faceless, pale people meant just for whaling on. After my first punch tipped the bag over, I realized the amount I was holding back was not enough. I didn't quite have a handle on my newfound strength yet. Evan, smooth like normal, made a joke of the bizarre display.

"Aaaaand she's back with a vengeance," he chimed, causing the four women to laugh and bat their eyes at him. I taught a few new moves but mostly watched Evan instruct. His particular favorite was jab placement, where you punch with pointed knuckles directly above where the leg connects to the hip. It wasn't that I didn't want to lead class, but my wound was throbbing after that first punch, and I wasn't sure how many slip-ups Evan could gloss over for me.

After class, I was left with a weird feeling of closure. I had thought it was this life I wanted back. That these classes and teaching were so much a part of my identity that not being able to do it had somehow stripped me of who I was. But after this class, I was less sure of that. It was great to see my old students, to know most of them were doing well and being in the familiar setting of Evan teaching class, but it wasn't enough. I no longer felt my purpose emanating from this.

We cleaned up in relative silence as I reflected on my emotional discovery. Evan broke the silence first as he locked the main entrance door.

"You really gonna make me ask how you did that earlier?"

I smiled and, upon failing to think of a believable lie, told him the truth. "I'm not normal, and honestly couldn't even begin to explain it to you," I said with a shrug. Surprisingly, he just smiled back at me, shoved my shoulder, and joked that he already knew I wasn't 'normal.'

I stuck my tongue out at him before giving him a quick hug and grabbing my bag.

"Hey, Evan. I may kinda fall off the face of the Earth again soon. I'm fine, just moving," I said unconvincingly.

"Starting a new life in a new place with your scary, non-titled friend?" he asked jokingly.

"Yeah. That about sums it up," I said, chuckling.

"He's a scary puta madre, so I approve. He seems more than capable of keeping your disaster self safe." I smiled a bit too wide at this. If only he knew just how hard that job really was.

"He does," I agreed. He pulled me into a goodbye bear hug one more time and walked me out to the back.

"Check in when you're able. A postcard or something, so I know you're settled."

"I will." With that I took off, quickly out of view, not wanting him to see me cry. I couldn't believe I was crying. I never cried, and now to cry because of a temporary goodbye, good God, what was wrong with me?

Consciously, I made the unwise decision to disobey Jordan's direct orders to come straight home and decided to take a very scenic route through Central Park to clear my head, before stepping into the next chapter of my life and all of the unknown that lay before me.

I passed the Great Hall before I noticed the sun was starting to set; Jordan would be worried soon. When I turned around, I noticed two hooded figures walking a bit too briskly in my direction.

'Not a good idea, guys, that is if you value your health,' I thought sardonically to myself.

They were both roughly the same height and weight. Very average guys. No more than 5'10", one had a crooked nose, likely because he had broken it before. The other had a very low-quality face tattoo on his cheek.

Taking a deep breath, I centered myself and stopped walking. This must have surprised them because they hesitated for a second.

"Can I help you with something?" I asked, channeling my bitchiest of tones.

The response I got was both of them opening pocket knives. I suppressed rolling my eyes when I remembered the still stiff wound in my side from the last mortal knife I got shanked with.

"I really don't recommend it, boys." Can't say I didn't warn them.

I inhaled a very slow breath making sure to approach this with a level head. The last thing I needed was to lose my shit in Central Park and oust my people's existence because of a couple of bored losers.

Not making the same mistake as every action film ever, they didn't try the 'attack one at a time' method. Both lunged simultaneously with a smooth slicing speed, their knives glinting orange in the light of the setting sun.

With very little effort, I ducked between their two bodies and, while twisting to face them, pivoted and knuckled them both hard right beneath the ribs.

Closer now, I could see both of the men were younger. Early twenties, if I had to guess, and they looked very upset with me right about now; likely because I was grinning back at them.

The one with the face tattoo bared his teeth at me; it became clear why he needed the gnarly black ink up his face as a distraction. His eyes squinted, recognizing the disgust on my face at the display of his cigarette-blotched snaggle teeth. In my head, his botched tattoo earned him the name black teeth Tyson.

Loser number two thought I was distracted enough to begin edging his way around me, looking to stop any attempt I may make to flee. He was wrong. The temptation to set the ground at his feet aflame was strong, but I really wanted to avoid an incident.

"Last chance, boys."

'See, I can be a nice person. I warned them not once, but twice.'

Black teeth Tyson was to my front; loser number two was now behind me. The false confidence evident in his angry sneer.

"Go ahead, try that again, baby."

Taking a deep breath, I listened for and heard the predictable movement of the man behind me at the same time as his dentally impaired friend. They had been so focused on not missing me this time that they hadn't anticipated me making a very sudden movement to my left, resulting in them hitting each other.

Black-toothed Tyson took his friend's tiny knife in the side and, in turn, sliced his friend's bicep open.

"You guys must be new to this whole thug thing," I said, picking up the gym bag I had dropped, prepared to walk away unmarked; feeling like a powerful independent woman from rescuing myself. Like the Goddess I had begun to identify as, until the hairs on my arms stood straight up.

Savious stood, looking like a rich, dapper man on a mission. His thick hair, touched with gray, was slicked back, and his leather-gloved hands were tucked into his peacock pockets. He looked inconvenienced yet unsurprised.

As much as his presence sent me into high alert, I assumed Jordan hadn't trusted me to stay out of trouble. I no more than opened my mouth to tell him to fuck off when the two bleeding men in my company started screaming.

Red lines snaked along their visible skin. Their eyes screeched in a ghastly silent pain, bodies so overwhelmed they were unable to summon the air for an audible call for help.

"What are you doing to them? Stop!" I yelled, dropping to the crumpling bodies of my attackers. Getting closer, I noticed the red lines were being caused by rubbing and moving sand. Savious was manipulating the coarse sand particles to chafe and scratch the men's skin until, in many places, the skin was opening, blood oozing out.

I ran to Savious and shoved him, demanding he stop this unnecessary torture. The shove against his chest sent me back onto my ass. He snorted condescendingly at me, only adding to my fear as I remembered the same disinterested expression on his face as he walked into my parents' house all those years ago.

"My son may bend to your will, but I do not. These mortals you revere are so... temporary." He held his hand up. The men jerked, stilling with a sudden snap. I looked at their limp bodies and felt my stomach go sour. The acidic presence of brewing vomit unpleasantly invaded my taste and smell in response to the sight of two grown men being brutally murdered.

"Come now, isn't this where you spatter me with questions?" he asked tauntingly, crouching down to me and moving a curl out of my face. That one touch. His audacity in reaching out and touching my hair completely stilled my panic and fear. Replaced in full by sheer unfiltered rage.

I stood quickly, startling him and sending him falling over onto his side, leaving me in the upper position.

"To ask you questions begs the assumption I give any kind of fuck what your motives for doing anything are." My voice was unrecognizable to my own ears as I growled them at him. The wind had picked up, matching my chaotic temper as the wind battered the hair around my face.

Savious stood, unimpressed as he dusted his sleeves off. "I must commend your originality. At a minimum, everyone else I've slain has wanted to know why," he said.

Acting on sheer instinct, I brought my hands together and, while thrusting them out, sent a thick pulse of energy with it. It pushed Savious back a step but didn't put him on the ground as I would have hoped.

"And you are putting up a fight, more than I can say for your parents," he remarked simply, almost endearingly pissing me off more. That rage was boiling in me now, staring down the tormentor of my nightmares, the bogeyman I had spent my life running from. The man who robbed this world of my mother's sarcasm and my father's geeky passion.

The intensity of my breathing and the sickening feeling of fire charring my intestines distracted me from the fact that the wind had turned utterly violent around us. Grass was ripping from the ground in slices, and trees bent crooked, adorned leaves flapping like little SOS flags hanging on for dear life in a tornado.

Like the coward I knew him to be, he transported to the broken men and grabbed one of their knives, using it to lunge at me, the knife aimed towards my heart.

Using the palm of my hand, I quickly twirled and smacked his hand, making the knife fall out of it.

"Using a knife? How *mortal* of you. If you are trying to hide your involvement here, you shouldn't have manipulated the elements. Jordan will know," I goaded.

"I have been burdened by a Fated match. I know how all-consuming it can be. You are poisoning him with your influence. Causing him to make mistakes that will get him killed. Letting Pierce live, you truly are a stupid woman," he said admonishingly. This rattled me and gave him the opportunity to transport close enough to me to grab me by the neck. I didn't know Jordan had changed his plans. But of all the things to be angry about, why would he be so mad that Pierce lived?

His grip burned and broke its way through the barrier of energy I had been focusing on to protect myself. It surprised me to hear it fizzling under his pressurized heat.

"Savious. Face it. You aren't very good at killing me. You have a tendency of taking out the wrong target."

He looked to the crumpled men, and in a sardonic smile, he said the most chilling words to ever brush across my face, "Had you truly been my target, you would have been dead, my dear." In the span of a blink, I thrust my knee abruptly upwards, his jerk away allowing me to break free.

It would have been a smart move to summon Jordan. It would have been an understandable move to run. Neither of these options crossed my mind as red hazed my vision. Somehow knowing he set out to kill my parents, their murder seemed fresher in my mind. No longer something that was my burden, something that happened because they put themselves in between me and the threat. But an act of undeserved malice resulted in them being stolen away from me.

I breathed in as my arm swung back, gathering concentrated energy, and unleashed it with full force as I swung my fist forward, connecting with his face. The impact blew me backwards onto my back, stripping the nearby trees of leaves, and sent him face-first to the ground so hard it cracked the pavement of the sidewalk.

"Christine!" I blinked through the haze, not realizing I had blacked out; it must have only been for a second because

Savious hadn't yet regained his footing. Kielius, of all people, was hovering above me with clear concern etched in his voice. He mouthed two words, 'Summon him,' as Savious bargained behind him.

"Jordan doesn't need to know. This little witch is going to get your brother killed. We can say she came into the park and vanished, by the time we found her, it was too late. He will blame Pierce. I'll even let you have some fun with her first." The bargain sent a chill of panic up my spine as Kielius's fingers flexed his hold on me.

Raising my hand, I traced the mark and tapped the top.

All three sets of eyes looked at Jordan, darkness pooling around him menacingly. After taking one, very quick, inky look at me, his eyes snapped to his father.

"You would dare..." Jordan began in a deep, deathly timbre, transporting to Savious and punching him back to the ground. As he finished his sentence, black ooze rose from the ground. Jordan's eyes were inking over. The darkness wrapping itself around Savious began to shimmer, and Savious began to scream, "... to take her from me?" Jordan finished his question softly, letting his malice show via the pain he inflicted.

I had never seen darkness used as a weapon; it was the most tremor-inducing sight I had ever witnessed. Savious was disappearing into it, jolting as it stung him. It looked like he was drowning in a void of sharp electricity born of the night.

Kielius tensely set me down on my feet, both of us holding our breath at the sight before us. The dark haze was fully shrouding Savious now as Jordan stood above him, head tilted, mumbling under his breath in a language I didn't know. Jordan reached towards his father; the haze melted away, revealing Savious. It looked like he had been the victim of an acid burn as Jordan held him by the shirt. He reached his arm back to land a blow to Savious's face when Kielius intervened.

"Jordan!" Kielius called, trying to break the concentration of his rage.

Watching Jordan bludgeon Savious gave me an eerie sense of clarity that I hated. I stepped forward and into Jordan's deathly darkness, reaching forward and placing a hand on his shoulder. Immediately his shoulder dropped some of its tension. He dropped Savious as if discarding a sack of potatoes, looking back at me.

I didn't see his expression because I was too busy examining Savious. His eye was already swelling into a grotesque plum. His skin was cherry red and shiny, but he was definitely alive. A few seconds ago, I pieced together that what Jordan was doing was for me. Killing his father to make me feel safe, ending a threat to my life and as much as I wanted to let him do it, I couldn't.

My left hand was still resting on his shoulder. I was holding my right arm to my side; it had a pulsating shooting pain running up it. When I finally met Jordan's eyes, he wasn't looking at me softly as I had expected. The shadow of death was still lingering in his eyes.

I tried to say, "It's enough," but Savious must have squeezed my throat harder than I thought because air painfully hissed through my throat with no words following it. At this, Jordan fully turned to me; the softness I had expected presented itself. He folded me into his arms; I could hear him breathing my scent in as deeply as possible as I did the same with his, burrowing my face into his chest.

"Thank you for stepping in," Jordan said over my head to Kielius. Warm breath hit my lungs as the lighting around me changed. We were back in the skyline flat.

BLOOD RUNS THICKER

Azazel sat in his untidy living room, twirling his favorite throwing knife on his pointer finger while watching his contraband Middle Earth TV. A good friend of his had somehow made it able to play cable directly from Middle Earth. He used it to monitor top news stories in hopes nothing about his sister popped up. The last time he had spent time with his family, Christine was only three years old.

She had long braided pigtails, eyes that were way too big for her head, chubby fingers, and was told he was her 'Uncle' Axel. He had worn a glamor covering his markings and shortening his hair.

It was some consolation that she grew up with pictures in her home of him. The story their parents told her was that he had been killed in a motorcycle accident. Once she was old enough, they had planned to tell her the truth, and he would get to come back into the mix and make her own choice. He and his parents had very different political beliefs.

The day his parents told him they were leaving Heaven was the worst day of his life. He watched his father give up his wings by having his mother cut them off his body. He watched his mother roam around the home she had lived in for seventy-five years with her family and say goodbye, all the while their hometown burned in the aftermath of an uprising.

Meeting the Fates was considered an honor, but when they came stumbling through his parents' door, bloody and desperate, he knew they were really more of a curse.

They warned his parents that they would have the daughter they always dreamed of, but she would grow into the woman from the prophecy that started the panic and unrest two days before that resulted in a High God being forced from the throne.

Cyx had told him directly, while his parents listened, that this girl needed to be raised in the mortal realm in secret and kept as far away from Pierce as possible.

Did they warn him his parents would be murdered? No. And he would pray for the end of their eternal lives until his own death. Had he known, he would have gone with them; he could have helped. His father and mother weren't easy targets, but Savious wouldn't have gotten through him. He had even laid Pierce out a time or two.

He had been tempted to move to the Middle realm after the death of his parents and support Christine, but he couldn't do that under the radar; he had been too blindly loyal to Pierce and too close to him already to just vanish. So he kept his distance and did what he could from afar.

He hadn't known about his parents' death until the day Christine was brought to Heaven, and her arrival was announced. Most people had projections in place of the clunky television sets mortals were still using, and those projections echoed her story throughout the city of Castofel.

He had listened intently while making his way to the castle to come forward, but he stalled on one sentence, 'After her parents were gruesomely murdered by Savious.' It was Pierce's voice that read the announcement. And it was Pierce's voice that echoed in his mind.

'Her parents were murdered by Savious'
'Parents were murdered'
'Parents murdered'
'Parents'

He would never forget the limpness of his body as he fell to his hands and knees. Hearing from endless directions the echo that his parents had been killed years ago, and he hadn't even known, all because he disagreed with their choice to listen to the Fates. He had called his father a conspiratorial fool to listen to the Fates' warning against his endorsement of Pierce's character.

Now he knew better. He knew Pierce was scum who could force an innocent and naive girl into a very public relationship she didn't want. Sure, she seemed shy and sweet and amenable to the people. But Azazel knew her.

The child he had known was pure fire, just like his mother. She only got shy OR sweet when she was uncomfortable. There was no way she should be so consistently ill at ease while being hand in hand with her 'fated' match.

Now, Azazel clung to the TV while scanning the internet, looking for any sign of her in hopes he could get to her before Pierce this time. He needed her to know she wasn't alone. He needed her to know her big brother never stopped looking after her and was so sorry he had failed her.

"Fuck me," he complained, wiping a tear from his eye. He had no problem with processing emotions, but this wasn't going to help him. Sitting here and dwelling wasn't his normal style, but he was at a loss for what to do. A spike of frustration shot through him. He chucked the knife he had been playing with backward toward one of the many targets he had throughout his house. It landed dead center, but he cut his thumb on the release.

"I didn't mean literally, ya damned Fates. Haven't you screwed me enough?" he said angrily toward the ceiling. His mother had been a gifted healer and had taught him some simple energy stitching when he was young because he was careless around anything sharp, shiny, or dangerous.

She could heal a cut without leaving a trace. His magic wasn't that strong, so when he healed himself, it left a raised mark. When he would come home for dinner, she would sit him down and correct his scars, smoothing his skin again.

He could remember the scoldings she gave him on numerous occasions, "I made you perfect. So, if you could please stop damaging my good work, I would appreciate it." Always with a kiss on the forehead, then a light smack to the back of the head.

Looking at his hands, he stretched his long narrow fingers out, then clenched them again, looking at the marred skin. His hands were more scar tissue than not these days; he couldn't bring himself to let anyone else heal him. Each scar was a reminder of the time passing without his family and without making things right. Each scar drove him.

His eyes drew their attention back to the screen as an image of central park came into view. A helicopter was circling a small portion of the Northern bit of the park. The news anchor pointed to the destruction and was talking about a possible terrorist attack. The trees were all bending away from one spot, the grass had slices in it, and signs were ripped from the ground.

New York. Feathers poofed into the air as he jumped from the couch. He tried not to get his hopes up as he clipped his vest on carefully so as to not knock any of the concealed daggers, or as he called them, his ladies, ajar as he threw it on.

He had stitched it himself, he concealed ten different-sized knives, brazenly displaying five. Because he was going to Middle Earth, where people were a bit jumpier than his kind, he threw on a jacket over the vest. It was winter there anyway, not that he needed a coat. Temperature changes didn't bother guardians as they did most people. He could hardly feel the difference between thirty-five and seventy-five degrees.

He went to the fridge and pulled out a small golden bottle labeled 'Intent,' and downed the sour juice in one gulp. Intent was the Angelican equivalent of cocaine. He needed the focus if he was going to go investigate around New York while trying to glamor his wings the entire time.

Placing the small bottle on the full trash bin, he left his home, ready to make his way to Middle Earth to hopefully find and save his baby sister.

***

Savious could melt into the ground with the embarrassment and betrayal he felt at that moment. He lay, broken and bleeding from the pummeling his son had given him. Having been in a Fated match himself, Savious couldn't blame Jordan for his reaction.

Had anyone threatened Elmyra the way he had just threatened Christine, he wouldn't have walked away until they had taken their last breath, even if she had asked him to.

They really had made a mess of things. This girl's arrival could not have been more inconvenient, and now Jordan planned to speak with Pierce and reason with him, which would not do.

Coughing up a nice lungful of blood, he forced himself to sit. Hating the prickling feeling of his body healing, he would heal slower on Earth but as a pure-blooded Angelican, not by much. There was only one option for him now, and he didn't like it but knew the day had been coming for a long time.

"What were you thinking?" Kielius asked him with his arms splayed wide at the destruction, completely bewildered.

A blood-stained, toothy smile was the only response Savious had before closing his eyes and surprising his son by transporting.

"Shit," Kielius muttered. He looked around at the sheer destruction, admiring Christine's propensity for damage, figuring if he behaved himself, they might be able to be good friends. Lord knows she was entertaining.

Bracing himself to be a messenger of bad news, he sighed and transported outside of Jordan's door in his New York apartment, on the assumption he won't risk transporting Christine further until after she could be examined. His brother was predictable in that one area.

He felt stupid knocking, but knew Jordan would be a bit touchy and didn't feel like just popping in on them.

"How bad?" Thad signed after ripping open the door.

"Hello to you too. I'm fine, thanks for the concern," Kielus responded snippily. "He was already healing, to the point of being able to transport away. He, like Jordan, enjoys flaunting the ever-distant conveniences of being fully Angelican," he added.

"He transported?" Thad signed, and then signed again after his brother ignored him.

"Can I come in and talk about it? I really don't feel like explaining to you just to repeat myself to Jordan." Nodding, Thad stepped aside as his brother brushed past him.

Jordan had propped Christine up on the counter and was inspecting her very burnt and bruised neck. It looked a lot worse in direct light, and even Kielius couldn't help but flinch, feeling a bit of guilt remembering the burn he himself had given her. Knowing now what she was, he dreaded the ways he had yet to pay for that mistake.

"Well, you've been hotter," Kielius snarked. Christine shot him an unamused, scrunched face in response to his jest. He thought he was funny until noticing Jordan's facial expression, promptly flattening his own smile.

"Watch that acid tongue, brother. I will not allow anyone to kick her while she is down," Jordan warned. Christine nodded in approval.

"Since when is she incapable of giving me a verbal scolding herself?" Kielius asked.

"Fated matches are legally considered one; therefore, I have every right to speak for her." Her glare turned to Jordan until he elaborated, "And her for me when it better suits." Thad didn't miss the warmth Jordan had added into his tone on that last sentence and rolled his eyes at the blatant pandering.

"Don't worry, I find them insufferable too," Thad said, putting a hand on Kielius's shoulder.

"Fine, I'll be nice. There's always Amy to pick on," Kielius said.

"Where is she, by the way?" Thad asked, directing the question to a very distracted Jordan.

Outwardly Jordan was putting on a calm front, but everyone in the room could sense it was a farce. A thin one at that. This was the second instance in which he had almost lost her in a very short time span.

The ghost of his father's fingers silhouetted against her neck in red and deepening with blue and purple, and the longer he looked at her, the more his resolve to leave his father alive slipped from his grasp.

Jordan reached out again, hovering just above her injury, reaching out and feeling the damaged cells, the misfiring electric signals between her atoms where his father had damaged her on a cellular level. He was lucky she had, in fact, been Angelican.

A gifted mortal would not have survived this. Meeting her eyes, he watched her face soften in contrast with her firm warning eyes. She was reading his mind and knew what he was thinking and regretting.

A full breath was needed to push the words past her battered throat, but she managed the raspy, one-word demand.

"No." Her nose scrunched up in a way Jordan had come to recognize every time she tried to appear authoritative. To most anyone else, the sharpness of her eyes would hold their intended threat. But to him, the attempt was just adorable. He reached out with a finger and tapped the tip of her nose. Communicating his thoughts on her attempted command.

"No, what?" Thad asked.

"She doesn't want me to track down and kill our father," Jordan informed them, never breaking his eye contact with her.

"So, you heard he got away."

"I expected as much. He holds greater power than both of you combined and has spent much more time than all three of us honing them. The question is, where will he slither off to?" Jordan's pointer finger was wrapped around his own chin, thumb tapping his jaw as he thought of Savious's limited options.

"Obviously, Hell, duh," Thad chimed in. "He detests mortals enough to disown me for marrying one, and he has built a life in the underworld. It seems like an easy choice to me." Jordan raised his chin a bit indigantly to this.

"Make a move against the queen of my realm; you quickly lose privileges to it." Both brothers' eyes widened ever so slightly in response to the obvious warning.

"So, you blocked his ass from going home. Finding him should be easy; he won't be able to go long trying to blend in with Mortals," Kielius said.

Christine knew tracking Savious seemed important at the moment, but in her mind, she was more concerned with deciphering what he said.

'Had you been my intended target, you would be dead.'

Was it just a taunt?

Jordan could see the wheels turning in Christine's head and turned his attention back to her while Kielius and Thad turned away and flicked on the TV to feign distraction, attempting to give them some sort of privacy.

"I will not let him near you again, I swear." She shook her head at his assumption of her fear.

"He said," she started the words and broke into a fit of coughing and couldn't help but notice the ever-perfect timing of a commercial coming across the screen for Ricola.

Jordan shifted, grabbing a glass she had used earlier and filling it from behind the sink and handing it to her. She sipped some and decided it wasn't as helpful as it was a hindrance. "What did he say that has you concerned?"

"I was never his target." She forced the words out quickly; each syllable was like regurgitating a screw up her windpipe. Jordan's jaw clenched, and his head went back as he huffed out a breath of hate.

"Son of a bitch."

She wanted to ask him what it was he had pieced together, but she didn't get the chance. The images flashing from the TV stopped her.

Very quickly, she became aware of her own breathing because it was all she could hear. Kielius and Thad both turned back to face them, looking from the long flat screen to the girl who was starring on it.

A news program was talking over crudely shot footage of Christine's encounter with Savious at Central Park. She was hovering above the ground, arms slightly raised with debris and wind scattering as if to escape her very presence.

A stone-like quality hardened Jordan's features, his complexion dusting.

"What are you so worried about?" Kielius asked, trying to break the unearned tension in the room.

"Give it two weeks, and they will deconstruct this as an elaborate hoax," he said flippantly, pointing the remote back at the box and shutting the program off.

"Christine has been exposed in a big way," Jordan said, mostly to himself. He was referring to her having abilities and her being in New York and that Pierce would likely be scouring the streets any second. Kielius took his meaning in an entirely different direction connecting Jordan's words and fears to the darkness of his past.

"Brother. I doubt any Empaths escaped to this realm that would see this. You are way too thorough for that." The second his words hit Jordan, he wished he could suck them back down his throat. Thad didn't help by immediately directing a worried look to Christine.

For Jordan, seeing the look on Christine's face as she tried to process what his brother had meant made his world stop. There was no breathing or beating heart at this moment as he knew she would likely turn from him now. This bliss he had experienced the past several months was coming to its inevitable end as she discovered him in his entirety. It was lucky for Kielius that Jordan was experiencing his first-ever bout of fear paralysis because had he not, he likely would have killed him.

"What did you do?" Her words were broken from more than just the strain of her injuries. In her mind, she saw a foggy image of Kielius's meaning, but her brain was refusing to see it clearly.

There were many things Jordan knew he should regret. But he had decided long ago that regret did not have a place in his existence. Eternal life is too long to live second-guessing your actions and choices. Yet, on this particular subject, the shame he felt was too heavy to acknowledge, let alone attempt to process what he had done.

Looking away from her, he answered as concisely as he could. "The Empath bloodlines didn't die out over time. I ended them." Her hand resting in his had become so common and comfortable that his palm felt a keen sting as she ripped her hand from his.

He hadn't known what to expect from her at this moment, a moment he had hoped would never come. Would she look at him with disgust, anger, rejection? But of all things, he was not prepared for his Christine, his Goddess, his scrappy little fighter to look at him with fear; it devastated him.

"Why?" she asked, lowering herself from the counter and

distancing herself from him. Each step away felt like another break in their bond and any connection he had made with her.

"What could I possibly say that would justify...."

She finished the sentence for him in judgment. "Genocide."

In her mind, she waged a war against her own stupidity. She had been foolish enough to trust him. He had played a martyr so well, believing in him was the easiest thing in the world. How had she fought Pierce so fiercely yet thrown herself to Jordan's feet?

Pierce had been right; he had been good. The clearer things became in her mind, the angrier and more confused she grew.

Her mind was reeling.

'Of course, Pierce dethroned Jordan. His best friend had committed genocide against their people. Pierce was right to remove him from power and feel betrayed himself in the process. And to think Pierce didn't even expose what Jordan did; he protected his friend from the tarnishing that would do to his image.'

Yet, looking at the man before her, she didn't see a genocidal tyrant. She saw the dark eyes of a man she knew capable of deep affection and tenderness. A man who had given her freedom and tricked her into trusting him. She felt her connection to a soul and heart that would end worlds for her; now she knew just how capable of that he truly was.

Without another word, she turned away from him and walked, shakily, towards the door.

She flinched when he reached for her and cursed herself for feeling guilty in response to the hurt in Jordan's eyes. She didn't want to fear him. She knew he wouldn't hurt her, but she couldn't free herself from the image of him using his electric darkness to torture and kill groups of his own people.

To end bloodlines, he must have killed innocents, children, and civilians. People who trusted him as she did, possibly more, as he was their God on High. Their leader and savior turned to murder.

He had transported in between her and the door masking his emotions. Showing her nothing of the turmoil boiling inside of him. This was the first time since their meeting that her energy was not reaching out for him. Even fate knew their future was entirely dependent on Christine now.

He reached to cup her face in a way he had done countless times before, desperate to feel their connection, but this time she didn't lean into him. She pushed him away, tears stinging to break free. Resisting the urge to reach out to her again, he straightened, composure unbroken.

"Christine, feel how you will towards me, but we can't do this right now." Knowing he would try to justify locking her back up again, she scoffed.

"We agree. I know I can't do this right now. I'm not sure I'll be able to do this," she pointed rapidly from herself to him, "again." The colors of his eyes were darker somehow. Prompting her to remember if they had ever truly been black or if she had always just dismissed it as such.

Glancing around the room, over Jordan's two very still brothers, her shoulders slacked. Her eyes had touched everything in the room but him; he felt the slight keenly.

"I need at least a little bit of space to process this. Considering my recent discovery about the quality of the man I am tied to, I think my request is more than reasonable. A walk, one before we leave. Before I'm trapped and unsure of how independent my own thoughts are." Gritting his teeth, he stepped aside, allowing her to push past him and out the door.

Thad patted Jordan's shoulder, trailing behind Christine.

"I thought she knew," Kielius said in a pleading whisper. Jordan knew Kielius was right to fear him, but he also knew Kielius was not the one in the wrong.

"She should have." That was the only response he had. He needed to make his way to a broadcasting station.

Convincing one of the syndicates to begin spreading the spin of the newsreel that just played had been doctored. He grabbed a large sum of cash, avoiding looking at Kielius. Hearing a slight fizzling, he paused before transporting from the room and glanced to the door as it fell from its hinges. A faintly familiar face walked through the door, spinning a knife around his finger.

"Where the fuck is my baby sister?"

***

I had fled the confines of Jordan's penthouse expecting to be overwhelmed with images of his evil and instead tortured myself by running through possible justifications and then getting angry at myself for trying to justify such an awful thing.

'Was there a reason?'

'YEAH Christine, what kind of reason makes that okay.'

'Maybe there weren't all that many of them?'

'Even one death is too many.'

'You KNOW that.'

His very own words echoed in my head and were now so much clearer to me.

'Everyone has their own idea of what evil looks like. To many, I am the face of that evil, but that does not mean I need to be yours.'

I had known evil men. They Made a full career of teaching women how to fight against them, but this, how did I manage this? He was no man; he was a God. Did that mean he had different rules of morality? And if he did, was I someone who could accept those rules?

Being plastered all over the news meant even I could admit it wasn't wise to be walking around downtown without so much as a hoodie to cover my face. Tonight, I didn't have the luxury to care. I needed to seek refuge, somewhere I could think and form my own opinions without Jordan's kind eyes deceiving my reason.

Thad was blatantly following me; it was pissing me off.

Had I exposed our people to a world not yet ready? Kinda, yes. Had I very recently almost been killed? Also, yes. But neither of those things made me feel as though I needed a babysitter.

My great threat was bloody to a pulp, bleeding out somewhere after the beat-down Jordan gave him. So, I was in no mood to be 'looked after.' I turned on him and crossed my arms.

"I'm warning you, Thad. Go home before I become less friendly. I'm not in the fucking mood."

He didn't respond, just continued to follow me. Completely ignoring me, like normal.

I glared at him before turning and crossing the street to the only place I could think of going, Evans' gym.

"How would you know? You didn't even ask him. You just assumed the worst." I ignored his jab at me and unlocked the door with my new key.

I opened my mouth to snap at Thad as we walked into the studio. My throat turned into flypaper, catching the words before they could escape. An almost forgotten feeling of safety filled my chest with a warmth like sunlight itself.

Pierce stepped out of the doorway of Evans' office, and as our eyes met, I could see tears welling in his.

Thad gasped from behind me. "Christine, summon Jordan or run; I'll hold him off," he continued, positioning himself between us.

The soft excitement in Pierce's eyes went ablaze with possessiveness.

"Are you high?" I asked, pushing Thad aside. "He's not gonna hurt me. I need space anyway. I'm going with him."

Pierce reacted more violently than I would have expected. Either because of the broken sound of my voice, thanks to the festering burns, or the fact that Thad had grabbed my arm to stop me. He had a history of overreacting to anyone putting their hands on me; this was no exception.

Pierce had transported to us and effortlessly braced Thad

in an arm bar. I thought I had even caught a glimpse of a smile as Pierce shifted, snapping Thad's arm at the elbow.

Thad caught Pierce off guard with the lack of pain he displayed. In a fluid motion, Thad kicked his legs out from under him, springing back to his feet.

Considering the fuss Thad made the one time I knocked him down, I was a bit impressed with his composure. Not enough to warrant his overreaction, though.

"Christine, you don't know what you're doing!" he barked at me.

Pierce apparently didn't like his tone because he threw him roughly to the other side of the room before making his way toward me with a warm and relieved look on his face.

It shocked me when I felt Thad's hand on my shoulder. With his injury, I hadn't expected him to transport, especially with how much he feared it to begin with, yet he had. I whipped around and shoved him off me.

"Enough. I am a grown woman and will go where I choose. You can tell Jordan as much." I was exhausted and very much over the Savious family for the night, so when Thad glared at me and reached for me again, I blasted him with a wall of energy and pinned him to the wall.

Self-centeredness had consumed me. I had forgotten that the two men in the room with me were not just sparring over me but, in fact, were in the middle of a brewing war.

Thad's look of betrayal burned into my memory, the brand setting in and sizzling as Pierce appeared before him, a long white spear forming in his hand. I raised my hand in protest, beginning to scream, "don't," as he thrust the spear deep into Thad's chest, pinning him against the wall.

Blood spit from Thad's mouth and speckled across Pierce's shirt. My hands covered my mouth; my vision of him began to waver behind tears as Thad's head lolled to the side, his skin graying.

Thad hated me, and I wasn't his biggest fan. But I knew

him. He was good and loyal and the only person on this planet Jordan fully trusted; because of me and my damned temper, he was gone.

Pierce's chest obscured my vision, his arms wrapping tightly around me.

"It's okay, my love. You are safe now."

***

Jordan had paced for exactly twenty minutes when his impatience got the best of him. He decided he needed to go after Christine this time. He knew she needed space, but he also knew he could give her more context and then give her space as well.

His knee-jerk reaction to any situation was to let the dust settle and to push down any reaction he had to people's possibly changing perceptions of him. He was a divine leader; that kind of position would and should breed scrutiny.

He felt like an idiot for trying to apply that philosophy to Christine. Considering it was one taught to him by Arcane should have also tipped him off that it wasn't the best way to go about an argument or misunderstanding with the person you love.

He knew full well that Arcane couldn't have recognized love if Cupid himself smacked the rigid old bastard in the face. Truth be told, it would have been wise to take the advice Thad had given him the first week of having Christine.

When Thad had discovered his brother was Fated, he initially found it hysterical to imagine Jordan, of all people, wrapped around a woman's finger. But Thad could remember the feeling well and knew this was the only time he would likely be a resource for his brother.

He was, after all, the only one in Jordan's life that had known love and was willing to talk about it. Savious had been Fated to Jordan's mother, but made it clear to everyone that she was a topic not to be discussed.

Thad had given Jordan several pieces of advice, but the one he stressed the most and often reminded him was, 'tell her everything. Do not let someone else expose a deep dark secret of yours because then you aren't only guilty of whatever you didn't tell her, but of hiding it from her.'

The years he had lived had not prepared him to navigate the amount of weight one person's opinion would hold over him.

And now he would need to find her and do something he had never done in his long existence, grovel. Grovel and beg her to listen and try to understand. He would also need to let her go if that is what she chose. It wouldn't be an easy thing to walk away from Fate, but if there was ever a reason, this would be it.

"You look like your head is going to explode," Kielius said from the couch, looking at his disheveled brother.

"It feels that way too. You couldn't have waited to drop this bomb until a less chaotic night?" Jordan said, throwing an arm into his jacket and glaring over at Kielius.

The winged man who had broken in only moments ago crossed his arms impatiently. They had told him to wait. He could meet Christine as she should be back anytime now.

"YOU couldn't have told her one of the many nights you had her lavishly locked up in Hell?" he retorted. "Are you really running after her?"

"Yes. I can't just sit here. I handled that horribly."

"You should summon some rain. That always works in the movies."

Jordan chuckled, considering it briefly, knowing how fond of romantic comedies she was.

"She should be there about now, so she'll be inside. This city only houses one other refuge for her. The gym. We should be back soon. Do me a favor and start packing my things, will you?"

"Yes, Sir," Kielius said, throwing Jordan a loose salute causing Jordan to grin as he transported to the studio.

His grin evaporated instantly. Pierce had his arms wrapped around Christine. After making eye contact with Jordan, he grinned and transported her from the room. As they disappeared, his brother's limp body came into view, the long white spear glistening and dripping scarlet as it held Thad to the wall.

His instinct was to transport to Heaven, to go after Christine right now. But his brother needed him. The spear was lodged deep into the right side of Thad's chest, but after quickly checking, he confirmed his heart was still beating.

"Thad, buddy, come on. Wake up," Jordan said, wiping the blood from Thad's mouth and lightly smacking him. It took more than Jordan would have liked to rouse him and showed him how bad this wound really was. Thad drifted briefly back into consciousness, and upon seeing Jordan, tears welled in his tired eyes.

"I'm sorry. I..." He sputtered. Jordan felt his heart constrict in shame that his brother could be in this position and think he owed him an apology.

"Stop that. You did what you could. Just need to get rougher in training, I guess," Jordan teased. Thad needed to be moved. "I know how much you hate to transport, but I can't get you the help you need here. I need to take this out and cauterize the wound, okay?"

Thad limply nodded in acknowledgment. Jordan's fingers wrapped around the marble shaft, trying to ignore the familiar twinge it gave him. He had watched Pierce create his first one of these and had helped him hone this very skill.

He ripped it out quickly, and Thad fell from the wall into Jordan, who was prepared to catch him, leaving a dripping circle of crimson inked against the white-painted brickwork. He rested his brother on the floor and made a mental note of the way his eyes were dimming.

"This is going to hurt," Jordan warned, making sure his brother saw him form the words before pressing his hand to the oozing wound on Thad's chest. He summoned enough heat to cauterize the wound and cursed himself for not spending more time learning how to heal.

"Thad, stay awake." Thad's eyes had blinked a few times before his skin went a darker shade of gray. His eyes fluttered closed, as his body went completely limp.

New York would never forget that night. The night a young girl was broadcast everywhere, suspected of having superpowers, bearing a significant resemblance to a missing self-defense instructor named Christine.

But mostly for the storm born of Jordan's grief that ravaged the city and for the strange damage it had caused.

Three square miles had cracks throughout their brickwork and the asphalt in the streets. No window had been left unbroken; the wind shifted and flipped cars. No one had an explanation. The most perplexing thing about the storm wasn't only that it created the damage of both a tornado and an earthquake but the fact that it had been completely silent, as if, for the five minutes it ravaged the streets, sound had ceased to exist.

Asphalt against the metal of a rolling vehicle didn't screech. The powerful winds that broke thousands of windows didn't howl. For those five minutes, anyone unlucky enough to be within that three-mile radius had been certain they were experiencing the end of the world itself.

THE TRUTH WILL NOT, IN FACT, SET YOU FREE

The second I had made the decision to not only willingly but actively go with Pierce, the violence of regret ravaged my foundation. It was the first time in my life I was confident that I had made a genuine mistake.

For many reasons. I knew without a doubt that Jordan could show up anytime and drag my ass back to Hell. My biggest regret was the whole thing felt like a childish attempt to punish him for keeping such a monumental part of his past from me. It sickened me to know that in a moment I had chosen, based on my gut instinct, to do something as disgusting as using Pierce to hurt Jordan.

I wished I were the type of person who thought things through. Someone who slowed things down and calmed situations instead of someone who inflamed them. Wars of self-deprivation were waging battle, scarring the inside of my skull with vicious blows articulating the weakness of my character.

Although I did have to admit, the self-loathing was preferable to facing the image of Thad stuck up on that wall with his skin graying, life draining away, back to the river, flowing through the town he once labored over.

I was so preoccupied wallowing in worry over Thad that I hadn't even processed Pierce backing me up and gently sitting me down on the edge of my old bed. Looking around the room, it was strange that I wasn't greeted by a sense of homecoming.

This room had been my refuge. I had grown comfortable in its walls, but now, looking around, something had changed. The light gray and whites of the room had seemed clean and safe before, offering me comfort after long days of emotional overexposure to a world and people who were all always new. But now, the bleached color scheme of the paint on the walls and the starched fabrics of the furniture damn-near blinded me.

"My love, look at me. You must be in shock." Blinking the brightness of that Pierce-specific sunshine warmth from my eyes, I began to register he was kneeling before me, snapping his fingers, a concerned look defining the lines of his regal face.

"I..." Instead of creating words with their vibrations, my vocal cords protested their primary function, sending out a rough, high-pitched squeak instead. He flinched in response, eyes darting to the wreckage of my neck.

A small and unexpected half laugh escaped him.

"I apologize... You can't imagine how many times over the last several months I have envisioned this moment, and never in my wildest imaginings did you appear to me as silent." He pinched my chin affectionately before running his thumb along my jaw. I squirmed at the warmth of the moment. Guilt raced up my spine as he pulled away, noticing my discomfort.

He stood, hardening the mood as he looked me sternly in the eyes. "You are safe now. He will never put his hands on you again. A Medic will heal you, you will get some much-needed rest. I will see you for a private breakfast in the morning."

The fog I was shifting through was still only allowing me

to process new information bits at a time and the part of his statement I felt stuck on, repeating in my head, was that I was safe now.

Why would he bother assuring me? Of course I was safe now, but it had nothing to do with him. In fact, Savious hurting me again was the least of my worries. Jordan had beaten him within an inch of his life. I would not only be surprised but downright impressed to see him alive. There was something about watching a man curl into the fetal position after getting his teeth punched into the back of his throat that really stole his menace.

Glancing back at me from the doorway, Pierce paused, meeting my eyes with a severity I didn't recognize from our past time spent together. Within the expression he had tried but failed to hide, I could almost feel the turmoil raging within him at letting me out of his sight. I shot him an attempted reassuring smile to alleviate his worry, if only a little. It was a relief that it worked when he did, in fact, to my immediate relief, leave.

Letting out the breath I hadn't realized I had been holding, I slumped over, hiding my face in my hands. Taking a moment to just breathe and remind myself why I was here and that I was very much on borrowed time.

My soul cracked as it frosted over while I dug through the books Pierce had approved of for me back during my life of restricted access. Having access to unlimited information was something I was not giving up by coming back here. Pierce could not and would not be steamrolling me into submission on that topic again, not after I had spent, however long, un-restricted.

Before my time with Jordan, I had felt like a cold person, not intentionally, of course, but I always saw myself that way. I had always pulled away from opportunities to connect with others, and I sure as hell wouldn't have faced adversity to see the best in someone.

In truth, I didn't believe in giving people the benefit of the doubt. To me, everyone was garbage until proven otherwise; sadly, I had endless examples of people who proved that theory correct.

The books Pierce had allowed me weren't few, but they were lacking. Stacks of them still cluttered each corner of the room and just about any crevice. Most of them had been committed to memory, yet here I was digging. Desperately looking for some hint of acknowledgment that a genocide had taken place.

Of all the things I received a crash course on, nothing in print even hinted at such a crucial piece of this world's history. The books I had been 'approved' were of the geographical makeup of Heaven and its different territories. They touched on brief political histories of the different territories and the impact Pierce's ancestors had on them as the Gods on High.

After what felt like an eternity of skimming book after useless book, I was jarred by an abrupt knocking at the door.

I didn't bother to attempt calling out an invitation. I figured Pierce would warn them I was, at the moment, vocally challenged. Being back in a gracious realm meant my wounds were healing on their own but given their severity, it was always a possibility I would experience permanent scarring.

Seeing a medic was a good idea. Plus, I couldn't help but appreciate the unselfish way Pierce just knew I needed some time to readjust. I filed the example away in my brain for any future arguments I may have with Jordan on the possibility of Pierce threatening my safety.

I snapped back into an old habit of standing for my introduction to a new person. I straightened my back, and a flare skipped across my chest. Hand flying to Jordan's mark, I found I was unnervingly relieved at the discovery that there was fabric covering it, hiding it. I was not ready for Pierce or any of his admirers to see that quite yet.

It wasn't lost on me that my disdain for meeting new people

was a bit unfair to the admiring masses of this realm. Granted, to them I needed to appear worthy of their admiration, worthy of being this Goddess on high. After falling in love with Jordan, any act I put on for the sake of making a new acquaintance would make me feel like a fraud. That discomfort and pressure weighed extra on me for this first interaction.

While I debated the most appropriate stance I should be in, arms crossed, hands on hips, hands folded in front of me, the Medic let herself in. The woman who entered didn't look like any doctor I had ever seen. Some women have been described as brightening a room when they enter it. This one seemed to darken it in a deep and sultry sort of way. Her legs were graciously wrapped in tight black silk, and she had a flowing deep green shirt that set the vibrant red in her hair ablaze and warmed the brown embers of her calculating gaze.

I instantly decided the next time I glamor my hair, I was going to try that color because it gave this woman, who was, to the best of my knowledge, a healer, a seriously fierce look that I would revel donning.

I was admiring her, standing with my arms crossed in front of me, as she reached out to shake my hand. I met her gaze just as she had finished giving me a narrow-eyed once-over.

"Christine. Interesting to finally make your acquaintance. Name's Nacentra." I hesitantly took her hand, not sure if she was going to help heal me or try and kill me based on the look in her eyes and the edge in her voice.

"Well, let's get to it. I need you to answer a question for me, and if I make you talk in this condition, I have a strong inkling Jordan will string me up by my toes when he reclaims the throne here soon." She gave me a conspiratorial grin in response to my shock, not bothering to be gentle as she grabbed my neck in the same way Savious had.

As she squeezed, I could feel the pain, the burning as fresh as it had been while Savious scorched me. But then, as quickly as that pain had been there, her hand pulled away from my neck by only a few centimeters. Her eyes reminded me of perfectly mixed coffee and creamer. I could swear her gaze was just as hot as a fresh pot as she stared intently at my injury.

"This is going to burn again; there are several layers of damage here, and I don't want you to scar, so I am being thorough. Unfortunately, the more precise I am, the more it will hurt," she warned, grabbing my neck again and squeezing. This time there was no heat; in place of the burning, it felt like she was crystalizing my neck with ice shards.

We stayed like that, the ice invading deeper and deeper into my throat, scraping its way past my vocal cords and esophagus before she changed expressions. It astounded me that this was healing me and not causing more damage.

She abruptly yanked her hand away; its absence was met with the sweet cooling effect of an aloe she most certainly did not use. Triumph shone from the whites of the perfectly straight teeth of her smile.

"On the souls of the Gods on high, I am good," she lamented, playfully hitting my shoulder, grabbing me and turning me to face the mirror hanging above the antique dresser that held nothing because I refused to allow someone else to fold my clothes, so I insisted on hanging my own clothes up in the closet and leaving the ugly antique empty.

I didn't bother hiding how impressed I was. Where I had been practically broiled at skin level, there was now just a hint of red. Testing her work, I attempted to speak.

"Thank you." My throat felt dry, but there was no longer any pain.

"You, you unlucky gal, are very welcome." She was sincere in both statements as she sat heavily at my desk, tipping the chair back and propping her feet up on the desk. "Can we speak without you reporting my every word to Pierce?"

She had me more than intrigued. "Sure..."

Confidently, she sat up, her pointy elbows rested on her

knees; her chin was resting on her bundled-together fists.

"Did you tell Pierce Jordan did that to you?" She wiggled a red polished nail at me. "Or did he just assume?" Blankly, I stared back at her. Surely looking daft as her question took its time registering for me.

"Neither... I assume he knows this was Savious's handiwork since it was all over the news... and that's how he found me in the first place. Why would you think he blames Jordan for this?" I asked.

Shaking her head, she snorted disapprovingly at my ignorance.

"Well, I have made it clear to anyone who would listen that Jordan is inaccurately represented not only in the media but in our teachings of history. Pierce isn't a fan of having someone like me out there singing Jordan's praise, as someone people are aware knew him. I am not the best Medic he could have sent. He himself is one of the realm's finest. But he asked me to heal you in hopes that I would see the damage 'Jordan' inflicted on you, and it would change my opinion of him. If there had been video evidence of what Savious did to you, he hasn't seen it yet."

"If that newsreel hasn't made it here yet, how did you know Pierce was wrong?" Nacentra cleared her throat, blushing regally.

"Jordan and I were close for some time. And during that time, I encouraged him to handle me in a way that left the indents of his hands on me. And his hands are bigger than the ones that burnt you." Now I was the one blushing at her bold declaration.

"So, you and Jordan were 'very' close...?" I asked, unable to help myself. The heat burning my face wasn't just discomfort, but anger and jealousy. He was mine; I didn't like the thought of his hands on her in any way.

Her smile was a sad one, as if knowing my thoughts. It was a sad but very genuine smile of knowing.

"Not as close as I would have liked. I appreciate the fact that you look like you could burn a hole through my brain right now. It confirms a suspicion of mine." My head tilted in question.

"Jordan and you, you're fated together, aren't you?" she asked, a desperate twinge to it. Looking around nervously, I found myself pausing.

"Pierce won't hear it from me if you are," she promised. I wasn't sure if I was relieved that my conviction in my link to him hadn't wavered with being worlds apart, or concerned me, given his history.

"Yes, we are," I admitted. She let out a long-staggered breath.

"Thank you. I needed to hear that. Knowing it was always you he was waiting for and knowing it wasn't anything I was lacking, it was something I needed to hear. Be careful in your delivery, though. Pierce is dangerous, and he is certain you are his. This is going to shake him to his foundation. Empaths are skilled at confusing you, so stay resolute when you tell him."

She pinned me with a 'got it?' stare and pushed her hair back away from her face getting up to leave, but I stopped her with my question.

"An Empath?" She whirled to meet my gaze.

"Please, for the love of Jordan, tell me this isn't the first you're hearing of this?"

"Hearing of what?"

"Pierce is an Empath. Able to manipulate your emotions, reactions, hormones...." She motioned in a continuous gesture.

I shook my head. "He couldn't be. He has spent waaaay too long convinced I am just confused about not feeling enough for him. There is no way he could literally feel that whole time how specifically what I was feeling."

"I assure you; Pierce has been tuned into your emotions since the second he met you."

***

336

Jordan was sitting against the wall while Mother busily worked around Thad's body. Having blood crusting his hands had become an unfamiliar feeling, and now, thrust into a new time of war, he tried to accept the fact this would likely not be the last time.

Looking at his brother stirred a lust for action he, at this very moment, was unable to satiate. His motivation was so acute he had to fight off the temptation not to pop over to Heaven and end things right now, but that would be a much bloodier and much more selfish method of regaining control.

Staring at the vaguely familiar way the dried blood cracked as he flexed the straightened his fingers, he tried distracting himself from worry by thinking about how disappointed he was in Christine.

She saw an out. A way of temporarily delaying having to make the decision to accept or reject his sins. For the first time in her life, she chose the coward's path and ran. That disappointment was strong but unfortunately not nearly enough to dampen the anger festering within him towards the person he knew was truly responsible for this mess. Himself.

He had failed to warn Christine of Pierce's inclination. He had failed to be the one to reveal the darkest stain on his soul. And he had been so ashamed of a mistake made long ago that he allowed his judgment to lapse, his guard to drop, leading to the possible death of his brother. Once Thad was stabilized, he would get Christine, regardless of if she were willing to come home.

After what the Fates had confessed to him what they had done, there wasn't a chance in any of the three realms she would be spending a minute more than necessary in the same world as Pierce. Let alone in his direct company.

'Fuck, how could I not tell her that he is an Empath, or tell her what she is, for that matter? I am just as bad as him, just less clever at what information I conceal.'

"Do ya plan to keep brooding or help me?" Mother chided,

cocking a bony hand on her hip, eyebrows raised expectantly.

"All-powerful God, my ass, can't even heal a stab wound, pathetic," she added.

This was not the first time she had scolded him for neglecting this area of training. She had warned him when they met that being selfish and focusing on strength alone because he himself didn't need much healing would, 'come back to bite him in the ass,' and she was right.

He pulled himself up and was stunned to see she had already finished stitching Thad's wound closed. His complexion was tinted again, not pale. Christine didn't know, but Thad regularly wore a glamor to hide the gray complexion of his skin.

Jordan could understand why; he wanted to be known as one of the brothers instead of just another one of the people. Savious had spent enough time treating him as if he were 'just another person of Hell' instead of family that Thad would do anything to exist more comfortably around his family.

"He is very lucky whoever stabbed him didn't know a damned thing about a Givi's anatomy."

"Had his heart been where yours is, there would be nothing I could do." She sighed, looking at Azazel. He was leaning in the corner, using his wings to prop him up straighter than he otherwise would be.

"What about you, Feathers? If you joined the team, I might need to stitch you up; anything I should know now about the locations of your vital organs." Until Mother had addressed Azazel, Jordan had forgotten the Guardian had grabbed his shoulder as he transported Thad into Hell.

"Don't worry, baby doll; I'm not so easily shish kebabbed," Azazel retorted flippantly, eyes never leaving Thad's scarred chest.

"Shish kebab?" Mother asked. Jordan cleared his throat, regaining her sole attention. "Calm down. Thad will heal. It's going to take some time. But he's one of us, so he'll heal. We both know my people are stronger than yours," she added with a wink.

She paused once to rest a hand on Jordan's shoulder and, with a look, let him know she would be back to check on his damaged little brother again soon. Grabbing the last of the bloodied rags, she tossed them in the trash and sauntered from the room.

"Well, you hitchhiked, literally on my back, to my realm. What do you plan to do now?" Jordan asked Azazel.

Back at the condo, before he had decided to go after Christine, they had gotten introductions out of the way. Jordan knew he was looking to protect his sister, but he didn't know why he had waited until now to do so. Or why he followed them here while she was in Heaven, unprotected.

"I lead the Old Guard. In my experience, rashly jumping into a fight never beats out assessing a situation first. We need to get Christine away from Pierce, but I am open to any suggestions from you on how we do that." Jordan didn't miss the fact that Azazel's gaze continued to dart back to his brother.

"Unlike you, I am not bound by the inconveniences of regular extraction methods. If my brother wakes up, tell him I will be back shortly and that I waited until he was stable enough to leave," Jordan said, glancing at his brother. "He's sensitive about stuff like that," he added with a softer tone before disappearing from view.

Azazel had to admit it did look much more convenient than flying. But not nearly as stylish.

***

She stood, hands pressed against the stonewall of the shower, letting cold water wash over her. Nacentra had healed her wounds but completely decimated her resolve. According to her, Pierce had the ability to control the emotions of others. But if that were true, and he was willing to use those gifts as

Nacentra suspected, wouldn't he have used them to make her love him?

Her burning scar was delightfully cooled by the bite of cold water on her chest. She banished her condemning thoughts against Pierce. There was no proof that Pierce had ever manipulated her. Nothing to go on other than the words of Jordan's self-declared ex-girlfriend. Even this, the time alone, the space to readjust, gave weight to her desire to give him the benefit of the doubt.

The space between her and Jordan did nothing to lessen her love for him. And she found that infuriating. Her hope was that Nacentra had been right.

"My theory is that you were put in their lives to be a person capable of brokering peace between them. They may not be willing to negotiate with one another, but they are desperate to win your favor. I'm guessing even if that means putting their pride and plans aside at your request," she had explained.

This theory was too appealing for Christine to dismiss outwardly. She needed it, something or someone believing she had the ability to do more than simply exist as someone's wife.

Closing her eyes, a sense of calm wrapped around her. She allowed herself to give in to the all-encompassing warmth, distracting her from her current trials. She allowed herself to enjoy the feeling of power flowing through her veins, of the world electrifying all of the nerves in her body with unlimited potential.

That was one of the many addicting attributes about Jordan. He had a knack for bringing this side of her out, fueling her and strengthening her in a way that made her think she would one day be able to fight her own battles.

Her eyes snapped open as the thought occurred to her that she had been taking a very cold shower and had only felt this specific type of warmth under very specific circumstances. Eyes open, she now knew she was being eclipsed by the shadow of a large body over hers. There were long masculine fingers spread over her own, still pressing against the tile of the shower.

"Showering without me, my Goddess?" Her heart jumped into her throat. Her feet leapt from the ground, and her back landed against a solid torso as a smoke-wrapped arm caught her. A strong hand clamped over her mouth, muffling her scream.

"Shh, shh, shh. Sorry. I didn't expect to catch you off guard; I assumed you sensed my presence." Registering it was only Jordan, her hammering heart slowed but only slightly.

"Don't take me," she blurted out the instant his hand left her mouth. An air of worry settled between them as he said nothing in response. The black hue of his loose cotton shirt darkened from the spray water still flowing from the shower head. "And... I am so sorry."

Thinking of Thad once again, tears burned the back of her eyes as she expected him to ice over, to renounce his love for her and her selfish ways.

No such thought was possible for him as she blinked her big blue eyes at him, brimming with fresh pain, of which he took a great part.

 Cupping her face in between both his hands, he brushed the softest of kisses to her lips, whispering against them. "Any fault is shared between us. We should both save our apologies for Thad himself."

"Wait, hold up," she said, pressing her hands to his chest. "Thad's, okay?" He smiled at the hopeful glitter in her eyes.

"I wouldn't use 'okay' to describe his current condition. He needs to heal. Pierce completely missed any vital organs. It helps that he has not a clue what differences Thad's anatomy holds." Her face scrunched.

"Different anatomy?"

"Yes... His mother was Givi, and her DNA overwhelmed our father's Angelican contributions." She had learned some of the basic anatomical differences while in Hell.

One of the largest differences being that the people born of that world, Givi as they called themselves, had no heart. Their blood flowed easily throughout their body without a pump.

"So, his skin graying... Oh my God, is he DEAF?" She smacked her own forehead, so many of their interactions making way more sense.

She felt like an idiot for not piecing together Thad and Kielius were part Givi. It made sense. Savious was a resident of Hell, and therefore for him to have kids, it made sense it was with Givi women. But she had never heard either of them mention their mothers.

"He is, yes. But he can speak and read lips; I taught him very well. If you don't mind, I would much rather discuss this back home and not dripping wet." He looked ridiculous standing there, fully clothed, water dripping down his face as he continued to basically surround her.

"No." One word but delivered with a resounding authority that spoke volumes on a conviction he couldn't help but adore.

He had expected this but hadn't come to barter. Leaning in, closing off the already small distance between them, he placed one foot between her bare legs. His hands were on each side of her as he leaned slowly in, waiting until her back arched from the cold of the tiles to bend down and part her wanting lips with his.

At that moment, her mind blinded itself from what she knew him guilty of and registered only this connection. Their energies compounded between them, power colliding, tying them tighter together. Tightening the knot of their already taut thread of Fate. Ravaging them both with a spine-tingling sensation of desired oneness.

Feeling as though he would snap from the tension building, he loosened the moment by lifting his face away from hers until they were nose to nose.

"You don't get to just say *no*, my demanding Goddess. Not this time." Remorse dripped from his words. Choice was something he desperately wanted her to have, but it was not a gift she had yet to prove she was capable of safely handling.

"Fine... *please* no." Blinking innocently up at him and attempting a sweet smile, she thought maybe she could get him to grin or laugh. Something to break the seriousness of the moist air hanging around them.

The blank moroseness of his expression didn't waver. After a moment of looking her in the eye, he simply shook his head, singularly to each side.

"I need to tell him the truth. He deserves to be freed from the lie he is living, and he has earned, at the very least, the right to hear that truth from me," she pleaded.

His eyes darkened, narrowing protectively. "Absolutely not."

His voice had dropped to a timbre she registered as his attempt at sounding 'authoritative.' What he didn't know, and what she planned to never tell him, was that it was completely ineffective towards her as she found his attempted gruffness sexy, not scary.

"Jordan, I owe him that," she begged, bunching the chest of his shirt in her hands.

"No, the fuck, you don't," he said disbelievingly, looking at her like she had completely lost her mind.

The thought that she felt she owed anything to Pierce had fueled the rage burning within the depth of his soul and forced him to step away from her. His hand ran through his hair as he spun away from her, trying to get himself under control before he started having an effect on the spaces around them, alerting everyone to his presence.

"Nacentra also brought up a good point," she started quickly, hoping this would stall him from just grabbing her and going.

"WAIT. You met Nacentra?" The velocity at which he turned back around had almost made her think her attempt backfired until, instead of putting his hands on her, they both pressed against his forehead as if he were warding off a migraine.

"Leggy, perfect, Nacentra, your ex? Yes. She is the healer Pierce called in to fix my neck. At Least you had good taste before me. Listen... I am not ready to come back. I need to ask Pierce some questions, tell him the truth, and while I'm at it, try and broker peace between you two. Your fan girl was a bit jealous, but she made some good points."

"She isn't my fan. She is a very good friend. Or, I had thought so until this. I am going to kill her."

"Jordan. I can do this."

"Christine. I am not doubting your capabilities. But even you must see how unreasonable your ask is." What he deemed as unreasonable, she knew, was the only chance either of them had of coming out of this whole mess unbloodied.

"Unreasonable? I'm asking you for a day. That's it," she stated as if that cleared things up; by the further clenching of his jaw, she hurried along.

"You obviously have no trouble getting to me. I can still summon you if I need you. Just give me until tomorrow at this time. You two may not be willing to talk to each other, but maybe that's why I was thrown into this mess. You both seem willing to talk to me."

He contemplated her words, trying not to warm to her at this moment as she pressed her hands together in mock prayer, staring at him, fully naked, in a cold shower, hope brimming in her eyes.

"I am not looking for peace. I am looking to regain my lost kingdom and unite worlds." It was important to him that she understood the difference.

"If I can convince him to step down peacefully from a position he never wanted in the first place, we can avoid a war. Maybe all he needs is to have it on good authority that you aren't the same person who committed genocide against everyone like him."

Her point was solid and stated so simply it even sounded possible. But Jordan knew the allure of power. Those who claimed to never want it generally had the hardest time relinquishing it.

"Nacentra told you about him?"

"Yes. And I'm glad it came from her and not you. It was more digestible that way. Jordan, I need to do this. If anyone can get him to correct the people's current view of you and ensure a smooth transition, it is me." Her confidence in her sway of Pierce left him feeling unbalanced and uneasy.

"My Goddess, he will never do that. The admission that I am not the evil being of his spun narrative would open up the opportunity for far too many questions. The answers of which would drastically dim that overly fluorescent light of his," he chided.

"I need to stay, Jordan. I don't want to do this. I need to."

He gritted his teeth, fighting with the many things she needed to know when a knock sounded on the door. Pierce had her being watched around the clock and her thirty minutes of timed shower privileges were apparently over. "Twenty-four hours, Christine. Not a minute more. If you feel even remotely threatened, you summon me immediately. Do NOT try and fight him under any circumstances. I mean it." She nodded excitedly.

"Promise me." For the first time since knowing him, she heard desperation in his voice. It made her hesitate before grabbing his face the way he always grabbed hers and kissed him.

"I promise."

The door handle wiggled; in a swift movement, he pulled her as close as he could. Time stilled as their energy collided, their tethered coil strumming in appreciation of this kiss. All too quickly, he disappeared, leaving her fighting the urge to gasp from the shock to her senses at his absence.

She was surprised it wasn't anyone she knew at the door.

Pierce had always been so restrictive to the people he had tending to her. The woman who had knocked was a soft-faced, elderly woman who let her know it had been thirty minutes and Pierce was insistent she get a good night's sleep.

The small, hunched woman left her in peace, and after drying, Christine sat at the end of the bed she once hid contraband books beneath and sighed out in frustration. Fearing the lack of sleep she would get without Jordan beside her, and then fearing what it meant about her that she could so desperately want someone capable of such terrible things.

She woke in the morning in the same place she had sat down the night before. Her arms sprawled, reaching to the side for someone who wasn't there. The turmoil of the day had hit her hard enough that she had passed out before even crawling up and pulling the covers over her.

Taking the time she hadn't the day before, she admired the way Pierce had made sure everything in her room had been kept clean and exactly how she had left it. It floored her that it had only been six months since Jordan had taken her to Hell and blown up her world again, but this time, she didn't want to change it.

She wasn't upset to have met him or to have fallen for him. She was his, and he was hers and looking at the room around her, she felt a ghost of the guilt that once plagued her.

Digging through the dresser, she pulled out a black turtleneck, cotton, knee-high dress to hide her mark for now. As gentle as Pierce had been with her in the past, she wanted to be careful around him out of respect for the promise she made to Jordan. She had done a terrible job of living up to her promises thus far and wanted to be able to hold true to at least one.

She was just finishing shimmying into her dress when she heard a gentle knock on the door.

"It's open!" she called from the small dressing room. Grabbing a pair of slip-on flats, she walked into the main room of her suite and saw Pierce sitting rigidly at the end of her bed with his head in his hands.

"Pierce?" she asked, concerned. She had never seen him break his stoic composure. He looked up at her abruptly, his sharp eyes stunning her in place. Her heart broke for him seeing the strain leave his eyes as they made their way up her body and stilled on her face.

"You bought that dress on our first excursion to town. I had been delighted that you had chosen something that suited you so nicely, yet you never wore it in the whole of your time here."

She could see the amused glint in his eyes, one he had once described as existing solely for her. That little well of guilt pooled a bit deeper.

The dress just seemed like the natural thing to grab, something Jordan would have picked out for her and she would have pretended to hate, but secretly loved. A dress that made her feel strong, sexy and confident. A not-so-confident blush ran across her cheeks now at the uncomfortable attention it was getting her.

His smile widened; he sat up a bit taller and relaxed.

"Oh, Darling, I didn't mean to make you insecure; I'm sorry. I just, seeing you in something other than jeans threw me off. I forgot how beautiful you are."

Guilt added a deeper crimson to the flush in her face, and his smile widened dangerously, pulling himself off the bed and making his way towards her.

"I will not deny I am appreciating still having some effect on you after being separated all this time."

He didn't seem to notice her backing away as he advanced. She could feel, aware now of his gifts, that he was attempting to root through her emotions. It was strange; now that she was aware of it, his manipulations felt obvious. So out of place within her body. It made her a bit irritated, knowing all the time she spent dwelling over her being broken and that being why her emotions never made sense.

She internally blocked him. As he pulled her in for a kiss, she raised her hand between their lips. Ducking and stepping out from the circle of his arms, he stilled, looking confused.

"What's wrong? What did he do to you?"

'Not sure there is anything he hasn't done to me, but I enjoyed it all,' she thought, suppressing a nervous laugh.

"Pierce." His eyes flamed; he stepped close again, and again she backed away, "You need to know... You found me on Middle Earth because I asked to be there. Jordan wasn't keeping me captive. You told me countless times I was only here for my safety. I don't need protection from Jordan, and he has secured my protection from his father." An unfamiliar stillness had settled over him.

"You claim he simply released you on Middle Earth? If that were true, why did I have to kill someone to get to you?" he questioned.

"Thad was there to make sure no harm came to me. He's protective and has more enemies than just you, or so he says. He also helps train me." She tried to explain without giving out too much.

"If he released you, why would he care about protecting you, if not to keep you from me?" Pierce inched closer again.

"You have it wrong. Those years of you valiantly trying to spark something between us, and me never being able to give you enough... We aren't fated, Pierce. It's Jordan. I'm so sorry." She rambled the words out, guilt ebbing with each one at the pain in his eyes as she said them.

His head rocked back and forth. Again, she felt the itchy presence of Pierce attempting to manipulate her emotions and though she tried to resist she didn't know if such a thing was even possible, if this interaction was proving anything, it was that defending against an emotional attack was fruitless.

"Jordan has spent a lifetime perfecting manipulation, Christine. We *are* fated. You and me." He inched closer again, and again she backed away, trying to keep at least a foot of distance between them; she knew the closer he was, the easier it was for him to get inside her.

"Was he patient with you, gentle and always kind?" Pierce clipped accusingly.

'Not always,' she thought, 'but I loved it because it was him.'

The feeling of want was invading the space between her legs. Her mind screamed in protest to the violation. Any guilt fiercely evaporated.

"You want to talk about manipulation. Okay, let's talk. But first, please retract yourself from my hormones." His eyes widened.

"Yeah, I know what you are, and I don't care, but stop trying to force me to feel things I don't. I want Jordan, not you. Fucking with my hormones isn't going to change that." For a brief second, he lost composure, and palpable rage was evident on his face, but the feeling receded from her body none-the-less.

"And what exactly am I?" The words were too flat, too pressed, as if he were putting in a bit too much effort to wring out any reaction. She composed herself, standing a bit taller and taking another step back as he had again advanced on her.

"An Empath. As far as Jordan knows, you are the only living Angelican left with these abilities because he protected you from the genocide committed against the others."

In her heart, she knew she meant what she said, and that although Jordan wasn't innocent, she couldn't fully fault him for his part in the atrocity. There had to be more to that story.

"A shining example of why information needs to be delivered in a specific order. He did not protect me, per se. He was the only one who knew what I was, and he didn't say anything when he and my father started murdering my kind."

Christine flinched. She had no idea that Arcane was involved in what had happened and had made the assumption Jordan had protected him.

ALLYSON KUEPFER

"Do you see now how information can be manipulated based on how it is delivered? I have always done everything I can to protect you, and I always will. I have proven that."

"Stop." She held up her hands; to both his advancing and his words.

"Jordan made sure to give me any information I wanted as unbiasedly as possible. I had access to news from all of the worlds. He is incredibly powerful and capable of manipulation, I'm sure. But that doesn't change the fact that he didn't need to manipulate me. I wanted him. I want him. Only him. Go ahead and 'prove it' again. Take. Me. Home."

She was done dancing around the subject. Pierce shifted then. She couldn't tell if it was the slightly stiffer way he was standing or the irritated way he had clenched his jaw. But something about him had become new. New and starkly cold in comparison with the sunbeam she had gotten used to.

"Marry me." She blanched at the random and completely out of place words, so taken aback she almost missed the new steel in his tone.

"What about anything I just said makes you think I would marry you?"

She knew marriage was another tradition copied from the Angelicans. When it came to their leaders, they took it much more seriously. To them, 'till death did you part' really did mean eternity; divorce symbolized failure and would result in your people losing faith in you.

"What about my tone makes you assume I was asking?" The threat he was emanating was dense and elicited a gulp from her. She traced the hidden mark and tapped the top.

A spike of warmth left her. Pierce's eyes narrowed at her hand, and his jaw clenched again. He teleported in front of her so quickly she had barely let out a surprised yelp as he ripped the neck of the dress down to her breasts, revealing Jordan's now glowing symbol.

He stumbled back as if she had struck him as she gathered

the ripped pieces of cloth together, trying to cover up.

"He disfigured you, marked you, and I'm the monster for making small adjustments to your emotions in an attempt to help you adapt?" His words were heavy with disbelief and landed their intended blow.

Afraid as she was at this moment, she couldn't deny there was some truth in what he was saying. His eyes shimmered, unable to pull his gaze away from the scar.

"Summon him all you want. Go ahead, torture him for me. I assure you he isn't coming." Grabbing her arm, he led her to the dressing room and shoved her toward her clothes.

"Change; I need you to cover up."

"Seeing his mark on me is that bothersome, huh?" she shot back, grabbing a pair of jeans and a cotton shirt with a high neckline. She ignored his remark about Jordan not coming. He underestimated Jordan if he really thought he could keep him from her. Pierce looked her up and down without regard to her protest as she changed.

"'Bothersome' is not nearly strong enough a word. But I'm more concerned with how poorly I may handle seeing you like this, exposed. I have been patient to not push you these last few years, but that patience has just run out." The implication sped her dressing up significantly and added slime to the distinct feel of his violating gaze.

"You are confused right now. But once we are married and you have had some time to heal, things will be back on track for us. Until then, it would help me if you could try and lessen the temptation." He broke it down for her slowly, as if she was some temptress who needed convincing, and he wasn't the one who had just exposed her by force.

She marched angrily over to him, now fully dressed, and crossed her arms aggressively.

"There is no way, on any of these three planes of existence, I would ever marry you, so you're just gonna have to go fuck yourself."

His hand cracked across the side of her face, breaking the skin and knocking her to the ground. He knelt above her and grabbed her chin, inspecting the broken skin with startling concern.

"Great, that is going to need to be glamoured now for the wedding," he scolded himself.

She looked up at him, wide-eyed, in utter shock. Stunned that this was the same man she had lashed out at continually, who had never shown anything but warmth in response to her icy remarks. The gentle, kind man she gave Jordan her word was no threat. She smacked his hand and pulled herself up, standing away from him.

"Really, nothing to say. Is that all you've needed to be compliant all this time after all?" His tone was light and taunting as he joked like he hadn't just smacked the breath out of her.

"Slapping me around won't change anything. I am not yours, Pierce. There are plenty of women here who would happily be your queen, but you cannot force me. This," she pointed to her face, "doesn't help your case. You so much as touch me again, and I'll break your fucking hand." She crossed her arms and cocked a hip, pretending to be unfazed as pain radiated on the side of her face.

Jordan's words of warning drummed in her ears. She couldn't fight him; if she lost it, he might know what her inclination was, and that could put her in danger. She just wished Jordan had told her in what way so she could weigh the odds on whether it was worth the risk. Assuming he meant his threats, she figured Jordan would probably be okay with her fighting back in this scenario.

Pierce backed her up to a wall and pinned her to it. His elbows dug into her chest as he clasped her head between his hands, inspecting her. Leaning forward, he placed his forehead to hers and whispered very gently.

"Let me make this very clear. What I want more than anything in all the worlds, is you sitting on the throne next to me, crown on your head, and pride in your eyes," He paused, forcing a soft but unreciprocated kiss onto her lips, the scar on her chest flared in protest, "but I will happily settle for you sitting at my feet with a collar around your neck." He chuckled as he felt the sensation of absolute terror pulsing through her veins, sending pleasurable electric shivers down his legs.

"Do you really think the people will keep you on that moral pedestal of yours if they see this side of you?" she asked, hating herself for being this blind. Had the women she helped experienced this? Had she known other women who had witnessed this kind of complete personality deception?

He was running his fingers through her hair and running the tip of his nose up her neck. He slowed by her ear and spoke sensually into it.

"Every great man in history has had their vice. Angry drunk, repeat cheater, gambler, drugs... Mine, as it appears, is you. Besides, I am sure I can find a way to help you behave in public." She tried to get out of his grasp, but he countered her movement and thrust her harder against the wall, his smile widening playfully and her terror growing.

"You don't know me at all, do you?" she said, leaning forward as if to kiss him, distracting him just enough she was able to raise one of her feet up along the wall enough to push herself with enough momentum to break free. He laughed darkly behind her as she ran to the door and pulled; nothing happened, it wouldn't budge.

"I begged Jordan to spare your life, said you were a good man, a great leader. My God, I feel like an idiot." He was ignoring her, punching something into his phone. She felt the space of the doorway open up behind her and turned to see Victor there, looking at her apologetically, holding Amy by the arm. She was only half conscious, bloodied badly.

Victor pulled Amy inside the room and closed the door behind them, tossing Amy to the ground. Christine rushed to her.

"What did you do!? What is wrong with you!?" she sobbed, trying to get Amy's attention, but as soon as she noticed Christine's face, her glare had settled on Pierce.

Amy's voice was a rasp but filled with vile, "You better hope that heals before Jordan sees her again, or your death will be drastically drawn out." The pre-existing humor had left his face.

"Amy here," Pierce indicated, "has been convicted of elevated treason. She was the mole who informed Jordan when and where you were going to be the day he took you. She also programmed Jordan's DNA into the shields system so he could come and go as he pleased." He feigned a tsk tsk sound before continuing.

"Putting you in harm's way like that is not something I take lightly, and is an offense punishable by death, but I know how much you care for her. So, I wanted to let you make the decision regarding what to do with her. Now, however, knowing they have confused you so thoroughly, she can serve a different purpose."

Victor grabbed Amy's hair lifting her slightly from the ground as Pierce wrapped an arm around Christine's waist and pulled her to her feet, away from them.

He held her tightly against him as she sobbed, using his hand to force her to keep looking at Amy's broken figure, tears running over his tightly clamped hand. She struggled as Victor drew a knife from his waistband and held it reluctantly to Amy's neck.

"Killing Amy, it isn't ideal. You love her. I know that. She is simply trying to be loyal to you. But I will do what I must. Trust me when I tell you I would prefer not to, for your sake. I offer you this; if you can promise to behave, at least in public, we can pardon her and let her live," he whispered into the crook of her neck, the words meant as a means of connection. A failed attempt at offering her something he figured she would want.

Taking a deep breath, she calmed herself, trying to level the teeter-totter flipping within her stomach. She felt his arms relax around her as he registered the stillness of her emotions. Hoping, praying, that he would misunderstand where her new serenity was coming from.

Amy finally looked at her, a look that only Christine would be able to read. And Christine knew at that moment, Empath or not, only someone interested in knowing her, the real her, would be able to ever truly read her, as her friend knew, with just that look what she was planning to do.

"The thing about Amy, she has this complex that my safety is her responsibility," Pierce's shoulder rolled back slightly into place, his hold losing some of its vice as he misread her resoluteness, her stillness as compliance.

"She needs to learn family protects each other." The words came out raw and deep, falling over one another, each bounding over the last, building in tensile conviction.

With that, Christine thrust her hands forward, creating a dense energy block to form over Victor's dagger taking him by surprise. She threw one hand to the side, pulling with that black energy, flinging the dagger across the room.

She stomped down hard on Pierce's foot and shoved off of him, focusing a blast of energy to leave her body, knocking both Pierce and Victor back against their respective walls; she tried to summon Jordan again just in case while running to Amy.

Pierce was quicker to recover than she had hoped. She wouldn't have time to run from the room, so she threw her body across Amy's and lifted her hands in the air defensively, creating a bubble of energy around them as a shield.

"I shouldn't be surprised you learned this much in the last six months; he always was a good teacher," Pierce said, his image and garbled words making it through to her. Sweat was already beading on her forehead.

He created a blast of force of his own; it looked like an

explosion of lightning cracking through the colorless shield she had created. She could feel the hits within her, her bubble getting a little bit smaller with each blow.

"I would know, I was his first student, the foundation off which he built his skills. It's almost a shame all the knowledge he has gathered will go to waste when I kill him." A floodgate within her snapped; she exploded from within, outward.

Amy looked up at her friend and sister; broken, horrified as she raged with absolute power, colors of which she had never seen coming out in sharp blasts cutting Pierce's surprised face, wind and density blasts pushing him back.

"Amy," Christine called. "Run."

It was a demand; Amy knew there was no way they were both going to make it out of that room alive. If she stuck around, Pierce would use her as a tool to manipulate Christine. She needed to get to Jordan.

With a final intense surge, Christine's energy waning, she held Pierce and Victor down as Amy bolted as fast as her damaged legs could carry her. Luck willing she plowed into a friend in the hallway.

His wings unfurled in surprise as she plastered against him. He grabbed her shoulders, looking past her to see his sister going practically nuclear with power. Even from the Hall outside the room, the sound was deafening. He went to move Amy aside; she stopped him.

"We need to get out of here! We are the only two people alive he can use against her. We need Jordan!" For the first time, Azazel peeled his worried eyes off his baby sister and looked at her captor. A wide grin was plastered on Pierce's face, not one hint of concern at the sheer power erupting from her.

Amy was right. If that wasn't enough to scare Pierce, neither he nor Amy would be able to do anything but put her at further risk right now. With a pained snarl, Azazel grabbed a tight hold of Amy and used concentrated matter to blast through the wall nearest to him as Christine wavered, crumpling to her knees.

With Amy in his arms, they blasted into the sky and towards the gate at top speeds. Pierce didn't even notice the blast of the break in the sound barrier as they left.

The room around them was in shambles, paint peeled from the walls, gashes in the ceiling, floorboards ripped up; and Pierce stared at her in gleeful amazement while Victor looked on in disbelief.

Her skin felt like it was vibrating. She was hot everywhere and so nauseous. Breathing heavily, she knew she had pushed her limits too far. An unbalanced laugh radiated from Pierce's chest. Christine pulled herself up painfully and moved away from him the best she could.

"He warned you, didn't he?" Pierce said through the laughter. "He warned you not to fight me. Did he even tell you why my little creationist?"

He stalked towards her with triumph in his step, "Your inclination is undeniable proof you were put in my path, my Fated match." His sheer giddiness rattled her. She had never felt so miserable, so weak, and had never seen him so blatantly gleeful.

"Christine, my love, your abilities will even the scales. Because of you, we will be able to keep the peace between three separate worlds and fight a man who would wish to rule over them all."

"You should know by now I would never help you, and I sure as hell wouldn't give you any of my abilities." It shamed her how shaky the words were coming out.

Standing above her now, a predator's grin stretched along his face leaving no trace of the man she once trusted and shared soft kisses with. He placed his thumbs to both her temples and rubbed them in circles. His thumbs on her skin felt like hot coal, gaining intensity as they circled.

"My sweet, ignorant Christine. You don't need to give them

to me. Being an Empath, I can *take* them." The heat turned into a searing pain as if he had jabbed spikes into her temples.

"Shhh, don't worry. The true beauty of your abilities is that they, unlike anyone else's, will regenerate." His words were soft but in no way calming.

"With time, this will become less painful, I promise."

She could feel what was left of her strength being extracted from her in hot waves of searing pain. As the flow weakened, almost every bit of her energy was stolen, he leaned in and kissed her hard as she fell unconscious.

***

Searing light invade my senses as I woke to what I thought was someone shaking me roughly back and forth. Disoriented, I tried and failed to sit up. There were words trying to make it through to me, but everything sounded like I was underwater. I could vaguely make out my name and the words 'time' and 'up.'

With immense effort, I worked to force open my heavy lids, fighting through the unkind and abrasive glow of the room. Nothing I saw helped me to feel better. I recognized nothing. There were books stacked everywhere that I hadn't read. The sheets were white and airy; my breathing intensified as my memory began beating me with the reminder of my recent terror.

I resisted sitting straight up, not knowing if I were alone or not. Looking and feeling inward, I confirmed no one was manipulating me at this moment. I dared to lift my head slightly to get a better idea of my surroundings. Upon moving, I realized someone was lying beside me, unmoving. I became frigid and energized all in the same moment, adrenaline and panic spiking.

A chuckle rattled within Pierce's exposed chest next to me. I tried to move but was hit with exhaustion at the attempt.

"Refrain from over-extending yourself, little one. You pushed your limits and transferred gifts for the first time. You are nearly mortal at the moment, and broken to boot. Go back to sleep; you're so amenable when you're sleeping, soft and affectionate. It's nice." Ice ran through my veins.

"At least take me to my own room to recover." The words stumbled out of my mouth, hoarse and broken.

"Our engagement has been announced; this *is* your room now." He rolled over and propped himself above me. My panic rose; I became acutely aware of how thin the pajama shorts and top I had been wearing were.

I shocked him by laughing with a dark and rueful sneer.

"Thank you. I would also like Jordan to hurry up and get here." It was satisfying to feel him go rigid, although I would have preferred not to be able to literally feel it.

"His surprise visits are over. If he could get here, he already would have. It's been six hours since I harvested your abilities. It's time to accept reality; he isn't coming, little one. Even if he wanted to, he can't."

"And I can't have purple eyes, and he can't teleport thirty people. Jordan and I are the types of people who enjoy defying the word 'can't.'"

I spit the word at him, hoping it would frustrate him and cause him to remove himself from my space, or at least hit me. Anything would have been better than the hungry way he was looking at me, brushing his nose along my face. He was only in loose sweatpants; I could feel the reaction he was having to our proximity.

Never had I felt so close to death, yet I knew for a certainty this man had no desire to kill me. Fear growing angrily up my spine gave me just enough energy to rock my body and hit my shoulder against his right arm to break free of him.

But he didn't budge. Instead, he dipped his head lower as if to kiss me while sinking his body on top of mine slowly, giving me too much time to register his stiff want. I fought back panic-driven tears at the completely debilitating feeling of being at the mercy of someone I feared.

"I'm not that tired. Did my power strengthen you that much?" I didn't want the answer, but I needed it. Was I weak, or was he already that much stronger?

"Eventually, I *will* be that much stronger because of you, my sweet fate, but currently you are that much weaker and will thankfully remain that way for the foreseeable future. For now, you will live similarly to the mortals you identify with, just as you've wanted. The only difference being your existence will be eternal." One of his hands was exploring my stomach underneath my satin shirt, slowly running his fingers up and down my side.

"I have made adjustments for you, though. Any restricted books I've withheld from you have been brought to this room, so no need to check to see if my shelves house fake books, they may not be for entertainment, but they will be interesting, nonetheless."

A memory sent ice water through my veins of the blue-eyed therapist I saw before meeting Pierce, and the strangeness of the interaction. Gulping, it became another bit clearer just how much he had been interfering in my life before I was brought here.

This man had introduced me to his version of my power. Another had looked to unleash me from within, to help me harness it. Both had led to me wanting more, not for the sake of wielding it, but for what I could do with it. Jordan had shown me what was possible with power. It could literally assist in the restoration of an entire civilization, and I wanted that. My own world, my home, had people who were suffering, people I could help with my born gifts.

Gifts that had now been ripped from me by someone out of greed. I hadn't known it would be possible to regret empowering someone, yet here I was. His theft of my strength made me feel empty and exposed. The backs of my eyes were burning as my stomach flipped and rotated.

"Most do not understand the sheer amount an Empath is exposed to with each interaction. We sense different emotions and reactions in various ways." Still pinning me down and looming above me, he rested his forehead against mine and continued in a delicate whisper.

"I want you to understand me. I experience it all... My palms sweat when I feel another deeply in love. I can smell the sea whenever I'm near someone who is completely tranquil. But with you, everything is a bit different. I have always harbored guilt over this, but for some reason, your emotions have a stronger effect on me. Intoxicatingly..." He lowered his face to mine and whispered against my lips.

"Your anger tastes like the powder at the bottom of bags of sour candy. Your appreciation warms my skin in the most calming of ways. But my favorite has always been your panic. It scares me sometimes how badly I want it. The adrenaline and desire I feel in reaction to it is confounding. I appreciate no longer needing to hide it." Capturing my mouth with his, he got exactly what he wanted. My panic went into overdrive; tears stung my cheeks.

A desperate moan escaped him as he pulled away, leaving me huffing in complete relief at the gifted space.

"Soon, love. But your body has over-performed today. I don't want to further over-exert you." He pulled me into his arms and kissed my cheek. Pulling back, I returned his look of surprise with disbelief.

"Why are you crying, little one?"

"How can you ask me that? I don't want this; I don't want you." He looked at me unconcerned.

"Don't worry yourself. You will." His tone left no room for argument. "In your improved state, I can assist you more thoroughly." In demonstration, he placed a hand on my abdomen, moved it to my side and pulled me closer.

From the point of contact, a tingling sensation grew into

an impossible-to-deny lust. Impossible as it was, I tried. Images of Jordan pounded in my brain, but they were growing foggy. I could feel my dampness grow and knew he was aware of his success by the growing heat in his eyes.

Along with that heat, he had an aura of approval at my body's newfound pliability as he reveled in my forced desire. All the while suppressing the violation my body was reeling with, deep in my silenced heart.

Soon my hormones were controlling both my body and mind to his enjoyment. I was his puppet. I don't know how long he watched me squirm with the desire he was forcing me to feel before he was back above me, his lips brushing mine slowly and with excruciating tenderness. Each brush of his tongue on my lips was a betrayal as he held me down in this weakened and malleable state.

22

PERCEPTION IS EVERYTHING

After reappearing back home, their home, without her, he debated changing his mind and facing her wrath by going back for her, but in his hesitation noticed Thad was sitting up now, speaking to Azazel.

"What's wrong? You look like your head is going to pop," Azazel asked, shifting his focus to Jordan. Looking worried.

"I'm a fool, is all," was Jordan's response as he made his way to his kitchen and dug an untouched bottle of whiskey from his fridge. Thad, still gray and slouching with a deflated look to him, cracked a knowing grin.

"You are so under her thumb," he croaked out.

"Well, aren't you sassy for someone who was literally just flattened out by an Empath?" Jordan had filled Azazel in briefly before he had gone after Christine initially back in NY. Thad glared back at him with a slight tint to his cheeks.

"Don't call me - whatever you just called me," he demanded.

"I'll call you whatever you want, doll," Azazel added with a wink. Jordan downed his drink. "Seriously though, where is Christine? Your demeaning comment before leaving had me believing you would be able to get to her. So, what happened?" In response, Jordan poured and downed another drink before capping the whiskey and putting it back in the fridge.

"Give him a minute and he'll answer. He's just being dramatic," Thad explained with a roll of his eyes.

"She demanded I leave her there. That's why I am a fool. I listened to her," Jordan said, leaning heavily on the table Thad was still seated on. He looked at his brother for understanding; he got it.

"You are a fool. Love does that." Jordan appreciated the warm comment from his brother and was worried about how hollow his eyes seemed.

"Well, thank you for fucking nothing. I guess I'll go get her myself," Azazel said, a dismissive flutter of his wings sending a few feathers flying around the room. "Fucking waste of time, Gods, I swear," he sputtered angrily, heading for the door.

"Hold on a minute, Feathers," Jordan said. "I gave her twenty-four hours. She is confident she can convince him to step down peacefully." Azazel looked back at him with wide eyes.

"You're kidding, right?" he asked.

"Unfortunately, not. She also wants to be the one to tell him he was wrong this whole time, and she knows she is Fated to me." Azazel's eyes were aflame with disapproving anger.

"I only agreed because I can get to her whenever she needs me. She is able to summon me at will. This time tomorrow she will be here, safely among the people who care about her," Jordan explained. Thad didn't miss the way it sounded like he was explaining it more to himself than the other two men in the room.

"You two care. I would have had him had she not intervened."

"She intervened?" Jordan asked, surprised.

"She pinned me to the wall, allowing Pierce to stab me," Thad explained, only signing the communication, a bit embarrassed. Jordan put a hand on his knee and made eye contact with him before signing in response.

"Thank you for going after her. I'm sorry for the result of my mess. If it helps, she feels terrible."

"Ah yes, her regret helps so much. It's like the wound is healing already." The word dripped with a hard-learned sarcasm. He didn't miss the enjoyment he got at knowing he had made Azazel smile.

"Look. I don't care how much of a sway her eye-batting has with you. She is not safe there. I am going to get her. You haven't seen how distraught Pierce has been. Rejecting him is not going to go well. I won't lose her too."

Jordan could see the sincerity in his statement, the palpable fear behind the strong bravado he was putting forth.

"Leave her tonight. She is asleep and needs it. I can check in on her in the morning if that will alleviate your fears. Do you think you can still get into heaven, or will they suspect you?" Jordan asked, the wheels in his head turning.

If Christine was going to put herself at risk to give them an opportunity, he wasn't going to waste it for all of its potential.

***

The joyous nature of the staff continually bustling around her did nothing to lighten her mood. Pity had always grated her, but misdirected pity had proved to be more provoking. Pierce had ordered the staff to avoid conversing with her as she 'came to terms with and healed from the trauma' she recently went through.

Trauma, yes, but not in the ways they assumed. In their eyes, Jordan stole her away to Hell and did unspeakable things to her. Sure, a good chunk of the things he did to her shouldn't be spoken about in polite conversation. But everything he did was done with love. Unlike their presumed hero of the story, their shiny sunshine God, Pierce.

He had invited himself inside her. Manipulated her, slithering his way through her very veins, forcing her to feel exactly what he wanted. She had woken with a weight she had never known.

The sheer slime of it was palpable as she walked through what she previously considered 'their' garden. That slime of his trailed along behind her, thick, weighty, and above all else, suffocating.

Hate him as she did, this was still the most beautiful place she had ever seen. In her sour mood, she wanted to cut each peppy rose peddle from the stem and set the roots ablaze.

Training was no longer scheduled into her days. Pierce had gone before she had woken up from her anxious sleep. She was appreciative that she had been brought a tray of fruits to eat and even coffee within the privacy of Pierce's room. The fact that he had moved her into his quarters announced their 'engagement,' after everything, floored her.

Her face was still split open. She left it visible for the staff to see, hoping someone, anyone, had seen her before their confrontation and could maybe piece together Pierce had done this to her.

In the center of the garden was a large tacky fountain Christine had always joked was just missing a marble, baby cupid in the center. She had walked through the outstretched rose bushes that led its way here, brushing her hands along the thorny vines, enjoying the rough scrapes against her hands.

Bored and agitated, she sat on the edge of the fountain and dared a look at herself.

She had seen herself in the mirror earlier that morning. Her split open face, the bruises, the darkened eyes, purple still fading, but it gave her fuel each time she glanced at it. He had turned her into the woman she had tried to save.

Admittedly, she had judged some of her students and felt the earned irony now.

'How could they stay in that situation?' she had ignorantly

thought. Knowing there were obviously hurdles to leaving any abusive relationship, but nothing so difficult it would stop someone with real drive.

'God, I was an ignorant Bitch,' she thought, glaring at her reflection before reaching up to her cheek and daring to touch it.

She winced at the sting from the pressure of her fingertips and debated pulling the scab off to flow her blood, perhaps purge some of the slime-infected cells.

Before getting the chance to further consider ways of purging Pierce from her system, she noticed movement under one of the arched stone entrances to the garden and became alert, not thrilled with being so available to the royal sunburn of a man.

However, it wasn't Pierce who rounded the hedged corner to meet her eyes. He was familiar, but she couldn't place him, which felt odd since he had wings. It occurred to her he could have been one of the 'birdmen' she had observed running drills back when Pierce had introduced her to the clan all that time ago.

Then it occurred to her. This is a Guardian. They are loyal to the people and the people only. Pierce does not own them or their loyalty. Maybe he could get her out of here.

The man had large black wings that looked as if they had been dipped to the tips in silver, glinting just as the many exposed knives all along his chest and abdomen did.

"Well, fuck. I actually made it to you. Take that, ya almighty pain in the ass," he breathily muttered, fisting his hands onto his hips proudly.

"How am I an almighty pain in the ass? I don't even know you?" she asked with a half-hearted laugh. With this, he truly looked at her and that proud smile of his faded.

He let out a tight hitch of breath and reached up, approaching her, looking intently at the scab cracking along her bruised cheekbone.

"He will die slowly for this." There was a surety in his words that was largely in contrast with the amusement seeping from them.

"Who the fuck are you?" she demanded, her shortened fuse going off.

"Come on; you don't recognize me?" he said, arms outstretched, hands tilted in, motioning to the many tattoos up his arms as if that should jog a memory.

"Should I?" she asked bitterly. "Let me guess, one of Pierce's training buddies? Look, that's great for you. But... Look. I am incapable of being anything other than bitchy right now, so it's not the time for introductions, okay?"

The ever-present void she often shoved her emotions in seemed to regurgitate some of her acid fury, causing her eyes to burn, the precursor to tears. Tears that she had no interest in shedding, let alone in front of a stranger.

Knives, tattoos, and scars in abundance had tricked her. She could tell with the drop of his smile. As it fully dissipated and the softest concern she had ever seen warmed his eyes, that recognition sparked again, deep within her.

He sighed heavily. Clearly battling his own war of tears.

"It'll be okay, Krissy. Everything will be just fine. I'm here now."

She stumbled back, the tears sizzling her waterline, on the brink of escape as his words compounded within her, repeating but changing from his voice to her mother's.

It was then she noticed her mom's cheekbones and her father's eyes.

"I'm your brother, and I am so sorry I waited this long... We don't have a lot of time. I am having this area cloaked so no one can hear us, but that will raise flags soon."

She was defeated; her tears flowed freely down her face; memories projected in her skull. Memories of an uncle she had, covered in tattoos. Mom had said he was a pilot.

He was still talking, but she couldn't hear him for the brief moment she rushed him, throwing herself into him. Scarred arms and feathers surrounded her in a safe embrace. They stood for a few seconds in solidarity, in shared, unprocessed mourning, both of them trying to hold on to the brief spark of hope this light had gifted them.

He unfurled his wings and placed his hands on her shoulders, stepping back from her.

"We both deserve time we don't have right this moment, but we will soon, okay?" Wiping her tears away, she nodded yes back at him.

"So, you aren't my ride outta here, huh?" she asked, only half joking.

"I can be." His words were confident. That gave her what she needed to stand up straighter. She wanted to be filled in on whatever was happening. Other than discovering she had blood family left alive, who had wings of all things.

"I lead the Old Guard. Given your condition, I could free you, and there wouldn't be a damn thing Pierce could do about it publicly. Jordan seems to think you will like his plan better." Her hand flew to her chest in an automatic response, but he grabbed it before it made contact.

"Don't summon him."

"He can't get to me anyway...." she explained longingly.

Dropping her hand, he snorted. "The fuck he can't."

Now she was confused. He had better not be able to get to her, or she was going to kill him for leaving her here when she had needed him.

"Coming to get you right now means taking down the shield. That is a huge displacement of energy and would likely cause a devastating tsunami in the Asmal region. He assured me, for you, casualties be damned, summon him again, he is coming through." She believed it and not because of the things he had done in the past, but because, if the situation were reversed, she would do the same for him.

"Okay, so what is going on?" she asked, eager to catch up.

"I haven't left my station as Head of the Old Guard and can use that as a guise to remain in touch with you, but you must pretend to not know me."

"That should be easy since I really don't."

"It's more than that, Christine. He will sense if you get hopeful around me."

He was right. She knew that now more than ever.

"Well, how the fuck do I block that and why even take the risk. Talking to him did not go well. I can eat crow once I tell Jordan he was right again, but Pierce is wrapped up in his own delusion. He thinks we are getting married," she explained with Amy-like speed.

"I know. He is overconfident. We want to use that to our advantage. I got Amy out of here, but her discovery left us a mole down. You are in a position to gather intelligence and set him up with a false sense of confidence. Here," He reached behind him and glanced around them quickly before handing her a bag, "it's from Jordan. I have no idea what's in there. He said, 'she will need these to get through' and gave me that to give to ya." Doing her own cursory glance, she looked around before setting the blank, glossy white bag on the smooth marble of the fountain and reached in.

She pulled out the shirt he got for her that said, 'if you can read this shirt, you're too close to me' first and smiled, pressing it to her face and inhaling Jordan's lingering scent. Setting it down, she then pulled out a thick book.

The Cover said, '**Matter enhancement - Glamor for beginners**.' Confused as to why he would send her a book on a skill she felt confident with, she opened it up and discovered the slipcover was for another book.

The Cover page held the real title. 'Ability Blocking – from Empaths to Medics,' what you need to know. She smiled and enjoyed the warming sensation spreading deep within her chest, noticing there was a handwritten note beneath the title.

Nowhere to hide, I'll be coming for you soon.
Give him Hell like the Goddess you are,
J

From the first moment she had breathed Angelican air upon arriving back here, she felt unbalanced.

"What's it gonna be? Jordan thinks you're relatively safe until the wedding he has no intention of allowing to take place. Do you? Neither of us has any clue how long it will take for your power to regenerate enough for that leech to drain you again."

"Pierce doesn't know either. And Jordan's right. I can endure. How do I get you the information I manage to gather?" I asked.

"I will make opportunities arise. Just be ready for them." Looking up, he nodded at someone behind me. "Time's up. Look. The Guardians know what is happening. Shit hits the fan, you run for feathers, you got it?" I nodded yes as I ripped a blank spacing page from the book.

"Do you have a pen?"

"Oh, for the love of the Gods on High, you aren't making me play carrier pigeon are you?" he asked, reaching into one of his many pockets and pulling out a pen.

"I am." She smiled, writing on the page, folding it hastily and handing it to him.

A long time ago, she had believed she was plagued with anxiety. Before learning an Empath had suppressed her emotions. He had caused her to suffer from attacks so severe she had even tried therapy.

One of the useful tricks she had picked up was anxiety control. Slowly squeezing her fists together while breathing in, and then slowly releasing the pressure while breathing out.

Her brother walked away from her, his large wings casting an ominous shadow against the sparkling cathedral glass wall. It grew as he approached a door that was housed snuggly in the middle of it. With him leaving, she practiced that technique now.

Reminding herself discovering family is a good thing.

Having an ally is a good thing. As long as it doesn't get said ally killed.

***

Azazel attempted to avoid being seen as he reluctantly navigated his way out of Pierce's Garden. Being a Guardian very rarely involved stealth, so it was a skill he wasn't very well practiced with. Having expansive, silver-tipped wings and being lined with blades didn't help either.

This plan of action was still not something he agreed with, and he had made that very clear to Jordan before coming up here.

The only reason he hadn't protested more had been the starkly apparent anguish on Jordan's face at his realization that Pierce had re-armed the shields against him. A discovery made upon being summoned by Christine.

Azazel and Thad had needed to tackle Jordan to the ground and restrain him in order to convince him to take a second and think through what he was doing rationally. Not an easy task considering Thad was still broken.

He could get through, but that would involve breaking through and causing massive damage.

Azazel had lost both of his parents while being on the outs with them. He had been an arm's length away from his baby sister for years, the whole time feeling as though she was in mortal danger. He had felt, truly, like someone abandoned to this world, destined to save and protect the lives of others, yet never fully connect with its people.

All that, and he knew he had never experienced the worst pain life had to offer. That anguish lived in the eyes of his sister's Fated match as he was denied going to her aid when he knew she needed him.

Jordan had taken little comfort in the joke Azazel had attempted to lighten his mood with. Telling him he should feel pretty good, considering when Pierce was denied access to Hell, it caused him to seize. Whereas Jordan was simply unable to get through, undergoing no physical harm.

Jordan was unimpressed. Simply stating, "He is a mere Angelican. I am a God. If a shield harms me, I do not deserve my title."

Azazel refrained from mentioning his 'title' was 'technically' not his at the moment, figuring it wasn't the time to test his boundaries for jokes.

It was excruciating knowing he was not going to be returning to their ragtag group with good tidings. If he reported his findings honestly, they might need to full-on drug Jordan to prevent him from busting though the barrier this time.

Christine's face was broken open, just as Amy had said it was, and still swollen. Despite having had a day to heal. He was grateful he hadn't been in a spot to notice it the day before when everything had blown up, and the wound was still fresh. It wasn't an image he wanted in his mind of her.

Azazel knew it would be up to Thad to de-escalate Jordan again. The two seemed to have a strong trust between them. They had told him of their other brother. Going as far as to warn him of the 'little toad's' lack of manners. They had tasked him with attempting to locate their father in hopes it would avoid him causing any other issues.

Everything taking place right now was new for Jordan and his team. As a Guardian, Azazel knew you could never plan for every situation. Tactical strategy was necessary in almost every aspect of his position. Yet, he had never seen such an acute redirection of planning than watching Jordan reconstruct the reclaiming of his throne with Thad.

Being an outsider, Azazel had made sure to watch on as they readjusted their planning and found, to his surprise, they didn't need his input. They had the information they needed and the skillset to pull it off.

Had someone told him a God was being dethroned, he would never, in his extended life, assume the aggressing party would do it via the method Jordan had constructed. He couldn't help but be a bit impressed with the man for it.

It made him feel almost guilty for being on the opposing side of the revolt. Granted, only in spirit, as he was a good Guardian and had remained neutral. Not joining in the riots but instead clearing streets and attempting to minimize the damage occurring.

Jordan had been a mysterious leader who seemed to grant or deny the wishes of the people from the shadows by his own prerogative. Pierce had been his friend. Fuck, Pierce had been everyone's friend.

He was the prince fate tossed aside who could laugh about it. The shiny, relatable guy who defended his moody and distant brother. His parents had been right in their last fight not to trust Pierce. He could only look back now and wish he had listened to them.

He had almost made it out of the palace grounds without attracting too much attention. Then he saw Pierce turn the corner. Azazel had many skills; deceit was not among them. The problem he faced now was that Pierce considered him a friend, and he would not let him simply walk away.

"Hey, Axe! I see you are fully clothed today! How have you been, friend?" Pierce's tone was friendly, but his eyes held worry.

Azazel watched Pierce place his fingertips to the center of his chest while half bowing. A sign of respect and a greeting customary to the Leader of the Old Guard he normally ignored.

"I am doing better now that I know Christine has been located," Azazel said honestly. He couldn't help but enjoy the way Pierce's ass seemed to pucker at the thought of Christine and himself talking.

"I can relate to that sentiment. Did you see the news, or perhaps bump into her here?" he asked in a perfectly casual tone.

"I knew she was here and wanted to check in on her. As you know, the whole department has been worried. I told them I would keep them updated and would be taking a personal interest in her recovery." It was a relief to Azazel how much truth he could speak without condemning himself.

Pierce smiled at him, and a sensation of campfire adjacent warmth spread up his back.

'Attempting to make me friendly for ya, huh, well, go fuck yourself.' Azazel's thoughts were contemptuous, but his emotions weren't. He was happy just knowing Pierce had signed his own fate.

"I appreciate that. You are always welcome here. However, if any of your men, or even yourself, would like to see her, at least until she is recovered, please let me know so I can make sure she is in the right headspace for visitors."

"We sure will. You know, she seemed to be in a pretty good head space for someone who obviously experienced great trauma at the hands of a monster," Azazel threw in, getting a bit too cocky.

"Yes... She is strong. Well, speaking of her, I am afraid I'm sure she's missing me, so I will catch up with you later."

'I'm sure.' Azazel sneered in his head.

Unable to verbalize a civil response, he looked to the marble tile in a half bow of respect. Making a good effort not to read too far into the inquisitive glint in Pierce's eye as he brushed past him and out the expansive arched doorway to the castle's exit.

***

Entering their garden, he took stock of the world within it. The energies ebbing and flowing from life point to life point, reaching out and searching for her. He knew she had spent the morning sulking in here while he attended to the people and their needs.

Seeing Azazel would normally leave him unruffled but considering he had yet to set any clear boundaries for her in regard to what aspects of their personal life she should be disclosing, he was a bit nervous.

The Old Guard was not an organization he wanted cognizant of the current arrangement between him and Christine. Under Jordan's rule, the previous Leader of the Old Guard had been such a fearsome protector of women he had been transitioned into a general. Azazel took over after winning a competition of skill and intelligence for the title.

Being in service to the people and not the crown, the Old Guard could legally attack him and attempt to remove her from him. They would do just that if they felt she was unsafe in any way. She was considered 'one of the people,' and they took on any needed protection services for groups of large or independent citizens.

The previous leader of the Old Guard was not someone Pierce had ever been personally acquainted with; he was glad for it. He had either failed to protect the Empaths of this world or had intentionally turned a blind eye to their slaughter.

Both had earned him the grim fate he met while cowering away on Middle Earth. Azazel was a good man. Pierce trusted him to have an equal interest in all of their citizens. Unfortunately, that meant he knew if Christine had said the wrong thing he would be back and with his Men.

To resist the Old Guard's removal of anyone would not go well. They were wise and brought media crews to all extractions where domestic abuse was indicated, and to do so to him would be a political nightmare. One not lessened by his killing of the beloved Old Guard, which he would if they attempted to take her from him.

That wasn't happening again. She was home, permanently. He had been wise not to boast his abilities; only Jordan fully knew his strength. There were some benefits that came with being the product of parents who had chosen to bond for the sake of a powerful match instead of love.

He was blessed, knowing his children would benefit from both.

Her energy was much more difficult to locate in her drained state. Although it caused him temporary inconvenience, he appreciated it. Struggling to sense her power meant it was contained. And it being contained meant he would have an easier time protecting her from herself.

Reaching out, he ran his hands along the tops of the rose bushes as he had walked past them, knowing Christine enjoyed pruning them and enjoyed the feeling of the soil on her hands. He was right, her presence lingered here. He clicked his tongue, sensing Azazel's presence as well, meaning the Guardian had been here long enough for his energies to linger.

He pinched the spine of one of the white roses, one without any wilting, and snapped it off. Sticking it, spine only into his back pocket and making his way out of the Garden on the other side, leaving the feel of plush grass underfoot behind him for cold Marble once again.

'Where would she be hiding?' he pondered, fighting a wicked smile and attempting to ignore the invigorating bubbling in his stomach at the possibility of a chase.

He paused. Laughter. He heard laughter. What was strange is that he was almost certain it was her laughter. That was something he hadn't expected but was thrilled to be hearing ricochet through the halls of their estate.

Following the addictive sound of her joy, he reached out as an Empath, breathing in her happiness, letting its sweet, perfume-like scent flow through him. He followed it until he was sure he was close to its remarkable origin. Peeking around the corner of one of the corridor-like halls, he spotted her.

'Finally.'

***

"How did she appear while agreeing to this?" The question was a loaded one; Azazel measured his words. She looked terrible, plainly speaking.

Her fear was evident. No matter how hard she had attempted to hide it from him. Her eyes had been evasive, her stance unsteady. But her spine had been straight, and her shoulders had been squared.

This was a challenge she wanted and one he had faith in her ability to complete. Pierce was operating with a confidence his known abilities did not warrant. With the threat of Jordan coming for him, he should be more anxious, shield able to detect him or not. They needed to know what they were missing.

"She looked afraid but also confident and, more than anything, determined. Threatening Amy's life was not wise; she wants to see him pay for it. She sent me with this, for you." Azazel filled him in, glancing once over at Amy, who was sitting on a couch nearby.

Her arm was in a sling, and she was hunched over but actively listening for word on her friend. He handed Jordan the note Christine had sent for him.

Jordan unfolded it with a deliberate delicacy, taking his time, as if he were almost afraid of what the note may contain. The years he had spent hardening himself under Arcane's rules flared up in him at reading the words, forcing him to suppress the tears burning his eyes. Azazel had just confirmed she was okay, not great, but okay. Seeing her handwriting, it somehow acted as its own proof of life. One he hadn't known he needed this badly.

I've got this...
But, don't be late.
Yours, C

'Yours.' That word quirked his lips.

With that one word, she was letting him know she hadn't

written him off. In truth, one of the benefits of her staying put was the access to information she had there. He knew her; she would use that access to snoop.

What she found would not absolve him of his crimes in her mind. He knew and accepted that. One of the very first things she had ever said to him had hit so close to the mark it had caused him to snap. He could remember the well-aimed barb clearly.

'Leaders make their own choices.'

There was no way she could have known how personal that blow was, but that hadn't stopped it from landing on him with devastating force. He remembered the expression on Pierce's face as he registered the words.

Pierce's knowing grimace had reflected the shared pain they felt. A bond of pain and history that caused him a moment of remorse at having to kill his old friend soon, and for threatening the woman he thought fated to Pierce as well. Then he looked into her eyes, and that remorse flitted and faded away as the ember of their friendship officially dissolved within him.

He folded the paper back up as delicately as he had opened it. Slipping it into his back pocket, he allowed himself a brief moment to feel this fear. The terror of her being in such a vulnerable position, before allowing the darkness within him to grab that pain and fear and pull it deep down within him. Hiding it in shrouds until she was back in his arms, allowing him to focus on getting her there.

"What date has he set for the," he took a moment to force the word out.

"Wedding?"

***

Pierce admired her from this safe distance, peeking behind a wall and knowing her mood would dampen once he tried to approach her. An unfortunate ramification of their current cir-cumstances. But, with time, she would begin to accept things. She would need to, and hopefully, if he could locate the Fates, he could even fix her.

It shattered him to feel how disconnected she was from him every time she was close enough for his energy to reach out to hers, only for her energy in response to retreat from him. This wasn't how it was supposed to be.

He knew they were Fated. Her being a creationist solidified that knowledge. Being Fated was something you could feel, something you knew, and he understood that now. Because he knew it about her, he felt it every time her name danced through his mind.

The first time he had met her, he was operating under the possibility of her being Fated to Jordan. He figured locating her gave him a possible bargaining chip in case Jordan ever came for his head.

Thanks to the Fates' carelessness on the day of the upris-ing, and a mutual trip they had made to Azazel's residence, he had heard them warn her parents.

The Snowfall family had been assigned to watch over them the next day and report when or if a child was born. A long time passed before that day came. Pierce himself met her while she was still a child; he substituted one of her classes. She had still been a child and not yet susceptible to the pull of a Fated match

He had been prepared for the unlikely possibility of a match. What he hadn't been prepared for was how resistant she would be to their connection because of whatever the Fates had done to their tied thread.

She had possessed him and then rejected him. The first Creationist born in thousands of years was fated to the last of the Empaths. The Fates would not have liked that, given their fondness for Jordan and his reign. He would locate them and have them brought before him for questioning.

He had two overpriced bounty hunters looking for the two women currently. It was inconvenient that they had requested their pay in Euros, the currency used on Middle Earth. That was not as easily accessible to him as the Angelican coin, otherwise referred to as Drux units. But he would make it work. They were skilled at their jobs and hopefully would be successful in their hunt.

He laughed at the sight before him. One of the younger boys he had moved to the castle was showing Christine the trick he had recently taught them. He was asking her to let Pierce know most of them had figured it out, so they were ready to learn the new game.

This had lightened her soul a little. He could feel it, even from this distance. She was also already healing, regaining power. She must have felt it too as she knelt to the boy mischievously.

Glancing around suspiciously, she couldn't see through his glamoured camouflage. She placed her fingertips together, pulling them apart and recreating the light tendrils the boy had just shown her. The boy squealed as she snapped her fingers, causing the tendrils to burst apart into all the different colors of the rainbow – like little fireworks.

The sparks of her magic glittered in her smiling eyes as the young boy looked up at her with awe. Appreciating her and beginning to worship her in her own right. Pierce could not have been more touched at witnessing such a perfect display of Goddess-like affection. Those were the small things he needed her to do, inspire the people, and make their jaws drop in unconditional admiration.

Deciding he didn't want to cheapen the moment by announcing himself and spoiling her mood just yet, he left her back in the children's wing, transporting to his office.

Upon arrival, he groaned at the unexpected presence of an irritating problem, but necessary alliance.

"Savious. I thought you were still recovering. What are

you doing in my office?" Pierce asked, not bothering to hide the agitation from his tone. He may have formed an uneasy alliance with the man based on needed mutual benefit, but he did so while holding onto his scorn. Friends or not, Pierce couldn't forget everything he had witnessed this man put Jordan through; there was no excuse for treating your child that way.

"We need to talk next steps," he said plainly.

"There are no next steps for you," Pierce answered, sitting down roughly in the large chair behind his efficiently arranged desk.

"Come on now, boy. We both know even with the girl, you are severely outmatched. You announced a wedding. He will bring your protective barrier down upon us and everyone inhabiting this realm before he lets you marry his Fated match. Trust me; I am a good source on the matter," Savious explained, motioning to his still discolored and swollen features.

They both stiffened at the sound of Victor's disciplinary voice.

"Roto, I would not consider you a reliable source on what one Fated match would do to keep the other safe, given the current state of yours. Your role is complete. Go back to cowering and leave us." Victor was a calm man. As cool as a fresh spring, his current was not easily quickened, but Savious was perhaps the only person who could flood the man simply by breathing the same air as him.

Savious forced his broken body to a hard standing stance and glared back at Victor. This friction was the exact reason Pierce put constant effort into keeping the two separated. He couldn't help but cross his arms and lean back in his chair, allowing them to get it out of their system.

"I do not go by that name."

"Savious is your family name. Calling someone by their family name is a sign of respect I will not grant you."

"That name died the last time it left her lips, as did the

man it represented," Savious said. Pierce almost thought he could detect a bit of wavering in his voice.

"That's nice. I'm sure Elmyra would have been touched by the sentiment. Well, except for the fact that you have used it as an excuse to be the very example of everything in this world she hated, and to neglect and abuse her child," Victor jabbed. This sparked a newly recovered drive for Savious; he took a menacing step toward the right hand of God.

"Don't presume to have known her well enough for such grand assumptions. She was my Fated match, not yours." Savious's tone dripped with possessiveness.

"She was my wife." The words left Victor quietly. The same words he spoke as he brought her charred and unrecognizable body back to this realm for proper last rites after Savious had abandoned her corpse on Middle Earth.

"You had been separated for two years when she was killed." Savious had gotten himself back under control. That, or his energy could not keep up with the fight. He collapsed back down onto the chair, dismissively waving his hand at Victor, attempting to end the conversation.

"And married for seventy-five when you met her!" Victor surprised Pierce by fully yelling the words, allowing them to drip with a previously unspoken hatred.

"Enough." Pierce was not loud or commanding.

He said the word resolutely; both men grumbled low in their chests but silenced. Guilt was gnawing at him for bringing Savious into the mix, knowing the bad blood between him and his mentor.

He had needed someone unaffiliated with Heaven to remove any Earthly ties that would have prevented Christine from relinquishing her hold on her mortal life. As well as give him a leg of trust to stand on; saving her life was the surest way he could think of gaining fast trust.

He just hadn't expected Savious to go rogue and attack her again without orders this time.

"Now that your jaw has healed, allowing you to articulate again, would you care to explain to me what you were doing when you attacked her without orders? Or, for that matter, why you fell off the grid the day she was taken from me."

"Pierce. We both know the only reason I assisted you was for my own benefit. I know now my suspicions were correct. She is Fated to my son. Not you. And that makes her a weakness to him, especially if she develops the full capacity of a Creationist. Our deal stands. I will help you keep her as long as you keep my son firmly in Hell, and alive."

Pierce kept eye contact while slowly standing, reading the emotions pulsing through the broken, fallen angel. He was sincere, but he not only caused Victor a great deal of pain anytime he was around but had recently attempted to end Christine's life.

"Any alliance we shared is over. You may remain in the Heed until you have recovered. Once you can travel, you must relocate to any other territory. I am allowing you to seek refuge in my realm solely because you have, until recently, been an asset to me, and I need to know where you are if the need for your assistance arises once again. But you are not to meddle, or I will personally hand you over to Jordan to finish you off."

Feeling the discontent coming at him from both men, Savious knew this was as good of a deal as he was getting and didn't bother to waste his breath bartering. He stood, nodding, and slowly exited the room, desperately missing the convenience of transporting.

BREAKING THE BONDS
THAT BIND US

It had been two years since Pierce had lost his first trainee. And one year since that trainee's husband had been found dead after taking his own life. Jordan and he had briefly escaped the watchful scrutiny of Arcane by going on a mock holiday to Middle Earth.

The true purpose of the holiday was to use the mortal realm as a testing ground for Pierce's recently discovered Empathic abilities. One of the largest influences of Arcane's rule on the people was their distrust and hatred of the Empaths, mirroring their leaders' bias. Neither of the young men wanted to imagine the sort of unkind response Arcane would have if he discovered his only son had grown into his worst fears.

It didn't take Jordan long to comfortably develop the ability to sense and block any sort of manipulation Pierce had accidentally forced his way. They had quickly discovered how erratic his newfound gifts were.

Testing on the mortals had not improved Pierce's control. If anything, it panicked him. He could fully adjust someone's attitude, remove their feeling of fear, and give them the courage usually only earned after several stiff drinks. His biggest complaint was how difficult it was to keep his own emotions from leaching out to those around him. The only thing he reaped enjoyment from was the different sensations he had while experiencing the emotions of others; how unique each person's effect on him was.

It was Jordan's unwavering strength and faith in him that had convinced him to leave home to learn to better control his powers.

Jordan wasn't thrilled at the prospect of being the only person available to Arcane at any given time. The God was a handful and did not believe in downtime. But he did agree that Pierce needed to find others like him and learn what he could.

Arcane had been hurt with each excuse Jordan made for Pierce's absence at holidays and large events. It had been a tricky conversation to navigate, considering Arcane was right. Pierce could transport and really had no reason for not visiting more often.

The story they had told him was that he was leaving to connect with the people, to not only find himself but hopefully discover his purpose among them. Arcane understood the need for this in Pierce's life but was growing more persistent in his son visiting him.

Jordan, on the other hand, had visited him often. Keeping tabs and being available as a sounding board for concerns and excitement regarding the progress his friend had made.

The last time Jordan had seen Pierce was several months ago now. He was confident he had located a settlement of Empaths, all of them residing together, avoiding the suspicious treatment they received from otherly gifted Angelicans. If Jordan's recollection served, he had even found a teacher. A kind and soft elderly woman who had enough patience to deal with him.

They had gotten a good laugh out of the fact that his instructor was a woman. Pierce was terrible with women due entirely to his inexperience with them. Both had lost their mothers the day they were born, leaving them in Arcane's 'nurturing' hands.

Today was the largest festival in the territory. The Fates' festival drew people from all over the realm. Jordan knew what the Fates displayed to them was a facade, a show, but it appeased the people, and that was valuable. This one day a year allowed them peace to live as they pleased without constant pandering for information from citizens.

This year they had already been given approval to display a prediction about his future love life. It was sure to be a crowd-pleaser. He was happy he wouldn't be there when they put on that particular show. The stage and decorations were still being set up along the glass-lined streets of the cityscape. Soon, frosted tendrils would hang above the streets along with glittering images of predictions past.

While the people celebrated, he sat in his childhood fortress, waiting on the arrival of his friend and brother.

"Do you have an expression other than brooding?" Jordan heard from behind him. He had been standing in the center of the room, staring at the door, arms crossed, patiently waiting for Pierce to show up.

"Do you have a stylist for that hair? There is no way you keep maintenance up on your own," he joked back, commenting on his friend's shoulder-length, golden ringlets.

They grabbed each other's forearms in greeting before Pierce pulled his brother into a warm hug.

"Seriously though, compensating for your missing eyebrow still?" Jordan laughed, squeezing him back before pulling away from him and lightly shoving Pierce's shoulder with affection. He hadn't noticed how large of an ache Pierce's absence had caused in his gut until this moment.

"Why compensate for something fixable with glamor?" Pierce responded lightly.

"It's been months since you came last. I didn't know if I

should expect you. Are you prepared to be around your father yet? I would love some company at the Fates' festival." Jordan asked, attempting to avoid pressuring Pierce into going.

"If he was less adept at angering me, I would say yes. I have gotten decent control in the last few months. But, when agitated, that irritation spreads from me, strong enough that he would sense it. But, the woman training me says I am progressing along faster than she's ever seen. Likely due to the strength of my bloodline, within the year. You can tell him to expect me at the next Fates' festival."

Pierce's smile was weak. Knowing Jordan didn't want to be given this task again. Arcane was not an easy man to keep at bay, and was starting to get more and more demanding about why his son had been dodging him.

"You are not an easy friend to keep," Jordan said. He smiled earnestly then, placing a hand on each of Pierce's shrugging shoulders and looking him in the eye.

"I need you to come home soon. So, focus in, will you?" he asked, covering up the desperation as well as he could.

While Pierce had been training to contain his abilities, Jordan had been suffering through a war Arcane was leading within the shadows. Discontent was thrumming through his people, rumors spreading, particularly within the ranks of their soldiers.

A general had resigned that very day, demanding Jordan step up and look into the military bases Arcane had ordered be neutralized, go himself, versus sending his men to do their dirty bidding. But that sort of reaction to war was expected from someone who had run the Old Guard during his previous profession. It was likely he was lashing out, bitter and angry at Jordan for rejecting his request for retirement.

Arcane had assured Jordan once Pierce had returned home, Jordan would be approved to assign him a general status. Then the two of them could look into things together. But now, there was only one base left; he had their final raid in an hour. Had

Pierce been another ten minutes, they would have missed each other again.

"You look haunted. Is there anything I should know?" Pierce asked. Jordan stopped himself from spilling his concerns out to his friend. Pierce and he had burdened each other with their problems their whole lives. Now they were men, growing into their roles. As his was that of a High God, he could no longer expect his friend to shoulder his weighty burdens.

"I am. It isn't anything I can't handle, though. Your father is a handful. Practice hard, come home soon, and cut your damn hair, will you?"

Pierce's smile grew into the warmth only he could produce as he hugged him once more.

"Whatever you say, great leader of ours." And with a wink, he left Jordan standing alone in their old fortress, parting as friends for the last time.

***

I had buried the most valuable of contraband books I had ever hidden in the garden. The High Gods of past could only know when Pierce would decide to just pop in on me. He wouldn't appreciate catching me with a book on how to resist his manipulations.

Luckily, Pierce knows I love playing with plant life. Mostly, playing in dirt and the satisfaction of seeing something I had a positive impact on thriving.

He had relocated me to his quarters, assaulted me; then run off before I woke up. I had debated running through the halls screaming his sins, but given the propaganda of my so-called 'trauma' at Jordan's hands, I would be dismissed as 'confused.'

There was so much I needed to focus on, a plan I needed to set in place, yet I couldn't focus. I had a brother. My parents had a son before moving to Middle Earth; he had been here the whole fucking time.

I would kick his ass someday for that. But first, I needed to get out of this situation and figure out what I could in the process; then I could learn everything about my winged big bro.

I had stopped in to see the children that resided in the far wing of the castle just a few minutes ago. Kids were honest and genuine; their complete adoration of Pierce helped calm my nerves. A complete sadist couldn't be so good with children. Maybe I wasn't in complete mortal danger by staying here.

Hopefully, Jordan and I were right about the wedding. Pierce was being pushy, and I had not been honest about the extent of that pushiness to the feathered relative I had discovered today. If I had been, he would have pulled me out right then and there. That and if he reported the truth back to Jordan, he would be on his way, shield or not, casualties or not.

It was a pleasant surprise that Pierce hadn't kept me confined to his quarters as I had expected him to. I guess he was confident I wasn't going anywhere. Unfortunately, he wasn't wrong.

Even if I tried to get away from him, the guards stationed around the palace grounds had been told to keep me in. With the small amount of power I had regenerated, I wouldn't be able to get through them.

Running my hands over the intricately patterned etchings in the stonework, I recognized a familiar pattern. Bending to inspect closer, one hand traced a little distinct mark; the other touched her chest. They were the same. "It's Enochian." The realization fascinated me, and I again yearned to be home with Jordan to look up what the translation of this mark was.

'Home.' It was strange; when I thought of the word now, I didn't envision a place. The word had become synonymous with Jordan.

I had been walking down a corridor towards the banquet hall, tracing my hands along a stretch of colored tiles that lined the wall, patterned with what I now saw as a fascinating language, not just patterns.

There was a large screen at one end of the hall. The same two-hour broadcast had been playing on loop since I had returned. Obnoxious reels of Pierce and I, ending with an announcement from the secret psycho himself about my safe recovery.

Being told I could create energy was a lot to grasp. It brought with it so many questions. The largest of which was could I give gifts to anyone? If I could, there were several people on Middle Earth I would like to empower.

Another question I had was if my gifts were simply generated for the purpose of empowering others, could I wield them? I hoped Jordan would know, because if that were possible, I could use these gifts to assist in the unification of Heaven and Hell.

More importantly, I could get the ball rolling in these people pulling their heads out of the sand and providing much-needed assistance to the people I was raised amongst.

I felt his presence for the first time since the night before and had to stop myself from gulping, fearing he would appreciate the effect too much.

"I have looked forward to concluding with meetings all day to be able to spend some time with you," he whispered, stepping now, still behind me to press against my back. A cool sliver of a chill slithered down my spine.

I wanted to retort with a snarky remark but couldn't find the words. In this neutral environment, my winning emotion towards him was a tried sort of disappointment. Thus far he had restrained himself to only manipulating my emotions and kissing me. There was an always itching fear I carried with me everywhere that he would snap, taking things too far.

"Come now. There is no use being upset. I have come to bargain." His fingers flexed a few times playfully as they wrapped around each side of my waist. Reaching my tolerance level with his contact, I swiftly elbowed him in the stomach and stepped out of his reach.

"Keep your hands off me." My nostrils flared. I felt as though I was capable of biting till I drew blood if he tried again. Expecting to see annoyance, it irritated me that he seemed humored more than anything.

"Those terms are not on the table, my love. We are soon to be bonded. Married in your people's vernacular. Couples on the cusp of a lifetime together tend to enjoy the other's touch," he countered, forcibly grabbing my waist again. With a smile, he pulled me into him again, this time front-facing. Leaving me no reprieve from his charring heat.

"That should be a fun day. I can't wait to see everyone's faces as I spit in your face and say, 'I do fucking NOT.'"

His grip tightened to an uncomfortable pressure causing me to try and wiggle out of his grasp in vain. Cool calmness rested on the soft angles of his face as he squeezed.

"I came to bargain to avoid just that. Our wedding will be your first large public appearance since your abduction, and I don't want you ruining it with that mouth of yours. So, let's talk." Looking around again, I could see we were in his office now; it was the room one over from his sleeping quarters, and I had not often been inside it.

He released me; I jolted away from him, hastily making my way to the other side of his desk. I sat in one of the dark wooden chairs, hoping it would provide me with some protection from his touch.

"Negotiations tend to happen between people who both have something the other wants. There is nothing you will give me that I want."

"How do you know? You haven't asked," he said simply, sitting with intended authority on the boss's side of his desk, hands wrapping around the arms of his chair.

"I have, though. I want to be free of you. I want you to keep your hands off me and your creepy Empath-ness out of me." My arms crossed bitterly as I awaited his scorn. But it didn't come.

"I could be persuaded to keep my hands off you until the wedding," he conceded. "And if you really want, I can attempt to desist from correcting your emotions, but I can't promise I will have no effect on you. I don't have full control of that and likely never will."

The control bit was news to me, but what had intrigued me just as much was the possibility of him keeping his hands to himself.

Walking through the Castle today, I had overheard one of the frequent news updates on TV in the children's room. He had announced our wedding was set for the day after tomorrow. Not a lot of guaranteed time, but Jordan would be coming before then anyway, so that wasn't really a concern.

"Why are you forcing me to marry you anyway? Wedding ceremonies aren't a thing here. And aren't bonding ceremonies done in private, just the couple in attendance? Why negotiate at all?"

The question had been there, but just now it forced itself forward, out of my mind, landing abruptly on the desk between us. His face scrunched, and he leaned, defeated, back in his chair.

"For you. To respect the culture you were raised in." This is not the answer I had expected.

"Well, that was a kind thought. But I don't want this marriage as it is, so it's completely unnecessary. Feel free to cancel."

"It's too late for that. The people are looking forward to a large royal wedding. So, as angry with me as you are now, you will have it." I rolled my eyes at him.

There was one thing I wanted. Information on the Empaths. Getting access to that collection of information would be worth keeping quiet and, by Pierce's archaic terms, 'behaved' for the short time I planned to be here.

"I want to know what happened to the Empaths. I don't want to hear you tell me a story. I want to know everything;

see everything you have about the event, and I want you to answer my questions about anything and everything anytime I
ask them. Call it the 'freedom of information pact.' That on top
of you keeping your distance until we are married." I surprised
him. I could see it. He wasn't expecting me to cave, and he was
far too happy about it.

"The freedom of information pact it shall be. I will not
touch your body or emotions until we have been bound, and
you shall be given all information I have regarding what happened to my people. I will answer any questions you have," he
practically cooed at me. It took every ounce of will I possessed
not to spit in his pleased face.

'You think you've won something. Fucking fool.' I thought,
feeling for once like I had a leg up against him.

The only concern I had was that he had made the wedding
so soon, not giving me much time to absorb the information.

I would need to attempt to get some time alone tomorrow after research to make my way to the gardens and read
anything and everything possible within that book Jordan had
sent to me.

***

*Jordan had left the small room he had once referred to as 'fort
Goldilocks' after speaking too briefly with Pierce. He had been
gone for almost two years and broke the news today that he
would not be attending the Fates' festival. A declaration Jordan
would get to now go and deliver to Arcane.*

*'This should go well.' Jordan thought sarcastically. He ap-
proached the main building of the castle, pausing for a moment
to breathe in the calm, content air of the soft spring day. The
sun felt radiant on his skin as his pores begged for more. It was
unlikely he would get a chance to enjoy it beyond this moment.*

*He huffed out a sigh, resigning to his fate and pushing the
doors open to find Arcane. It wasn't hard, the man had been in*

the war room expecting him. He and one of the silent generals were crouched over some coordinates, speaking in hushed tones.

Jordan swore silent generals would be phased out as soon as Arcane relented the reigns to him as more than just a public spectacle. It never sat right with him that someone in charge of the team drawing blood and life in a war remain faceless, unaccountable for their actions, even if they were only taking orders.

"My boy!" Arcane boomed, jarring the faceless man beside him to the point the man's feature-blurring glamor almost dropped. Jordan cringed at his immediate change in demeanor as he asked if his 'other' boy would be joining them.

"I'm afraid not. He told me to send his best, though; he promises to make it to the next Fates' festival." Jordan filled in as hastily as he could, hoping they could move on from the subject.

"I have been a great leader, but I fear I may have failed my son as a father if he can comfortably avoid me at length such as this." Jordan didn't know how to respond, so he opted not to. Pierce wasn't a fan of his Father's company even before he had needed to fear his Father discovering what he was. The man always found a way to lessen him by comparing both of them, Pierce rarely coming out the better son.

"No matter, you are not his keeper. Shall we proceed?" Arcane asked; a simple nod was all Jordan could offer his mentor.

They spent little time rehashing the optics of the operation already in motion. Arcane had been clear in all his instructions; what makes a leader great is his ability to delegate what needs delegating and handling anything too sensitive to trust in the hands of another. That strong teaching was what had him so uneasy with the entire war they were standing on the cusp of winning.

Arcane had forced him to join in the battles as he led optics, guiding their teams from here, the castle. Jordan would take out the defenses of any military base they were striking, then report back to the castle and observe how Arcane led his men.

He hated taking life. The first man he killed in battle had looked him in the eyes and asked 'why,' and he would never forget the confusion and panic he saw as his life left his body.

Today, they had located the last of the uprising. The sect they were fighting was led by rouge Empaths. They had gone unnoticed until it had been uncovered that they were trafficking members of high-powered bloodlines and forcibly taking their abilities.

Today, Jordan would not be drawing blood. He, instead, would be leading optics from base as Arcane felt he had observed enough.

Jordan did not need a headset as the large table before him projected their signal and showed their exact location in coordination with their targets. The hologram did not show the men themselves but formless figures moving around one another, through one another; mostly, the red heat signatures of his men blotted out the white opposing forces as they were the highest-ranking men in the realm.

He hated watching the figures move, listening for any disturbance and barking orders like 'ten inbound, next left corner, advancing.' He felt like a puppeteer; he hated it.

If he were going to be directing men in battle, he felt he should at least be involved in it.

Almost zoning out due to his unimportance, he almost missed one of his men going down, then another. Arcane and he crowded the table worriedly.

"Come in. Is there a disturbance?" Jordan asked, pressing the button on the table that would relay his audio to the earpieces of their men. He got no response.

One by one he watched a single, menacing white figure blot out the signatures of his men.

"Jordan, do not do it," Arcane ordered, knowing in an instant what Jordan was thinking. His command fell on deaf ears as Jordan transported to the coordinates of his dying men.

On appearing, the scene was not at all what he would have expected. He had been operating under the assumption he would be appearing in some military compound as a hero to save his men from morally corrupt Empaths who were stealing innocent lives.

Instead, he was greeted by the sight of a quaint, vibrant village. Toys were resting against the walls of red clay houses; clothes were hanging from lines. The gentle spring sun and the vibrant green grass were casting an eerie friendliness upon the battered corpses of his men.

The white uniforms that bore his mark were blotted with blood. Their bodies were scattered in a circle surrounding one singular man, his shoulders heaving with the heavy breaths earned from utilizing well-honed battle skills to demolish an entire battalion, tears escaping his blue eyes, icy in their fury with crimson smeared through his long, curly, blond hair.

***

Sometimes, feeling things was a terrible burden. Looking at pictures of slaughtered children after reading through documents and watching video footage of the massacres had made her heart slow in its beating. It strained and struggled in its labored beating beneath the weight of this knowledge and the sight of these atrocities.

Pierce told her the Empaths had known they were being hunted, but they hadn't known by what or who. Men patrolled their gated communities in shifts while armed. It did not help protect them.

Jordan dispensed with the men on patrol easily. She had seen it in more than one video. He would transport, appearing and disappearing, the angel of death, cloaked in black, and take each Father, son, whoever, out in a quick attack and then vanish.

Men would enter then, casually, quickly and efficiently,

rounding up the people of the town and, using a local weapon similar to an assault rifle, gun the innocent civilians down before burying them in a mass grave.

The Empaths lived in remote sections of their born territories, attempting to escape persecution for their gifts, ultimately allowing them to be easily dispensed of for having them.

Pierce sat, leaning against his desk where Christine sat, pale-faced, eyes flicking from the gruesome pictures he had taken before burying his people and the video footage playing on a small projected screen on his desk. He had recovered the videos of their operations in his father's belongings.

She was fighting tears. Hot, rancid anger festered in her stomach, and he let it. That anger was but a star in the galaxy of his pain; he was happy to have finally shared it with someone.

"Why did you cover this up? You sneakily slander him constantly. Putting doubts and ideas in people's minds without ever being too overt. I don't understand. Why not release this?" The images almost crumpled in her trembling fingers as she shook the pictures at him. He made direct eye contact with her then.

"To condemn him fully is to condemn my father. I thought about it. Obviously." He motioned to all the evidence he had collected. He sighed, and it slightly wheezed.

This had been something he had shared with Victor, but Victor had already hated Jordan and Savious, so there was no element of betrayal or shock. Christine understood; he almost regretted that for her.

"I loved my father. He wasn't the warmest of Men, but he was good to me, and he did love me. I could not allow his name to be forever stained in blood. Even though it's what he and Jordan both deserve."

She wanted to argue but given the fear in the lifeless eyes of a child staring blankly back at her from the snapshot Pierce had taken, she couldn't.

Jordan had been right. There was no excuse. Pierce hadn't tried to heighten Jordan's involvement. Christine was appreciative of that. He had been completely honest that Jordan, while the massacres were occurring, strongly believed his and Arcane's men were fighting soldiers; that he was fighting a war.

That was no excuse. Not to Christine nor Pierce. Jordan had stepped into the role and worn the title of High God at the time. His failure to demand clarity surrounding the goings-on of his own war allowed a genocide to happen.

The last photo Christine held was of a pile of small and adolescent bodies stacked carelessly near a large, crudely dug hole in the ground. Fresh unearthed soil lay loosely in mounds up against the nearest building. The building had a large window; with the sun shining against it, it reflected an image like a mirror.

An image of Pierce.

His blond hair stood in every direction, crusted black with the dried blood of the people who had housed him.

His shirt was smeared with the earth he had hollowed for the graves of those who had validated his existence and taken him into their community with open arms.

His face had two perfectly clean streaks down each of his cheeks as he cried. Photographing the lifeless bodies of his friends and found family who had held the answers he needed to exist in this world without constantly feeling the emotions of everyone in it.

Christine stood and placed the photo down. Pierce watched her without moving, concentrating tightly on keeping his emotions to himself, not wanting to overwhelm her with his usually well-buried grief.

He went rigid in shock as she threw her arms around him in an act of comfort. It took him a few seconds to register what was happening before he hugged her back tightly. A wall of unprocessed grief and anger broke loose from him; for the first time since that day, he wept.

***

There were two balconies that peeked out of Castle Jordan looking out to the city and damned forests of hell. Azazel stood on the opposite of the one his little sister had frequented. This one rested outside a large strategy room that had begun to feel claustrophobic. Large wings and confined spaces did not mix well, even if he had more practice than most.

The majority of his people, Active or pedestrian Guardians, lived in bungalows several miles above the ground, with open walls and high ceilings. Their settlement was small as they were a rare breed, but it earned them free living in the sky-nestled city of Pownall, several miles above the largest Ocean of the Realm, Pesoindo. They lived solely off seafood and waterborne plant life the freshwater ocean provided them.

He had lived amongst them after his parents fled their family home. He only bought his apartment in The Heed to be nearer to Christine, even if she didn't know of their relationship.

A trickle of blood was running down his elevated arm from a nick of which he was not yet conscious. One he made with the knife he was still twirling in contemplation and agitation.

Thad noticed his absence and labored his way to check on him. Jordan was meeting with a group of volunteer Givi for an important lesson and test of glamor, leaving him alone and bored. Growing up down here set up youthful expectations of a dreary life ahead of oneself.

But Jordan had rescued him from that. At night, Jordan would gather Thad and Kielius up and tell the stories of Heaven and Middle Earth. Of worlds with rays of rejuvenating sunshine and people that were plainly stupid with hope and mostly unearned joy. Those were the bedtime stories of his youth. Just one of the many ways Jordan had been more of his father than his brother.

One of the stories Thad had requested be repeated almost nightly was of the winged Guardians of Heaven. Men and women who were above the pettiness of power and spent their lives dedicated to people's safety. Jordan's tales seeped with admiration and respect; those emotions very much infected Thad's imagination.

Now, the leader of that very civilization was leaning against the thick mortar balcony before him. Azazel looked puzzled and strikingly sensual as he stood, licking a bit of blood from the knife he had been spinning moments ago. Thad stopped and audibly gulped in response to the sight and its effect on him.

The knife glinted, casting a refracted bit of light into Thad's appreciative gaze, temporarily blinding him. After blinking away the bright obtrusion, he was met with an autumn spring glare piercing him into place.

"If you're admiring me, I not only allow but encourage it, but if you're planning to attack me, I really don't recommend it," Azazel warned from his straightened stance, wings menacingly unfurled.

Thad's mouth opened, closed, and opened again as he struggled with words. The menace in Azazel's eyes melted into a knowing smirk as his body relaxed and he leaned, once again, onto the balcony.

"Admiring me it is. It's good to know I'm sexy to every species," Azazel said with a sultry laugh and a flirty wink.

Composing himself, Thad found strength in a long-waged battle of shame-laden identity.

"My species is Angelican. Like that of my Father and brothers. Being from the realm of Heaven, I would assume you are familiar with other Angelicans," Thad snapped. Azazel glanced slowly over at him; one brow dipped slightly.

"Angelicans don't have gray skin. And they have hearts," he remarked.

"Angelicans often don't have wings, yet I am sure you identify as such." Azazel held back a laugh, attempting to avoid insulting him further but finding it a bit fun, nonetheless.

"From what I have heard, these people look up to you almost as much as they do Jordan. I would think you would honor them in proudly displaying your shared features, your proof of solidarity."

"I thought Guardians didn't partake in politics," Thad snipped.

"We don't. I know nothing of politics. But I am an expert on people and what makes them feel safe. Being governed by those you don't know, by those you cannot see yourself within, leads to fear and unrest. Neither of which is safe in the minds of the masses. Trust me," he said, staring out into the unlikely foliage surrounding the castle, his mind flashing briefly back to the day of the uprising.

Thad contemplated his words without directly respond-ing. He had never considered that before. His entire life he had been so concerned with trying to appear as one of 'The Sav-ious's' he hadn't thought about the positive impact he could have had by also just allowing himself to be known as being born of the Givi.

It wasn't like everyone didn't already know it; they did. It just wasn't something anyone spoke of. Fueled by his Fathers disgust with the Givi side of his DNA prevailing and of the way he spent his entire life diminishing him for it.

"I didn't mean to break you," Azazel said in his way of apol-ogy. Thad's attention snapped back to him as his lips started moving.

"Enlightenment shouldn't be apologized for. You are the second person, second only to Jordan to tell me I should be proud of my lineage instead of hiding it. Thank you."

They were shoulder to shoulder now; Thad was resisting looking at the winged tempter. Refusing to allow himself to get distracted, to allow himself to betray Alyk's memory. He hadn't wanted a man since his husband was murdered, and he was dreadfully out of practice at managing the symptoms of such.

Azazel enjoyed the attraction immensely. He was a firm believer that a bit of distraction was good during a crisis. It was useful for perspective and for clearing the mind.

He could tell Thad was struggling with it, so to heighten the moment, he leaned into their touching shoulders. A deliberate breath helped hide the way he was expanding the reach of his wings, allowing his silver-tipped feathers to gently brush along Thad's thick shoulder blades.

He was rewarded with Thad noticeably shivering.

Azazel hopped away from Thad at the sound of Kielius's voice, startling Thad into letting out a squeak to both Kielius and Azazel's amusement.

"Stare at that forest long enough with such heat, and it may actually grow." His laugh lines were creased in amusement as he watched the two redden as if they had been caught in a scandalous moment.

'At least bird boy is better at hiding it,' Kielius thought with admonishment for his very red brother.

"Have you located Savious?" Thad asked, standing up a bit taller.

"He isn't here or in Middle Earth, so I'll let you deduce his location. Where's Amy? I need to ask her something."

"Amy is with Jordan. He needed her assistance preparing the volunteers for the wedding. It's tomorrow. And Jordan is adamant everything goes smoothly for obvious reasons," Thad explained, catching Azazel's agreeing nod.

24

UNTIL DEATH DO WE PART

Pierce had spent his evening grinning like a fool after having had a sincere moment of warmth with his love. She had embraced him in shared pain and betrayal. The majority of the marriages between his ancestors had been built on less.

Thick and palpable hope was radiating from him as he looked out around the large open space, white chairs lined up on each side of a long narrow row. White flowers hung from every possible surface adorned with accents of fluffed and flowing white lace. Christine had told him to cancel the wedding, but he had changed her view after explaining its significance to their people.

An Earth-born mortal would be marrying their God. Their realm would be able to enjoy and celebrate an American wedding, just like in the movies. Excitement was buzzing along the streets. Pierce had lifted any printing restrictions for the time being, allowing the news and media affiliates to publish more extensively on this joyous occasion.

It didn't matter to him that Christine had not reciprocated his touch since that moment. For now, that moment was enough.

There was a surprise waiting for her tonight. An important custom she knew little about that he truly looked forward to educating her on. For now, he allowed her time alone. Self-reflection was a valuable thing, and time spent alone would not be a common luxury in her future.

The part of him that had felt saddened by her hesitation had slowly been muted by irritation over the last couple of days, not with her but with the Fates.

He had it formerly worked out in his head now that Christine was in no way feeling their Fated matches pull. And he knew it was likely the malicious will of the Fates that caused her thread to lay limp and unresponsive.

Over time, he hoped, she would heal. That, and once the Fates had been discovered, the injustice could be righted. Once her thread was unblocked, the clouds of confusion would lift, and they would be able to move forward, unified, stronger than they would have been elsewise.

***

"Damn your bleeding heart."

I was pacing nervously in Pierce's room, refusing to unpack my own belongings and concede that I in any way belonged here. In a moment of weakness, he had seemed to me so ill-fated and damaged by everything that happened to his fellow Empaths, I became overwhelmed with the strong urge to comfort him.

It was in no way a romantic moment, and luckily, he hadn't tried to turn it into one. But I could see it. A treacherous gleam of success and hope shining glaringly through his watery eyes, illuminating the newest in my thick list of mistakes.

In the moment, I had lacked the words to crush his hope even. Still seeing in him the ravaged man who snapped photos of the slaughtered in hopes of, in some way, preserving their memory. That man, the one who loved those people. The one who keeps their history and future within him deserved that brief moment of peace.

I was only regretful that it was tainted with false pretenses, completely fabricated in his own self-deceptive mind. The wedding was tomorrow. I hadn't heard from Azazel and hadn't had a single moment to go back and retrieve the book and shirt I had buried in the garden.

Nothing felt safe.

'Damn transporting.' Even internally the words were a growl. I really hated the skill more by the day.

It was already evening, and I was apprehensive of the coming day. Jordan coming or not, tomorrow would be eventful, to say the least, and I had decided, against my better, more intellectual judgment, where I stood.

I did not flinch when the door swung open in a burst; my nerves were already completely numb.

The older woman from the previous day stood in the entryway, arms overflowing with purple cloth and a pleasant smile on her wrinkled face.

"Good Greeting, my Lady. I have come to prepare your gown," she said the words as if she were filling me in but did not wait on a response before dropping the fabric and grabbing me, pushing my shoulders back and tapping the bottom of my chin.

"Stand up straight, dear girl. This is only easy the first time," she instructed. I, seeing no immediate advantage to resisting, abided.

"I am surprised Teena isn't involved in this. She was so adamant about it happening." The older woman physically stiffened with my words.

"She would have loved to be here. However, Teena passed on in your absence." I pulled away from her.

"What do you mean she passed on?"

"I did not know her and do not know the details, dear. Please, I have much to do today, and this needs to be ready within the hour." Wrapped up in the perplexity of Teena's premature death, I missed the implications of danger before me.

Pierce had shown me the wedding dress he had chosen for me. It had been imported from, and custom-made, back on Middle Earth.

Fabric was whirling around the air, wrapping around and caressing me before tearing and weaving itself into a very thin, nearly sheer dress that rested suspended in the air before me.

"This feels like a poorly written Disney movie. I don't get it. Why do I need another dress?" I asked with complete disinterest in her show of dancing purple fabric.

"This is for your real union. For the bonding ceremony. As our customs require." Her words were gentle, as if she were expecting me to be ignorant of normal proceedings.

"Why do both? He is already forcing the one?" I had more asked the question out loud to myself but literally fell stunned when she not only provided me an answer, but the answer put the most frigid of chills in the marrow of my bones.

"Oh, sweet bride. The bonding ceremony is what allows the couples of this realm to further their bloodline."

With that absolute fucking bombshell, she left the room and the dress. It hung, draped along the bottom of the bed, taunting me with the nauseating implications.

My hand flung to my festering scar, the absence of Jordan causing it to make me constantly sweat, but its current pain was nothing compared to what I felt while in Hell.

I half traced the mark, tears welling in my eyes, remembering what the ramifications of my actions would be if I were to summon him. He would come. Nothing would stop him. But it would be at too high a cost. I alone was not worth that price.

'Tomorrow. The wedding was tomorrow. Jordan wouldn't let the wedding happen; he wouldn't. I did not need to be afraid.'

My eyes were clenched shut. I had fallen to my knees, and

was working hard at reminding myself I had allies Pierce did not know of.

This time when the door opened again, I did flinch. I was healing, regaining power, enough so that I was able to reach out and sense energies again. And the one that walked through the door was positively garish.

***

Jordan had done everything he could to prepare for the morning assault, yet, he sat restless, tracing the colorful patterns of Christine's tiny coffee table out on their balcony. An unrest was churning within him like he had never known.

He was uneasy and even anxious on the day of the uprising, the day he found out he had played a role in genocide. But that was nothing compared to the sickness that had rooted itself in his stomach.

A heavier darkness settled into the unlit sky of his realm that night as he looked out across it, reminding himself that without the reclaiming of Heaven, this was all this realm would know. It had begun to heal and had only recently allowed food to seed, providing the opportunity for sustainable crops.

Hell couldn't thrive without more energy inhabiting it. Each realm needed copious amounts of energy to feed its life force. There is a symbiotic partnership between people and realm, present in all the worlds, but only faintly lingering in this one. It was a flame he had been blowing on so gently for years. He had been aching to watch it shine.

It would be worth it once he could toss some real fuel on it. To see just how brightly it could glow. Tomorrow that would happen. He didn't fear facing Pierce. He no longer mourned the need to take his old friends' life.

Yet something, something was very wrong. There was a cry reaching him. From somewhere in the three worlds, buzzing, breaking its way through the channels of all the energies between himself and its origination, following a direct path, and spearing his heart.

'She knows she can summon me. She knows I can get to her if needed. You will see her tomorrow. Trust her as she has trusted you.'

He whispered the words to himself while attempting to lock onto the thread of terror he sensed, somewhere in the great distance, so that he may try to send its origin strength and contentment.

***

Her wedding night had been the longest night she had ever survived. Yet, she wasn't sure she could even call it surviving. She had entirely felt the death of a large part of her soul.

The morning, in contrast, had been brief.

She had been dressed and congratulated by people she had never seen. Gushed over by the young man who had escorted her, excitedly babbling about her dress. The dress that felt as though it weighed twice her body weight and did a magnificent job of hiding the blank and broken look on her face with its feathers and excessive frill.

The music that had played as she walked down the aisle failed to ring in her eyes. Instead, it was drowned out by the drum beat of thunder. It came in waves, washing over her like the most unsettling of drumline melodies.

Pierce had kissed her in front of no less than fifteen hundred people. She hadn't even registered the transaction. It wasn't until she was turned to face the overcrowded audience that she processed that the wedding had just happened.

It was over.

Pierce had one arm wrapped around her, his smile beaming across the rolling meadows of faces, delighting in seeing their king, their chosen God, happy. So very content in his joy that they all completely overlooked her misery and the tears running from her eyes freely now.

Pierce pulled her into a private room while the banquet hall was cleared of people and rearranged for a reception with a much smaller guest list. Excitedly he pushed her against the wall. Although she felt hollow and broken, there was still anger within her, and she summoned it.

She roughly shoved his chest, pushing him away.

"My dear wife, I thought we were past this?" he said, pinching her chin and blasting her with an affectionate smile.

"We will never be past this. Your delusions don't extend to me." There was no venom in her words. She had exhausted her supply the night before and, at this very moment, didn't even consider him worth the effort.

"I would think you would be relieved," he said, giving her enough space to attempt a deeper breath, an attempt that was rather unsuccessful.

The well of her words for him had been depleted, run completely dry; she looked away from him.

"He didn't come. I had expected him to. Had planned on it, actually. I wasn't sure how he would slither his way up here, but I thought he would, at a minimum, try. So, I have been doing some research, and as you are my wife now, it is only fair I keep you involved in my operations."

It sickened her to hear a reference to Jordan drip from his lips almost as much as hearing herself referred to as his wife.

With a regretful smile, he pulled the coat of his jacket aside, revealing the broken-off, black, obsidian tip of a spear strapped to his side. She looked up at him, unimpressed.

"I know. It doesn't look like much. But, according to my family records, the only way to kill a high god, that is, without being one yourself, is with an object of their own manifestation. This is the spear he assaulted me with the day he began to poison you against me. It is only fitting I use it to end the constant threat he poses against our realm and our marriage."

He didn't wait for a response from her. He lowered the

jacket and smiled, parting her lips with another forced kiss. Greedy hands explored newly discovered skin as he dropped her glamor to enjoy the little marks he had left on her from the night before. Marks he craved to duplicate.

But he wanted to take his time, so for now, he lifted her glamor again before dragging her out of the room into a continuation of her worst possible nightmare.

Every Pierce lackey in Heaven was gathered before her. His dearest friends and followers. Blindly loyal to the kind and gentle leader he was to them. Completely ignorant of the scum he became in private quarters. She could scream his sins in this room; not a single person within it would come to her aide.

He squeezed her hand tightly, forcing her to look up at him.

"These are our most loyal friends and family; try to show some appreciation for their presence, please." She wasn't sure what prompted her response. Of all the ones she had popping forth in her mind, the one that escaped wasn't the intended.

"Please, your most loyal follower is dead. Teena would have performed the ceremony last night herself if she felt it was what you wanted."

Pierce sagged a little.

'Well, there's one small win for me today. Gotta take them where I can get them,' she thought triumphantly.

"Teena is a wonderful example of why today should be celebrated. Our union ensures a sacrifice like hers will never be needed again. Not while I have you, my wife, my creationist, my fate."

The words chewed in her mind during the feast that everyone but her seemed to enjoy. She would cut her toe off, in this very moment, for just one more taste of gray blob.

Then they broke out in an unexpected bit of torture she should have known was coming. Every reception she had ever heard of contained the terrible and completely unenjoyable tradition of dancing. Sweaty people, bobbing up and down together, not her idea of a good time unless she was able to punch someone during it.

Pierce didn't care about her distaste for the act. He gently lifted her from the ground, wrapping her in a lover's embrace as they swayed to their first dance. To him, that moment was filled with sparkling magic. He was floating on the clouds the humans dreamed his city rested upon. In his arms, his Fated match, his wife, forever bonded to him until death did they part.

To her, he had been smothering her by pressing her head to his chest, not allowing for comfortable breathing and making her skin feel as though it were boiling and blistering. She might as well have been swaying with the sun itself. Beautiful to admire from a distance, but soul blackening and body melting once you got too close.

With a kiss on the forehead, he demanded she partake in one of the group dances, as their guests had learned most of them just for her. She had responded that it was very much his fault and not hers that they had done so.

Yet, here she was, being passed from person to person in various, different dances. There had been a dull ache carving itself within the cavity of her chest all day. Not a sharp pain, not a scar-related pain, but as if scoop by scoop, it was being hollowed out with a rusty spoon.

Stranger upon stranger grabbed her politely. Making sure not to earn Pierce's fury at an inappropriate touch or a hand that was slightly too low.

Until being snagged by this current partner, her hand was wrapped tightly in one of his. His other hand dipped far deeper than anyone else's. She felt warm. Genuine warmth, not the kind she had grown wary of with Pierce.

There was no sting to this. No sweat to it. No overbearing potential of blindness, and instead, it was fuzzy. It sent static through her stomach and down her legs. Thawing her where she hadn't even realized chunks of ice had lodged themselves, causing her pain.

She didn't know why, but this person, who had twirled her slightly away from the others, had calmed her. With that, she decided to look at him.

As she did, she recognized a face she had seen only once. He spoke to her softly, mumbling under his breath. He had sandy blond hair and blue eyes; he didn't even remotely pull off being human.

"I heard a rumor that you prefer fighting to dancing. Given the occasion, I would assume fighting would be the better option." Through thick glamor, she recognized her devil's grin.

She collapsed against him. Allowing him to easily carry her in their movements.

"You are late." He stilled. The jagged and broken edge in her voice became the only thing he could hear. Disregarding the room entirely, he cupped her face, unable to enjoy the way she pushed against his palm again.

He ran his thumb along her plush lip and felt beneath the pad of his thumb, broken skin that was not visible to the naked eye. Examining every inch of her face intently, he looked beneath the expertly executed glamor, seeing several red blemishes on her neck.

The night sky inked out his fake blue irises, but that impending darkness no longer frightened her. It fueled her; she wanted to assist it, to encourage it to spread out and consume the entire room around them. For a brief moment, he put his anger aside in order to be her strength.

Wanting to draw at least one smile from her, he pulled her back into his embrace, lowering himself into the crook of her neck, taking in her scent and surrounding her with his. She inhaled him as deeply as her lungs would allow, enjoying his scent of early morning dawn. Cool, and crisp, like morning dew, he soothed the wounds that lay beneath her skin.

This feeling, her being in his arms and knowing it was

somewhere she felt safe, was the ember he needed to stroke the flame within him. It was the only fuel he would ever be able to stomach taking from her.

"This room is that of our dearest friends and family. How is it that I have yet to make acquaintance with you, someone comfortable handling my wife in such an inappropriate manner?" Jordan seemed like he would ignore Pierce's words, continuing to stare into her eyes as if witnessing through them everything she had endured up until this moment.

His glamor melted away from him, his features slowly catching up to his dark eyes as he morphed into the dark-wielding king of the underworld.

"You were not invited for a reason. Remove your hands from my wife's person," Pierce asked too calmly. His words intentionally landed on the word wife. The room flickered as darkness crept into the whites of Jordan's eyes.

Pierce looked completely unimpressed by the display.

"Christine," Jordan soothed. "It's time for you to leave." Upon her protest, he turned to her again.

"You are owed your pound of flesh, but I want you to be whole when you go to carve it." Azazel's unmistakable silhouette then shadowed the door frame. Jordan tilted his head in his general direction.

Reluctantly she began to make her way toward her brother, the new recipient of Pierce's glare. Azazel's only response to the betrayal etching his old friend's face was one very intentional finger.

Jordan's voice was guttural and the very nature of inhumanly divine.

"Out of respect for the friendship we once shared and Christine's aversion to murder, this is your last chance to step down peacefully." At this, Pierce finally lost some, but not all, of his composure.

"I will not allow you to rule this world on a throne of blood. What do you plan to do, wage war here, in a room of innocents, loyal followers of mine who would die to protect me?" Pierce asked him incredulously, feigning ignorance of having the upper hand.

A maniacal grin cracked confidently across Jordan's face. After a deep breath, he exhaled slowly, and as he did, the faces of the people in the room shimmered. Friend's faces melted into strangers with dark gray complexions.

"The days of you hiding behind the possibility of casualties is over. Your pretend people have abandoned you." Pierce shot a worried look to Victor, who was glancing around the room in Panic, doubtful that they would truly have been abandoned by everyone.

After a shared nod, Victor ran from the room, terror winning in Victor's mind at the thought of Jordan killing such good and loyal friends. Leaving Pierce wasn't something he wanted to do, but combat had never been a skillset of his, and the priority needed to be locating the friends that should have been attending today.

He ran, in a full sprint, looking for anyone, finding the palace empty. It was better than discovering bodies. Jordan must have evacuated everyone during the ceremony, also managing to stage the entire day, making them believe everything had been going rather smoothly.

"You have tried taking everything of mine, but now I'm taking it back."

"I never wanted anything you had, not your powers or your claim to the throne, but I am obligated to the people to protect them from enduring your further injustice. Only one thing that you somehow had, I wanted, *my* wife. *Officially*, as of last night," Pierce added, intentionally poking the bear.

Christine had almost been gone. She had been so close to making it to Azazel, but after hearing this, she turned starkly in her path, wanting to beat Pierce to death herself.

Azazel, not caring about what Christine wanted, rushed after her, grabbed her arm and began dragging her from the room. He was not liking the sensation of impending doom that was radiating off Jordan as the God practically vibrated in building fury and anticipation.

Jordan didn't care to give him time. He instead began beating him down with a black force while the Givi people ran from the room to make their way to the bridge room they had been told about.

He raised his hands, condensing the black aura above them into a solid mass, then, with thick force, swung them down. Making sure each pulse stung with devastating fury.

Pierce tried to transport, but Jordan would not allow it, giving him no room, no chance for escape.

Somehow, Christine managed to slip her arm from Azazel's grasp, pulling away from him as he had just managed to get her out into the hallway. An idea flashed in her mind then.

"We can help!" Azazel paused, panting, surprised at her strength and put both hands on his hips in annoyance as he listened to her. Her plan, he had to admit, was worth seeing through.

Christine charged back into the room. Pierce and Jordan's attentions both snapped to her.

Breathing in deeply, he summoned forth a new ability. He sent a thankful prayer into the cosmos to the citizen who had gifted it to him. Feeling the tile work beneath him, he reached within it and willed it to expand for him. Like sand, the once solid tile work engulfed him.

This gave Jordan a moment of hesitation. Pierce returned to the room, manifesting himself out of the woodwork of the wall behind Jordan. Sending a power blast of hurricane wind in his direction, blowing out the wall behind them but not budging Jordan's composure in the slightest.

Pierce had planned for this. Had known he would need to do this, but it still went against every fiber within the threads of his soul to see this plan through.

Fighting his fates and ambition and succumbing to a necessary evil, he made intentional eye contact with Christine. He pulled the spear shard from inside his jacket and threw it as hard as he could in Jordan's direction.

Jordan awaited the blade with little regard. But Christine knew of its intention and wanted nothing more, at that moment, than to be between Jordan and the spear he had crafted himself that could kill him.

There was a reason Pierce hadn't drained her. And this was it. It broke his heart to see her will for self-sacrifice, out of love for another, be strong enough for his plan to succeed. For Victor's plan to succeed.

In the time between heartbeats, she was stumbling backward into Jordan's outstretched arms, with the black spear protruding from her chest. From the Empaths Jordan had assisted in slaughtering, Pierce had learned the Creationist's greatest gift was manifesting abilities based on sheer will.

Jordan dropped to his knees with her in his lap, bleeding. The life was seeping from her into the cracks of the marble tiles beneath him. They were breaking apart as they came in contact with what Christine had previously seen as darkness emanating from Jordan.

Looking at him now, it didn't seem as dark to her as before. It looked layered. A black tint rested above a deep blue base of energy. The color of a rising Dawn. In her delirium, she judged herself for being so damn blind. He was the High God; of course he wielded mornings. What was a God if not new beginnings?

Azazel had quietly grabbed one of the transmitting devices used to broadcast the news and had turned it on. Broadcasting everything as it happened live. But at this, he dropped it, then dropped to his knees, feeling as if it had been him that was stabbed in the chest, until he saw the lack of fury and instead a look of resolve settling on Jordan's features.

Knowing he had won, Pierce stood aside and allowed Jordan a moment to say goodbye.

She expected blood to spurt from her mouth or for overwhelming pain to consume her, but mostly, she just felt cold.

Her fingers were going numb. All she could feel were little pinpricks as she looked up into her favorite set of eyes.

"I'm not sure what Thad's problem is. That wasn't so hard," she laughed.

He savored that laugh, the music to his soul, missing her already. He bent down, his energy calling its goodbyes to hers as he kissed her. It was deep but overwhelmingly soft, and this time, the connections between them sparked again. For the last time, little stems of color intertwined in flashing desperate pleas.

Unexpectedly, the cold in her chest began to hurt as it heated back up, her pulse quickening again and breath stabilizing. Thinking she had just experienced a miracle, she sat up in his arms slowly, still sore, noticing only then the growing dampness on his chest.

"One more promise, My Goddess. Can you do that for me?" Those easy breaths were choking now. A worse pain, one of fire and fear, took over her whole body as she reached out and touched his chest. Her hands came away crimson. She clawed at her own, feeling no arrow and no mark to suggest it had ever been there.

"No. Jordan. No." She shuddered.

"Let Thad and Azazel keep you safe. Please." There was an ache in his wheezed plea; through her tears she could only nod yes.

"You are a God. You can't die. Jordan, please," she sobbed in between gasps. "Not you too."

It was Pierce who answered.

"If that were true, my father would still be alive. Jordan here sealed his Fate. My Father died in the same way because of him." There was an unexpected lack of malice in his words, but Jordan didn't waste his final few moments on him. Pierce had stolen enough of his time.

"I love you, Christine. Find the Fates," he whispered, kissing her back with waning energy, enjoying for the last time the push and pull of the energies dancing against one another.

As Jordan's eyes closed and his hand went limp, Azazel leapt from the ground and beat his wings against the matter within the air. In one swift motion, he had cradled a screaming Christine in his arms and flown from the building.

They crash-landed in the bridge room, Azazel failing to contain the erupting force of Christine's grief.

The plan had originally been Jordan would bring this room down around them once he returned. Or Amy would per his instruction. But now, Azazel pulled Amy from the room while Christine sobbed.

With each breath, the room constricted around them, tightening, cracking. As the flames that once danced across her chest diminished, she let out an Earth-shattering scream, and the room from Heaven's side ceased to exist.

While Pierce saw to the body of his childhood friend, Victor turned on the news to see the people marching towards the castle. Fury was sizzling through them after the footage they had all witnessed, preparing to demand answers and action.

Christine wasn't aware she had started the next great revolt. She had no idea that this outcome had been something Jordan and his team had prepared for.

All she could comprehend was raw, agonizing loss and the way it consumed her. Black matter rushed to her from all depths of Hell as it, for the first time, opened itself for her.

She stood. Azazel and Amy looked on in shock as darkness shrouded her. Her tears stilled at a voice whispering through her mind in memory, calling her to a river.

"It's okay Krissy, everything will be just fine."

ABOUT ATMOSPHERE PRESS

Atmosphere Press is an independent, full-service publisher for excellent books in all genres and for all audiences. Learn more about what we do at atmospherepress.com.

We encourage you to check out some of Atmosphere's latest releases, which are available at Amazon.com and via order from your local bookstore:

Icarus Never Flew 'Round Here, by Matt Edwards

COMFREY, WYOMING: Maiden Voyage, by Daphne Birkmeyer

The Chimera Wolf, by P.A. Power

Umbilical, by Jane Kay

The Two-Blood Lion, by Nick Westfield

Shogun of the Heavens: The Fall of Immortals, by I.D.G. Curry

Hot Air Rising, by Matthew Taylor

30 Summers, by A.S. Randall

Delilah Recovered, by Amelia Estelle Dellos

A Prophecy in Ash, by Julie Zantopoulos

The Killer Half, by JB Blake

Ocean Lessons, by Karen Lethlean

Unrealized Fantasies, by Marilyn Whitehorse

The Mayari Chronicles: Initium, by Karen McClain

Squeeze Plays, by Jeffrey Marshall

JADA: Just Another Dead Animal, by James Morris

Hart Street and Main: Metamorphosis, by Tabitha Sprunger

Karma One, by Colleen Hollis

Ndalla's World, by Beth Franz

Adonai, by Arman Isayan

ABOUT THE AUTHOR

Allyson Kuepfer was raised in the whimsical woodlands of Traverse City, MI. In every stage of her life, she has

been known to have her nose in a book or a pen in her hand. In High School she participated in an advanced writers program named Front Street Writers and interned for a Publishing company directly after. She now lives in Columbus Ohio and is channeling what she has learned from the sudden loss of her mother into what she knows best, crafting a fantasy world for others to use to heal and enjoy along with her.

Where to Connect with Me:

Email: thetrueallykue@gmail.com
TikTok: @allykue
Facebook: Books by Ally Kue

CPSIA information can be obtained
at www.ICGtesting.com
Printed in the USA
JSHW020414180523
41823JS00001B/7